Troubled Blood

A *Strike* Novel

Part Two

Robert Galbraith

W F HOWES LTD

This large print edition published in 2021 by
W F Howes Ltd
Unit 5, St George's House, Rearsby Business Park,
Gaddesby Lane, Rearsby, Leicester LE7 4YH

1 3 5 7 9 10 8 6 4 2

First published in the United Kingdom in 2020
by Sphere

A CIP catalogue record for this book is available
from the British Library

ISBN 978 1 00405 199 1

Typeset by Palimpsest Book Production Limited,
Falkirk, Stirlingshire

and bound by
)ks in the UK

To Barbara Murray,
social worker, WEA worker, teacher,
wife, mother, grandmother,
demon bridge player
and
world's best mother-in-law

There they her sought, and euery where inquired,
Where they might tydings get of her estate;
Yet found they none. But by what haplesse fate,
Or hard misfortune she was thence conuayd,
And stolne away from her beloued mate,
Were long to tell . . .

Edmund Spenser
The Faerie Queene

For, if it were not so, there would be something disappearing into nothing, which is mathematically absurd.

Aleister Crowley
The Book of Thoth

CHAPTER 39

. . . they thus beguile the way,
Vntill the blustring storme is ouerblowne . . .
They cannot finde that path, which first was
*   showne,*
But wander too and fro in waies
*   vnknowne . . .*

Edmund Spenser
The Faerie Queene

Robin's alarm went off at half past six on Friday morning, in the middle of a dream about Matthew: he'd come to her in the Earl's Court flat, and begged her to return to him, saying that he'd been a fool, promising he'd never again complain about her job, imploring her to admit that she missed what they'd once had. He'd asked her whether she honestly liked living in a rented flat, without the security and companionship of marriage, and in the dream Robin felt a pull back towards her old relationship, before it had become complicated by her job with Strike. He

1

was a younger Matthew in the dream, a far kinder Matthew, and Sarah Shadlock was dismissed as a mistake, a blip, a meaningless error. In the background hovered Robin's flatmate, no longer the disengaged and courteous Max, but a pale, simpering girl who echoed Matthew's persuasions, who giggled when he looked at her and urged Robin to give him what he wanted. Only when she'd managed to silence her alarm, and dispel the fog of sleep, did Robin, who was lying face down on her pillow, realise how closely the dream-flatmate had resembled Cynthia Phipps.

Struggling to understand why she'd set her alarm so early, she sat up in bed, the cream walls of her bedroom a blueish mauve in the dawn light, then remembered that Strike had planned a full team meeting, the first in two months, and that he'd asked her to come in an hour earlier than the others again, so that they could discuss the Bamborough case before everyone else got there.

Extremely tired, as she always seemed to be these days, Robin showered and dressed, fumbling over buttons, forgetting where she'd put her phone, realising there was a stain on her sweater only when halfway upstairs to the kitchen and generally feeling disgruntled at life and early starts. When she reached the upper floor, she found Max sitting at the dining table in his dressing gown, poring over a cookbook. The TV was on: the breakfast television presenter was asking whether Valentine's Day was an exercise in commercial cynicism or an opportunity to inject some much-needed romance into a couple's life.

'Has Cormoran got any special dietary requirements?' Max asked her, and when Robin looked blank, he said, 'For tonight. Dinner.'

'Oh,' said Robin, 'no. He'll eat anything.'

She checked her emails on her phone as she drank a mug of black coffee. With a small stab of dread, she saw one from her lawyer titled 'Mediation'. Opening it, she saw that an actual date was being proposed: Wednesday March the nineteenth, over a month away. She pictured Matthew talking to his own lawyer, consulting his diary, asserting his power, as ever. *I'm tied up for the whole of next month.* Then she imagined facing him across a boardroom table, their lawyers beside them, and felt panic mixed with rage.

'You should eat breakfast,' said Max, still reading cookbooks.

'I'll get something later,' said Robin, closing her email.

She picked up the coat she'd left draped over the arm of the sofa and said,

'Max, you haven't forgotten my brother and his friend are spending the weekend, have you? I doubt they'll be around much. It's just a base.'

'No, no, all good,' said Max vaguely, lost in recipes.

Robin headed out into the cool, damp early morning, getting all the way to the Tube before she realised that she didn't have her purse on her.

'*Shit!*'

Robin was usually tidy, efficient and organised; she rarely made this kind of mistake. Hair flying, she ran back to the flat, asking herself what the hell she could have done with it, and wondering, now panicking, whether she'd dropped it in the street or had it stolen out of her bag.

Meanwhile, in Denmark Street, the groggy Strike was hopping on his one foot out of the shower, eyes puffy, and similarly exhausted. The after-effects of a week spent covering Barclay's and Hutchins's shifts were now catching up with him, and he slightly regretted having asked Robin to come into work so early.

However, just after pulling on his trousers, his mobile rang and with a stab of fear, he saw Ted and Joan's number.

'Ted?'

'Hi, Corm. There's no need to panic, now,' said Ted. 'I just wanted to give you an update.'

'Go on,' said Strike, standing bare-chested and frozen in the cold grey light filtered by the too-thin curtains of his attic flat.

'She's not looking too clever. Kerenza was talking about trying to get her to hospital, but Joanie doesn't want to go. She's still in bed, she – didn't get up, yesterday,' said Ted, his voice cracking. 'Couldn't manage it.'

'Shit,' muttered Strike, sinking down onto his bed. 'Right, Ted, I'm coming.'

'You can't,' said his uncle. 'We're surrounded by

4

flood water. It's dangerous. Police are telling everyone to stay put, not to travel. Kerenza can . . . she says she can manage her pain at home. She's got drugs they can inject . . . because she's not eating a lot now. Kerenza doesn't think it's . . . you know . . . she thinks it'll be . . .'

He began to cry in earnest.

'. . . not immediate, but . . . she says . . . not long.'

'I'm coming,' said Strike firmly. 'Does Lucy know how bad Joan is?'

'I called you first,' said Ted.

'I'll tell her, don't worry about that. I'll ring you when we've put a plan together, all right?'

Strike hung up and called Lucy.

'Oh God, no,' his sister gasped, when he'd given her an unemotional summary of what Ted had said. 'Stick, I can't leave right now – Greg's stuck in Wales!'

'The hell's Greg doing in Wales?'

'It's for work – oh God, what are we going to do?'

'When's Greg back?'

'Tomorrow night.'

'Then we'll go down Sunday morning.'

'How? The trains are all off, the roads are flooded—'

'I'll hire a jeep or something. Polworth'll meet us the other end with a boat if we have to. I'll ring you back when I've got things sorted.'

Strike dressed, made himself tea and toast,

carried them downstairs to the partners' desk in the inner office and called Ted back, overriding his objections, telling him that, like it or not, he and Lucy were coming on Sunday. He could hear his uncle's yearning for them, his desperate need for company to share the burden of dread and grief. Strike then called Dave Polworth, who thoroughly approved of the plan and promised to be ready with boat, tow ropes and scuba equipment if necessary.

'I've got fuck all else to do. My place of work's underwater.'

Strike called a few car hire companies, finally finding one that had a jeep available. He was giving his credit card details when a text arrived from Robin.

Really sorry, I lost my purse, just found it, on my way now.

Strike had entirely forgotten that they were supposed to be catching up on the Bamborough case before the team meeting. Having finished hiring the jeep, he began to assemble the items he'd intended to discuss with Robin: the blood-smeared page he'd cut out of *The Magus*, which he'd now put into a plastic pouch, and the discovery he'd made the previous evening on his computer, which he brought up on his monitor, ready to show her.

He then opened up the rota, to check what shifts

he'd have to reallocate now that he was heading back to Cornwall, and saw 'Dinner with Max' written in for that evening.

'*Bollocks*,' he said. He didn't suppose he could get out of it now, having agreed to it the previous day, but this was the last thing he needed.

At that very moment, Robin, who was climbing the escalator at Tottenham Court Road two steps at a time, heard her mobile ringing in her bag.

'Yes?' she gasped into the phone, as she emerged into the station, one among many bustling commuters.

'Hey, Robs,' said her younger brother.

'Hi,' she said, using her Oyster card at the barrier. 'Everything OK?'

'Yeah, fine,' said Jonathan, though he didn't sound quite as cheerful as the last time they'd spoken. 'Listen, is it all right if I bring another guy with me to crash at yours?'

'What?' said Robin, as she emerged into the blustery rain and controlled chaos of the intersection of Tottenham Court Road and Charing Cross Road, at which there had now been building works for three and a half years. She hoped she'd misheard what Jonathan had said.

'Another guy,' he repeated. 'Is that OK? He'll sleep anywhere.'

'Oh Jon,' Robin moaned, half-jogging along Charing Cross Road now, 'we've only got one sofa bed.'

'Kyle'll sleep on the floor, he doesn't care,' said

Jonathan. 'It's not that big a deal is it? One more person?'

'OK, fine,' sighed Robin. 'You're still planning on getting here at ten, though?'

'I'm not sure. We might get an earlier train, we're thinking of skipping lectures.'

'Yeah, but the thing is,' said Robin, 'Cormoran's coming over to dinner to talk to Max—'

'Oh great!' said Jonathan, sounding slightly more enthusiastic. 'Courtney'd love to meet him, she's obsessed with crime!'

'No – Jon, I'm trying to tell you, Max needs to interview Cormoran about a part he's playing. I don't think there'll be enough food for another three—'

'Don't worry about that, if we get there earlier, we'll just order ourselves a takeaway.'

How was she supposed to say, 'Please don't come during dinner'? After he'd hung up, Robin broke into a jog, hoping that Jonathan's time management, which she knew from experience could use improvement, might see him miss enough trains south to delay his arrival.

Taking the corner into Denmark Street at a run, she saw, with a sinking feeling, Saul Morris ahead of her, walking towards the office and carrying a small, wrapped bunch of pink gerberas.

They'd better not be for me.

'Hey, Robs,' he said, turning as she ran up behind him. 'Oh dear,' he added, grinning, 'someone overslept. Pillow face,' he said, pointing at the spot on his cheek where, Robin surmised, her own still bore a faint crease from the way she'd slept, face down and unmoving, because she was so tired. 'For Pat,' he added, displaying his straight white teeth along with the gerberas. 'Says her husband never gets her anything on Valentine's.'

God, you're smarmy, Robin thought, as she unlocked the door. She noticed that he was calling her 'Robs' again, yet another sign that his discomfort in her presence post-Christmas had evaporated over the succeeding seven weeks. She wished she could as easily shrug off the lingering, unreasonable but no less potent sense of shame she felt, forever having seen his erection on her phone.

Upstairs, the harassed Strike was checking his watch when his mobile rang. It was unusually early for his old friend Nick Herbert to be calling him, and Strike, now sensitised to expect bad news, picked up with a sense of foreboding.

'All right, Oggy?'

Nick sounded hoarse, as though he'd been shouting.

'I'm fine,' said Strike, who thought he could hear footsteps and voices on the metal stairs outside. 'What's up?'

'Nothing much,' said Nick. 'Wondered whether you fancied a pint tonight. Just you and me.'

'Can't,' said Strike, very much regretting that this was so. 'Sorry, I've got something on.'

'Ah,' said Nick. 'OK. What about lunchtime, you free then?'

'Yeah, why not?' said Strike, after a slight hesitation. God knew he could use a pint away from work, from family, from his hundred other problems.

Through the open door he saw Robin enter the outer office, followed by Saul Morris, who was holding a bunch of flowers. He closed the dividing door on them, then his tired brain processed the flowers and the date.

'Hang on. Aren't you busy with Valentine's shit?' he asked Nick.

'Not this year,' said Nick.

There was a short silence. Strike had always considered Nick and Ilsa, a gastroenterologist and a lawyer respectively, the happiest couple he knew. Their house on Octavia Street had often been a place of refuge to him.

'I'll explain over a pint,' said Nick. 'I need one. I'll come to you.'

They agreed a pub and a time and rang off. Strike checked his watch again: he and Robin had fifteen minutes left of what he'd hoped would be an hour on Bamborough. Opening the door, he said,

'Ready? We haven't got long.'

'Sorry,' said Robin, hurrying inside. 'You got my text, didn't you? About the purse?'

'Yeah,' said Strike, closing the door on Morris and pointing at the page from *The Magus*, which he'd laid in front of Robin's seat. 'That's the page from the book in the Athorns' house.'

He'd called Robin about finding the Athorns straight after leaving the ironmonger, and she'd responded with excitement and congratulations. His present grumpiness aggravated her. Presumably it was due to her lateness, but was she not allowed a little human fallibility, after all the extra hours she'd put in lately, covering her own work and Strike's, managing the subcontractors, trying as hard as she could not to put extra stress on him when his aunt was dying? However, outside she could hear Barclay and Hutchins entering the outer office, which reminded her that not so very long ago, she'd been the temp, that Strike had laid down his expectations of a partner in uncompromising terms at the start of their professional relationship. There were three men outside who undoubtedly considered themselves better qualified for her position than she was. So, Robin simply sat down, picked up the page and read the passage beneath the smear.

'The writing mentions blood.'

'I know.'

'How fresh does blood have to be, to analyse?'

'The oldest sample I've heard of that was successfully analysed was twenty-something years old,' said Strike. 'If this is blood, and it dates from when Gwilherm Athorn was alive, it's a good decade older. On the other hand, it's been kept away from light and damp, inside that book, which might help. Anyway, I'm going to call Roy Phipps and ask him what Margot's blood group was and then I'll try and find someone to analyse it for us. Might try that bloke your friend Vanessa used to date in forensics, what was his name?'

'Oliver,' said Robin, 'and he's now her fiancé.'

'Well, him, yeah. One other interesting thing came out of my conversation with Samhain . . .'

He told her about Uncle Tudor's belief that 'Nico and his boys' had killed Margot Bamborough.

'"Nico" – d'you think—?'

'Niccolo "Mucky" Ricci? Odds on,' said Strike. 'He wasn't living far away and he must've been a local personality, although no one from the practice seems to have realised who'd walked into their Christmas party.

'I've left a message with the Athorns' social worker, because I want to know how much store we can put in Deborah and Samhain's memories. Shanker's supposed to be digging around on Ricci for me, but I've heard sod all from him. Might give him a prod.'

He held out his hand and Robin passed the blood-smeared page back.

'Anyway, the only other development is that I've found C. B. Oakden,' said Strike.

'What? How?'

'Last night,' said Strike. 'I was thinking about names. Irene getting them wrong – Douthwaite and Duckworth, Athorn and Applethorpe. Then I started thinking about how people often don't stray too far from their original name if they change it.'

He swung his computer monitor around to face her, and Robin saw a picture of a man in early middle age. He was slightly freckled, his eyes fractionally too close together and his hair thinning, though he still had enough to sweep across his narrow forehead. He was still just recognisable as the boy screwing up his face at the camera, at Margot Bamborough's barbecue.

The story below read:

SERIAL SWINDLER GETS JAIL SENTENCE

'Despicable Betrayal of Trust'

A serial fraudster who conned over £75,000 from elderly widows over a two-year period has been jailed for four years, nine months.

Brice Noakes, 49, of Fortune Street, Clerkenwell, who was born Carl Oaken, persuaded a total of nine 'vulnerable and trusting women' to part with jewellery and cash, which in one case amounted to £30,000 of life savings.

Noakes was described by Lord Justice McCrieff as 'a cunning and unscrupulous man who capitalised shamelessly on his victims' vulnerability.'

Smartly dressed and well-spoken Noakes targeted widows living alone, usually offering valuations on jewellery. Noakes persuaded his victims to allow him to remove valuable items from their houses, promising to return with an expert assessment.

On other occasions he posed as a representative from the council, who claimed that the householder was in arrears with council tax and about to be prosecuted.

'Using plausible but entirely fraudulent paperwork, you pressured and bullied vulnerable women into transferring money into an account set up for your own benefit,' said Lord Justice McCrieff, while sentencing.

'Some of the women concerned were initially too embarrassed to tell their families that they'd let this individual into their homes,' said Chief Inspector Grant. 'We believe there may be many more victims who are too ashamed to admit that they've been defrauded, and we would urge them, if they recognise Noakes' picture, to contact us.'

'The paper's misspelled his real name,' said Robin. 'They've printed "Oaken", not Oakden.'

'Which is why he wouldn't have shown up on a basic Google search,' said Strike.

Feeling subtly criticised, because she was the one who was supposed to be looking for Oakden, Robin glanced at the date on the news story, which was five years old.

'He'll be out of jail by now.'

'He is,' said Strike, turning the monitor back towards himself, typing another couple of words and turning it to face Robin again. 'I did a bit more searching on variations of his name, and . . .'

She saw an author page of the Amazon website, listing the books written by an author called Carl O. Brice. The photograph showed the same man from the newspaper, a little older, a little balder, a little more creased around the eyes. His thumbs hooked in his jeans pockets, he wore a black T-shirt with a white logo on it: a clenched fist inside the Mars symbol.

Carl O. Brice

Carl O. Brice is a life coach, entrepreneur and award-winning writer on men's issues including masculism, fathers' rights, gyno-centrism, men's mental health, female privilege and toxic feminism. Carl's personal experience of the gynocentric family court system, cultural misandry and male exploitation give him the tools and skills to guide men from all walks of life to healthier, happier lives. In his award-winning book series, Carl examines the catastrophic impact that modern feminism has had on freedom of speech, the workplace, men's rights and the nuclear family.

Robin glanced down the list of books beneath the author biography. The covers were cheap and amateurish. All featured pictures of women in various slightly pornified costumes and poses. A scantily dressed blonde wearing a crown was sitting on a throne for *From Courtly Love to Family Courts, A History of Gynocentrism*, whereas a brunette dressed in a rubber stormtrooper outfit pointed at the camera for *Shamed: The Modern War on Masculinity.*

'He's got his own website,' said Strike, turning the monitor back to himself. 'He self-publishes books, offers to coach men on how to get access to their kids, and flogs protein shakes and vitamins. I don't think he'll pass up the chance to talk to us. He seems the type to come running at the sniff of notoriety or money.

'Speaking of which,' said Strike, 'how're you getting on with that woman who thinks she saw Margot at the window on—?'

'Amanda Laws,' said Robin. 'Well, I went back to her offering her expenses if she'll come into the office, and she hasn't answered yet.'

16

'Well, chase her,' said Strike. 'You realise we're now six months in—?'

'Yes, I do realise that,' said Robin, unable to help herself. 'I learned counting at school.'

Strike raised his eyebrows.

'Sorry,' she muttered. 'I'm just tired.'

'Well, so am I, but I'm also mindful of the fact we still haven't traced some fairly important people yet. Satchwell, for instance.'

'I'm working on him,' said Robin, glancing at her watch and getting to her feet. 'I think they're all out there, waiting for us.'

'Why's Morris brought flowers?' said Strike.

'They're for Pat. For Valentine's Day.'

'Why the hell?'

Robin paused at the door, looking back at Strike.

'Isn't it obvious?'

She let herself out of the room, leaving Strike to frown after her, wondering what was obvious. He could imagine only two reasons to buy a woman flowers: because you were hoping to sleep with her, or to avoid being criticised for not buying flowers on a day when flowers might be expected. Neither seemed to apply in this case.

The team was sitting in a cramped circle outside, Hutchins and Barclay on the fake leather sofa, Morris on one of the fold-up plastic chairs that had been bought when the team outgrew the existing seats, and Pat on her own wheeled desk chair, which left another two uncomfortable plastic

17

chairs for the partners. Robin noticed how all three men stopped talking when Strike emerged from the inner office: when she'd led the meeting alone, she'd had to wait until Hutchins and Morris finished discussing a mutual police acquaintance who'd been caught taking bribes.

The bright pink daisy-like gerberas sat in a small vase on Pat's desk now. Strike glanced at them before saying,

'All right, let's start with Shifty. Morris, did you get anywhere with that bloke in the tracksuit?'

'Yeah, I did,' said Morris, consulting his notes. 'His name's Barry Fisher. He's divorced with one kid and he's a manager at Shifty's gym.'

Appreciative, low-toned growls of approval and interest issued from Strike, Barclay and Hutchins. Robin contented herself with a slight eyebrow raise. It was her experience that the slightest hint of warmth or approval from her was interpreted by Morris as an invitation to flirtation.

'So, I've booked myself in for a trial session with one of their trainers,' said Morris.

Bet it's with a woman, thought Robin.

'While I was talking to her, I saw him wandering about talking to some of the other girls. He's definitely hetero, judging by how he was looking at one of the women on the cross-trainer. I'm going back Monday for a workout, if that's all right with you, boss. Try and find out more about him.'

'Fine,' said Strike. 'Well, this looks like our first

solid lead: a link between Shifty and whatever's going on inside Elinor Dean's house.'

Robin, who'd spent the night before last sitting in her Land Rover outside Elinor's house, said,

'It might not be relevant, but Elinor took an Amazon delivery yesterday morning. Two massive boxes. They looked quite light, but—'

'We should open a book,' Morris told Strike, talking over Robin. 'Twenty on dominatrix.'

'Never seen the appeal in bein' whipped,' said Barclay thoughtfully. 'If I want pain, I jus' forget to put the bins oot.'

'Bit mumsy-looking, though, isn't she?' said Hutchins. 'If I had SB's money, I'd go for something a bit more—'

He sketched a slimmer figure in mid-air. Morris laughed.

'Ach, there's no accountin' for taste,' said Barclay. 'Army mate o' mine wouldnae look at anythin' under thirteen stone. We usedtae call him the Pork Whisperer.'

The men laughed. Robin smiled, mainly because Barclay was looking at her, and she liked Barclay, but she felt too tired and demoralised to be truly amused. Pat was wearing a 'boys will be boys' expression of bored tolerance.

'Unfortunately, I've got to go back to Cornwall on Sunday,' said Strike, 'which I appreciate—'

'The fuck are ye gonna get tae Cornwall?' asked Barclay, as the office windows shook with the wind.

'Jeep,' said Strike. 'My aunt's dying. Looks like she's got days.'

Robin looked at Strike, startled.

'I appreciate that leaves us stretched,' Strike continued matter-of-factly, 'but it can't be helped. I think it's worth continuing to keep an eye on SB himself. Morris'll do some digging with this bloke at the gym and the rest of you can divvy up shifts on Elinor Dean. Unless anyone's got anything to add,' said Strike, pausing for comments. The men all shook their heads and Robin, too tired to mention the Amazon boxes again, remained silent. 'Let's have a look at Postcard.'

'I've got news,' said Barclay laconically. 'She's back at work. I've talked tae her. Yer woman,' he added, to Robin, 'short. Big round glasses. Ambled over and started askin' questions.'

'What about?' asked Morris, a smirk playing around his lips.

'Light effects in the landscapes o' James Duffield Harding,' said Barclay. 'What d'ye think I asked, who she fancied for the Champions League?'

Strike laughed, and so did Robin, this time, glad to see Morris looking foolish.

'Yeah, I read the notice by his portrait an' looked him up on my phone round the corner,' said Barclay. 'Wanted a way o' gettin' ontae the subject o' weather wi' her. Anyway,' said the Glaswegian, 'coupla minutes intae the conversation, talkin' light effects an' broodin' skies an' that, she brought up oor weatherman friend. Turned pink when she mentioned him. Said he'd described a viewer's picture as "Turneresque" last week.

'It's her,' said Barclay, addressing Robin. 'She wanted tae mention him for the pleasure of sayin' his name. She's Postcard.'

'Bloody well done,' Strike told Barclay.

'It's Robin's win,' said Barclay. 'She made the pass. I jus' tapped it in.'

'Thanks, Sam,' said Robin, pointedly, not looking at Strike, who registered both the tone and her expression.

'Fair point,' said Strike, 'well done, both of you.' Aware that he'd been short with Robin during their meeting about the Bamborough case, Strike sought to make amends by asking her opinion on which of the waiting list clients they ought to contact, now that the Postcard case was as good as wrapped up, and she said she thought the commodities broker who thought her husband was sleeping with their nanny.

'Great,' said Strike. 'Pat, can you get in touch and tell her we're ready to roll if she still wants him under surveillance? If nobody's got anything else—'

'I have,' said Hutchins, generally the quietest person in the agency. 'It's about that roll of film you wanted passed to the Met.'

'Oh yeah?' said Strike. 'Is there news?'

'My mate rang last night. There's nothing to be done with it. You won't get any prosecutions now.'

'Why not?' said Robin.

She sounded angrier than she'd meant to. The men all looked at her.

'Perpetrators' faces all hidden,' said Hutchins. 'That arm that appears for a moment: you can't build a prosecution case on an out-of-focus ring.'

'I thought your contact said the roll had come out of a raid on one of Mucky Ricci's brothels?' said Robin.

'He *thinks* it did,' Hutchins corrected her. 'You won't get DNA evidence off a can that old, that's been kept in a shed and an attic and handled by a hundred people. It's a no-go. Shame,' he said indifferently, 'but there you are.'

Strike now heard his mobile ringing back on the partners' desk, where he'd left it. Worried it might be Ted, he excused himself from the meeting and retreated into the inner office, closing the door behind him.

There was no caller ID on the number ringing his mobile.

'Cormoran Strike.'

'Hello, Cormoran,' said an unfamiliar, husky voice. 'It's Jonny.'

There was a brief silence.

'Your father,' Rokeby added.

Strike, whose tired mind was full of Joan, of the agency's three open cases, of guilt about being grumpy with his partner, and the logistical demands he was placing on his employees by disappearing to Cornwall again, said nothing at all. Through the dividing door, he could hear the team still discussing the roll of film.

'Wanted a chat,' said Rokeby. 'Is that all right?'

Strike felt suddenly disembodied; completely detached from everything, from the office, from his fatigue, from the concerns that had seemed all-important just seconds ago. It was as though he and his father's voice existed alone and nothing else was fully real, except Strike's adrenalin, and a primal desire to leave a mark that Rokeby wouldn't quickly forget.

'I'm listening,' he said.

Another silence.

'Look,' said Rokeby, sounding slightly uneasy, 'I don't wanna do this by phone. Let's meet. It's been too fucking long. Water under the bridge. Let's meet, let's . . . I wanna – this can't go on. This fucking – feud, or whatever it is.'

Strike said nothing.

'Come to the house,' said Rokeby. 'Come over. Let's talk, and . . . you're not a kid any more. There are two sides to every story. Nothing's black and white.'

He paused. Strike still said nothing.

'I'm proud of you, d'you know that?' said Rokeby. 'I'm really fucking proud of you. What you've done and . . .'

The sentence petered out. Strike stared, motionless, at the blank wall in front of him. Beyond the partition wall, Pat was laughing at something Morris had said.

'Look,' repeated Rokeby, with just a tiny hint of temper now, because he was a man used to getting his own way. 'I get it, I do, but what the fuck can I do? I can't time travel. Al's told me what you've been saying, and there's a bunch of stuff you don't know, about your mother and all her fucking men. If you just come over, we can have a drink, we can have it all out. And,' said Rokeby, quietly insinuating, 'maybe I can help you out a bit, maybe there's something you want I can help out with, peace offering, I'm open to suggestions . . .'

In the outer office, Hutchins and Barclay were taking their leave, ready to get back to their separate jobs. Robin was thinking only about how much she wanted to go home. She was supposed to have the rest of the day off, but Morris was hanging around, and she was sure he was waiting because he wanted to walk with her to the Tube. Pretending to have paperwork to look at, she was rifling through a filing cabinet while Morris and Pat chatted, hoping he'd leave. She'd just opened an old file on a prolific adulterer, when Strike's voice filled the room from the inner office. She, Pat and Morris turned their heads. Several pages of the file Robin was balancing on top of the drawer slid to the floor.

'. . . so GO FUCK YOURSELF!'

Before Robin could exchange looks with Morris or Pat, the dividing door between inner and outer offices opened. Strike looked alarming: white, livid, his breath coming fast. He stormed through the outer office, grabbed his coat and could be heard heading down the metal staircase outside.

Robin picked up the fallen pages.

'Shit,' said Morris, grinning. 'Wouldn't have wanted to be on the end of *that* call.'

'Nasty temper,' said Pat, who looked weirdly satisfied. 'Knew it, the moment I laid eyes on him.'

CHAPTER 40

Thus as they words amongst them multiply,
They fall to strokes, the frute of too much
  talke . . .

Edmund Spenser
The Faerie Queene

Robin found no polite way of avoiding walking to the Tube with Morris and in consequence was obliged to listen to two off-colour jokes, and to lie about her Valentine's plans, because she could just imagine Morris's response if she told him Strike was coming over. Pretending that she hadn't heard or registered Morris's suggestion that they should get together one night to compare notes on lawyers, she parted from him at the bottom of the escalator with relief.

Tired and mildly depressed, Robin's thoughts lingered on Morris as the Tube sped her back towards Earl's Court. Was he so used to women responding readily to his undeniable handsomeness

26

that he took it for granted he was eliciting a positive response? Or did the fault lie in Robin herself, who, for the sake of politeness, for the cohesion of the team, because she didn't want to make trouble when the agency was so busy, continued to smile at his stupid jokes and chose not to say, loudly and clearly, 'I don't like you. We're never going to date.'

She arrived home to find the flat full of the cheering and delicious smell of simmering beef and red wine. Max appeared to have gone out, but a casserole was sitting in the oven and Wolfgang was lying as close to the hot door as he could manage without burning himself, reminding Robin of fans who camped out overnight in hope of catching a glimpse of pop stars.

Instead of lying down on her bed and trying to get a few hours' sleep before dinner, Robin, who'd been stung by Strike's reminders that she hadn't chased up Amanda Laws or found Paul Satchwell, made herself more coffee, opened her laptop and sat down at the small dining table. After sending Amanda Laws another email, she opened Google. When she did so, each letter of the logo turned one by one into a pastel-coloured, heart-shaped candy with a slogan on it: MR RIGHT, PUPPY LUV and BLIND DATE, and for some reason, her thoughts moved to Charlotte Campbell. It would, of course, be very difficult for a married woman to meet her lover tonight. And who, she wondered, had Strike been telling to fuck off over the phone?

Robin set to work on Satchwell, trying to emulate Strike's success in finding C. B. Oakden. She played around with Satchwell's three names, reversing Paul and Leonard, trying initials and deliberate misspellings, but the men who appeared in answer to her searches didn't look promising.

Was it possible that Margot's tight-jeaned, hairy-chested artist had turned, over the space of four decades, into classic car collector Leo Satchwell, a rotund man with a goatee who wore tinted glasses? Unlikely, Robin decided, after wasting ten minutes on Leo: judging by the photographs on his Facebook page, in which he stood alongside other enthusiasts, he was barely five feet tall. There was a Brian Satchwell in Newport, but he had a lazy eye and was five years too young, and a Colin Satchwell in Eastbourne who ran an antiques business. She was still trying to find an image of Colin when she heard the front door open. A few minutes later, Max walked into the kitchen, with a bag of shopping in his hand.

'How's the casserole doing?' he asked.

'Great,' said Robin, who hadn't checked it.

'Get out of the way, Wolfgang, unless you want to be burned,' said Max, as he opened the oven door. To Robin's relief, the casserole appeared to be doing well, and Max shut the door again.

Robin closed her laptop. A feeling that it was rude to sit typing while someone else was cooking in her vicinity persisted from the days when she'd

28

lived with a husband who'd always resented her bringing work home.

'Max, I'm really sorry about this, but my brother's bringing another friend with him tonight.'

'That's fine,' said Max, unpacking his shopping.

'And they might be arriving early. They aren't expecting to eat with us—'

'They're welcome. This casserole serves eight. I was going to freeze the rest, but we can eat the lot tonight, I don't mind.'

'That's really nice of you,' said Robin, 'but I know you want to talk to Cormoran alone, so I could take them—'

'No, the more the merrier,' said Max, who seemed mildly cheerful at the prospect of company. 'I told you, I've decided to give up the recluse life.'

'Oh,' said Robin. 'OK, then.'

She had some misgivings about what she feared might be quite an ill-assorted group, but telling herself her tiredness was making her pessimistic, she retired to her bedroom, where she spent the rest of the afternoon trying to find a photograph of Colin Satchwell. Finally, at six o'clock, after a great deal of cross-referencing, she located a picture on the website of a local church, where he appeared to be an alderman. Portly, with a low hairline, he in no way resembled the artist she sought.

Aware that she really ought to change and go

upstairs to help Max, she was on the point of closing her laptop when a new email arrived. The subject line was one word: 'Creed', and with a spurt of nervous excitement, Robin opened it.

Hi Robin,

Quick update: I've passed the Creed request to the two people I mentioned. My Ministry of Justice contact was a bit more hopeful than I thought he'd be. This is confidential, but another family's been lobbying for Creed to be interviewed again. Their daughter was never found, but they've always believed a pendant in Creed's house belonged to her. My contact thinks something might be achievable if the Bamborough family joined forces with the Tuckers. I don't know whether Cormoran would be allowed to conduct the interview, though. That decision would be taken by the Broadmoor authorities, the Ministry of Justice and the Home Office and my MoJ contact thinks it more likely to be police. I'll let you know what's going on as soon as I hear anything else.

Best, Izzy

Robin read this email through and allowed herself a flicker of optimism, though she didn't

30

intend to tell Strike what she was up to just yet. With luck, they'd be allowed to talk to the police interviewer before he or she went into Broadmoor. She typed an email of thanks, then began to get ready for dinner.

Her slightly improved mood survived looking in the mirror and seeing how tired she looked, with grey shadows under her slightly bloodshot eyes, and hair that definitely needed washing. Making do with dry shampoo, Robin tied back her hair, changed into clean jeans and her favourite top, applied undereye concealer and was on the point of leaving her room when her mobile rang.

Afraid that it would be Strike cancelling, she was positively relieved to see Ilsa's name.

'Hi, Ilsa!'

'Hi, Robin. Are you with Corm?'

'No,' said Robin. Instead of leaving her bedroom, she sat back down on the bed. 'Are you OK?'

Ilsa sounded odd: weak and numb.

'D'you know where Corm is?'

'No, but he should be here in ten minutes. D'you want me to give him a message?'

'No. I – d'you know whether he's been with Nick today?'

'No,' said Robin, now worried. 'What's going on, Ilsa? You sound terrible.'

Then she remembered that it was Valentine's Day and registered the fact that Ilsa didn't know where her husband was. Something more than worry overtook Robin: it was fear. Nick and Ilsa were the happiest couple she knew. The five weeks she'd lived with them after leaving Matthew had restored some of Robin's battered faith in marriage. They couldn't split up: not Nick and Ilsa.

'It's nothing,' said Ilsa.

'Tell me,' Robin insisted. 'What—?'

Wrenching sobs issued through the phone.

'Ilsa, what's happened?'

'I . . . I miscarried.'

'Oh God,' gasped Robin. 'Oh no. Ilsa, I'm so sorry.'

She knew that Nick and Ilsa had been trying for some years to have a child. Nick never talked about it and Ilsa, only rarely. Robin had had no idea she was pregnant. She suddenly remembered Ilsa not drinking, on the night of her birthday.

'It happened – in the – in the supermarket.'

'Oh no,' whispered Robin. 'Oh God.'

'I started bleeding . . . at court . . . we're in the middle of a . . . massive case . . . couldn't leave . . .' said Ilsa. 'And then . . . and then . . . heading home . . .'

She became incoherent. Tears started in Robin's eyes as she sat with the phone clamped to her ear.

'. . . knew . . . something bad . . . so I got out of the cab . . . and I went . . . into the supermarket . . . and I was in . . . the loo . . . and I felt . . .

felt . . . and then . . . a little . . . blob . . . a tiny bod – bod – body . . .'

Robin put her face in her hands.

'And . . . I didn't know . . . what to do . . . but . . . there was a woman . . . in the loo with . . . and she . . . it had happened . . . to her . . . so kind . . .'

She dissolved again into incoherence. Snorts, gulps and hiccups filled Robin's ear before words became intelligible again.

'And Nick said . . . it was my fault. Said . . . all my fault . . . working . . . too hard . . . I didn't take . . . enough care . . . didn't put . . . the baby first.'

'He didn't,' said Robin. She liked Nick. She couldn't believe he'd have said such a thing to his wife.

'He did, he said I should've . . . come home . . . that I . . . put w – work . . . before the b – baby—'

'Ilsa, listen to me,' said Robin. 'If you got pregnant once, you can get pregnant again.'

'No, no, no, I can't,' said Ilsa, dissolving again into tears, 'it was our third go at IVF. We agreed . . . agreed . . . no more after this. No more.'

The doorbell rang.

'Ilsa, I've got to get the door, it might be Cormoran—'

'Yes, yes, go . . . it's fine . . . it's all fine.'

Before Robin could stop her, Ilsa had hung up. Hardly knowing what she was doing, Robin ran downstairs and flung open the door.

But naturally, it wasn't Strike. He'd never arrived on time for any out-of-work event to which she'd invited him, whether drinks, house-warming party or even her wedding. Instead she found herself facing Jonathan, the brother who most resembled her: tall and slender, with the same strawberry blond hair and blue eyes. The resemblance was even closer this evening, because both siblings looked peaky. Jonathan, too, had shadows under his eyes, not to mention a slightly grey cast to his skin.

'Hey, Robs.'

'Hi,' said Robin, accepting Jonathan's hug and trying to act pleased to see him, 'come in.'

'This is Courtney,' said Jonathan, 'and that's Kyle.'

'Hiya,' giggled Courtney, who was holding a can. She was an exquisitely pretty girl, with large dark eyes and long black hair, and she seemed slightly tipsy. Kyle, who accidentally bashed Robin with his large rucksack on entering, was a couple of inches taller than she was, skinny, with a high-fade haircut, large, bloodshot eyes and a neatly groomed beard.

'Hi there,' he said, holding out his hand and smiling down at Robin. A stranger might have thought he was welcoming her to his flat, rather than the other way around. 'Robin, yeah?'

'Yes,' said Robin, forcing a smile. 'Lovely to meet you. Come upstairs; we're eating on the top floor.'

Lost in thoughts of Ilsa, she followed the three

students. Courtney and Kyle were giggling and whispering together, Courtney a little clumsy on her feet. On reaching the living area, Robin introduced all three guests to Max, while Kyle dumped his none-too-clean rucksack on their host's cream sofa.

'Thanks very much for letting us stay,' said Jonathan to Max, who'd laid the table for six. 'Something smells really good.'

'I'm vegan,' piped up Courtney. 'But I can just eat, like, pasta, or whatever.'

'I'll do some pasta, don't you worry about that,' Robin told Max hastily, as she surreptitiously lifted Kyle's dirty rucksack off the sofa, trying not to make a big deal of what she was doing. Courtney promptly knelt on the sofa with her damp trainers still on, and said to Robin,

'Is this the sofa bed?'

Robin nodded.

'We'll have to sort out who sleeps where,' said Courtney, with a glance at Kyle. Robin thought she saw her brother's smile falter.

'Actually, why don't we put all the bags in my bedroom for now?' Robin suggested, as Jonathan swung his holdall onto the sofa, too. 'And keep this area clear for after dinner?'

Neither Courtney nor Kyle showed any inclination to move, so Robin and Jonathan took the bags downstairs together. Once they were in Robin's room, Jonathan took a box of chocolates out of his holdall and gave them to his sister.

'Thanks, Jon, that's lovely. D'you feel OK? You look a bit pale.'

'I was blunted last night. Listen, Robs . . . don't say anything to Courtney about her being, like, my girlfriend or whatever.'

'I wasn't going to.'

'Good, because . . .'

'You've split up?' Robin suggested sympathetically.

'We weren't ever – we hooked up a couple of times,' muttered Jonathan, 'but – I dunno, I think she might be into Kyle now.'

Courtney's laugh rang out from the upper floor. With a perfunctory smile at his sister, Jonathan returned to his friends.

Robin tried to call Ilsa back, but her number was engaged. Hoping this meant that she'd located Nick, Robin texted:

Just tried to call you. Please let me know what's going on. I'm worried about you. Robin xxx

She went back upstairs and started cooking pumpkin ravioli for Courtney. Apparently sensing that the casserole would soon be leaving the oven, Wolfgang slunk around Max's and Robin's ankles. Checking her watch, Robin noted that Strike was already fifteen minutes late. His record was an hour and a half. She tried, without much success, not to feel angry. After the way he'd treated her for being late this morning . . .

Robin was just draining the ravioli when the doorbell finally rang.

'D'you want me—?' said Max, who was pouring drinks for Jonathan, Courtney and Kyle.

'No, I'll do it,' said Robin shortly.

When she opened the door, she knew immediately that Strike, who was peering down at her with unfocused eyes, was drunk.

'Sorry I'm late,' he said thickly. 'Can I have a pee?'

She stood back to let him pass. He reeked of Doom Bar and cigarettes. Tense as she was, Robin noted that he hadn't thought to bring Max a bottle of anything, in spite of the fact he'd apparently spent all afternoon in the pub.

'The bathroom's there,' she said, pointing. He disappeared inside. Robin waited on the landing. He seemed to take a very long time.

'We're eating up here,' she said, when at last he emerged.

'More stairs?' mumbled Strike.

When they reached the open-plan living area, he seemed to pull himself together. He shook hands with Max and Jonathan in turn and said quite coherently that he was pleased to meet them. Courtney temporarily abandoned Kyle and bounced over to say hello to the famous detective, and Strike looked positively enthusiastic as he took in her looks. Suddenly very conscious of her own washed-out and puffy-eyed appearance, Robin turned back to the kitchen area to put Courtney's ravioli in a bowl for her. Behind her, she heard Courtney saying,

'And this is Kyle.'

'Oh, yeah, you're the detective?' Kyle said, determinedly unimpressed.

Jonathan, Courtney, Kyle and Max already had drinks, so Robin poured herself a large gin and tonic. While she was adding ice, a cheerful Max came back into the kitchen to fetch Strike a beer, then got the casserole out of the oven and on to the table. Wolfgang whined as the object of his devotion was lifted out of his reach.

While Max served everyone at the table, Robin set Courtney's ravioli down in front of her.

'Oh God, no, wait,' said Courtney. 'Is this vegan? Where's the packet?'

'In the bin,' said Robin.

'Tuh,' said Courtney, and she got up and walked into the kitchen. Max and Robin were the only two people at the table whose eyes didn't automatically follow Courtney. Robin downed half her gin before picking up her knife and fork.

'No, it's OK,' called Courtney, from beside the bin. 'It's vegan.'

'Oh good,' said Robin.

To Robin's left, Max began asking Strike's opinion on various aspects of his character's personality and past. Courtney returned to the table and began to wolf down her pasta, drinking and topping up her wine regularly as she went while telling Jonathan and Kyle her plans about a protest march at university. Robin joined in neither conversation, but ate and drank in silence, one eye on the mobile beside her plate in case Ilsa texted or rang back.

'. . . couldn't happen,' Strike was saying. 'He wouldn't've been allowed to join up in the first place, conviction for possession with intent to supply. Total bollocks.'

'Really? The writers did quite a lot of research—'

'Should've known that, then.'

'. . . *so* yeah, basically, you dress up in your underwear and short skirts and stuff,' Courtney was saying, and when Kyle and Jon laughed she said, '*Don't*, it's serious—'

'. . . no, this is useful,' said Max, scribbling in a notebook. 'So if he'd been in jail before the army—'

'If he'd done more than thirty months, the army wouldn't've taken him . . .'

'I'm not wearing *suspenders*, Kyle – anyway, Miranda doesn't want—'

'I don't know how long he's supposed to have done,' said Max. 'I'll check. Tell me about drugs in the army, how common—?'

'—so she says, "D'you not understand how problematic the word 'slut' is, Courtney?" And I'm like, "Er, what d'you think—"'

'"What d'you think a fucking SlutWalk's *for*?"' said Kyle, talking over Courtney. He had a deep voice and the air of a young man who was used to being listened to.

The screen of Robin's mobile lit up. Ilsa had texted back.

'Excuse me,' she muttered, though nobody was paying her any attention, and she headed into the kitchen area to read what Ilsa had said.

> **Didn't mean to worry you. Nick home, shitfaced. He's been in the pub with Corm. We're talking. He says he didn't mean it the way I took it. What other way was there? X**

Robin, who felt entirely on Ilsa's side, nevertheless texted back:

> **He's a dickhead but I know he really loves you. Xxx**

As she poured herself another double gin and tonic, Max called to her, asking her to bring Strike another beer from the fridge. When Robin set the open bottle down in front of Strike he didn't thank her, but merely took a long pull on it and raised his voice, because he was having difficulty trying to make himself heard over Kyle and Courtney, whose conversation had now migrated to the unknown Miranda's views on pornography.

'. . . so I'm, like, you *do* understand that women can actually *choose* what to do with their own bodies, Miran – Oh shit, sorry—'

Courtney's expansive gesture had knocked over her wine glass. Robin jumped up to get the kitchen roll. By the time she got back, Courtney's glass had been refilled by Kyle. Robin mopped up the wine while the two separate conversations grew steadily louder on either side of her, binned the sodden kitchen roll, then sat back down, wishing she could just go to bed.

'. . . troubled background, that's fucking original, guess what, plenty of people join the army because they want to serve, not to escape . . .'

'Pure whorephobia,' boomed Kyle. 'I s'pose she thinks waitresses love every fucking minute of their jobs, does she?'

'. . . and he can't have been in 1 Rifles if he's your age. The battalion was only formed . . .'

'. . . labour for hire, where's the fucking difference?'

'. . . think it was end 2007 . . .'

'. . . and some women enjoy *watching* porn, too!'

Courtney's words fell loudly into a temporary lull. Everyone looked round at Courtney, who'd blushed and was giggling with her hand over her mouth.

'It's all right, we're talking feminism,' said Kyle, with a smirk. 'Courtney isn't suggesting, y'know – after-dinner entertainment.'

'*Kyle!*' gasped Courtney, slapping his upper arm and dissolving into further giggles.

'Who wants pudding?' Robin asked, standing up

41

to collect the empty plates. Max, too, got to his feet.

'I'm sorry Strike's so pissed,' Robin murmured to Max, as she tipped a few uneaten pieces of ravioli into the bin.

'Are you kidding?' said Max, with a slight smile. 'This is pure gold. My character's an alcoholic.'

He'd gone, bearing a homemade cheesecake to the table, before Robin could tell him that Strike didn't usually drink this much; indeed, this was only the second time she'd ever known him drunk. The first time he'd been sad and quite endearing, but tonight there was a definite undercurrent of aggression. She remembered the shouted 'Go fuck yourself' she'd heard through the office door that afternoon and again wondered to whom Strike had been talking.

Robin followed Max back to the table, carrying a lemon tart and a third large gin and tonic. Kyle was now treating the entire table to his views on pornography. Robin didn't much like the expression on Strike's face. He'd often displayed an instinctive antipathy towards the kind of young man you could least imagine in the army; she trusted he was going to keep his feelings to himself tonight.

'. . . form of entertainment, just like any other,' Kyle was saying, with an expansive gesture. Fearful of more accidents, Robin discreetly moved the almost empty wine bottle out of hitting range. 'When you look at it objectively, strip it from all the puritanical bullshit—'

'Yeah, exactly,' said Courtney, 'women have got agency over their own—'

'—movies, gaming, it all stimulates the pleasure centres in your brain,' said Kyle, now pointing at his own immaculately groomed head. 'You could make an argument that movies are emotional pornography. All this moralistic, manufactured outrage about porn—'

'I can't eat either of those if they've got dairy in them,' Courtney whispered to Robin, who pretended she hadn't heard.

'—women want to make a living out of their own bodies, that's the literal definition of female empowerment and you could argue it has more societal benefit than—'

'When I was in Kosovo,' said Strike unexpectedly and all three students turned to look at him, with startled expressions. Strike paused, fumbling to get his cigarettes out of his pocket.

'Cormoran,' said Robin, 'you can't smo—'

'No problem,' said Max, getting up, 'I'll bring an ashtray.'

It took Strike three attempts to make his lighter work and in the meantime everybody watched him in silence. Without raising his voice, he'd dominated the room.

'Who'd like cheesecake?' Robin said into the silence, her voice artificially cheery.

'I can't,' said Courtney, with a slight pout. 'But I might be able to have the lemon tart, if it's—?'

'When I was in Kosovo,' Strike repeated, exhaling

as Max returned, placed an ashtray in front of him and sat back down again, '—cheers – I investigated a porn case – well, human trafficking. Coupla soldiers had paid for sex with underage girls. They were filmed without their knowledge an' the videos ended up on PornHub. Case ended up part of an international civilian investigation. Whole load of pre-pubescent boys and girls had been trafficked into porn. The youngest was seven.'

Strike took a large drag of his cigarette, squinting through the smoke at Kyle.

'What societal benefit would you say that had?' he asked.

There was a short, nasty silence in which the three students stared at the detective.

'Well, obviously,' said Kyle, with a small half-laugh, 'that's – that's a completely different thing. Nobody's talking about kids – that's not – that's illegal, isn't it? I'm talking about—'

'Porn industry's full of trafficking,' said Strike, still watching Kyle through his smoke. 'Women and kids from poor countries. One of the little girls in my case was filmed with a plastic bag over her head, while a bloke anally raped her.'

Out of the corner of her eye, Robin saw Kyle and Courtney throw her darting looks and knew, with an elevator drop in the area of her solar plexus, that her brother must have shared her history with his friends. Max was the only person at the table who seemed entirely relaxed. He was watching Strike with the dispassionate attention of a chemist checking an ongoing experiment.

'The video of that kid was viewed over a hundred thousand times online,' said Strike. Cigarette jammed in his mouth, he now helped himself to a large piece of cheesecake, effectively demolishing it to get a third of it onto his plate. 'Plenty of pleasure centres stimulated there, eh?' he went on, looking up at Kyle.

'No, but that's completely different, though,' said Courtney, rallying to Kyle's defence. 'We were talking about women who – it's up to women, grown women, to decide what they want to do with their own bod—'

'Did you cook all this?' Strike asked Max through a mouthful of cheesecake. He still had a lit cigarette in his left hand.

'Yes,' said Max.

'Bloody good,' said Strike. He turned back to Kyle. 'How many waitresses d'you know who got trafficked into it?'

'Well, obviously none but – I mean, you're bound to've seen that bad stuff, aren't you, being police—'

'As long as you don't have to see it, all good, eh?'

'Well, if you feel like that . . .' said Kyle, red in the face now, 'if you're so against it, you must never've – you've never used porn, then, you don't—?'

'If nobody else wants pudding,' said Robin

loudly, standing up and pointing towards the sofa area, 'shall we have coffee over there?'

Without waiting for an answer, she headed for the kitchen area. Behind her, she heard the scraping of a couple of chairs. After switching on the kettle, she headed downstairs to the bathroom, where, after she'd peed, she sat for five minutes on the toilet with her face in her hands.

Why had Strike turned up drunk? Why did they have to talk about rape and porn? Her attacker had been a voracious consumer of violent pornography, with a particular emphasis on choking, but his internet search history had been deemed inadmissible evidence by the judge. Robin didn't want to know whether Strike used porn; she didn't want to think about trafficked children being filmed, just as she didn't want to remember Morris's dick pic on her phone, or the snuff movie Bill Talbot had stolen. Tired and low, she asked herself why Strike couldn't leave the students alone, if not out of consideration for his host, then for her, his partner.

She headed back upstairs. Halfway to the living area she heard Kyle's heated voice and knew the argument had escalated. Arriving on the top floor, Robin saw the other five sitting around the coffee table, on which stood a cafetière, a bottle and the chocolates Jonathan had brought. Strike and Max were both holding glasses of brandy while Courtney, who was now very obviously drunk, though nowhere near as much as Strike, was nodding along with Kyle's argument, a cup of coffee balanced precariously in her hands. Robin sat back down at the abandoned dining table, away from the rest of the group, took a piece of beef out of the casserole and fed it to a pathetically grateful Wolfgang.

'The *point* is to destigmatise and reclaim derogatory language about women,' Kyle was saying to Strike. 'That's the *point.*'

'And that'll be 'chieved by a bunch'f nice middle-class girls going f'ra walk in their underwear, will it?' said Strike, his voice thick with alcohol.

'Well, not necessar'ly *under*—' began Courtney.

'It's about ending victim-blaming,' said Kyle loudly. 'Surely you can—?'

'An' how's it end victim-blaming?'

'Well, *obv'sly,*' said Courtney loudly, 'by changing the adertu – the underlying attitudes—'

'You think rapists'll see you all marching 'long and think "better jack in the raping", do you?'

Courtney and Kyle both began shouting at Strike. Jonathan glanced anxiously at his sister, who felt another of those sickening drops in her stomach.

'It's about destigmatising—'

'Oh, don't get me wrong, plen'y of men will enjoy watching you all strut past in your bras,' said Strike, taking a sloppy gulp of brandy, ''n 'I'm sure you'll look great on Instagram—'

'It's not about Instagram!' said Courtney, who

47

sounded almost tearful now. 'We're making a serious point about—'

'Men who call women sluts, yeah, you said,' said Strike, talking over her again. 'I'm sure they'll feel properly rebuked, watching you prounce – prance by in your mini-skirt.'

'It's not about *rebuking*,' said Kyle, 'you're missing the—'

'I'm not missing your super-subtle fucking point,' snapped Strike. 'I'm telling you that in the *real* world, this f'cking Whore Walk—'

'SlutWalk,' said Kyle and Courtney loudly.

'—'ll make fuck-all difference. The kind of man who calls women sluts'll look at your fucking sideshow and think "there go a load of sluts, look". Reclaim fucking language all you fucking like. You don't change real altit – att – real-world attitudes by deciding slurs aren't derug – derogat'ry.'

Wolfgang, who was still quivering at Robin's ankle in the hope of getting more beef, emitted a loud whimper, which made Strike glance around. He saw Robin sitting there, pale and impassive.

'What *d'you* think 'bout all this?' Strike asked her loudly, waving his glass in the direction of the students, so that brandy slopped over the rim onto the carpet.

'I think it would be a good idea to change the subject,' said Robin, whose heart was beating so fast it hurt.

'Would *you* go on a fucking Whore—?'

'I don't know, maybe,' said Robin, blood thumping in her ears, wanting only for the conversation to end. Her rapist had grunted 'whore' over and over again during the attack. If her would-be killer had squeezed her neck for another thirty seconds, it would have been the last word she heard on earth.

'She's b'ng polite,' said Strike, turning back to the students.

'Talking for women now, are you?' sneered Kyle.

'For an *actual* rape victim!' said Courtney.

The room seemed to warp. A clammy silence descended. On the edge of Robin's field of vision she saw Max turn to look at her.

Strike got to his feet at the second attempt. Robin knew he was saying something to her, but it was all noise: her ears felt full of cotton wool. Strike lurched off towards the door: he was leaving. He bounced off the doorframe and disappeared from sight.

Everyone continued to stare at Robin.

'Oh God, I'm really sorry if I shouldn't have said that,' whispered Courtney through the fingers she'd pressed to her mouth. Her eyes were brimming with tears. From downstairs came the sound of the door slamming.

'It's fine,' said a distant voice that sounded quite like Robin's own. 'Excuse me a moment.'

She got to her feet, and followed Strike.

CHAPTER 41

With that they gan their shiuering speares to
  shake,
And deadly points at eithers breast to bend,
Forgetfull each to haue bene euer others frend.

Edmund Spenser
The Faerie Queene

The dark, unfamiliar road took the exceptionally drunk Strike by surprise. Rain and high winds battered him as he stood, swaying, wondering which direction the Tube was. His usually reliable sense of direction was telling him to turn right, so he lurched off that way, searching his pockets for cigarettes as he went, savouring the delicious release of tension and temper he'd just enjoyed. The memory of what had just happened presented itself in a few scattered fragments: Kyle's angry red face. *Tosser. Fucking students.* Max laughing at something Strike had said. Lots of food. Even more drink.

Rain sparkled in the street lights and blurred

Strike's vision. Objects seemed to shrink and enlarge around him, particularly the parked car that suddenly put itself in his path as he attempted to walk in a straight line down the street. His thick fingers fumbled fruitlessly in his pockets. He couldn't find his cigarettes.

That last brandy might have been a mistake. He could still taste it. He didn't like brandy, and he'd had a hell of a lot of Doom Bar with Nick in the pub.

It was a mighty effort to walk in these high winds. His glow of well-being was wearing off, but he definitely didn't feel sick, even after all that beef casserole and a sizeable bit of cheesecake, though he didn't really want to think about them, nor about the forty or so cigarettes he'd consumed in the past twenty-four hours, nor about the brandy he could still taste.

Without warning, his stomach contracted. Strike staggered to a gap between two cars, bent double and vomited as copiously as he'd done at Christmas, over and over, for several minutes, until he was standing with his hands on his knees, still heaving, but bringing nothing else up.

Sweaty-faced, he stood up, wiping his mouth on the back of his hand, pistons banging in his head. It was several seconds before he became aware of the pale figure standing watching him, its fair hair blowing wildly in the wind.

'Wh—? Oh,' he said, as Robin came into focus. 'It's you.'

It occurred to him that she might have followed him to bring his forgotten cigarettes and looked hopefully at her hands, but they were empty. Strike moved away from the puddle of vomit in the gutter and leaned up against another parked car.

'I was in the pub with Nick all afternoon,' he said thickly, under the impression that Robin might be concerned about him.

Something hard was pressing into his buttock. Now he realised that he did have his cigarettes on him, after all, and he was glad of this, because he'd rather taste tobacco than vomit. He tugged the pack out of his back pocket and, after a few false starts, managed to light up.

At last, it penetrated his consciousness that Robin's demeanour was unusual. Focusing on her face, he registered it as white and oddly pinched.

'What?'

'"What?"' she repeated. 'Fucking "*what?*"'

Robin swore far less often than Strike did. The damp night air, which felt icy on Strike's sweaty face, was rapidly sobering him up. Robin appeared to be angry: angrier, in fact, than he'd ever seen her. But drink was still slowing his reactions, and nothing better occurred to him than to repeat,

'What?'

'You arrive late,' she said, 'because of *course* you do, because when have you ever shown me

52

the common *fucking* courtesy of turning up on time—'

'Wha—?' said Strike again, this time less because he was looking for information than in disbelief. She was the unique woman in his life who'd never tried to change him. This wasn't the Robin he knew.

'You arrive *rat-arsed*, because of *course* you do, because what do I matter? It's only *Robin* who'll be embarrassed, and *my* flatmate, and *my* fam—'

'He wasn't bothered,' Strike managed to say. His memories of the evening weren't particularly distinct, but he was sure of that, at least: Max hadn't minded him being drunk. Max had given him more booze. Max had laughed at a joke he'd made, which he couldn't now remember. He liked Max.

'And then you launch an attack on my guests. And then,' said Robin, 'you lay me open to having something I wanted to keep priv – to keep—'

Her eyes were suddenly wet, her fists clenched, her body rigid.

'—to keep private bandied about in a fucking argument, in front of strangers. Did it *once* occur—'

'Hang on,' said Strike, 'I never—'

'—*once* occur to you that I might not want *rape* discussed, in front of people I barely know?'

'*I* never—'

'Why were you asking me whether I think SlutWalks are a good idea?'

'Well, obv'sly b'cause—'

'Did we need to talk about child rape over dinner?'

'I was making a p—'

'And then you *walk out*, and leave me to—'

'Well,' said Strike, 'by the sounds of it, the sooner I left, the bett—'

'Better for *you*,' she said, advancing on him, her teeth bared: he'd never seen her like this before, 'because you got to dump all your aggression at my house, then walk out and let me clean up your fucking mess, as per usual!'

'"As per fucking usual?"' said Strike, eyebrows raised. 'Wait a—'

'Now I've got to go back in there, and make it all right, soothe everyone's feelings—'

'No, you haven't,' Strike contradicted her. 'Go to fucking bed if you—'

'It's. What. I. DO!' shouted Robin, thumping herself hard on the sternum with each word. Shocked into silence, Strike stared at her. 'Like I remember to say *please* and *thank you* to the secretary, when you don't give a toss! Like I excuse your bad moods to other people when they get offended! Like I suck up a ton of shit on your behalf—'

'Whoa,' said Strike, pushing himself off the stationary car, and looking down at her from his full height. 'Where's all this—?'

54

'—and you can't be *fucking* bothered, with all I do for you, to arrive sober for *one dinner*—'

'If you must know,' said Strike, temper rising anew from the ashes of his previous euphoria, 'I was in the pub with Nick, who—'

'—whose wife just lost their baby! I know – and what the *fuck* was he doing in the pub with you, leaving her to—'

'She threw him out!' barked Strike. 'Did she tell you that, during the Great Sisterhood Grievance Meeting? And I'm not going to apologise for wanting some fucking R&R after the week I've just had—'

'—whereas *I* don't need R&R, do I? *I* haven't forfeited half my annual leave—'

'How many times have I thanked you for covering for me when I'm in Corn—?'

'So what was with you being an arsehole to me this morning, when I was late for the *first fucking time ever*—'

'I'd had three and a half hours' sleep—'

'You live over the bloody office!'

'Fuck this,' said Strike, throwing his cigarette down. He began to walk away from her, certain now of the direction to the Tube, thinking of the things he could have said: that it was guilt about the pressure he was putting on Robin that had kept him in London, when he should be in St Mawes with his dying aunt; Jonny Rokeby on the phone that morning; and Nick's tears in the pub, and the relief it had been to sit with an old mate

55

and drink, and listen to someone else's troubles instead of fret about his own.

'And *don't*,' bellowed Robin from behind him, 'buy me any more *fucking flowers*!'

'No danger of that!' yelled Strike over his shoulder, as he strode away into the darkness.

CHAPTER 42

. . . his late fight
With Britomart, so sore did him offend,
That ryde he could not, till his hurts he did
amend.

Edmund Spenser
The Faerie Queene

When Strike woke on Saturday morning, with a thumping headache and a foul-tasting mouth, it took him a while to piece together exactly what had happened the previous evening. Aside from the memory of vomiting, which he felt he'd done far too much of lately, all he could at first recall were Kyle's bright red face and Robin's pinched white one.

But then, slowly, he reconstructed Robin's complaints: arriving late and drunk, being rude to her brother and upsetting a dinner party by telling a couple of students what he considered home truths about the real world. He also thought

57

there'd been mention of him being insufficiently touchy-feely with staff.

Gingerly, he got out of bed and, with the aid of the furniture, hopped his way to the bathroom and then into the shower.

As Strike washed, two separate impulses did battle within him. One was the urge to self-justify, which patted him on the back and awarded him a win for what he could remember of his argument with the students. The other was an innate honesty about his motives that forced him to recognise that his instant antagonism to Robin's guests had been rooted in their resemblance to the kinds of people towards whom his mother would have instantly gravitated.

Leda Strike's whole life had been a battle against constraint of any kind: going for a march in her underwear would have seemed to her just one more fabulous blow against limitations. Strike, who never forgot Leda's generous heart or her ineradicable love of the underdog, was nevertheless clear-eyed about the fact her activism had mostly taken the form of enthusiastic exhibitionism. Not for Leda the tedious toil of door-to-door canvassing, the difficult business of compromise, or the painstaking work structural change entailed. Never a deep or critical thinker, she'd been a sucker for what Strike thought of as intellectual charlatans. The basis for her life's philosophy, if such a word could be used for the loose collection of whims and kneejerk reactions she called beliefs, was that everything of which the bourgeoisie disapproved must be good and right. Naturally, she'd have sided with Kyle and Courtney in championing pornography and SlutWalks, and she'd have seen her son's quibbles as something he must have picked up from her killjoy sister-in-law.

While Strike dried himself and put on his prosthesis, moving cautiously in deference to his throbbing head, the idea of phoning Robin occurred, only to be dismissed. His long-established habit, in the aftermath of a row with a woman, was to wait for her to make the next move, which he considered mere common sense. If she apologised, all well and good; if she wanted further discussion, there was a chance she'd be calmer after a spell of reflection; if she was still angry, it was simply masochistic to volunteer for further grief until she came looking for it. While Strike wasn't in principle opposed to offering an unsolicited apology in the event that he felt himself to have been in the wrong, in practice his apologies tended to be delivered late, and only when it became clear that resolution would come no other way.

This modus operandi owed much to his experiences with Charlotte. Attempting to make up with Charlotte before every last ounce of her fury had been spent had been like trying to rebuild a house during an earthquake. Sometimes, after he refused to accede to some new demand – usually leaving the army, but sometimes giving up contact with another female friend or refusing to spend money he didn't have, all of which were seen by Charlotte as proof he didn't love her – Charlotte would walk out, and only after she came back, by which time Strike might well have met or slept with someone else, would the row be discussed. Their arguments had often lasted a week or more. A couple of times, Strike had returned to postings abroad before anything was resolved.

Yet, as he ate a much-needed bacon roll, drank coffee and downed a couple of Nurofen; after he'd called Ted, heard that Joan was still holding out, and assured him that he and Lucy would be there the following day; while opening a couple of bits of post, and ripping up a large gilt-edged invitation to the Deadbeats' fiftieth anniversary party in May; while food shopping in the everlasting wind and rain, stocking up for what might be a journey of many hours; while he packed clothes for the trip, spoke to Lucy and checked the weather forecast, his thoughts kept returning to Robin.

Gradually he realised that what was bothering him most was the fact that he'd got used to Robin being on his side, which was one of the main reasons he tended to seek reasons to call her if he was at a loose end or feeling low. Over time, they'd developed a most soothing and satisfying camaraderie, and Strike hadn't imagined it could be disrupted by what he categorised as a dinner party row.

When his phone rang at four o'clock in the afternoon, he surprised himself by snatching it up in the hope that it was his partner, only to see yet another unknown number. Wondering whether he was about to hear Rokeby again, or some other unknown blood relative, he answered.

'Strike.'

'What?' said a sharp, middle-class female voice.

'Cormoran Strike here. Who's this?'

'Clare Spencer, the Athorns' social worker. You left a message for me.'

'Oh, yes,' said Strike, pulling out a kitchen chair and sitting down. 'Thanks for getting back to me, Mrs – er – Ms Spencer.'

'Mrs,' she said, sounding very slightly amused. 'Can I just ask – are you *the* Cormoran Strike?'

'I doubt there are many others,' said Strike.

He reached for his cigarettes, then pushed them away again. He really did need to cut down.

'I see,' said Clare Spencer. 'Well, it was a bit of a shock to get a message from you. How d'you know the Athorns?'

'Their name came up,' said Strike, thinking how very inaccurate a statement that was, 'in the course of a case I'm investigating.'

'Was it *you* who went into their downstairs neighbour's shop, and threatened him?'

'I didn't threaten him,' said Strike. 'But his attitude seemed aggressive, so I pointed out that they had friends who might take it amiss if he bullied them.'

'Ha,' said Clare, sounding warmer. 'He's a horror, that man. He's been trying to get them out of that flat for ages. Wants to buy the whole building. He removed a supporting wall, then tried to blame Deborah and Samhain for his ceiling sagging. He's caused them a lot of stress.'

'The flat was—' Strike almost said 'mucked out', but tried to find a politer way of saying it, '—thoroughly cleaned recently, he said?'

'Yes. I'm not denying it was pretty messy, but we've sorted that out now, and as for saying they've caused structural damage, we got a surveyor in who went through the whole place and agreed there's nothing wrong with it. *What* a chancer the man is. Anyway, you did a good thing, there, warning him off. He thinks because they haven't got many close relatives, he can get away with browbeating them. So, what's this case you're investigating?'

Briefly, Strike told her about Margot Bamborough, her disappearance in 1974, and the information that had led him to the Athorns' door.

'. . . and so,' he concluded, 'I wanted to talk to someone who could tell me how much reliance I can put on what they've told me.'

There was a brief silence.

'I see,' said Clare, who sounded a little more guarded now. 'Well, I'm afraid I've got a duty of confidentiality as their social worker, so—'

'Could I ask you some questions? And if you can't answer, obviously I'll accept that.'

'All right,' she said. He had the impression that his actions with regard to the bullying iron-monger had put her on his side.

'They're clearly competent to live alone,' said Strike.

'With support, yes,' said Clare. 'They've done very well, actually. They've got a strong mutual bond. It's probably kept both of them out of institutionalised care.'

'And what exactly—?' Strike wondered how to word the question sensitively. Clare came to his aid.

'Fragile X syndrome,' she said. 'Deborah's relatively high-functioning, although she's got some social difficulties, but she can read and so forth. Samhain copes better socially, but his cognitive impairment's greater than his mother's.'

'And the father, Gwilherm—?'

Clare laughed.

'I've only been their social worker for a couple of years. I never knew Gwilherm.'

'You can't tell me how sane he was?'

There was a longer pause.

'Well,' she said, 'I suppose . . . it seems to be common knowledge that he was very odd. Various family members have spoken to me about him. Apparently he thought he could hex people. With black magic, you know.'

'Deborah told me something I found . . . slightly concerning. It involved a doctor called Dr Brenner, who was a partner of Dr Bamborough's at the St John's practice. She might've been referring to a medical examination, but—'

He thought Clare had said something.

'Sorry?'

'No, nothing. What exactly did she tell you?'

'Well,' said Strike, 'she mentioned having to take her pants off, and not wanting to, but she said Gwilherm told her she had to. I assumed—'

'This was a doctor?'

'Yes,' said Strike.

There was another, longer pause.

'I don't really know what to tell you,' said Clare finally. 'It's possible that was a medical examination, but . . . well, a lot of men used to visit that flat.'

Strike said nothing, wondering whether he was being told what he thought he was being told.

'Gwilherm had to get drink and drugs money somewhere,' said Clare. 'From what Deborah's disclosed to social workers over the years, we think he was – well, not to put too fine a point on it, we think he was pimping her out.'

'Christ,' muttered Strike, in disgust.

'I know,' said Clare. 'From bits and piece she's told caregivers, we think Gwilherm used to take Samhain out whenever she was with a client. It *is* dreadful. She's so vulnerable. On balance, I can't be sorry Gwilherm died young. But please – don't mention any of this to Deborah's family, if you speak to them. I've no idea how much they know, and she's happy and settled these days. There's no need to upset anyone.'

'No, of course not,' said Strike, and he remembered Samhain's words: *old Joe Brenner was a dirty old man.*

'How reliable would you say Samhain's memory is?'

'Why? What's he told you?'

'A couple of things his Uncle Tudor said.'

'Well, people with Fragile X usually have quite good long-term memories,' said Clare cautiously. 'I'd say he'd be more reliable about things his Uncle Tudor told him than on many subjects.'

'Apparently Uncle Tudor had a theory about what happened to Margot Bamborough. It involved some people called "Nico and his boys".'

'Ah,' said Clare, 'yes. D'you know who that is?'

'Go on.'

'There was an old gangster who used to live in Clerkenwell,' said Clare, 'called Niccolo Ricci. Samhain likes talking about "Nico and his boys". Like they're folk heroes, or something.'

They talked for a couple more minutes, but Clare had nothing more of interest to tell.

'Well, thanks very much for getting back to me,' said Strike. 'Social workers work Saturdays as well as detectives, I see.'

'People don't stop needing help at weekends,' she said drily. 'Good luck. I hope you find out what happened to that poor doctor.'

But he could tell by her tone, however friendly, that she thought it highly unlikely.

Strike's headache had now settled into a dull throb that increased if he bent over or stood up too suddenly. He returned to his methodical arrangements for next day's departure to Cornwall,

65

emptying his fridge of perishables, making sand-wiches for the trip; listening to the news, which told him that three people had died that day as a result of the adverse weather conditions; packing his kit bag; ensuring his emails were up to date, setting up an out-of-office message redirecting potential clients to Pat, and checking the rota, to make sure it had been altered to accommodate his absence. Through all these tasks he kept an ear out for his mobile, in case a text from Robin arrived, but nothing came.

Finally, at eight o'clock, while he was finishing cooking the fry-up he felt he was owed given his hangover and how hard he'd worked all day, his mobile buzzed at last. From across the table, he saw that three long consecutive texts had arrived. Knowing that he was leaving the following morning without any clear idea of when he'd be back, Robin appeared to have begun the reconciliation process as women were wont to do, with an essay on her various grievances. He opened the first message, magnanimously prepared to accept almost any terms for a negotiated peace, and only then real-ised that it was from an unknown number.

I thought today was Valentine's day but I've just realised it's the 15th. They've got me on so many drugs in here I can hardly remember my name. I'm in a place again. This isn't my phone. There's another woman here who's allowed one

& she lent it to me. Yours is the only mobile number I know by heart. Why didn't you ever change it? Was it because of me or is that my vanity. I'm so full of drugs I cant feel anything but I know I love you. I wonder how much they'd have to give me before that went too. Engouh to kill me I suppose.

The next message, from the same number, read:

How did you spent valentines day. Did you have sex. I'm here partly because I don't want sex. I cant stand him touching me and I know he wants more kids. Id rather die than have more. Actually I'd rather die than most things. But you know that about me. Will I ever see you again? You could come and see me here. Today I imagined you walking in, like I did when your leg. I imagined you telling them to let me go because you loved me and you'd look after me. I cried and

The third message continued:

the psychiatrist was pleased to see me crying because they like emotion. I don't know what the whole address is but it's called Symonds House. I love

**you don't forget me whatever hpapens
to me. I love you.**

A fourth and final message read:

It's Charlotte in case that isn't obvious.

Strike read the entire thread through twice. Then
he closed his eyes, and like millions of his fellow
humans, wondered why troubles could never come
singly, but in avalanches, so that you became
increasingly destabilised with every blow that hit
you.

CHAPTER 43

And you faire Ladie knight, my dearest Dame,
Relent the rigour of your wrathfull will,
Whose fire were better turn'd to other flame;
And wiping out remembrance of all ill,
Graunt him your grace . . .

Edmund Spenser
The Faerie Queene

To Robin's relief, her three guests got up early the next morning, because they wanted to spend a full day in London. All were subdued after what Robin thought of as the Nightmare Dinner. She dreaded a tearful plea for forgiveness from Courtney, who seemed especially low, so Robin faked a cheery briskness she certainly didn't feel, making recommendations for cheap places to eat and good things to see before waving the students off. As Robin was due to run surveillance on Elinor Dean overnight, she'd given Jonathan a spare key, and wasn't sorry that she'd probably still be in Stoke Newington when the

69

students returned to Manchester, because they intended to catch a mid-morning Sunday train.

Not wanting to be alone with Max, in case he wanted a post-mortem on the previous evening, Robin made herself a voluntary prisoner in her own bedroom all day, where she continued to work on her laptop, attempting to block out waves of anger towards Strike, and a tearfulness that kept threatening to overcome her. Hard as she tried to concentrate on finding out who'd been living in Jerusalem Passage when Margot had disappeared, however, her thoughts kept returning to her partner.

Robin wasn't in the least surprised not to have heard from him, but was damned if she'd initiate contact. She couldn't in good conscience retract a word of what she'd said after watching him vomit in the gutter, because she was tired of being taken for granted in ways Strike didn't recognise.

But as the afternoon wore on, and the rain continued to fall outside her window, and while she hadn't been nearly as drunk as Strike, she developed a dull headache. Equal parts of misery and rage dragged at her every time she remembered last night's dinner, and all the things she'd shouted at Strike in the street. She wished she could cry, but the tightness in her chest prevented her doing so. Her anger boiled anew every time she remembered the drunk Strike attacking her guests, but then she found herself re-running Courtney and Kyle's arguments in her head. She was sure none of the students had ever brushed up against the ugliness Robin had encountered, not merely under that dark stair in her hall of residence, but during her work with Strike: battered women, raped girls, death. They didn't want to hear Strike's stories, because it was so much more comforting to believe that language alone could remake the world. But none of that made her feel more kindly to her partner: on the contrary, she resented agreeing with him. He'd been looking for someone or something to attack, and it was she who'd paid the price.

Robin forced herself to keep working, because work was her one constant, her salvation. By eight in the evening, Robin was as sure as a thorough perusal of online records could make her that nobody living in Jerusalem Passage had been there for forty years. By this time, she was so hungry that she really did need to eat something, which she feared meant facing Max, and discussing Strike.

Sure enough, when she reached the living area, she found Max sitting watching TV with Wolfgang on his lap. He muted the news the moment he saw her, and Robin's heart sank.

'Evening.'

'Hi,' said Robin. 'I'm going to make myself something to eat. D'you want anything?'

'There's still a bit of casserole, if you want it.'

'Strike didn't finish it all, then?'

She mentioned him first in the spirit of getting

71

it over with. She could tell that Max had things to say.

'No,' said Max. He lifted the sleepy Wolfgang onto the sofa beside him, stood up and moved to the kitchen. 'I'll heat it up for you.'

'There's no need, I can—'

But Max did so, and when Robin was settled at the table with her food and a drink, he sat down at the table with her with a beer. This was highly unusual and Robin felt suddenly nervous. Was she being softened up for some kind of unwelcome announcement? Had Max decided, after all, to sell up?

'Never told you how I ended up in such a nice flat, did I?' he said.

'No,' said Robin cautiously.

'I had a big payout, five years ago. Medical negligence.'

'Oh,' said Robin.

There was a pause. Max smiled.

'People usually say, "Shit, what went wrong?" But you never probe, do you? I've noticed that. You don't ask a lot of questions.'

'Well, I have to do a lot of that at work,' said Robin.

But that wasn't why she hadn't asked Max about his finances, and it wasn't why she didn't ask now what had gone wrong with his body or his treatment, either. Robin had too many things in her own past that she didn't want endlessly probed to want to cause other people discomfort.

'I was having palpitations seven years ago,' Max said, examining the label on his beer. 'Arrhythmia. I got referred to a heart specialist and he operated: opened me up and ablated my sinus node. You probably don't know what that is,' he said, glancing up at Robin, and she shook her head. 'I didn't either, until they ballsed mine up. Basically, they knackered my heart's ability to beat for itself. I ended up having to be fitted with a pacemaker.'

'Oh no,' said Robin, a bit of beef suspended in mid-air on her fork.

'And the best bit was,' said Max, 'none of it was necessary. There wasn't anything wrong with my sinus node in the first place. Turned out I hadn't been suffering from atrial tachycardia at all. It was stage fright.'

'I – Max, I'm so sorry.'

'Yeah, it wasn't good,' said Max, taking a sip of his beer. 'Two unnecessary open-heart surgeries, endless complications. I lost jobs, I was unemployed for four years and I'm still on anti-depressants. Matthew said I *had* to pursue a claim against the doctors. I probably wouldn't have done, if he hadn't nagged me. Lawyers' fees. Ton of stress. But I won in the end, got a big payout, and he persuaded me to sink it all into a decent property. He's a barrister, he earns great money. Anyway, we bought this place.'

Max pushed his thick blond hair out of his face and glanced down at Wolfgang, who'd trotted to the table to savour the smell of casserole once more.

'A week after we moved in, he sat me down and told me he was leaving. The ink was barely dry on the mortgage. He said he'd struggled against it, because he felt a loyalty to me, because of what I'd been through, but he couldn't fight his feelings any longer. He told me,' said Max, with a hollow smile, 'he'd realised pity wasn't love. He wanted me to keep the flat, didn't want me to buy him out – as if I could have done – so he signed over his half. That was to make him feel less guilty, obviously. And off he went with Tiago. He's Brazilian, the new guy. Owns a restaurant.'

'That,' said Robin quietly, 'sounds like hell.'

'Yeah, it was . . . I really need to stop looking at their bloody Instagram accounts.' Max heaved a deep sigh and absent-mindedly rubbed the shirt over the scars on his chest. 'Obviously I thought of just selling up, but we barely lived here together, so it's not as though it's got a ton of memories. I didn't have the energy to go through more house-hunting and moving, so here I've stayed, struggling to make the mortgage every month.'

Robin thought she knew why Max was telling her all this, and her hunch was confirmed when he looked directly at her and said,

'Anyway, I just wanted to say, I'm sorry about what happened to you. I had no idea. Ilsa only told me you were held at gunpoint—'

'Oh, I didn't get raped *then*,' said Robin, and to

74

Max's evident surprise, she started to laugh. Doubtless it was her tiredness, but it was a relief to find dark comedy in this litany of terrible things humans did to each other, though none of it was really funny at all: his mutilated heart, the gorilla mask in her nightmares. 'No, the rape happened ten years ago. That's why I dropped out of university.'

'Shit,' said Max.

'Yeah,' said Robin, and echoing Max, she said, 'it wasn't good.'

'So when did the knife thing happen?' asked Max, eyes on Robin's forearm, and she laughed again. Really, what else was there to do?

'That was a couple of years ago.'

'Working for Strike?'

'Yes,' said Robin, and she stopped laughing now. 'Listen, about last night—'

'I enjoyed last night,' said Max.

'You can't be serious,' said Robin.

'I'm completely serious. It was really useful for building my character. He's got some proper big man, take-no-bullshit energy about him, hasn't he?'

'You mean he acts like a dick?'

Max laughed and shrugged.

'Is he very different sober?'

'Yes,' said Robin, 'well – I don't know. Less of a dick.' And before Max could ask anything else about her partner, she said quickly, 'He's right about your cooking, anyway. That was fantastic. Thanks so much, I really needed that.'

Having cleared up, Robin returned downstairs, where she showered before changing for the night's surveillance. With an hour to go before she needed to take over from Hutchins, she sat back down on her bed and idly typed variations on the name Paul Satchwell into Google. *Paul L Satchwell. LP Satchwell. Paul Leonard Satchwell. Leo Paul Satchwell.*

Her mobile rang. She glanced down. It was Strike. After a moment or two, she picked it up, but said nothing.

'Robin?'

'Yes.'

'Are you OK to talk?'

'Yes,' she said again, her heart beating faster than usual as she frowned up at the ceiling.

'Calling to apologise.'

Robin was so astonished, she said nothing for several seconds. Then she cleared her throat and said,

'Can you even remember what you're apologising for?'

'Er . . . yeah, I think so,' said Strike. 'I . . . didn't mean *that* to get dragged up. Should've realised it wasn't a subject you'd want discussed over dinner. Didn't think.'

Tears started in Robin's eyes at last.

'OK,' she said, trying to sound casual.

'And I'm sorry for being rude to your brother and his friends.'

'Thank you,' said Robin.

There was a silence. The rain still fell outside. Then Strike said,

'Have you heard from Ilsa?'

'No,' said Robin. 'Have you heard from Nick?'

'No,' said Strike.

There was another silence.

'So, we're OK, yeah?' said Strike.

'Yes,' said Robin, wondering whether it was true.

'If I've taken you for granted,' said Strike, 'I'm sorry. You're the best I've got.'

'Oh, for *fuck's* sake, Strike,' said Robin, abandoning the pretence that she wasn't crying as she snorted back tears.

'What?'

'You just . . . you're bloody infuriating.'

'Why?'

'Saying that. Now.'

'That's not the first time I've said it.'

'It is, actually.'

'I've told other people.'

'Yeah, well,' said Robin, now laughing and crying simultaneously as she reached for tissues, 'you see how that isn't the same thing as telling *me*?'

'Yeah, I s'pose,' said Strike. 'Now you mention it.'

He was smoking at his small Formica kitchen table while the eternal rain fell outside his attic window. Somehow, the texts from Charlotte had made him realise he had to call Robin, had to make things right with her before he set off for Cornwall and Joan. Now the sound of her voice, and her laughter, acted on him as it usually did, by making everything seem fractionally less awful.

'When are you leaving?' Robin asked, drying her eyes.

'Tomorrow at eight. Lucy's meeting me at the car hire. We've got a jeep.'

'Well, be careful,' said Robin. She'd heard on the news that day about the three people who'd died, trying to travel through the wind and the floods.

'Yeah. Can't pretend I don't wish you were driving. Lucy's bloody terrible behind the wheel.'

'You can stop flattering me now. I've forgiven you.'

'I'm serious,' said Strike, his eyes on the relentless rain. 'You and your advanced driving course. You're the only person who doesn't scare the shit out of me behind the wheel.'

'D'you think you'll make it?'

'Possibly not all the way in the jeep. But Polworth's standing by to rescue us. He's got access to dinghies. We've got to do it. Joan might only have days.'

'Well, I'll be thinking about you,' said Robin. 'Keeping everything crossed.'

'Cheers, Robin. Keep in touch.'

After Strike had hung up, Robin sat for a while, savouring the sudden feeling of lightness that had filled her. Then she pulled her laptop towards her, ready to shut it down before she left for her night's surveillance in the Land Rover. Casually, as she might have thrown the dice one last time before turning away from the craps table, she typed 'Paul Satchwell artist' into Google.

. . . artist Paul Satchwell has spent most of his career on the Greek island of . . .

'*What?*' said Robin aloud, as though the laptop had spoken to her. She clicked on the result, and the website of the Leamington Spa Museum and Art Gallery filled the screen. She hadn't once seen it, in all her hours of searching for Satchwell. This page had either just been created or amended.

Temporary Exhibition March 3rd – 7th 2014
Local Artists

The Leamington Spa Museum and Art Gallery will be hosting a temporary exhibition of artists from the Warwickshire area. Entrance free.

Robin scrolled down the page past sundry artists' photos until she saw him.

It was, without a doubt, the same man. His face might be leathery and cracked, his teeth might have yellowed, his thick, curly hair turned whiter and thinner, but it still hung to his shoulders, while his open shirt showed thick white chest hair.

Born in Leamington Spa and raised in Warwick, artist Paul Satchwell has spent most of his career on the Greek island of Kos. Working mainly in oils, Paul's Hellenic-influenced exploration of myths challenge the viewer to face primal fears and examine preconceptions through sensual use of line and colour . . .

CHAPTER 44

Huge sea of sorrow, and tempestuous griefe,
Wherein my feeble barke is tossed long,
Far from the hoped hauen of reliefe,
Why doe thy cruel billowes beat so strong,
And thy moyst mountaines each on others
*   throng,*
Threatning to swallow vp my fearefull lyfe?

Edmund Spenser
The Faerie Queene

The storm water, rain and gales they faced were real enough, yet Strike and Lucy's battle to reach St Mawes had a strange, dreamlike quality. Both knew death lay at the end; both were resolved that if they managed to reach Joan alive, they would stay with her until she died.

Trees swayed and creaked as they sped along the motorway. They had to divert around great wide lakes where lately there had been fields, forcing them miles out of their way. Twice they were halted at roadblocks and told, by irate police, to turn back. They pressed on, at one point driving fifty miles to progress fifteen, listening to every weather update on the radio and becoming progressively more certain that there would come a point where they had to abandon the jeep. Rain lashed the car, high winds lifted the windscreen wipers from the glass, and brother and sister took it in turns to drive, bound by a single objective, and temporarily freed from all other concerns.

To Strike's grateful surprise, the crisis had revealed a different Lucy, just as illness had uncovered a different Joan. His sister was focused entirely on what needed to be done. Even her driving was different, without three noisy sons in the back seat, squabbling and thumping each other if the journey lasted longer than twenty minutes. He'd forgotten how efficient and practical Lucy could be, how patient, how resolute. Her calm determination only broke when they reached an impasse thirty miles from St Mawes, where flooding and fallen trees had rendered the road impassable.

While Lucy sat slumped at the steering wheel, sobbing with her face in her arms, Strike left the jeep to stand outside under a tree, where, sheltering from the perennial rain and taking the opportunity to smoke, he called Dave Polworth, who was holding himself ready to assist them.

'Yeah, we thought that's where you'd have to stop,' said Polworth, when Strike had given him their position.

'Who's "we"?'

'Well, I can't fucking do this alone, can I, Diddy? Should be with you in an hour. Stay in the car.'

And an hour later, true to his word, Dave Polworth and five other men, two of them members of the local lifeguard, three old school-friends of Strike's, emerged out of the gathering gloom. Dressed in waterproofs, and carrying waders ready for the worst passages, the men took charge of Strike and Lucy's bags. Leaving the jeep parked up a side street, the party set off on foot.

The end of Strike's stump began to chafe long before they had walked for two hours solid over boggy ground and slippery tarmac. Soon, he had to abandon pride and allow two of his old school-friends to support him on either side. Darkness fell before they reached a couple of dinghies that Polworth had arranged to carry them over flooded fields. Using oars to alternately row and punt themselves along, they navigated with the aid of torches and compasses.

Polworth had called on every friend and acquaintance he knew to arrange Strike and Lucy's passage across the storm-ravaged peninsula. They covered several miles by tractor pulling a trailer, but at some passages were forced to wade through feet of icy flood water, the diminutive Lucy accepting a piggyback from the largest lifeboat man.

Four hours after they'd abandoned the jeep, they reached St Mawes. At the gate of Ted and Joan's house, brother and sister hugged each of their escorts goodbye.

'Don't start,' said Polworth, as the weary and sore Strike tried to put into words what he felt to be incommunicable. 'Get inside, or what the fuck was it all for?'

Ted, whom they'd updated regularly through their journey, greeted them in pyjamas at the back door, tears running down the deep folds in his craggy face.

'I never thought you'd get here,' he kept saying, as he made them tea. '*Never* thought you'd make it.'

'How is she?' asked the shivering Lucy, as the three of them sat in the kitchen, their hands around mugs of tea, eating toast.

'She managed a bit of soup today,' said Ted. 'She's still . . . she sleeps a lot. But when she's awake, she likes to talk. Oh, she'll be over the moon to have you two here . . .'

And so began days that had the same strange, outside-time quality of their journey. Initially Strike, the end of whose stump was rubbed raw after the painful exigencies of their journey, abandoned his prosthesis and navigated the small house by hopping and holding onto chair backs and walls. He read and responded to Robin's emails about the agency's work, but her news seemed to come from a place far more remote than London.

Joan was now bird-like in her frailty, her bones visible through the translucent skin. She'd made it clear that she wished to die at home, not in the hospital in Truro, so she lay, tiny and shrunken, in the large double bed that dominated the bedroom, a bed that had been purchased to accommodate Ted's bulk back when he'd been a tall, fit and muscular man, late of the Royal Military Police and subsequently a stalwart member of the local lifeguard.

By day, Strike, Ted and Lucy took it in turns to sit beside Joan's bed, because awake or asleep, she liked to know that one of them was nearby. Kerenza came morning and afternoon, and these were the only times when her family left the room. Joan was no longer able to swallow medication, so Kerenza began injecting the morphine through a syringe driver. Strike knew that she washed his aunt, and helped her perform still more private functions: the long convalescence after his amputation had left him under no illusion about what nurses dealt with. Kind, efficient and humane, Kerenza was one of the few people Strike welcomed gladly into the draughty kitchen.

And still Joan clung on. Three days after their arrival, four: she slept almost constantly, but still she clung to life.

'It's you two,' said Ted. 'She doesn't want to go while you two are here.'

Strike was coming to dread silences too large for human voices to fill. His nerves were stretched by the constant clinking of teaspoons in hot drinks made for something to do, by the tears shed by Uncle Ted when he thought nobody was looking, by the hushed enquiries of well-meaning neighbours.

On the fifth day, Lucy's husband Greg arrived with their three boys. Husband and wife had debated how sensible it was to take the boys out of school, and risk a journey that remained tricky, though the storms had at last subsided, but Lucy could bear their absence no longer. When Greg arrived, the boys came running out of the car towards their mother and the whole family clung to each other, while Strike and Ted looked on, united in their aloneness, unmarried man and soon-to-be widower. The boys were led up to Joan's bedroom to see her, and she managed smiles for all of them. Even Luke was subdued afterwards, and Jack cried.

Both spare rooms were now needed to accommodate the new arrivals, so Strike returned, uncomplaining, to sleep on the sofa.

'You look like shit,' Polworth informed him bluntly on day six, and indeed Strike, who'd woken every hour on the horsehair sofa, felt it. 'Let's get a pint.'

'Can I come?' asked Jack hopefully. He was showing a tendency to hang around Strike rather than his father, while Lucy sat upstairs with Joan.

'You can if your dad says it's OK,' said Strike.

Greg, who was currently walking around the garden with his phone clamped to his ear, trying to contribute to a conference call with his London office while Luke and Adam played football around him, agreed with a thumbs up.

So Strike, Polworth and Jack walked down into St Mawes together. Though the sky was dark and the roads still wet, the winds had at last dropped. As they reached the seafront, Strike's mobile rang. He answered it, still walking.

'Strike.'

'It's Shanker. Got your message.'

'I left that ten days ago,' said Strike.

'I've been busy, you ungrateful piece of shit.'

'Sorry,' said Strike.

He waved the other two on and paused again at the harbour wall, looking out at the green-grey sea and the hazy horizon.

'I've nosed around a bit,' said Shanker, 'and you're not gonna find out 'oo that bint was, Bunsen. The one on the film. Nobody knows. She'll 'ave done somethin' fucking serious to get that, though.'

'Deserved it, you reckon,' said Strike, as he surveyed the flat sea. It didn't look capable, now, of the violence it had inflicted upon the town.

'I'm not saying she *deserved* – I'm sayin' even Mucky Ricci didn't make 'an 'abit of *that*,' said Shanker impatiently. 'Are you in solitary?'

'What?'

'Where the fuck are you? There's no noise.'

'In Cornwall.'

For a moment, Strike expected Shanker to ask where that was. Shanker was almost impressively ignorant of the country that lay beyond London.

'The fuck are you doin' in Cornwall?'

'My aunt's dying.'

'Oh shit,' said Shanker. 'Sorry.'

'Where is he now?'

''Oo?'

'Ricci.'

''E's in an 'ome. I told you.'

'All right. Thanks for trying, Shanker. Appreciate it.'

For perhaps the first time ever, it was Shanker who shouted at Strike to stop him hanging up.

'Oi – oi!'

'What?' said Strike, raising the mobile to his ear again.

'Why d'you wanna know where 'e is? You ain't gonna go talkin' to Ricci. You're done.'

'I'm not done,' said Strike, eyes screwed up against the sea breeze. 'I haven't found out what happened to the doctor, yet.'

'*Fuck's* sake. D'you wanna get shot through the fuckin' 'ead?'

'See you, Shanker,' said Strike, and before his old friend could say anything else, he cut the call and muted his phone.

Polworth was already at a table with Jack when

Strike reached the Victory, two pints and a Coke on the table.

'Just been telling Jack,' Polworth told Strike, as the detective sat down. 'Haven't I, eh?' he asked Jack, who nodded, beaming. 'For when he's older. *This* is his local.'

'A pub three hundred miles from where he lives?'

'He was born in Cornwall. He was just telling me.'

'Oh yeah,' said Strike. 'I forgot about that.'

The family had been staying with Ted and Joan when Lucy went into labour a month early. Jack had been born in the same Truro hospital as Strike himself.

'And you're a Nancarrow on your mum's side,' Polworth told Jack, who was greatly enjoying Polworth's approval. 'So that makes you a Cornishman, born and bred.'

Polworth turned to Strike.

'Who was the pearly king on the phone there? We could hear his cockney a mile off.'

'Guy called Shanker,' said Strike. 'I've told you about him. My mum scraped him off the street one night when he'd been stabbed. He adopted us.'

Strike sipped his pint, wondering how Polworth and Shanker would get on, in the unlikely event of them ever meeting. He fancied they might end up punching each other. They seemed to Strike like pieces from entirely different jigsaw puzzles: no point of connection. At the mention of stabbing, Polworth had glanced at Jack, but lowering his pint Strike said,

'Don't worry about him. He wants to be a Red Cap, like me and Ted.'

Jack beamed some more. He was having a great time.

'Can I try some of that beer?' he asked his uncle.

'Don't push it,' said Strike.

'Look at this,' said Polworth, pointing at a page in the newspaper he'd picked up. 'Westminster trying to bully the Scots, the bast—'

Strike cleared his throat. Jack giggled.

'Sorry,' said Polworth. 'But come on. Telling them they can't keep the pound if they vote for independence? 'Course they'll keep the pound. It's in everyone's interests . . .'

He talked on for the next ten minutes about small nationalism, the obvious arguments for both Scottish and Cornish independence and the idiocy of those who opposed them, until Jack looked glazed and Strike, as a last resort, dragged the conversation back to football. Arsenal, as he'd foreseen, had lost to defending champions Bayern Munich, and he didn't doubt the second leg would see them knocked out. He and Ted had watched the game together and done a good job of pretending they cared about the result. Strike permitted Polworth to pass censorious comment on the foul that had seen Szcz esny sent off, and politics was mercifully dropped.

Strike thought about Polworth later that night, as he lay in the dark on the horsehair sofa again, unable to sleep. His tiredness now had a feverishness about it, exacerbated by the aching of his body, the perpetual strain of being here, in this overcrowded house, waiting for the tiny body upstairs to give up.

In this near fever state, a jumble of ideas circulated in Strike's mind. He thought of categories and boundaries, of those we want to create and enforce, and those we seek to escape or destroy. He remembered the fanatic glint in Polworth's eye as he argued for a harder boundary between his county and the rest of England. He fell asleep thinking about the spurious groupings of astrology, and dreamed of Leda, laying out her tarot cards in the Norfolk commune of long ago.

Strike was woken at five by his own aching body. Knowing that Ted would be awake soon, he got up and dressed, ready to take over the bedside vigil while his uncle ate breakfast.

Sure enough, hearing Strike's footstep on the upstairs landing, Ted emerged from the bedroom in his dressing gown.

'Just made you tea,' whispered Strike. 'It's in the pot in the kitchen. I'll sit with her for a bit.'

'You're a good lad,' whispered Ted, clapping Strike on the arm. 'She's asleep now, but I had a little chat with her at four. Most she's said for days.'

The talk with his wife seemed to have cheered

him. He set off downstairs for his tea and Strike let himself quietly into the familiar room, taking up his position on the hard-backed chair beside Joan.

The wallpaper hadn't been changed, so far as Strike knew, since Ted and Joan had moved into the house, their only home since he'd left the army, in the town where both had grown up. Ted and Joan seemed not to notice that the house had grown shabby over the decades: for all that Joan was meticulous about cleanliness, she'd equipped and decorated the house once and seemed never to have seen any need to do so again. The paper was decorated with small bunches of purple flowers, and Strike could remember tracing geometric shapes between them with his forefinger as a small child, when he climbed into bed with Ted and Joan early in the morning, when both were still sleepy and he wanted breakfast and a trip to the beach.

Twenty minutes after he'd sat down, Joan opened her eyes and looked at Strike so blankly that he thought she didn't know him.

'It's me, Joan,' he said quietly, moving his chair a little closer to her bed and switching on the lamp, with its fringed shade. 'Corm. Ted's having breakfast.'

Joan smiled. Her hand was a tiny claw, now. The fingers twitched. Strike took it into his own. She said something he couldn't hear, and he lowered his large head to her face.

'What did you say?'

'. . . you're . . . good man.'

'Oh, I don't know about that,' muttered Strike.

He held her hand in a light clasp, scared of putting pressure on it. The *arcus senilis* outlining the irises of her pale eyes made the blue seem more faded than ever. He thought of all the times he could have visited, and hadn't. All those missed opportunities to call. All those times he'd forgotten her birthday.

'. . . helping people . . .'

She peered up at him and then, making a supreme effort, she whispered,

'I'm proud of you.'

He wanted to speak, but something was blocking his throat. After a few seconds, he saw her eyelids drooping.

'I love you, Joan.'

The words came out so hoarsely they were almost inaudible, but he thought she smiled as she sank back into a sleep from which she was never to wake.

CHAPTER 45

Of auncient time there was a springing well,
From which fast trickled forth a siluer flood,
Full of great vertues, and for med'cine good.

Edmund Spenser
The Faerie Queene

Robin was still at the office when Strike called that evening with the news that Joan had died.

'I'm sorry about this, but I think I'm going to have to stay down here until we get this funeral sorted,' said Strike. 'There's a lot to do and Ted's in pieces.'

He'd just shared Joan's plan for her funeral with Ted and Lucy, thereby reducing both of them to sobs at the kitchen table. Ted's tears were for the poignancy of his wife making arrangements for his own comfort and relief, as she'd done for the fifty years of their marriage, and for the news that she'd wanted, at the end, to enter the sea and wait for him there. In Lucy's case, the sobs were for the

94

lost possibility of a grave she'd hoped to visit and tend. Lucy filled her days with voluntary obligations: they gave purpose and form to a life she was determined would never be like her flighty biological mother's.

'No problem,' Robin reassured him. 'We're coping fine.'

'You're sure?'

'Completely sure.'

'There's a backlog at the crematorium, because of the floods,' said Strike. 'Funeral's pencilled in for March the third.'

This was the day Robin was planning to spend in Leamington Spa, so she could attend the opening of Paul Satchwell's exhibition. She didn't tell Strike this: she could tell that he had limited mental capacity right now for anything other than Joan, and his life in Cornwall.

'Don't worry,' she repeated. 'I'm so sorry, Cormoran,' she added.

'Thanks,' said Strike. 'I'd forgotten what it's like. Planning a funeral. I've already had to referee one argument.'

After he'd shared Joan's plans for her send-off, and Lucy and Ted had mopped up their tears, Ted had suggested they ask mourners for donations to the Macmillan Cancer Support in lieu of flowers.

'. . . but Lucy says Joan would've wanted flowers,' Strike told Robin. 'I've suggested we say either. Ted says that'll mean people do both and they can't afford it, but fuck it. Lucy's right. Joan *would* want flowers, and as many as possible. That's how she always judged other people's funerals.'

After they'd bidden each other goodbye, Robin sat for a while at the partners' desk, wondering whether it would be appropriate for the agency to send flowers to Strike's aunt's funeral. She'd never met Joan: she worried that it would seem odd, or intrusive, to send condolences. She remembered how, when she'd offered to pick Strike up from Joan's house in St Mawes the previous summer, he'd quickly cut her off, erecting, as ever, a firm boundary between Robin and his personal life.

Yawning, Robin shut down the computer, closed the completed file on Postcard, which she'd been updating, got to her feet and went to get her coat. At the outer door she stopped, her reflection blank-faced in the dark glass. Then, as though responding to an unheard command, she returned to the inner office, switched the computer back on and, before she could second-guess herself, ordered a sheaf of dark pink roses to be delivered to St Mawes church on March the third, with the message 'With deepest sympathy from Robin, Sam, Andy, Saul and Pat'.

Robin spent the rest of the month working without respite. She conducted a final meeting with the persecuted weatherman and his wife, in which she revealed Postcard's identity, gave them Postcard's real name and address, and took their final payment. She then had Pat contact their waiting list client, the commodities broker who suspected her husband of sleeping with their nanny and, next day, welcomed the woman to the office to take down her details and receive a down payment.

The commodities broker didn't bother to hide her disappointment that she was meeting Robin instead of Strike. She was a thin, colourless blonde of forty-two, whose over-highlighted hair had the texture, close up, of fine wire. Robin found her unlikeable until the end of the interview, when she talked about her husband, whose business had gone bankrupt and who now worked from home, giving him many long hours alone with the nanny.

'Fourteen years,' said the broker. 'Fourteen years, three kids and now . . .'

She hid her eyes behind her shaking hands and Robin, who'd been with Matthew since she was at school, felt, in spite of the woman's brittle façade, an unexpected glow of sympathy.

After the new client had left, Robin called Morris into the office and gave him the job of the first day's surveillance of the nanny.

'Okey-doke,' he said. 'Hey, what d'you say we call the client "RB"?'

'What does that stand for?' Robin asked.

'Rich Bitch,' said Morris, grinning. 'She's loaded.'

'No,' said Robin, unsmiling.

'Whoops,' said Morris, eyebrows raised. 'Feminist alert?'

'Something like that.'

'OK, how about—?'

'We'll call her Mrs Smith, after the street they live on,' said Robin coldly.

Over the next few days, Robin took her turn tailing the nanny, a glossy-haired brunette who somewhat reminded her of Strike's ex-girlfriend Lorelei. The commodities broker's children certainly seemed to adore their nanny, and so, Robin feared, did their father. While he didn't once touch the nanny in any amorous way, he showed every sign of a man completely smitten: mirroring her body language, laughing excessively at her jokes, and hurrying to open doors and gates for her.

A couple of nights later, Robin dozed off at the wheel for a few seconds while driving towards Elinor Dean's house in Stoke Newington. Jerking awake, she immediately turned on the radio and opened the window, so that her eyes streamed with the cold, sooty night air, but the incident scared her. Over the next few days, she increased her caffeine consumption in an effort to keep awake. This made her slightly jittery, and she found it hard to sleep even on the rare occasions the chance presented itself.

Robin had always been as careful with the firm's money as Strike himself, treating every penny spent as though it were to be deducted from her own take-home pay. The habit of parsimony had stayed with her, even though the agency's survival no longer depended on extracting money from clients before the final demands came in. Robin was well aware that Strike took very little money out of the business for his own needs, preferring to plough profits back into the agency. He continued to live a Spartan existence in the two and a half rooms over the office, and there were months when she, the salaried partner, took home more pay than the senior partner and founder of the firm.

All of this added to her feeling of guilt at booking herself into a Premier Inn in Leamington Spa on the Sunday night before Satchwell's art exhibition. The town was only a two-hour drive away; Robin knew she could have got up early on Monday morning instead of sleeping over in the town. However, she was so exhausted, she feared dozing off at the wheel again.

She justified the hotel room to herself by leaving twenty-four hours ahead of the exhibition's opening, thus giving herself time to take a look at the church where Margot had allegedly been sighted a week after her disappearance. She also packed photocopies of all the pages of Talbot's horoscope notes that mentioned Paul Satchwell, with the intention of studying them in the quiet of her hotel room. To these, she added a second-hand copy of Evangeline Adams's *Your Place in the Sun*, a pack of unopened tarot cards and a copy of *The Book of Thoth*. She hadn't told Strike she'd bought any of these items and didn't intend claiming expenses for them.

Much as she loved London, Yorkshire-born Robin sometimes pined for trees, moors and hills. Her drive up the nondescript M40, past hamlets and villages with archaic names like Middleton Cheney, Temple Herdewyke and Bishop's Itchington, gave her glimpses of flat green fields. The cool, damp day bore a welcome whiff of spring on the air, and in the breaks between scudding white clouds, hard, bright sunshine filled the old Land Rover with a light that made a pale grey ghost of Robin's reflection in the dusty window beside her. She really needed to clean the car: in fact, there were sundry small, personal chores piling up while she worked non-stop for the agency, such as ringing her mother, whose calls she'd been avoiding, and her lawyer, who'd left a message about the upcoming mediation, not to mention plucking her eyebrows, buying herself a new pair of flat shoes and sorting out a bank transfer to Max, covering her half of the council tax.

As the hedgerows flashed by, Robin consciously turned her thoughts away from these depressing mundanities to Paul Satchwell. She doubted she'd find him in Leamington Spa, being unable to imagine why the seventy-five-year-old would want to leave his home on Kos merely to visit the provincial art gallery. Satchwell had probably sent his paintings over from Greece, or else given permission for them to be exhibited. Why would he leave what Robin imagined as a dazzling white-walled villa, an artist's studio set among olive groves? Her plan was to pretend an interest in buying or commissioning one of his paintings, so as to get his home address. For a moment or two, she indulged herself in a little fantasy of flying out to Greece with Strike, to interrogate the old artist. She imagined the oven-blast of heat that would hit them on leaving the plane in Athens, and saw herself in a dress and sandals, heading up a dusty track to Satchwell's front door. But when her imagination showed her Strike in shorts, with the metal rod of his prosthetic leg on display, she felt suddenly embarrassed by her own imaginings, and closed the little fantasy down before it took her to the beach, or the hotel.

On the outskirts of Leamington Spa, Robin followed the sign to All Saints church, which she knew from her research was the only possible candidate for the place where Charlie Ramage had seen Margot. Janice had mentioned a 'big church'; All Saints was a tourist attraction due to its size. None of the other churches in Leamington Spa had graveyards attached to them. Moreover, All Saints was situated directly on the route of anyone travelling north from London. Although Robin found it hard to understand why Margot would have been browsing headstones in Leamington Spa, while her husband begged for information of her whereabouts in the national press and her Leamington-born lover remained in London, she had a strange feeling that seeing the church for herself would give her a better idea as to whether Margot had ever been there. The missing doctor was becoming very real to Robin.

She managed to secure a parking space in Priory Terrace, right beside the church, and set off on foot around the perimeter, marvelling at the sheer scale of the place. It was a staggering size for a relatively small town; in fact, it looked more like a cathedral, with its long, arched windows. Turning right into Church Street, she noted the further coincidence of the street name being so similar to Margot's home address. On the right, a low wall topped with railings provided an ideal spot for a motorbike rider to park, and enjoy a cup of tea from his Thermos, looking at the graveyard.

Except that there was no graveyard. Robin came to an abrupt standstill. She could only see two tombs, raised stone caskets whose inscriptions had been eroded. Otherwise, there was simply a wide stretch of grass intersected with two footpaths.

'Bomb fell on it.'

A cheery-looking mother was walking towards Robin, pushing a double pushchair containing sleeping boy twins. She'd correctly interpreted Robin's sudden halt.

'Really?' said Robin.

'Yeah, in 1940,' said the woman, slowing down. 'Luftwaffe.'

'Wow. Awful,' said Robin, imagining the smashed earth, the broken tombstones and, perhaps, fragments of coffin and bone.

'Yeah – but they missed them two,' said the woman, pointing at the aged tombs standing in the shadow of a yew tree. One of the twin toddlers gave a little stretch in his sleep and his eyelids flickered. With a comical grimace at Robin, the mother took off again at a brisk walk.

Robin walked into the enclosed area that had once been a graveyard, looking around and wondering what to make of Ramage's story, now. There hadn't been a graveyard here in 1974, when he claimed to have seen Margot browsing among tombstones. Or had an intact cemetery been assumed by Janice Beattie, when she heard that Margot was looking at graves? Robin turned to look at the two surviving tombs. Certainly, if Margot had been examining these, she'd have been brought within feet of a motorcyclist parked beside the church.

Robin placed her hands on the cold black bars that kept the curious from actually touching the old tombs, and examined them. What could have drawn Margot to them? The inscriptions etched on the mossy stone were almost illegible. Robin tilted her head, trying to make them out.

Was she seeing things? Did one of the words say 'Virgo', or had she spent too much time dwelling on Talbot's horoscope notes? Yet the more she studied it, the more like 'Virgo' the name looked.

Robin associated that star sign with two people, these days: her estranged husband, Matthew, and Dorothy Oakden, the widowed practice secretary at Margot's old place of work. Robin had become so adept at reading Talbot's horoscope notes, that she routinely heard 'Dorothy' in her head when looking at the glyph for Virgo. Now she took out her phone, looked up the tomb and felt mildly reassured to discover that she wasn't seeing things: this was the last resting place of one James Virgo Dunn.

But why should it have been of interest to Margot? Robin scrolled down a genealogy page for the Virgos and the Dunns and learned that the man whose bones now lay in dust a few feet from her had been born in Jamaica, where he'd been the owner of forty-six slaves.

'No need to feel sorry for *you*, then,' Robin muttered, returning her phone to her pocket, and she walked on around the perimeter to the front of the church, until she reached the great oak and iron double front doors. As she headed up the stone steps towards them, she heard the low hum of a hymn. Of course: it was Sunday morning.

After a moment's hesitation, Robin opened the door as quietly as possible and peered inside. An immense, sombre space was revealed: chilly parabolas of grey stone, a hundred feet of cold

104

air between congregation and ceiling. Doubtless a church of this gigantic size had been deemed necessary back in Regency times, when people had flocked to the spa town to drink its waters, but the modern congregation didn't come close to filling it. A black-robed verger looked around at her; Robin smiled apologetically, quietly closed the door and returned to the pavement, where a large modern steel sculpture, part squiggle, part coil, was evidently supposed to represent the medicinal spring around which the town had been built.

A pub nearby was just opening its doors and Robin fancied a coffee, so she crossed the road and entered the Old Library.

The interior was large but hardly less gloomy than the church, the décor mostly shades of brown. Robin bought herself a coffee, settled herself in a tucked-away corner where she couldn't be observed, and sank into abstraction. Her glimpse of the church's interior had told her nothing. Margot had been an atheist, but churches were some of the few places a person could sit and think, undisturbed. Might Margot have been drawn to All Saints out of that unfocused, inchoate need that had once driven Robin herself into an unknown graveyard, there to sit on a wooden bench and contemplate the parlous state of her marriage?

Robin set down her coffee cup, opened the messenger bag she'd brought with her and took out the wad of photocopies of those pages of Talbot's notebook that mentioned Paul Satchwell. Smoothing them flat, she glanced up casually at the two men who'd just sat down at a nearby table. The one with his back to her was tall and broad, with dark, curly hair, and before she could remind herself that he couldn't be Strike, because her partner was in St Mawes, a thrill of excitement and happiness passed through her.

The stranger seemed to have felt Robin looking at him, because he turned before she could avert her eyes. She caught a glimpse of eyes as blue as Morris's, a weak chin and a short neck before she bowed her head to examine the horoscope notes, feeling herself turning red and suddenly unable to take in the mass of drawings and symbols in front of her.

Waves of shame were crashing over her, entirely disproportionate to catching a stranger's eye. In the pit of her stomach, the last sparks of the excitement she'd felt on thinking that she was looking at Strike glimmered and died.

It was a momentary error of perception, she told herself. *There's absolutely nothing to worry about. Calm down.*

But instead of reading the notes, Robin put her face in her hands. In this strange bar, her resistance lowered by exhaustion, Robin knew she'd been avoiding the question of what she really felt about Strike for the past year. Busy trying to disentangle herself from Matthew, familiarising herself with a new flat and a new flatmate, managing and deflecting her parents' anxiety and judgement, fending off Morris's constant badgering, dodging Ilsa's infuriating determination to matchmake and working twice as hard as ever before, it had been easy not to think about anything else, even a question as fraught as what she really felt for Cormoran Strike.

Now, in the corner of this dingy brown pub, with nothing else to distract her, Robin found herself thinking back to those honeymoon nights spent pacing the fine white sand after Matthew had gone to bed, when Robin had interrogated herself about whether she was in love with the man who'd then been her boss, not her partner. She'd worn a deep channel on the beach as she walked up and down in the dark, finally deciding that the answer was 'no', that what she felt was a mixture of friendship, admiration and gratitude for the opportunity he'd given her to embark on a once-dreamed-of career, which she'd thought was closed to her forever. She liked her partner; she admired him; she was grateful to him. That was it. That was all.

Except . . . she remembered how much pleasure it had given her to see him sitting in Notes Café, after a week's absence, and how happy she was, no matter the circumstances, to see Strike's name light up her phone.

Almost scared now, she forced herself to think about how bloody aggravating Strike could be:

grumpy, taciturn and ungrateful, and nowhere near as handsome, with his broken nose and hair he himself described as 'pube-like', as Matthew, or even Morris . . .

But he was her best friend. This admission, held at bay for so long, caused an almost painful twist in Robin's heart, not least because she knew it would be impossible ever to tell Strike so. She could just imagine him lumbering away from her like a startled bison at such a naked statement of affection, redoubling the barriers he liked to erect if ever they got too close to each other. Nevertheless, there was a kind of relief in admitting the painful truth: she cared deeply for her partner. She trusted him on the big things: to do the right thing for the right reasons. She admired his brains and appreciated his doggedness, not to mention the self-discipline all the more admirable because many whole-bodied men had never mastered it. She was often astonished by his almost total lack of self-pity. She loved the drive for justice that she shared, that unbreakable determination to settle and to solve.

And there was something more, something highly unusual. Strike had never once made her feel physically uncomfortable. Two of them in the office, for a long time the only workers at the agency, and while Robin was a tall woman, he was far bigger, and he'd never made her feel it, as so many men did, not even in an attempt to intimidate, but because they enjoy the Parade, as a peacock spreads its tail. Matthew hadn't been able to get past the idea of them together all the time, in a small office space, hadn't been able to believe that Strike wasn't capitalising on the situation to make advances, however subtle.

But Robin, who'd forever be hypersensitive to the uninvited touch, the sidelong, lecherous glance, the invasion of personal space, the testing of conventional limits, had never once experienced, with Strike, that shrinking sensation within her own skin evoked by attempts to push a relationship into a different space. A deep reserve lay over Strike's private life, and while that sometimes frustrated her (had he, or had he not, called Charlotte Campbell back?), his love of privacy extended to a respect for other people's boundaries. Never had there been an ostensibly helpful but unnecessary touch, no hand on the small of the back, no grasping of the arm, no look that made her skin prickle, or made her want to cover herself: the legacy of those violent encounters with men that had left her scarred in more ways than the visible.

In truth (why not admit everything to herself now, when she was so tired, her defences lowered?) she was aware of only two moments in four years where she'd been sure that Strike had seen her as a desirable woman, not as a friend, or an apprentice, or a younger sister.

The first had been when she'd modelled that green Cavalli dress for him, in the course of their first investigation together, when he'd looked away from her as a man would if shunning too-bright light. She'd been embarrassed by her own behaviour, afterwards: she hadn't meant to make him think she was trying to be seductive or provocative; all she'd been trying to do was get information out of the sales assistant. But when he'd subsequently given her the green dress, thinking he'd never see her again, she'd wondered whether part of the message Strike had been trying to convey was that he didn't disavow that look, that she had, indeed, looked wonderful in the dress, and this suspicion hadn't made her feel uncomfortable, but happy and flattered.

The second moment, far more painful to remember, had been when she'd stood at the top of the stairs at her wedding venue, Strike below her, and he'd turned when she called his name, and looked up at her, the new bride. He'd been injured and exhausted, and again, she'd seen a flicker of something in his face that wasn't mere friendship, and they'd hugged, and she'd felt . . .

Best not to think about it. Best not to dwell on that hug, on how like home it had felt, on how a kind of insanity had gripped her at that moment, and she'd imagined him saying 'come with me' and known she'd have gone if he had.

Robin swept the horoscope papers off the pub table, stuffed them back into her messenger bag and went outside, leaving half her coffee undrunk.

Trying to walk off her memories, she crossed a small stone bridge spanning the slow-flowing River Leam, which was spotted with clumps of duckweed, and passed the colonnade of the Royal Pump Rooms, where Satchwell's exhibition would open the following day. Striding briskly, her hands in her pockets, Robin tried to focus on the Parade, where shopfronts disfigured what had once been a sweeping white Regency terrace.

But Leamington Spa did nothing to raise her spirits. On the contrary, it reminded her too much of another spa town: Bath, where Matthew had gone to university. For Robin, long, symmetrical curves of Regency buildings, with their plain, classical façades, would forever conjure once-fond memories disfigured by later discoveries: visions of herself and Matthew strolling hand in hand, overlain by the knowledge that, even then, he'd been sleeping with Sarah.

'Oh, bugger everything,' Robin muttered, blinking tears out of her eyes. She turned abruptly and headed all the way back to the Land Rover.

Having parked the car closer to the hotel, she made a detour into the nearby Co-op to buy a small stash of food, then checked in at a self-service machine in her Premier Inn and headed upstairs to her single room. It was small, bare but perfectly clean and comfortable, and overlooked a spectacularly ugly town hall of red and white brick, which was over-embellished with scrolls, pediments and lions.

A couple of sandwiches, a chocolate éclair, a can of Diet Coke and an apple made Robin feel better. As the sun sank slowly behind the buildings on the Parade, she slipped off her shoes and reached into her bag for the photocopied pages of Talbot's notebook and her pack of Thoth tarot cards, which Aleister Crowley had devised, and in which Bill Talbot had sought the solution to Margot's disappearance. Sliding the pack out of the box into her hand, she shuffled through the cards, examining the images. Just as she'd suspected, Talbot had copied many motifs into his notebook, presumably from those cards which had come up during his frequent attempts to solve the case by consulting the tarot.

Robin now flattened a photocopy of what she thought of as the 'horns page', on which Talbot had dwelled on the three horned signs of the zodiac: Capricorn, Aries and Taurus. This page came in the last quarter of the notebook, in which quotations from Aleister Crowley, astrological symbols and strange drawings appeared far more often than concrete facts.

Here on the horns page was evidence of Talbot's renewed interest in Satchwell, whom he'd first ruled out on the basis that he was an Aries rather than a Capricorn. Talbot had evidently calculated Satchwell's whole birth horoscope and taken the trouble to note various aspects, which he noticed were *same as AC. Same as AC. AND DON'T FORGET LS connection.*

To add to the confusion, the mysterious Schmidt kept correcting signs, although he'd allowed Satchwell to keep his original sign of Aries.

And then an odd idea came to Robin: the notion of a fourteen-sign zodiac was clearly ludicrous (but why was it more ludicrous than a twelve-sign zodiac? asked a voice in her head, which sounded remarkably like Strike's), but certainly if you were going to squeeze in an extra two signs, dates would have to shift, wouldn't they?

She picked up her mobile and Googled 'fourteen-sign zodiac Schmidt'.

'Oh my God,' said Robin aloud, into her still hotel room.

Before she could fully process what she'd read, the mobile in her hand rang. It was Strike.

'Hi,' said Robin, hastily turning him to speakerphone so she could continue reading what she'd just found. 'How are you?'

'Knackered,' said Strike, who sounded it. 'What's happened?'

'What d'you mean?' asked Robin, her eyes rapidly scanning lines of text.

'You sound like you do when you've found something out.'

Robin laughed.

'OK, you won't believe this, but I've just found Schmidt.'

'You've what?'

'Schmidt, first name, Steven. He's a real person! He wrote a book in 1970 called *Astrology 14*, proposing the inclusion of two extra signs in the zodiac, Ophiuchus the Serpent-Bearer, and Cetus the Whale!'

There was a brief silence, then Strike muttered, 'How the hell did I miss that?'

'Remember that statue of the man holding the serpent, at Margot's old house?' said Robin, falling back on her pillows among the scattered tarot cards.

'Asclepius,' said Strike. 'Ophiuchus was the Roman form. God of healing.'

'Well, this explains all the changing dates, doesn't it?' said Robin, 'and why poor Talbot got so confused! He was trying to put everyone into Schmidt's adjusted dates, but they didn't seem to fit. And all the other astrologers he was consulting were still using the twelve-sign system, so—'

'Yeah,' said Strike, talking over her, 'that'd make a crazy man crazier, all right.'

His tone said, 'This is interesting, but not important.' Robin removed the Three of Disks from beneath her and examined it absent-mindedly. Robin was now so well-versed in astrological symbols that she didn't need to look up the glyphs to know that it also represented Mars in Capricorn.

'How are things with you?' she asked.

'Well, the church isn't going to hold everyone who's coming tomorrow, which Joan would've been thrilled about. I just wanted to let you know I'll be heading back up the road again on Tuesday.'

'Are you sure you don't need to stay longer?'

Note St John's cross
"And the Light
shineth in Darkness
and the Darkness
comprehended
it not"
St John
1:5

The Emperor = ♈
sudden, violent
activity
Crowley
equates
Baphomet

SCHMIDT CHANGES
♓ AND ♒ TO ♑
Change ♒ to ♀
But ♃ and ⚸ both in 12th with ♓
♀ IN 10th HOUSE: ELEVATION

Solve et Coagula
No resolution without
BREAKING DOWN

?
nurturing
and protective
denies contact
with ⚸
(wives and
infidelity)
Is ♌ right?)

But
♀ in
in 7th – House
of Marriage
FITS and ♀ in
11th – House
of Career? At
work?

'LUST/BABALON
'yet of their own poison
do they
perish'

♍

♑

SORNS are the universal hieroglyph of energy, particularly of Phallic energy

The wicked are estranged from
the womb, they go astray as soon
as they be born, speaking lies,

BAPHOMET

This poison is the poison
of the serpent
Psalm 58

BANEBDJEDET
EGYPTIAN RAM GOD
LINKED TO BAPHOMET

♂ ♑   Same as AC: strong willed, determined,
          but prone to accidents
♀ ♈ 10 ♀ close to his ☉ destined for him /
          soulmate, in 10th, she is his ambition
☊ ♌   Same as AC: Adams: 'no sense of
          moderation'/'resent any demands on them
☽ ♓   Same as AC: neuroses/personality
          disorders/excuses/dishonesty
Vs. ♐ ♄   Same as AC: transit could
          indicate BIRTH or significant relationship
MC. ♈   Same as AC: public image: forceful,
          masculine, possibly aggressive
REMEMBER LS CONNECTION
IF SCHMIDT says ♈ remains ♈

♀♂

BAPHOMET IS A FORM OF
THE BULL GOD

The Hierophant/♉ secretive/
secretly LAUGHING This woman
represents Venus as she is now in this aeon
ARMED AND MILITANT'
Clearly resentful, suspect ♄ rising
Adams: women with ♄ rising
have expression intense/bitter/sad
Also spare & lanky
Resentment, sullen silence
Conceals and broods
Power of earth – does she have magick?
Contrast power of ♀
White moon/black moon

SCHMIDT SAYS ♀
BECOMES ♈

THE FOOL is SILENCE
The Twin of Horns.

'The neighbours are all promising they're going to look after Ted. Lucy's trying to get him to come up to London for a bit afterwards. Any other news your end?'

'Er . . . let's see . . . I wrapped up Postcard,' said Robin. 'I think our weatherman was quite disappointed when he saw who his stalker was. His wife cheered up no end, though.'

Strike gave a grunt of laughter.

'So, we've taken on the commodities broker,' Robin continued. 'We haven't got pictures of anything incriminating between the husband and nanny yet, but I don't think it's going to be long.'

'You're owed a long stretch off for all this, Robin,' said Strike gruffly. 'I can't thank you enough.'

'Don't be silly,' she said.

They hung up shortly afterwards.

Robin's room seemed to have become suddenly much darker. The sun had gone down; in silhouette, the town hall resembled a monstrous Gothic palace. She turned on her bedside lamp and looked around at the bed strewn with astrological notes and tarot cards. Seen in the light of Strike's lack of enthusiasm, Talbot's doodles looked like the determinedly weird drawings in the back of a teenager's jotter, leading nowhere, done purely for the love of strangeness.

Yawning, she refolded the photocopied notes and put them back in her bag, went for a shower, returned in her pyjamas to the bed and gathered up the tarot cards, putting them in order as she did so, to make sure none of them were missing. She didn't particularly want the cleaner to think of her as the kind of person who left tarot cards strewn in her wake.

On the point of replacing the deck in its box, Robin suddenly sat down on the bed and began to shuffle it instead. She was too tired to attempt the fifteen-card layout advocated in the little booklet that accompanied the tarot, but she knew from her exhaustive examination of his notes that Talbot had sometimes tried to see his way through the investigation by laying out just three cards: the first representing 'the nature of the problem', the second, 'the cause', and the third, 'the solution'.

After a minute's shuffling, Robin turned over the top card and laid it down in the pool of light cast by her bedside lamp: the Prince of Cups. A naked blueish-green man rode an eagle, which was diving towards water. He held a goblet containing a snake in one hand and a lotus flower in the other. Robin pulled *The Book of Thoth* out of her bag and looked up the meaning.

> The moral characteristics of the person pictured in this card are subtlety, secret violence, and craft. He is intensely secret, an artist in all his ways.

She thought immediately of Dennis Creed. A master of murder, in his way.

She turned over the next card: the Four of Cups, or Luxury. Another lotus was pouring water over four more goblets, golden this time. Robin turned to the book.

> The card refers to the Moon in Cancer, which is her own house; but Cancer itself is so placed that this implies a certain weakness, an abandonment to desire.

Was the tarot criticising her for soft living? Robin glanced around her little box of a room, then turned over the last card.

More cups and yet more lotuses, and two entwined fish, pouring out water into two more golden chalices which stood on a green lake.

> Love . . . The card also refers to Venus in Cancer. It shows the harmony of the male and the female: interpreted in the largest sense. It is perfect and placid harmony . . .

Robin inspected the card for a few more seconds, before laying it down beside the other two. They were all cups. As she knew from her study of the Thoth tarot, cups meant water. Well, here she was in a spa town . . .

Robin shook her head, though nobody was there to see her do it, returned the tarot cards to their box, climbed into bed, set her alarm and turned out the light.

CHAPTER 46

Whereas that Pagan proud him selfe did rest,
In secret shadow by a fountaine side:
Euen he it was, that earst would haue
  supprest
Faire Vna . . .

Edmund Spenser
The Faerie Queene

Robin's night was punctuated with sudden wakings from a succession of anxious dreams: that she'd fallen asleep at the wheel again, or had overslept and arrived at the gallery to find Satchwell's exhibition gone. When the alarm on her mobile rang at 7 a.m., she forced herself immediately out of bed, showered, dressed and, glad to leave the impersonal bedroom, headed downstairs with her packed holdall to eat muesli and drink coffee in the dining room, which was painted an oppressive sludge green.

The day outside was fresh but overcast, a cold silver sun trying to penetrate the cloud. Having returned her holdall to the parked Land Rover, she headed on foot towards the Royal Pump Rooms, which housed the gallery where Satchwell's exhibition was about to open. To her left lay the ornamental Jephson Gardens, and a fountain of pinkish stone that might have been the model for one of Crowley's tarot cards. Four scallop-patterned basins sat at the top.

. . . a certain weakness, an abandonment to desire . . .

You're getting like Talbot, Robin told herself crossly. Speeding up, she arrived at the Pump Rooms with time to spare.

The building had just been opened; a young woman in black was walking away from the glass doors, holding a bunch of keys. Robin entered, to find little trace of the Regency pump rooms left inside: the floor was covered in modern grey tiles, the ceiling supported by metal columns. A café took up one wing of the open-plan space, a shop another. The gallery, Robin saw, lay across opposite, through more glass doors.

It comprised one long room, brick-walled and wooden-floored, which had been temporarily given over to an exhibition of local artists. There were only three people inside: a stocky, grey-bobbed woman in an Alice band, a small man with a hang-dog air whom Robin suspected was her husband, and another young woman in black, who she assumed worked there. The grey-haired woman's voice was echoing around the room as though it was a gymnasium.

'I *told* Shona that Long Itchington needs an accent light! You can barely *see* it, this corner's so dark!'

Robin walked slowly around, looking at canvases and sketches. Five local artists had been given space for the temporary exhibition, but she identified Paul Satchwell's work without difficulty: it had been given a prominent position and stood out boldly among the studies of local landmarks, portraits of pallid Britons standing at bus stops, and still lifes.

Naked figures twisted and cavorted in scenes from Greek mythology. Persephone struggled in the arms of Hades as he carried her down into the underworld; Andromeda strained against chains binding her to rock as a dragonish creature rose from the waves to devour her; Leda lay supine in bulrushes as Zeus, in the form of a swan, impregnated her.

Two lines of Joni Mitchell floated back to Robin as she looked at the paintings: '*When I first saw your gallery, I liked the ones of ladies . . .*'

Except that Robin wasn't sure she liked the paintings. The female figures were all black-haired, olive-skinned, heavy-breasted and partially or entirely naked. The paintings were accomplished, but Robin found them slightly lascivious. Each of the women wore a similar expression of vacant abandon, and Satchwell seemed to have a definite preference for those myths that featured bondage, rape or abduction.

121

'Striking, aren't they?' said the meek-faced husband of the angry painter of Long Itchington, appearing at Robin's side to contemplate a picture of a totally naked Io, whose hair streamed behind her and whose breasts gleamed with sweat as she fled a bull with a gargantuan erection.

'Mm,' said Robin. 'I was wondering whether he was going to come to the exhibition. Paul Satchwell, I mean.'

'I think he said he's going to pop back in,' said the man.

'Back—? You mean he's here? In England?'

'Well, yes,' said the man, looking somewhat surprised. 'He was here yesterday, anyway. Came to see them hung.'

'Visiting family, I think he said,' said the young woman in black, who seemed glad of a reason to talk to somebody other than the fuming artist in the hairband.

'You haven't got contact details for him, have you?' asked Robin. 'Maybe the address of where he's staying?'

'No,' said the young woman, now looking intrigued. Evidently local artists didn't usually engender this much excitement. 'You can leave your name and address, though, if you like, and I'll tell him you want to speak to him if he drops by?'

So Robin accompanied the young woman back to the reception area, where she scribbled her name and phone number onto a piece of paper and then, her heart still beating fast in excitement, went to the café, bought herself a cappuccino and positioned herself beside a long window looking out onto the Pump Room Gardens, where she had a good view of people entering the building.

Should she book back into the Premier Inn and wait here in Leamington Spa until Satchwell showed himself? Would Strike think it worth neglecting their other cases to remain here in the hope of Satchwell turning up? It was Joan's funeral today: she couldn't burden him with the question.

She wondered what her partner was doing now. Perhaps already dressing for the service. Robin had only ever attended two funerals. Her maternal grandfather had died just before she dropped out of university: she'd gone home for the funeral and never gone back. She remembered very little of the occasion: it had taken everything she'd had to preserve a fragile façade of well-being, and she remembered the strange sense of disembodiment that underlay the eggshell brittleness with which she'd met the half-scared enquiries of family members who knew what had happened to her. She remembered, too, Matthew's hand around hers. He hadn't once dropped it, skipping lectures and an important rugby game to come and be with her.

The only other funeral she'd attended had been four years previously, when she and Strike had attended the cremation of a murdered girl in the course of their first murder investigation, standing together at the back of the sparsely populated, impersonal crematorium. That had been before Strike had agreed to take her on permanently, when she'd been nothing but a temp whom Strike had allowed to inveigle her way into his investigation. Thinking back to Rochelle Onifade's funeral, Robin realised that even then, the ties binding her to Matthew had been loosening. Robin hadn't yet realised it, but she'd found something she wanted more than she'd wanted to be Matthew's wife.

Her coffee finished, Robin made a quick trip to the bathroom, then returned to the gallery in the hope that Satchwell might have entered it while she wasn't watching, but there was no sign of him. A few people had drifted in to wander around the temporary exhibition. Satchwell's paintings were attracting the most interest. Having walked the room once more, Robin pretended an interest in an old water fountain in the corner. Covered in swags and lion's heads with gaping mouths, it had once dispensed the health-giving spa waters.

Beyond the font lay another a room, which presented a total contrast to the clean, modern space behind her. It was octagonal and made of brick, with a very high ceiling and windows of Bristol blue glass. Robin stepped inside: it was, or had once been, a Turkish *hammam* or steam room, and had the appearance of a small temple. At the highest point of the vaulted ceiling was a cupola decorated with an eight-pointed star in glass, with a lantern hanging from it.

'Nice to see a bit of *pagan* influence, innit?'

The voice was a combination of self-conscious cockney, overlain with the merest whiff of a Greek accent. Robin spun around and there, planted firmly in the middle of the *hammam*, in jeans and an old denim shirt, was an elderly man with his left eye covered in a surgical dressing, which stood out, stark white against skin as brown as old terracotta. His straggly white hair fell to his stooping shoulders; white chest hair grew in the space left by his undone buttons, a silver chain hung around his crêpe-skinned throat, and silver and turquoise rings decorated his fingers.

'You the young lady 'oo wanted to talk to me?' asked Paul Satchwell, revealing yellow-brown teeth as he smiled.

'Yes,' said Robin, 'I am. Robin Ellacott,' she added, holding out her hand.

His uncovered eye swept Robin's face and figure with unconcealed appreciation. He held her hand a little too long after shaking it but Robin continued to smile as she withdrew it, and delved in her handbag for a card, which she gave him.

'Private detective?' said Satchwell, his smile fading a little as he read the card, one-eyed. 'The 'ell's all this?'

Robin explained.

'Margot?' said Satchwell, looking shocked. 'Christ almighty, that's, what . . . forty years ago?'

'Nearly,' said Robin, moving aside to let some tourists claim her spot in the middle of the *hammam*, and read its history off the sign on the wall. 'I've come up from London in hopes of talking to you about her. It'd mean a lot to the family if you could tell me whatever you remember.'

'*Éla ré*, what d'you expect me to remember after all this time?' said Satchwell.

But Robin was confident he was going to accept. She'd discovered that people generally wanted to know what you already knew, why you'd come to find them, whether they had any reason to worry. And sometimes they wanted to talk, because they were lonely or felt neglected, and it was flattering to have somebody hang on your words, and sometimes, as now (elderly as he was, the single eye, which was a cold, pale blue, swept her body and back to her face) they wanted to spend more time with a young woman they found attractive.

'All right, then,' said Satchwell slowly, 'I don't know what I can tell you, but I'm hungry. Let me take you to lunch.'

'That'd be great, but I'll be taking you,' said Robin, smiling. 'You're doing *me* the favour.'

CHAPTER 47

. . . the sacred Oxe, that carelesse stands,
With gilden hornes, and flowry girlonds
* crownd . . .*
All suddeinly with mortall stroke astownd,
Doth groueling fall . . .
The martiall Mayd stayd not him to lament,
But forward rode, and kept her ready
* way . . .*

Edmund Spenser
The Faerie Queene

Satchwell bade the attendant in the art gallery
farewell by clasping her hands in a double
handshake and assuring her he'd look in
later in the week. He even took fulsome leave of
the disgruntled painter of Long Itchington, who
scowled after him as he left.

'Provincial galleries,' he said, chuckling, as he
and Robin headed out of the Pump Rooms.
'Funny, seeing my stuff next to that old bat's postcard pictures, though, wasn't it? And a bit of a

kick to be exhibited where you were born. I haven't been back here in, Christ, must be fifty-odd years. You got a car? Good. We'll get out of here, go froo to Warwick. It's just up the road.'

Satchwell kept up a steady stream of talk as they walked towards the Land Rover.

'Never liked Leamington.' With only one eye at his service, he had to turn his head in exaggerated fashion to look around. 'Too *genteel* for the likes of me . . .'

Robin learned that he'd lived in the spa town only until he was six, at which point he and his single mother had moved to Warwick. He had a younger half-sister, the result of his mother's second marriage, with whom he was currently staying, and had decided to have his cataract removed while in England.

'Still a British citizen, I'm entitled. So when they asked me,' he said, with a grand wave backwards at the Royal Pump Rooms, 'if I'd contribute some paintings, I thought, why not? Brought them over with me.'

'They're wonderful,' said Robin insincerely. 'Have you got just the one sister?' She had no aim other than making polite conversation, but out of the corner of her eye, she saw Satchwell's head turn so that his unbandaged eye could look at her.

'No,' he said, after a moment or two. 'It was . . . I 'ad an older sister, too, but she died when we were kids.'

128

'Oh, I'm sorry,' said Robin.

'One of those things,' said Satchwell. 'Severely disabled. Had fits and stuff. She was older than me. I can't remember much about it. Hit my mum hard, obviously.'

'I can imagine,' said Robin.

They had reached the Land Rover. Robin, who'd already mentally calculated the risk to herself, should Satchwell prove to be dangerous, was confident that she'd be safe by daylight, and given that she had control of the car. She unlocked the doors and climbed into the driver's seat, and Satchwell succeeded in hoisting himself into the passenger seat on his second attempt.

'Yeah, we moved froo to Warwick from 'ere after Blanche died,' he said, buckling up his seatbelt. 'Just me and my mum. Not that Warwick's much better, but it's *aufentic*. Aufentic medieval buildings, you know?'

Given that he was Midlands born and raised, Robin thought his cockney accent must be a longstanding affectation. It came and went, mingled with an intonation that was slightly foreign after so many years in Greece.

'Whereas this place . . . the Victorians 'ad their wicked way with it,' he said, and as Robin reversed out her parking space he said, looking up at the moss-covered face of a stone Queen Victoria, 'there she is, look, miserable old cow,' and laughed. 'State of that building,' he added, as they passed the town hall. 'That's somefing me and Crowley had in common, for sure. Born 'ere, hated it 'ere.'

Robin thought she must have misheard.

'You and . . .?'

'Aleister Crowley.'

'Crowley?' she repeated, as they drove up the Parade. 'The occult writer?'

'Yeah. 'E was born here,' said Satchwell. 'You don't see that in many of the guidebooks, because they don't like it. 'Ere, turn left. Go on, it's on our way.'

Minutes later, he directed her into Clarendon Square, where tall white terraced houses, though now subdivided into flats, retained a vestige of their old grandeur.

'That's it, where he was born,' said Satchwell with satisfaction, pointing up at number 30. 'No plaque or nothing. They don't like talking about him, the good people of Leamington Spa. I had a bit of a Crowley phase in my youth,' said Satchwell, as Robin looked up at the large, square windows. 'You know he tortured a cat to death when he was a boy, just to see whether it had nine lives?'

'I didn't,' said Robin, putting the car into reverse.

'Probably 'appened in there,' said Satchwell with morbid satisfaction.

Same as AC. Same as AC. Another moment of enlightenment had hit Robin. Talbot had gone looking for identical components between Satchwell's horoscope and Crowley's, the self-proclaimed Beast, Baphomet, the wickedest man in the West. *LS connection.* Of course: Leamington Spa.

Why had Talbot decided, months into the investigation, that Satchwell deserved a full horoscope, the only one of the suspects to be so honoured? His alibi appeared watertight, after all. Had the return of suspicion been a symptom of Talbot's illness, triggered by the coincidence of Satchwell and Crowley's place of birth, or had he uncovered some unrecorded weakness in Satchwell's alibi? Satchwell continued to talk about his life in Greece, his painting and about his disappointment in how old England was faring, and Robin made appropriate noises at regular intervals while mentally reviewing those features of Satchwell's horoscope that Talbot had found so intriguing.

Mars in Capricorn: strong-willed, determined, but prone to accidents.

Moon in Pisces: neuroses/personality disorders/ dishonesty

Leo rising: no sense of moderation. Resents demands on them.

They reached Warwick within half an hour and, as Satchwell had promised, found themselves in a town that could hardly have presented a greater contrast to the wide, sweeping white-faced crescents of Leamington. An ancient stone arch reminded Robin of Clerkenwell. They passed timber and beam houses, cobbles, steep sloping streets and narrow alleyways.

'We'll go to the Roebuck,' said Satchwell, when Robin had parked in the market square. 'It's been there for ever. Oldest pub in town.'

'Wherever you like,' said Robin, smiling as she checked that she had her notebook in her handbag.

They walked together through the heart of Warwick, Satchwell pointing out such landmarks as he deemed worth looking at. He was one of those men who felt a need to touch, tapping Robin unnecessarily upon the arm to draw her attention, grasping her elbow as they crossed a street, and generally assuming a proprietorial air over her as they wove their way towards Smith Street.

'D'you mind?' asked Satchwell, as they drew level with Picturesque Art Supplies, and without waiting for an answer he led her into the shop where, as he selected brushes and oils, he talked with airy self-importance of modern trends in art and the stupidity of critics. *Oh, Margot*, Robin thought, but then she imagined the Margot Bamborough she carried with her in her head judging her, in turn, by Matthew, with his endless store of anecdotes of his own sporting achievements, and his increasingly pompous talk of pay rises and bonuses, and felt humbled and apologetic.

At last, they made it into the Roebuck Inn, a low-beamed pub with a sign of a deer's head hanging outside, and secured a table for two towards the rear of the pub. Robin couldn't help but notice the coincidence: the wall behind Satchwell was dotted with horned animal heads, including a stuffed deer and bronze-coloured models of an antelope and a ram. Even the menus had silhouettes of antlered stag heads upon them. Robin asked the waitress for a Diet Coke, all the while trying to repress thoughts of the horned signs of the zodiac.

'Would it be all right,' she asked, smiling, when the waitress had departed for the bar, 'if I ask a few questions about Margot now?'

'Yeah, of course,' said Satchwell, with a smile that revealed his stained teeth again, but he immediately picked up the menu card and studied it.

'And d'you mind if I take notes?' Robin asked, pulling out her notebook.

'Go ahead,' he said, still smiling, watching her over the top of his menu with his uncovered eye, which followed her movements as she opened the book and clicked out the nib of her pen.

'So, I apologise if any of these questions—'

'Are you sure you don't want a proper drink?' asked Satchwell, who had ordered a beer. 'I 'ate drinking on me own.'

'Well, I'm driving, you see,' said Robin.

'You could stay over. Not with me, don't worry,' he said quickly, with a grin that on a man so elderly, resembled a satyr's leer, 'I mean, go to an 'otel, file expenses. I s'pect you're taking a good chunk of money from Margot's family for this, are you?'

Robin merely smiled, and said,

'I need to get back to London. We're quite busy. It would be really useful to get some background on Margot,' she continued. 'How did you meet?'

He told her the story she already knew, about how he'd been taken to the Playboy Club by a client and seen there the leggy nineteen-year-old in her bunny ears and tail.

'And you struck up a friendship?'

'Well,' said Satchwell, 'I don't know that I'd call it *that*.'

With his cold eye upon Robin he said,

'We 'ad a very strong *sexual* connection. She was a virgin when we met, y'know.'

Robin kept smiling formally. He wasn't going to embarrass her.

'She was nineteen. I was twen'y-five. Beau'iful girl,' he sighed. 'Wish I'd kept the pictures I took of her, but after she disappeared I felt wrong about 'aving them.'

Robin heard Oonagh again. 'He took pictures of her. *You* know. *Pictures*.' It must be those revealing or obscene photos Satchwell was talking about, because after all, he'd hardly have felt guilty about having a snapshot.

The waitress came back with Satchwell's beer and Robin's Diet Coke. They ordered food; after swiftly scanning the menu, Robin asked for a chicken and bacon salad; Satchwell ordered steak and chips. When the waitress had gone Robin asked, though she knew the answer,

134

'How long were you together?'

'Coupla years, all told. We broke up, then got back togevver. She didn't like me using other models. Jealous. Not cut out for an artist's muse, Margot. Didn't like sitting still and not talking, haha . . . no, I fell hard for Margot Bamborough. Yeah, there was a damn sight more to her than being a Bunny Girl.'

Of course there was, thought Robin, though still smiling politely. *She became a bloody doctor.*

'Did you ever paint her?'

'Yeah,' said Satchwell. 'Few times. Some sketches and one full-size picture. I sold them. Needed the cash. Wish I 'adn't.'

He fell into a momentary abstraction, his uncovered eye surveying the pub, and Robin wondered whether old memories were genuinely resurfacing behind the heavily tanned face, which was so deeply lined and dark it might have been carved from teak, or whether he was playing the part that was expected of him when he said quietly,

'Hell of a girl, Margot Bamborough.'

He took a sip of his beer, then said,

'It's her 'usband who's hired you, is it?'

'No,' said Robin. 'Her daughter.'

'Oh,' said Satchwell, nodding. 'Yeah, of course: there was a kid. She didn't look as though she'd 'ad a baby, when I met her after they got married. Slim as ever. Both my wives put on about a stone with each of our kids.'

'How many children have you got?' asked Robin, politely.

She wanted the food to hurry up. It was harder to walk out once food was in front of you, and some instinct told her that Paul Satchwell's whimsical mood might not last.

'Five,' said Satchwell. 'Two with me first wife, and three with me second. Didn't mean to: we got twins on the last throw. All pretty much grown up now, thank Christ. Kids and art don't mix. I love 'em,' he said roughly, 'but Cyril Connolly had it right. The enemy of promise is the pram in the bloody 'all.'

He threw her a brief glance out of his one visible eye and said abruptly,

'So 'er 'usband still thinks I had something to do with Margot disappearing, does 'e?'

'What d'you mean by "still"?' enquired Robin.

''E gave my name to the police,' said Satchwell. 'The night she disappeared. Thought she might've run off with me. Did you know Margot and I bumped into each other a coupla weeks before she disappeared?'

'I did, yes,' said Robin.

'It put ideas into what's-'is-name's head,' he said. 'I can't blame him, I s'pose it did look fishy. I'd've probably thought the same, if my bird had met up with an old flame right before they buggered off – disappeared, I mean.'

The food arrived: Satchwell's steak and chips looked appetising, but Robin, who'd been too busy concentrating on her questions, hadn't read the small print on the menu. Expecting a plate of salad, she received a wooden platter bearing various ramekins containing hot sausage slices, hummous and a sticky mess of mayonnaise-coated leaves, a challenging assortment to eat while taking notes.

'Want some chips?' offered Satchwell, pushing the small metal bucket that contained them towards her.

'No thanks,' said Robin, smiling. She took a bite of a breadstick and continued, her pen in her right hand,

'Did Margot talk about Roy, when you bumped into her?'

'A bit,' said Satchwell, his mouth full of steak. 'She put up a good front. What you do, when you meet the ex, isn't it? Pretend you think you did the right thing. No regrets.'

'Did you think she had regrets?' asked Robin.

'She wasn't 'appy, I could tell. I thought, nobody's paying you attention. She tried to put a brave face on it, but she struck me as miserable. Knackered.'

'Did you only see each other the once?'

Satchwell chewed his steak, looking at Robin thoughtfully. At last he swallowed, then said,

'Have you read my police statement?'

'Yes,' said Robin.

'Then you know perfectly well,' said Satchwell, waggling his fork at her, 'that it was just the once. *Don't* you?'

He was smiling, trying to pass off the implied

admonition as waggish, but Robin felt the spindle-thin spike of aggression.

'So you went for a drink, and talked?' said Robin, smiling, as though she hadn't noticed the undertone, daring him to become defensive, and he continued, in a milder tone,

'Yeah, we went to some bar in Camden, not far from my flat. She'd been on an 'ouse call to some patient.'

Robin made a note.

'And can you remember what you talked about?'

'She told me she'd met 'er husband at medical school, 'e was an 'igh-flier and all that. What was 'e?' said Satchwell, with what seemed to Robin a forced unconcern. 'A cardiologist or something?'

'Haematologist,' said Robin.

'What's that, blood? Yeah, she was always impressed by clever people, Margot. Didn't occur to 'er that they can be shits like anyone else.'

'Did you get the impression Dr Phipps was a shit?' asked Robin lightly.

'Not really,' said Satchwell. 'But I was told 'e had a stick up his arse and was a bit of a mummy's boy.'

'Who told you that?' asked Robin, pausing with her pen suspended over her notebook.

'Someone 'oo'd met him,' he replied with a slight shrug. 'You not married?' he went on, his eyes on Robin's bare left hand.

'Living with someone,' said Robin, with a brief

138

smile. It was the answer she'd learned to give, to shut down flirtation from witnesses and clients, to erect barriers. Satchwell said, 'Ah. I always know, if a bird's living with a bloke without marriage, she must be really keen on him. Nothing but 'er feelings holding her, is there?'

'I suppose not,' said Robin, with a brief smile. She knew he was trying to disconcert her. 'Did Margot mention anything that might be worrying her, or causing her problems? At home or at work?'

'Told you, it was all window dressing,' said Satchwell, munching on fries. 'Great job, great 'usband, nice kid, nice 'ouse: she'd made it.' He swallowed. 'I did the same thing back: told her I was having an exhibition, won an award for one of me paintings, in a band, serious girlfriend . . . which was a lie,' he added, with a slight snort. 'I only remember that bird because we split up later that evening. Don't ask me her name now. We 'adn't been together long. She had long black hair and a massive tattoo of a spider's web round her navel, that's what I mainly remember – yeah, anyway, I ended it. Seeing Margot again—'

He hesitated. His uncovered eye unfocused, he said,

'I was thirty-five. It's a funny age. It starts dawning on you forty's really gonna happen to you, not just to other people. What are you, twenty-five?'

'Twenty-nine,' said Robin.

'Happens earlier for women, that worrying about getting old thing,' said Satchwell. 'Got kids yet?'

'No,' said Robin, and then, 'so Margot didn't say anything to you that might suggest a reason for disappearing voluntarily?'

'Margot wouldn't have gone away and left everyone in the lurch,' said Satchwell, as positive on the point as Oonagh. 'Not Margot. Responsible was her middle name. She was a good girl, you know? School prefect sort.'

'So you didn't make any plans to meet again?'

'No plans,' said Satchwell, munching on chips. 'I mentioned to 'er my band was playing at the Dublin Castle the following week. Said, "drop in if you're passing", but she said she wouldn't be able to. Dublin Castle was a pub in Camden,' Satchwell added. 'Might still be there.'

'Yes,' said Robin, 'it is.'

'I told the investigating officer I'd mentioned the gig to her. Told 'im I'd've been up for seeing her again, if she'd wanted it. I 'ad nothing to hide.'

Robin remembered Strike's opinion that Satchwell volunteering this information seemed almost too helpful, and, trying to dissemble her sudden suspicion, asked:

'Did anyone spot Margot at the pub, the night you were playing?'

Satchwell took his time before swallowing, then said,

'Not as far as I know.'

140

'The little wooden Viking you gave her,' said Robin, watching him carefully, 'the one with "Brunhilda" written on the foot—'

'The one she had on her desk at work?' he said, with what Robin thought might have been a whiff of gratified vanity. 'Yeah, I gave her that in the old days, when we were dating.'

Could it be true, Robin wondered. After the acrimonious way Margot and Satchwell had broken up, after he'd locked her in his flat so she couldn't get out to work, after he'd hit her, after she'd married another man, would Margot really have kept Satchwell's silly little gift? Didn't private jokes and nicknames become dead and rotten things after a painful break-up, when the thought of them became almost worse than memories of rows and insults? Robin had given most of Matthew's gifts to charity after she'd found out about his infidelity, including the plush elephant that had been his first Valentine's present and the jewellery box he'd given her for her twenty-first. However, Robin could tell Satchwell was going to stick to his story, so she moved to the next question in her notebook.

'There was a printers on Clerkenwell Road I think you had an association with.'

'Come again?' said Satchwell, frowning. 'A printers?'

'A schoolgirl called Amanda White claims she saw Margot in an upper window belonging to this printers on the night—'

'Really?' said Satchwell. 'I never 'ad no association with no printers. 'Oo says I did?'

'There was a book written in the eighties about Margot's disappearance—'

'Yeah? I missed that.'

'—it said the printers produced flyers for a nightclub you'd painted a mural for.'

'For crying out loud,' said Satchwell, half-amused, half-exasperated. 'That's not an association. It'd be a stretch to call it a coincidence. I've never heard of the bloody place.'

Robin made a note and moved to her next question.

'What did you think of Bill Talbot?'

'Who?'

'The investigating officer. The first one,' said Robin.

'Oh yeah,' said Satchwell, nodding. 'Very odd bloke. When I 'eard afterwards he'd had a breakdown or whatever, I wasn't surprised. Kept asking me what I was doing on random dates. Afterwards, I worked out 'e was trying to decide wevver I was the Essex Butcher. He wanted to know my time of birth, as well, and what the hell that had to do with anything . . .'

'He was trying to draw up your horoscope,' said Robin, and she explained Talbot's preoccupation with astrology.

'*Dén tó pistévo!*' said Satchwell, looking annoyed. 'Astrology? That's not funny. He was in charge of the case – how long?'

'Six months,' said Robin.

'Jesus,' said Satchwell, scowling so that the clear tape holding the dressing over his eye crinkled.

'I don't think the people around him realised how ill he was until it got too obvious to ignore,' said Robin, now pulling a few tagged sheets of paper out of her bag: photocopies of Satchwell's statements to both Talbot and Lawson.

'What's all that?' he said sharply.

'Your statements to the police,' said Robin.

'Why are there – what are they, stars? – all over—'

'They're pentagrams,' said Robin. 'This is the statement Talbot took from you. It's just routine,' she added, because Satchwell was now looking wary. 'We've done it with everyone the police interviewed. I know your statements were double-checked at the time, but I wondered if I could run over them again, in case you remember anything useful?'

Taking his silence for consent, she continued:

'You were alone in your studio on the afternoon of the eleventh of October, but you took a call there at five from a Mr . . . Hendricks?'

'Hendricks, yeah,' said Satchwell. 'He was my agent at the time.'

'You went out to eat at a local café around half past six, where you had a conversation with the woman behind the till, which she remembered. Then you went back home to change, and out again to meet a few friends in a bar called Joe

Bloggs around eight o'clock. All three friends you were drinking with confirmed your story . . . nothing to add to any of that?'

'No,' said Satchwell, and Robin thought she detected a slight sense of relief. 'That all sounds right.'

'Was it one of those friends who'd met Roy Phipps?' Robin asked casually.

'No,' said Satchwell, unsmiling, and then, changing the subject, he said, 'Margot's daughter must be knocking on forty now, is she?'

'Forty last year,' said Robin.

'*Éla*,' said Satchwell, shaking his head. 'Time just—'

One of the mahogany brown hands, wrinkled and embellished with heavy silver and turquoise rings, made a smooth motion, as of a paper aeroplane in flight.

'—and then one day you're old and you never saw it sneaking up on you.'

'When did you move abroad?'

'I didn't mean to move, not at first. Went travelling, late '75,' said Satchwell. He'd nearly finished his steak, now.

'What made you—?'

'I'd been thinking of travelling for a bit,' said Satchwell. 'But after Creed killed Margot – it was such a bloody 'orrible thing – such a shock – I dunno, I wanted a change of scene.'

'That's what you think happened to her, do you? Creed killed her?'

144

He put the last bit of steak into his mouth, chewed it and swallowed before answering.

'Well, yeah. Obviously at first I 'oped she'd just walked out on 'er husband and was 'oled up somewhere. But then it went on and on and . . . yeah, everyone thought it was the Essex Butcher, including the police. Not just the nutty one, the second one, the one who took over.'

'Lawson,' said Robin.

Satchwell shrugged, as much to say as the officer's name didn't matter, and asked,

'Are you going to interview Creed?'

'Hopefully.'

'Why would he tell the truth, now?'

'He likes publicity,' said Robin. 'He might like the idea of making a splash in the newspapers. So Margot disappearing was a shock to you?'

'Well, obviously it was,' said Satchwell, now probing his teeth with his tongue. 'I'd just seen her again and . . . I'm not going to pretend I was still *in love* with her, or anything like that, but . . . have *you* ever been caught up in a police investigation?' he asked her, with a trace of aggression.

'Yes,' said Robin. 'Several. It was stressful and intimidating, every time.'

'Well, there you are,' said Satchwell, mollified.

'What made you choose Greece?'

'I didn't, really. I 'ad an inheritance off my grandmother and I thought, I'll take some time off, do Europe, paint . . . went through France and Italy, and in '76 I arrived in Kos. Worked in

145

a bar. Painted in my free hours. Sold quite a few pictures to tourists. Met my first wife . . . never left,' said Satchwell, with a shrug.

'Something else I wanted to ask you,' said Robin, moving the police statements to the bottom of her small stack. 'We've found out about a possible sighting of Margot, a week after she disappeared. A sighting that wasn't ever reported to the police.'

'Yeah?' said Satchwell, looking interested. 'Where?'

'In Leamington Spa,' said Robin, 'in the grave-yard of All Saints church.'

Satchwell's thick white eyebrows rose, putting strain on the clear tape that was holding the dressing to his eye.

'In All Saints?' he repeated, apparently astonished.

'Looking at graves. Allegedly, she had her hair dyed black.'

''Oo saw this?'

'A man visiting the area on a motorbike. Two years later, he told the St John's practice nurse about it.'

'He told the *nurse*?'

Satchwell's jaw hardened.

'And what else has the *nurse* told you?' he said, searching Robin's face. He seemed suddenly and unexpectedly angry.

'Do you know Janice?' asked Robin, wondering why he looked so angry.

'That's her name, is it?' said Satchwell. 'I couldn't remember.'

'You *do* know her?'

Satchwell put more chips in his mouth. Robin could see that he was trying to decide what to tell her, and she felt that jolt of excitement that made all the long, tedious hours of the job, the sitting around, the sleeplessness, worthwhile.

'She's shit-stirring,' said Satchwell abruptly. 'She's a shit-stirrer, that one, that nurse. She and Margot didn't like each other. Margot told me she didn't like her.'

'When was this?'

'When we ran into each other, like I told you, in the street—'

'I thought you said she didn't talk about work?'

'Well, she told me that. They'd had a row or something. I don't know. It was just something she said in passing. She told me she didn't like the nurse,' repeated Satchwell.

It was as though a hard mask had surfaced under the leather dark skin: the slightly comical, crêpey-faced charmer had been replaced by a mean old one-eyed man. Robin remembered how Matthew's lower face had tautened when angry, giving him the look of a muzzled dog, but she wasn't intimidated. She sensed in Satchwell the same wily instinct for self-preservation as in her ex-husband. Whatever Satchwell might have meted out to Margot, or to the wives who'd left him, he'd think better of slapping Robin in a crowded pub, in the town where his sister still lived.

'You seem angry,' Robin said.

'*Gia chári tou*, of course I am – that nurse, what's her name? Trying to implicate me, isn't she? Making up a story to make it look like Margot ran away to be with me—'

'Janice didn't invent the story. We checked with Mr Ramage's widow and she confirmed that her late husband told other people he'd met a missing woman—'

'What else has *Janice* told you?' he said again.

'She never mentioned you,' said Robin, now immensely curious. 'We had no idea you knew each other.'

'But she claims Margot was seen in Leamington Spa after she disappeared? No, she knows exactly what she's bloody doing.'

Satchwell took another chip, ate it, then suddenly got to his feet and walked past Robin, who looked over her shoulder to see him striding into the gents. His back view was older than his front: she could see the pink scalp through the thin white hair and there was no backside filling out his jeans.

Robin guessed he considered the interview finished. However, she had something else up her sleeve: a dangerous something, perhaps, but she'd use it rather than let the interview end here, with more questions raised than answered.

It was fully five minutes before he reappeared and she could tell that he'd worked himself up in his absence. Rather than sitting back down, he stood over her as he said,

'I don't think you're a fucking detective. I think you're press.'

Seen from below, the tortoise's neck was particularly striking. The chain, the turquoise and silver rings and the long hair now seemed like fancy dress.

'You can call Anna Phipps and check if you like,' said Robin. 'I've got her number here. Why d'you think the press would be interested in you?'

'I had enough of them last time. I'm off. I don't need this. I'm supposed to be recuperating.'

'One last thing,' said Robin, 'and you're going to want to hear it.'

She'd learned the trick from Strike. Stay calm, but assertive. Make them worry what else you've got.

Satchwell turned back, his one uncovered eye hard as flint. No trace of flirtation remained, no attempt to patronise her. She was an equal now; an adversary.

'Why don't you sit down?' said Robin. 'This won't take long.'

After a slight hesitation, Satchwell eased himself back into his seat. His hoary head now blocked the stuffed deer head that hung on the brick wall behind him. From Robin's point of view, the horns appeared to rise directly out of the white hair that fell in limp curls to his shoulders.

'Margot Bamborough knew something about you that you didn't want to get out,' said Robin. 'Didn't she?'

He glared at her.

'The pillow dream?' said Robin.

Every line of his face hardened, turning him vulpine. The sunburned chest, wrinkled beneath its white hair, caved as he exhaled.

'Told someone, did she? Who?' Before Robin could answer, he said, ''Er husband, I suppose? Or that fucking Irish girl, was it?'

His jaws worked, chewing nothing.

'I should never 'ave told her,' he said. 'That's what you do when you're drunk and you're in love, or whatever the fuck we were. Then I 'ad it playing on my mind for years that she was gonna . . .'

The sentence ended in silence.

'Did she mention it, when you met again?' asked Robin, feeling her way, pretending she knew more than she did.

'She asked after my poor mother,' said Satchwell. 'I fort at the time, are you 'aving a go? But I don't think she was. Maybe she'd learned better, being a doctor, maybe she'd changed her views. She'll have seen people like Blanche. A life not worth living.

'Anyway,' he said, leaning forwards slightly, 'I still think it was a dream. All right? I was six years old. I dreamed it. And even if it wasn't a dream, they're both dead and gone now and nobody can say no different. My old mum died in '89. You can't get 'er for anything now, poor cow. Single mother, trying to cope with us all on 'er own. It's

150

merciful,' said Satchwell, 'putting someone out of their misery. A mercy.'

He got up, drained beneath his tan, his face sagging, turned and walked away, but at the moment he was about to disappear he suddenly turned and tottered back to her, his jaw working.

'I think,' he said, with as much malevolence as he could muster, 'you're a nasty little bitch.'

He left for good this time.

Robin's heart rate was barely raised. Her dominant emotion was elation. Pushing her unappetising ramekins aside, she pulled the little metal bucket he'd left behind towards her, and finished the artist's chips.

CHAPTER 48

Sir Artegall, long hauing since,
Taken in hand th'exploit . . .
To him assynd, her high beheast to doo,
To the sea shore he gan his way apply . . .

Edmund Spenser
The Faerie Queene

Joan's funeral service finished with the hymn most beloved of sailors, 'Eternal Father, Strong to Save'. While the congregation sang the familiar words, Ted, Strike, Dave Polworth and three of Ted's comrades in the lifeboat service shouldered the coffin back down the aisle of the simple cream-walled church, with its wooden beams and its stained-glass windows depicting purple-robed St Maudez, for whom both village and church were named. Flanked by an island tower and a seal on a rock, the saint watched the coffin-bearers pass out of the church.

O Saviour, whose almighty word
The winds and waves submissive heard,
Who walked upon the foaming deep,
And calm amidst the rage did sleep . . .

Polworth, by far the shortest of the six men, walked directly behind Strike, doing his best to bear a fair share of the load.

The mourners, many of whom had had to stand at the back of the packed church, or else listen as best they could from outside, formed a respectful circle around the hearse outside as the shining oak box was loaded onto it. Barely a murmur was heard as the rear doors slammed shut on Joan's earthly remains. As the straight-backed undertaker in his thick black overcoat climbed back into the driver's seat, Strike put an arm around Ted's shoulders. Together, they watched the hearse drive out of sight. Strike could feel Ted trembling.

'Look at all these flowers, Ted,' said Lucy, whose eyes were swollen shut, and the three of them turned back to the church to examine the dense bank of sprays, wreaths and bunches that created a jubilant blaze against the exterior wall of the tiny church.

'Beautiful lilies, Ted, look . . . from Marion and Gary, all the way from Canada . . .'

The congregation was still spilling out of the church to join those outside. All kept a distance from the family while they moved crabwise along the wall of the church. Joan would surely have delighted in the mass of floral tributes and Strike drew unexpected consolation from messages that Lucy was reading aloud to Ted, whose eyes, like hers, were puffy and red.

'Ian and Judy,' she told her uncle. 'Terry and Olive . . .'

'Loads, aren't there?' said Ted, marvelling.

The now-whispering, milling crowd of mourners were doubtless wondering whether it would be heartless to set out immediately for the Ship and Castle, where the wake was to be held, Strike thought. He couldn't blame them; he too was craving a pint and perhaps a chaser too.

'"With deepest sympathy, from Robin, Sam, Andy, Saul and Pat",' Lucy read aloud. She turned to look at Strike, smiling. 'How lovely. Did you tell Robin pink roses were Joan's favourite?'

'Don't think so,' said Strike, who hadn't known himself.

The fact that his agency was represented here among the tributes to Joan meant a great deal to him. Unlike Lucy, he'd be travelling back to London alone, by train. Even though he'd been craving solitude for the past ten days, the prospect of his silent attic room was cheerless, after these long days of dread and loss. The roses, which were for Joan, were also for him: they said, you won't be alone, you have something you've built, and all right, it might not be a family, but there are still people who care about you waiting in London. Strike told himself 'people', because there were five names on the card, but he turned away thinking only of Robin.

Lucy drove Ted and Strike to the Ship and Castle in Ted's car, leaving Greg to follow with the boys. None of them talked in the car; a kind of emotional exhaustion had set in.

Joan had known what she was doing, Strike thought, as he watched the familiar streets slide past. He was grateful they weren't following to the crematorium, that they would reclaim the body in a form that could be clutched to the chest and borne on a boat, in the quiet of a sunny afternoon to come, just the family, to say their last, private farewell.

The Ship and Castle's dining-room windows looked out over St Mawes Bay, which was overcast but tranquil. Strike bought Ted and himself pints, saw his uncle safely into a chair among a knot of solicitous friends, returned to the bar for a double Famous Grouse, which he downed in one, then carried his pint to the window.

The sea was Quaker grey, sparkling occasionally where the silvered fringes of the clouds caught it. Viewed from the hotel window, St Mawes was a study in mouse and slate, but the little rowing boats perched on the mudflats below provided welcome dabs of cheerful colour.

'Y'all right, Diddy?'

155

He turned: Ilsa was with Polworth, and she reached up and hugged Strike. All three of them had been at St Mawes Primary School together. In those days, as Strike remembered it, Ilsa hadn't liked Polworth much. He'd always been unpopular with female classmates. Over Dave's shoulder, Strike could see Polworth's wife, Penny, chatting with a group of female friends.

'Nick really wanted to be here, Corm, but he had to work,' said Ilsa.

'Of course,' said Strike. 'It was really good of you to come, Ilsa.'

'I loved Joan,' she said simply. 'Mum and Dad are going to have Ted over on Friday night. Dad's taking him for a round of golf on Tuesday.'

The Polworths' two daughters, who weren't renowned for their good behaviour, were playing tag among the mourners. The smaller of the two – Strike could never remember which was Roz and which Mel – dashed around them and clung, momentarily, to the back of Strike's legs, as though he were a piece of furniture, looking out at her sister, before sprinting off again, giggling.

'And we're having Ted over Saturday,' said Polworth, as though nothing had happened. Neither Polworth ever corrected their children unless they were directly inconveniencing their parents. 'So don't worry, Diddy, we'll make sure the old fella's all right.'

'Cheers, mate,' said Strike, with difficulty. He hadn't cried in church, hadn't cried all these last horrible days, because there'd been so much to organise, and he found relief in activity. However, the kindness shown by his old friends was seeping through his defences: he wanted to express his gratitude properly, because Polworth hadn't yet permitted him to say all he wanted about the way he'd enabled Strike and Lucy to reach the dying Joan. Before Strike could make a start, however, Penny Polworth joined their group, followed by two women Strike didn't recognise, but who were both beaming at him.

'Hi, Corm,' said Penny, who was dark-eyed and blunt-nosed, and who'd worn her hair pulled back into a practical ponytail since she was five. 'Abigail and Lindy really want to meet you.'

'Hello,' said Strike, unsmiling. He held out his hand and shook both of theirs, sure that they were about to talk about his detective triumphs and already annoyed. Today, of all days, he wanted to be nothing but Joan's nephew. He assumed that Abigail was Lindy's daughter, because if you removed the younger woman's carefully pencilled, geometrically precise eyebrows and fake tan, they had the same round, flat faces.

'She was ever so proud of you,' said Lindy.

'We follow everything about you in the papers,' said plump Abigail, who seemed to be on the verge of giggling.

'What are you working on now? I don't suppose you can say, can you?' said Lindy, devouring him with her eyes.

'D'you ever get involved with the royals, at all?' asked Abigail.

Fuck's sake.

'No,' said Strike. 'Excuse me, need a smoke.'

He knew he'd offended them, but didn't care, though he could imagine Joan's disapproval as he walked away from the group by the window. What would it have hurt him, she'd have said, to entertain her friends by talking about his job? Joan had liked to show him off, the nephew who was the closest thing she'd ever have to a son, and it suddenly came back to him, after these long days of guilt, why he'd avoided coming back to the little town for so long: because he'd found himself slowly stifling under the weight of teacups and doilies and carefully curated conversations, and Joan's suffocating pride, and the neighbours' curiosity, and the sidelong glances at his false leg when nobody thought he could see them looking.

As he stumped down the hall, he pulled out his mobile and pressed Robin's number without conscious thought.

'Hi,' she said, sounding mildly surprised to hear from him.

'Hi,' said Strike, pausing on the doorstep of the hotel to pull a cigarette out of the packet with his teeth. He crossed the road and lit it, looking out over the mudflats at the sea. 'Just wanted to check in, and to thank you.'

'What for?'

'The flowers from the agency. They meant a lot to the family.'

'Oh,' said Robin, 'I'm glad . . . How was the funeral?'

'It was, you know . . . a funeral,' said Strike, watching a seagull bobbing on the tranquil sea. 'Anything new your end?'

'Well, yes, actually,' said Robin, after a fractional hesitation, 'but now's probably not the moment. I'll tell you when you're—'

'Now's a great moment,' said Strike, who was yearning for normality, for something to think about that wasn't connected to Joan, or loss, or St Mawes.

So Robin related the story of her interview with Paul Satchwell, and Strike listened in silence.

'. . . and then he called me a nasty little bitch,' Robin concluded, 'and left.'

'Christ almighty,' said Strike, genuinely amazed, not only that Robin had managed to draw so much information from Satchwell, but at what she'd found out.

'I've just been sitting here looking up records on my phone – I'm back in the Land Rover, going to head home in a bit. Blanche Doris Satchwell, died 1945, aged ten. She's buried in a cemetery outside Leamington Spa. Satchwell called it a mercy killing. Well,' Robin corrected herself, 'he called it a dream, which was his way of telling Margot, while retaining some plausible deniability, wasn't it? It's a traumatic memory to carry around with you from age six, though, isn't it?'

'Certainly is,' said Strike, 'and it gives him a motive of sorts, if he thought Margot might tell the authorities . . .'

'Exactly. And what d'you think about the Janice bit? Why didn't she tell us she knew Satchwell?'

'Very good question,' said Strike. 'Go over it again, what he said about Janice?'

'When I told him Janice was the one who said Margot was spotted in Leamington Spa, he said she was a shit-stirrer and that she was trying to implicate him somehow in Margot's disappearance.'

'Very interesting indeed,' said Strike, frowning at the bobbing seagull, which was staring at the horizon with concentrated intent, its cruel, hooked beak pointing towards the horizon. 'And what was that thing about Roy?'

'He said somebody had told him Roy was a "mummy's boy" who "had a stick up his arse",' said Robin. 'But he wouldn't tell me who'd said it.'

'Doesn't sound much like Janice, but you never know,' said Strike. 'Well, you've done bloody well, Robin.'

'Thanks.'

'We'll have a proper catch-up on Bamborough when I get back,' said Strike. 'Well, we'll need a catch-up on everything.'

'Great. I hope the rest of your stay's OK,' said

160

Robin, with that note of finality that indicated the call was about to end. Strike wanted to keep her on the line, but she evidently thought she oughtn't monopolise his time in his last afternoon with the grieving family, and he could think of no pretext to keep her talking. They bade each other goodbye, and Strike returned his mobile to his pocket.

'Here you go, Diddy.'

Polworth had emerged from the hotel carrying a couple of fresh pints. Strike accepted his with thanks, and both turned to face the bay as they drank.

'You back up to London tomorrow, are you?' said Polworth.

'Yeah,' said Strike. 'But not for long. Joan wanted us to take her ashes out on Ted's boat and scatter them at sea.'

'Nice idea,' said Polworth.

'Listen, mate – thanks for everything.'

'Shut up,' said Polworth. 'You'd do it for me.'

'You're right,' said Strike. 'I would.'

'Easy to say, you cunt,' said Polworth, without skipping a beat, 'seeing as my mum's dead and I don't know where the fuck my dad is.'

Strike laughed.

'Well, I'm a private detective. Want me to find him for you?'

'Fuck, no,' said Polworth. 'Good riddance.'

They drank their pints. There was a brief break in the cloud and the sea was suddenly a carpet

161

of diamonds and the bobbing seagull, a paper-white piece of origami. Strike was wondering idly whether Polworth's passionate devotion to Cornwall was a reaction against his absent Birmingham-born father when Polworth spoke up again:

'Speaking of fathers . . . Joan told me yours was looking for a reunion.'

'She did, did she?'

'Don't be narked,' said Polworth. 'You know what she was like. Wanted me to know you were going through a tough time. Nothing doing, I take it?'

'No,' said Strike. 'Nothing doing.'

The brief silence was broken by the shrieks and yells of Polworth's two daughters sprinting out of the hotel. Ignoring their father and Strike, they wriggled under the chain separating road from damp shingle and ran out to the water's edge, pursued a moment later by Strike's nephew Luke, who was holding a couple of cream buns in his hand and clearly intent on throwing them at the girls.

'OI,' bellowed Strike. 'NO!'

Luke's face fell.

'They started it,' he said, turning to show Strike a white smear down the back of his black suit jacket, newly purchased for his great-aunt's funeral.

'And I'm finishing it,' said Strike, while the Polworth girls giggled, peeking out over the rim of the rowing boat behind which they had taken refuge. 'Put those back where you got them.'

Glaring at his uncle, Luke took a defiant bite out of one of the buns, then turned and headed back into the hotel.

'Little shit,' muttered Strike.

Polworth watched in a detached way as his girls began to kick cold seawater and sand at each other. Only when the younger girl overbalanced and fell backwards into a foot of icy sea, eliciting a scream of shock, did he react.

'Fuck's sake . . . get inside. Come on – don't bloody whine, it's your own fault – come on, inside, now!'

The three Polworths headed back into the Ship and Castle, leaving Strike alone again.

The bobbing seagull, which was doubtless used to a tide of tourists, to the chugging and grinding of the Falmouth ferry and the fishing boats passing in and out of the bay every day, had been unfazed by the shrieks and yells of the Polworth girls. Its sharp eyes were fixed upon something Strike couldn't see, far out at sea. Only when the clouds closed again and the sea darkened to iron, did the bird take off at last. Strike's eyes followed it as it soared on wide, curved wings into the distance, away from the shelter of the bay for open sea, ready to resume the hard but necessary business of survival.

PART V

CHAPTER 49

After long storms and tempests overblown,
The sun at length his joyous face doth clear;
So whenas fortune all her spite hath shown,
Some blissful hours at last must needs appear;
Else would afflicted wights oft-times
* despair . . .*

Edmund Spenser
The Faerie Queene

At 8 a.m. on the morning she should have been meeting her estranged husband for mediation, Robin emerged from Tottenham Court Road station beneath a cerulean sky. The sunshine felt like a minor miracle after the long months of rain and storms and Robin, who had no surveillance to do today, had put on a dress, glad to be out of her everlasting jeans and sweatshirts.

Angry as she felt at Matthew for calling off the session with only twenty-four hours' notice ('My client regrets that an urgent matter of a personal nature has arisen. Given my own unavailability for the latter part of March, I suggest we find a mutually convenient date in April'), suspicious as she was that Matthew was dragging out the process merely to demonstrate his power and add pressure to give up her claim on their joint account, her spirits were raised by the dusty glow of the early morning sunshine illuminating the eternal roadworks at the top of Charing Cross Road. The truth, which had been borne forcibly upon Robin during the five days off that Strike had insisted she take, was that she was happier at work. With no desire to go home to Yorkshire and face the usual barrage of questions from her mother about the divorce and her job, and insufficient funds to get out of London to take a solitary mini-break, she'd spent most of her time taking care of her backlog of chores, or working on the Bamborough case.

She had, if not precisely leads, then ideas, and was now heading into the office early in the hope of catching Strike before the business of the day took over. The pneumatic drills drowned out the shouts of workmen in the road as Robin passed, until she reached the shadowy calm of Denmark Street, where the shops hadn't yet opened.

Almost at the top of the metal staircase, Robin heard voices emanating from behind the glass office door. In spite of the fact that it was not quite eight-fifteen, the light was already on.

'Morning,' said Strike, when she opened the

door. He was standing beside the kettle and looked mildly surprised to see her so early. 'I thought you weren't going to be in until lunchtime?'

'Cancelled,' said Robin.

She wondered whether Strike had forgotten what she'd had on that morning, or whether he was being discreet because Morris was sitting on the fake leather sofa. Though as handsome as ever, Morris's bright blue eyes were bloodshot and his jaw dark with stubble.

'Hello, stranger,' he said. 'Look at you. Proper advert for taking it easy.'

Robin ignored this comment, but as she hung up her jacket, she found herself wishing she hadn't worn the dress. She greatly resented Morris making her feel self-conscious, but it would have been easier just to have worn jeans as usual.

'Morris has caught Mr Smith at it, with the nanny,' said Strike.

'That was quick!' said Robin, trying to be generous, wishing Morris hadn't been the one to do it.

'Red-handed, ten past one this morning,' said Morris, passing Robin a night vision digital camera. 'Hubby was pretending to be out with the boys. Nanny always has a night off on Tuesdays. Silly fuckers said goodbye on the door-step. Rookie error.'

Robin scrolled slowly through the pictures. The voluptuous nanny who so resembled Strike's ex

Lorelei was standing in the doorway of a terraced house, locked in the arms of Mrs Smith's husband. Morris had captured not only the clinch, but the street name and door number.

'Where's this place?' Robin asked, flicking past pictures of the clinch.

'Shoreditch. Nanny's best mate rents it,' said Morris. 'Always useful to have a friend who'll let you use their place for a sneaky shag, eh? I've got her name and details, too, so she's about to get dragged into it all, as well.'

Morris stretched luxuriously on the sofa, arms over his head, and said through a yawn,

'Not often you get the chance to make three women miserable at once, is it?'

'Not to mention the husband,' said Robin, looking at the handsome profile of the commodity broker's husband, silhouetted against a street-lamp as he made his way back to the family car.

'Well, yeah,' said Morris, holding his stretch, 'him too.'

His T-shirt had ridden up, exposing an expanse of toned abdomen, a fact of which Robin thought he was probably well aware.

'Don't fancy a breakfast meeting, do you?' Strike asked Robin. He'd just opened the biscuit tin and found it empty. 'We're overdue a Bamborough catch-up. And I haven't had breakfast.'

'Great,' said Robin, immediately taking down her jacket again.

'You never take *me* out for breakfast,' Morris

told Strike, getting up off the sofa. Ignoring this comment, Strike said,

'Good going on Smith, Morris. I'll let the wife know later. See you tomorrow.'

'Terrible, isn't it,' said Robin, as she and Strike walked back out of the black street door onto the cool of Denmark Street, where sunlight still hadn't penetrated, 'this missing plane?'

Eleven days previously, Malaysia Airlines flight 370 had taken off from Kuala Lumpur and disappeared without trace. More than two hundred people were missing. Competing theories about what had happened to the plane had dominated the news for the last week: hijack, crew sabotage and mechanical failure among them. Robin had been reading about it on the way into work. All those relatives, waiting for news. It must, surely, come soon? An aircraft holding nearly two hundred and fifty people wasn't as easily lost as a single woman, melting away into the Clerkenwell rain.

'Nightmare for the families,' agreed Strike, as they headed out into the sun on Charing Cross Road. He paused, looking up and down the road. 'I don't want to go to Starbucks.'

So they walked to Bar Italia in Frith Street, which lay opposite Ronnie Scott's jazz club, five minutes from the office. The small metal tables and chairs outside on the pavement were all unoccupied. In spite of its sunny promise, the March morning air still carried a chill. Every high stool at the counter inside the café bore a customer gulping down coffee before starting their working day, while reading news off their phones or else examining the shelves of produce reflected in the mirror that faced them.

'You going to be warm enough if we sit out here?' asked Strike doubtfully, looking from Robin's dress to the counter inside. She was starting to really wish she'd worn her jeans.

'I'll be fine,' said Robin. 'And I only want a cappuccino, I already ate.'

While Strike was buying food and drink, Robin sat down on the cold metal chair, drew her jacket more tightly around her and opened her bag, with the intention of taking out Talbot's leather note-book, but after a moment's hesitation, she changed her mind and left it where it was. She didn't want Strike to think that she'd been concentrating on Talbot's astrological musings over the last few days, even though she had, in fact, spent many hours poring over the book.

'Cappuccino,' said Strike, returning to her and setting the coffee in front of her. He'd bought himself a double espresso and a mozzarella and salami roll. Sitting down next to her, he said,

'How come mediation was cancelled?'

Pleased he'd remembered, Robin said:

'Matthew claims something urgent came up.'

'Believe him?'

'No. I think it's more mind games. I wasn't looking forward to it, but at least it would've

172

been over. So,' she said, not wanting to talk about Matthew, 'have you got anything new on Bamborough?'

'Not much,' said Strike, who'd been working flat out on other cases since his return from Cornwall. 'We've got forensics back on that blood smear I found in the book in the Athorns' flat.'

'And?'

'Type O positive.'

'And did you call Roy to find out . . .?'

'Yeah. Margot was A positive.'

'Oh,' said Robin.

'My hopes weren't high,' said Strike, with a shrug. 'It looked like a smear from a paper cut, if anything.

'I've found Mucky Ricci, though. He's in a private nursing home called St Peter's, in Islington. I had to do a fair bit of impersonation on the phone to get confirmation.'

'Great. D'you want me to—?'

'No. I told you, Shanker issued stern warnings about upsetting the old bastard, in case his sons got wind of it.'

'And you feel, of the two of us, I'm the one who upsets people, do you?'

Strike smirked slightly while chewing his roll.

'There's no point rattling Luca Ricci's cage unless we have to. Shanker told me Mucky was gaga, which I hoped meant he was a bit less sharp than he used to be. Might even have worked in our favour. Unfortunately, from what I managed to wheedle out of the nurse, he doesn't talk any more.'

'Not at all?'

'Apparently not. She mentioned it in passing. I tried to find out whether that's because he's depressed, or had a stroke, or whether he's demented, in which case questioning him is obviously pointless, but she didn't say.

'I went to check out the home. I was hoping for some big institutional place where you might slip in and out unnoticed, but it's more like a B&B. They've only got eighteen residents. I'd say the chances of getting in there undetected or passing yourself off as a distant cousin are close to zero.'

Irrationally, now that Ricci seemed unreachable, Robin, who hadn't been more interested in him than in any of the other suspects, immediately felt as though something crucial to the investigation had been lost.

'I'm not saying I won't take a bash at him, eventually,' said Strike. 'But right now, the possible gains don't justify making a bunch of professional gangsters angry at us. On the other hand, if we've got nothing else come August, I might have to see whether I can get a word or two out of Ricci.'

From his tone, Robin guessed that Strike, too, was well aware that more than half their allotted year on the Bamborough case had already elapsed.

'I've also,' he continued, 'made contact with Margot's biographer, C. B. Oakden, who's playing hard to get. He seems to think he's far more important to the investigation than I do.'

'Is he after money?'

'I'd say he's after anything he can get,' said Strike. 'He seemed as interested in interviewing me as letting me interview him.'

'Maybe,' suggested Robin, 'he's thinking of writing a book about you, like the one he did on Margot?'

Strike didn't smile.

'He comes across as equal parts wily and stupid. It doesn't seem to have occurred to him that I must know a lot about his dodgy past, given that I managed to track him down after multiple name changes. But I can see how he conned all those old women. He puts up a good show over the phone of knowing and remembering everyone around Margot. There was a real fluency to it: "Yes, Dr Gupta, lovely man", "Oh yes, Irene, bit of a handful". It's convincing until you remember he was fourteen when Margot disappeared, and probably met them all a couple of times, tops.

'But he wouldn't tell me anything about Brenner, which is who I'm really interested in. "I'll need to think about that," he said. "I'm not sure I want to go into that." I've called him twice so far. Both times he tried to divert the conversation back onto me, I dragged it back to Brenner, and he cut the call short, pretending he had something urgent to take care of. Both times, he promised to phone me back but didn't.'

'You don't think he's recording the calls, do you?' asked Robin. 'Trying to get stuff about you he can sell to the papers?'

'It occurred to me,' Strike admitted, tipping sugar into his coffee.

'Maybe I should talk to him next time?'

'Might not be a bad idea,' said Strike. 'Anyway,' he took a gulp of coffee, 'that's all I've done on Bamborough since I got back. But I'm planning to drop in on Nurse Janice the moment I've got a couple of clear hours. She'll be back from Dubai by now, and I want to know why she never mentioned she knew Paul Satchwell. Don't think I'll warn her I'm coming, this time. There's something to be said for catching people unawares. So, what's new your end?'

'Well,' said Robin, 'Gloria Conti, or Jaubert, as she is these days, hasn't answered Anna's email.'

'Pity,' said Strike, frowning. 'I thought she'd be more likely to talk to us if Anna asked.'

'So did I. I think it's worth giving it another week, then getting Anna to prod her. The worst that can happen is another definite "no". In slightly better news, I'm supposed to be speaking to Amanda White, who's now Amanda Laws, later today.'

'How much is that costing us?'

'Nothing. I appealed to her better nature,' said Robin, 'and she pretended to be persuaded, but I can tell she's quite enamoured of the idea of publicity, and she likes the idea of you, and of

176

getting her name in the papers again as the plucky schoolgirl who stuck to her woman-in-the-window story even when the police didn't believe her. That's in spite of the fact that her whole shtick, when I first contacted her, was that she didn't want to go through all the stress of press interest again unless she got money out of it.'

'She still married?' asked Strike, taking his cigarettes out of his pocket. 'Because she and Oakden sound like a good match. Mightn't be a bad sideline for us, setting grifters up with each other.'

Robin laughed.

'So they can have dodgy children together, thus keeping us in business for ever?'

Strike lit his cigarette, exhaled and then said,

'Not a perfect business plan. There's no guarantee breeding two shits together will produce a third shit. I've known decent people who were raised by complete bastards, and vice versa.'

'You're nature over nurture, are you?' asked Robin.

'Maybe,' said Strike. 'My three nephews were all raised the same, weren't they? And—'

'—one's lovely, one's a prick and one's an arsehole,' said Robin.

Strike's loud burst of laughter seemed to offend the harried-looking suited man who was hurrying past with a mobile pressed to his ear.

'Well remembered,' Strike said, still grinning as he watched the scowling man march out of sight. Lately he, too, had had moods where the sound of other people's cheerfulness grated, but at this moment, with the sunshine, the good coffee and Robin beside him, he suddenly realised he was happier than he'd been in months.

'People are never raised the same way, though,' said Robin, 'not even in the same house, with the same parents. Birth order matters, and all kinds of other things. Speaking of which, Wilma Bayliss's daughter Maya has definitely agreed to talk to us. We're trying to find a convenient date. I think I told you, the youngest sister is recovering from breast cancer, so I don't want to hassle them.

'And there's something else,' said Robin, feeling self-conscious.

Strike, who'd returned to his sandwich, saw, to his surprise, Robin drawing from her bag Talbot's leather-bound notebook, which Strike had assumed was still in the locked filing cabinet in the office.

'I've been looking back through this.'

'Think I missed something, do you?' said Strike, through a mouthful of bread.

'No, I—'

'It's fine,' he said. 'Perfectly possible. Nobody's infallible.'

Sunshine was slowly making its way into Frith Street now, and the pages of the old notebook glowed yellow as Robin opened it.

'Well, it's about Scorpio. You remember Scorpio?'

'The person whose death Margot might have been worried about?'

'Exactly. You thought Scorpio might be Steve Douthwaite's married girlfriend, who killed herself.'

'I'm open to other theories,' said Strike. His sandwich finished, he brushed off his hands and took out his cigarettes. 'The notes ask whether Aquarius confronted Pisces, don't they? Which I assumed meant Margot confronted Douthwaite.'

In spite of his neutral tone, Strike resented remembering these star signs. The laborious and ultimately unrewarding task of working out which suspects and witnesses were represented by each astrological glyph had been far from his favourite bit of research.

'Well,' said Robin, taking out two folded photocopies, which she'd been keeping in the notebook, 'I've been wondering . . . look at these.'

She passed the two documents to Strike, who opened them and saw copies of two birth certificates, one for Olive Satchwell, the other for Blanche Satchwell.

'Olive was Satchwell's mother,' said Robin, as Strike, smoking, examined the documents. 'And Blanche was his sister, who died aged ten – possibly with a pillow over her face.'

'If you're expecting me to deduce their star signs from these birthdays,' said Strike, 'I haven't memorised the whole zodiac.'

'Blanche was born on the twenty-fifth of October, which makes her a Scorpio,' said Robin. 'Olive was born on the twenty-ninth of March. Under the traditional system, she'd be Aries, like Satchwell . . .'

To Strike's surprise, Robin now took out a copy of *Astrology 14* by Steven Schmidt.

'It was quite hard to track this down. It's been out of print for ages.'

'A masterwork like that? You amaze me,' said Strike, watching Robin turn to a page listing the dates of revised signs according to Schmidt. Robin smiled, but refusing to be deflected said,

'Look here. By Schmidt's system, Satchwell's mother was a Pisces.'

'We're mixing up the two systems now, are we?' asked Strike.

'Well, Talbot did,' Robin pointed out. 'He decided Irene and Roy should be given their Schmidt signs, but other people were allowed to keep the traditional ones.'

'But,' said Strike, well aware that he was trying to impose logic on what was essentially illogical, 'Talbot made massive, sweeping assumptions on the basis of people's original signs. Brenner was ruled out as a suspect solely because he was—'

'—Libra, yes,' said Robin.

'Well, what happens to Janice being psychic and the Essex Butcher being a Capricorn if all the dates start sliding around?'

'Wherever there was a discrepancy between the traditional sign and Schmidt sign, he seems to have gone with the sign he thought suited the person best.'

'Which makes a mockery of the whole business. And also,' said Strike, 'calls all my identifications of signs and suspects into question.'

'I know,' said Robin. 'Even Talbot seems to have got very stressed trying to work across both systems, which is when he began concentrating mainly on asteroids and the tarot.'

'OK,' said Strike, blowing smoke away from her, 'go on with what you were saying – if Satchwell's sister was a Scorpio, and her mother was Pisces . . . remind me,' said Strike, 'exactly what that passage about Scorpio says?'

Robin flicked backwards through Talbot's notebook until she found the passage decorated with doodles of the crab, the fish, the scorpion, the fish-tailed goat and the water-bearer's urn.

'"Aquarius worried about how Scorpio died, question mark",' she read aloud. 'And – written in capitals – "SCHMIDT AGREES WITH ADAMS". Then, "Did Aquarius challenge Pisces about Scorpio? Was Cancer there, did Cancer witness? Cancer is kind, instinct is to protect," then, in capitals, "INTERVIEW AGAIN. Scorpio and Aquarius connected, water, water, also Cancer, and Capricorn," in capitals, "HAS A FISH'S TAIL".'

Brow furrowed, Strike said:

'We're assuming Cancer still means Janice, right?'

'Well, Janice and Cynthia are the only two Cancerians connected with the case, and Janice

181

seems to fit this better,' said Robin. 'Let's say Margot decided she was going to act on her suspicion that Satchwell's mother killed his sister. If she phoned Olive from the surgery, Janice might have overheard a phone call, mightn't she? And if Janice knew the Satchwell family, or was involved with them in some way we don't know about, she mightn't have wanted to tell the police what she'd overheard, for fear of incriminating Olive.'

'Why would Margot have waited years to check out her suspicions about the pillow dream?' asked Strike, but before Robin could supply an answer, he did it himself. 'Of course, people do sometimes take years to decide what action to take on something like that. Or to muster up the courage to do it.'

He handed Robin back the two photocopies.

'Well, if that's the story behind the Scorpio business, Satchwell's still a prime suspect.'

'I never got his address in Greece,' said Robin guiltily.

'We'll get at him through his surviving sister if we have to.'

Strike took a swig of coffee then, slightly against his better judgement, asked,

'What did you say about asteroids?'

Robin flicked further on through the notebook, to show Strike the page she'd pored over in Leamington Spa, which she thought of as the 'horns page'.

'As the case went on, he seemed to give up on

normal astrology. I think Schmidt had confused him so much he couldn't work it any more, so he starts inventing his own system. He's calculated the asteroids' positions for the evening Margot disappeared. See here—'

Robin was pointing to the symbol ♀ . . .

'That symbol stands for the asteroid Pallas Athena – remember that ugly clock at the Phippses' house? – and he's using it to mean Margot. The asteroid Pallas Athena was in the tenth house of the zodiac on the night Margot disappeared, and the tenth house is ruled by Capricorn. It's also supposed to govern businesses, upper classes and upper floors.'

'You think Margot's still in someone's attic?'

Robin smiled, but refused to be deflected.

'And see here . . .' She angled the notebook towards him, 'assuming the other asteroids also refer to living people, we've got Ceres, Juno and Vesta.

'I think he's using Vesta, "keeper of the hearth", to represent Cynthia. Vesta was in the seventh house, which is the house of marriage. Talbot's written "FITS" – so I think he's saying Cynthia was in Margot's marital home, Broom House.

'I think "nurturing, protective Ceres" sounds like Janice again. She's in the twelfth house, and so's Juno, who's associated with "wives and infidelity", which might take us back to Joanna Hammond, Douthwaite's married girlfriend . . .'

'What's the twelfth house represent?'

'Enemies, secrets, sorrows and undoing.'

Strike looked at her, eyebrows raised. He'd indulged Robin because it was sunny, and he was enjoying her company, but his tolerance for astrology was now wearing very thin.

'It's also Pisces' house,' said Robin, 'which is Douthwaite's sign, so maybe—'

'You think Janice and Joanna Hammond were both in Douthwaite's flat when Margot was abducted, do you?'

'No, but—'

'Because that'd be tricky, given that Joanna Hammond died weeks before Margot disappeared. Or are you suggesting her ghost was haunting Douthwaite?'

'All right, I know it might mean nothing,' said Robin, half-laughing as she ploughed on, 'but Talbot's written something else here: "Ceres denies contact with Juno. Could Cetus be right?"'

She was pointing at the whale symbol representing Irene.

'I find it hard to imagine Irene Hickson being right about very much,' said Strike. He pulled the leather notebook towards him to look more closely at Talbot's small, obsessive writing, then pushed the notes away again with a slightly impatient shrug. 'Look, it's easy to get sucked into this stuff. When I was going through the notes I started making connections while I was trying to follow his train of thought, but he was ill, wasn't he? Nothing leads anywhere concrete.'

'I was just intrigued by that "Could Cetus be right?" because Talbot mistrusted Irene from the start, didn't he? Then he starts wondering whether she could have been right about . . . about something connected to enemies, secrets and undoing . . .'

'If we ever find out what happened to Margot Bamborough,' said Strike, 'I'll bet you a hundred quid you'll be able to make equally strong cases for Talbot's occult stuff being bang on the money, and completely off beam. You can always stretch this symbolic stuff to fit the facts. One of my mother's friends used to guess everyone's star signs and she was right *every single time*.'

'She was?'

'Oh yeah,' said Strike. 'Because even when she was wrong, she was right. Turned out they had a load of planets in that sign or, I dunno, the midwife who delivered them was that sign. Or their dog.'

'All right,' said Robin, equably. She'd expected Strike's scepticism, after all, and now put both the leather-bound notebook and *Astrology 14* back into her bag. 'I know it might mean nothing at all, I'm only—'

'If you want to go and see Irene Hickson again, be my guest. Tell her Talbot thought she might've had profound insight into something connected to asteroids and – I dunno – cheese—'

'The twelfth house doesn't govern *cheese*,' said Robin, trying to look severe.

185

'What number's the house of dairy?'

'Oh, bugger off,' she said, laughing against her will.

Robin's mobile vibrated in her pocket, and she pulled it out. A text had just arrived.

Hi Robin, if you want I can talk now? I've just agreed to work a later shift, so I'm not needed at work for a few hours. Otherwise it'll have to be after 8 tonight – Amanda

'Amanda White,' she told Strike. 'She wants to talk now.'

'Works for me,' said Strike, relieved to be back on firm investigative ground. Liar or not, Amanda White would at least be talking about an actual woman at a real window.

Robin pressed Amanda's number, switched the mobile to speakerphone and laid it on the table between her and Strike.

'Hi,' said a confident female voice, with a hint of North London. 'Is that Robin?'

'Yes,' said Robin, 'and I'm with Cormoran.'

'Morning,' said Strike.

'Oh, it's *you*, is it?' said Amanda, sounding delighted. 'I *am* honoured. I've been dealing with your assistant.'

'She's actually my partner,' said Strike.

'Really? Business, or the other?' said Amanda.

'Business,' said Strike, not looking at Robin. 'I

understand Robin's been talking to you about what you saw on the night Margot Bamborough disappeared?'

'That's right,' said Amanda.

'Would you mind if we take a recording of this interview?'

'No, I s'pose not,' said Amanda. 'I mean, I want to do the right thing, although I won't pretend it hasn't been a bit of a dilemma, because it was really stressful, last time. Journalists, two police interviews, and I was only fourteen. But I've always been a stubborn girl, haha, and I stuck to my guns . . .'

So Amanda told the story with which Strike and Robin were already familiar: of the rain, and the angry schoolfriend, and the upper window, and the retrospective recognition of Margot, when Amanda saw her picture in the paper. Strike asked a couple of questions, but he could tell that nothing would ever change Amanda's story. Whether she truly believed she'd seen Margot Bamborough at the window that night or not, she was evidently determined never to relinquish her association with the forty-year-old mystery.

'. . . and I suppose I've been haunted ever since by the idea that I didn't do anything, but I was fourteen and it only hit me later, I could've been the one to save her,' she ended the story.

'Well,' said Robin, as Strike nodded at her, signalling he had everything he wanted, 'thank you so much for talking to us, Amanda. I really—'

'There's something else, before you go,' said Amanda. 'Wait until you hear this. It's just an amazing coincidence, and I don't think even the police know about this, because they're both dead.'

'Who're dead?' asked Robin, while Strike lit himself another cigarette.

'*Well*,' said Amanda, 'how's this for strange? My last job, this young girl at the office's great-aunt—'

Strike rolled his eyes.

'—was in a hospice with, guess who?'

'I don't know,' said Robin politely.

'Violet Cooper,' said Amanda. 'You probably don't—'

'Dennis Creed's landlady,' said Robin.

'*Exactly!*' said Amanda, sounding pleased that Robin appreciated the significance of her story. 'So, anyway, isn't that just *weird*, that I saw Margot at that window, and then, all those years later, I work with someone whose relative met Vi Cooper? Only she was calling herself something different by then, because people hated her.'

'That *is* a coincidence,' said Robin, making sure not to look at Strike. 'Well, thank—'

'That's not all!' said Amanda, laughing. 'No, there's more to it than that! So, this girl's great-aunt said Vi told her she wrote to Creed, once, asking if he'd killed Margot Bamborough.'

Amanda paused, clearly wanting a response, so

188

Robin, who'd already read about this in *The Demon of Paradise Park*, said,

'Wow.'

'*I know*,' said Amanda. 'And apparently, Vi said – this is on her deathbed, so you know, she was telling the truth, because you would, wouldn't you? – Vi said the letter she got back, said he *had* killed her.'

'Really?' said Robin. 'I thought the letter—'

'No, but this is direct from Violet,' Amanda said, while Strike rolled his eyes again, 'and she said, he definitely did, he as good as told her so. He said it in a way only she'd understand, but she knew *exactly* what he meant.

'*Crazy*, though, isn't it? I see Margot at the window, and then, years later—'

'Amazing,' said Robin. 'Well, thanks very much for your time, Amanda, this has been really . . . er . . .'

It took Robin another couple of minutes, and much more insincere gratitude, to get Amanda off the line.

'What d'you think?' Robin asked Strike, when at last she'd succeeded in getting rid of Amanda.

He pointed a finger at the sky.

'What?' said Robin, looking up into the blue haze.

'If you look carefully,' said Strike, 'you might just see an asteroid passing through the house of bollocks.'

189

CHAPTER 50

Aye me (said she) where am I, or with
*   whom?*
Emong the liuing, or emong the dead?

Edmund Spenser
The Faerie Queene

Agency work unconnected with the
Bamborough case consumed Strike for
the next few days. His first attempt to
surprise Nurse Janice Beattie at home was fruitless.
He left Nightingale Grove, a nondescript street that
lay hard against the Southeastern railway line,
without receiving any answer to his knock.

His second attempt, on the following Wednesday,
was made on a breezy afternoon that kept threatening showers. Strike approached Janice's house
from Hither Green station, along a pavement
bordered to the right with railings and hedge,
separating the road from the rail tracks. He was
thinking about Robin as he trudged along, smoking,
because she'd just turned down the opportunity

of joining him to interview Janice, saying that there was 'something else' she needed to do, but not specifying what that something was. Strike thought he'd detected a trace of caginess, almost amounting to defensiveness, in Robin's response to the suggestion of a joint interview, where usually there'd have been only disappointment.

Since she'd left Matthew, Strike had become used to more ease and openness between him and Robin, so this refusal, coupled with her tone and lack of an explanation, made him curious. While there were naturally matters he might not have expected her to tell him about – trips to the gynaecologist sprang to mind – he would have expected her to say 'I've got a doctor's appointment', at least.

The sky darkened as Strike approached Janice's house, which was considerably smaller than Irene Hickson's. It stood in a terrace. Net curtains hung at all the windows, and the front door was dark red. Strike didn't immediately register the fact that a light was shining from behind the net curtains at the sitting-room window until he was halfway across the road. When he realised that his quarry must be in, however, he successfully pushed all thoughts about his business partner out of his mind, crossed the road at a quicker pace and knocked firmly on the front door. As he stood waiting, he heard the muffled sounds of a TV on high volume through the glass of the downstairs window. He was just considering knocking again, in case Janice hadn't heard the first time, when the door opened.

In contrast to the last time they'd met, the nurse, who was wearing steel-rimmed spectacles, looked shocked and none too pleased to see Strike. From behind her, two female American voices rang out from the out-of-sight TV: '*So you love the bling?*' '*I love the bling!*'

'Er – 'ave I missed a message, or—?'

'Sorry for the lack of warning,' said Strike insincerely, 'but as I was in the area, I wondered whether you could give me a couple of minutes?'

Janice glanced back over her shoulder. A camp male voice was now saying, '*The dress that Kelly is in love with is a one-of-a-kind runway sample . . .*'

Clearly disgruntled, Janice turned back to Strike.

'Well . . . all right,' she said, 'but the place is in a mess – and can you please wipe your feet properly, because the last bloke who turned up 'ere unannounced brought dog shit in wiv 'im. You can close the door be'ind you.'

Strike stepped over the threshold, while Janice strode out of sight into the sitting room. Strike expected her to turn off the TV but she didn't. While Strike wiped his feet on the coconut mat inside the door, a male voice said: '*This one-of-a-kind runway gown might be impossible to find, so Randy's on the search . . .*' After hesitating for a moment on the doormat, Strike decided that

Janice expected him to follow her, and entered the small sitting room.

Having spent a significant part of his youth in squats with his mother, Strike had a very different idea of 'mess' to Janice's. Although cluttered, with something on almost every surface, the only signs of actual disorder in the room were a copy of the *Daily Mirror* lying in one armchair, some crumpled packaging lying beside an open packet of dates on the low coffee table and a hairdryer, which was lying incongruously on the floor beside the sofa, and which Janice was currently unplugging.

'. . . *Antonella's pulling the closest gown to Kelly's pick, a blinged-out $15,000 dress . . .*'

'The mirror down 'ere's better for drying my 'air,' Janice explained, straightening up, pink in the face, hairdryer in her hand and looking slightly cross, as though Strike was forcing her to justify herself. 'I would've appreciated some warning, you know,' she added, looking as stern as such a naturally smiley-looking woman could. 'You've caught me on the 'op.'

Strike was unexpectedly and poignantly reminded of Joan, who'd always been flustered if guests dropped in while the Hoover or the ironing board were still out.

'Sorry. As I say, I happened to be in the area . . .'

'*Even as Kelly steps into dress number one, she still can't get her dream dress off her mind,*' said the narrator loudly, and both Strike and Janice glanced towards the TV, where a young woman was wriggling into a clinging, semi-transparent white dress covered in silver rhinestones.

'*Say Yes to the Dress*,' said Janice, who was wearing the same navy jumper and slacks as the last time Strike had seen her. 'My guilty pleasure . . . D'you want a cup of tea?'

'Only if it's no trouble,' said Strike.

'Well, it's always *some* trouble, innit?' Janice said, with her first glimmer of a smile. 'But I was going to make myself some at the first advert break, so you might as well 'ave some.'

'In that case, thanks very much,' said Strike.

'*If I don't find this dress*,' said the camp male wedding consultant on-screen, rifling urgently through racks of white dresses, his eyebrows so sharply plucked they looked drawn on, '*it's not gonna be—*'

The screen went blank. Janice had turned it off with her remote control.

'Wanna date?' she asked Strike, holding out the box.

'No thanks,' said Strike.

'Got boxes of 'em in Dubai,' she said. 'I was gonna give 'em as presents, but I just can't stop eating 'em. 'Ave a seat. I won't be two ticks.'

Strike thought he caught another downward glance towards his lower legs as she marched out of the room, hairdryer in one hand, dates in the other, leaving Strike to take an armchair, which creaked beneath his weight.

Strike found the small sitting room oppressive. Predominantly red, the carpet was decorated in a scarlet, swirling pattern, on top of which lay a cheap crimson Turkish rug. Dried flower pictures hung on the red walls, between old photographs, some black and white, and the coloured ones faded, displayed in wooden frames. A china cabinet was full of cheap spun-glass ornaments. The largest, a Cinderella carriage pulled by six glass horses, stood in pride of place on the mantelpiece over the electric fire. Evidently, beneath Janice's no-nonsense clothing, there beat a romantic heart.

She returned a few minutes later, holding a wicker-handled tray bearing two mugs of tea with the milk already added, and a plate of chocolate Hobnobs. The act of making tea seemed to have put her into slightly better humour with her guest.

'That's my Larry,' she said, catching Strike looking towards a double frame on the small side table beside him. On one side was a sleepy-eyed, overweight man with a smoker's teeth. On the other was a blonde woman, heavy but pretty.

'Ah. And is this—?'

'My little sister, Clare. She died '97. Pancreatic cancer. They got it late.'

'Oh, I'm sorry to hear that,' said Strike.

'Yeah,' said Janice, with a deep sigh. 'Lost 'em both around the same time. To tell you the truth,' she said, as she sat down on the sofa and her knees gave audible clicks, 'I walked back in 'ere after Dubai and I fort, I really need to get some new pictures up. It was depressing, coming back in 'ere, the number of dead people . . .

'I got some gorgeous ones of Kev and the grand-kids on 'oliday, but I 'aven't got 'em printed out yet. The lad next door's going to do it for me. All my old ones of Kev and the kids are two years out of date. I gave the boy the memory . . . *board*, is it?'

'Card?' suggested Strike.

'That's the one. The kids next door just laugh at me. Mind you, Irene's worse'n I am. She can 'ardly change a battery. So,' she said, 'why d'you want to see me again?'

Strike, who had no intention of risking an immediate rebuff, was planning to ask his questions about Satchwell last. Drawing out his notebook and opening it, he said,

'A couple of things that have come up since I last saw you. I asked Dr Gupta about this first one, but he couldn't help, so I hoped you might be able to. Would you happen to know anything about a man called Niccolo Ricci, sometimes nicknamed "Mucky"?'

'Old gangster, weren't 'e?' said Janice. 'I knew 'e lived local, in Clerkenwell, but I never met 'im. Why d'you want – oh, 'as Irene been telling you about the foundations thing?'

'The what?' asked Strike.

'Oh, it's nuffing, really. There was this rumour,

196

back when they were doing a load of redevelopment round Clerkenwell in the early seventies, that some builders 'ad found a body buried in concrete under one of the demolished buildings. The story was that Little Italy gangsters 'ad hidden it there, back in the forties. But Eddie – this is Irene's Eddie, the builder she ended up marrying – that's 'ow they met, local pub, when 'is firm was doing a lot of the redevelopment – Eddie told us it was all cobblers. *I* 'adn't ever believed it. I fink Irene 'ad, a bit,' Janice added, dunking a biscuit in her tea.

'How does this tie in with Margot?' Strike asked.

'Well, after Margot disappeared, there was a theory 'er body 'ad been put into one o' the open foundations and covered in concrete. They was still doing a bit of building round there in '74, see.'

'Were people suggesting Ricci had killed her?' asked Strike.

'Gawd, no!' said Janice, with a shocked little laugh. 'What would Mucky Ricci 'ave to do with Margot? It was only because of that old rumour. It put the idea in people's minds, you know, burying bodies in concrete. People can be bloody silly. My Larry said to me – 'e was a builder, you know – it's not like workmen wouldn't've noticed a load of fresh concrete when they turned up for work.'

'Were you aware that Ricci attended the St John's practice Christmas party?'

''E what?' said Janice, with her mouth full.

'He and another couple of men arrived towards the end of the party, possibly to escort Gloria home.'

'They – *what*?' Janice said, looking unaffectedly astonished. 'Mucky Ricci and *Gloria*? Come off it. Is this because – no, look, you don't wanna pay no attention to Irene, not about Gloria. Irene . . . she gets carried away. She never much liked Gloria. And she gets the wrong end of the stick sometimes. *I* never 'eard Gloria's family 'ad any criminal connections. Irene watched way too many *Godfather* movies,' said Janice. 'We saw the first one togevver, at the cinema, and I went back and saw it again twice more on me own. James Caan, you know,' she sighed. 'My dream man.'

'Ricci was definitely at the practice party,' said Strike. 'From what I can tell, he turned up right at the end.'

'Well then, I'd already left. I needed to get 'ome to Kev. Is 'e still alive, Ricci?'

'Yes,' said Strike.

'Must be really getting on, is 'e?'

'He is,' said Strike.

'That's odd, though. What on earth would Ricci be doing at St John's?'

'I'm hoping to find out,' said Strike, flipping over a page of his notebook. 'The next thing I wanted to ask you was about Joseph Brenner. You remember the family you thought might be called Applethorpe? Well, I found—'

'You never tracked 'em down!' said Janice, looking impressed. 'What *was* their name?'

'Athorn.'

'*Athorn!*' said Janice, with an air of relief. 'I *knew* it wasn't Applethorpe. That bugged me for days, after . . . 'Ow are they? It's Fragile X they've got, isn't it? They're not in an 'ome, or—?'

'Still living together in the old flat,' said Strike, 'and getting on reasonably well, I think.'

'I 'ope they're being well supported, are they?'

'There's a social worker involved, who seems very much on their side, which brings me to what I was going to ask you.

'The social worker says that since Gwilherm's death, Deborah's disclosed . . .' Strike hesitated, '. . . well, the way the social worker put it, was that Gwilherm was, er, pimping Deborah out.'

''E was what?' said Janice, the smile sliding off her face.

'It's an unpleasant idea, I know,' said Strike unemotionally. 'When I was talking to her, Deborah told me about Dr Brenner visiting her at home. She said he'd – er – asked her to take off her pants—'

'No!' said Janice, in what seemed instinctive revulsion. 'No, I'm sure – no, that's not right. That's not 'ow it would've 'appened, if she'd needed an intimate examination. It would have 'appened at the surgery.'

'You said she was agoraphobic?'

'Well – yeah, but . . .'

'Samhain, the son, said something about Dr Brenner being a "dirty old man".'

''E . . . but . . . no, it . . . it *must've* been an examination . . . maybe after the baby was born? But that should've been me, the nurse . . . that's upset me, now,' said Janice, looking distressed. 'You think you've 'eard everything, but . . . no, that's really upset me. I mean, I was in the 'ouse that one time to see the kid and she never said a word to me . . . but of course, 'e was there, the father, telling me all about 'is bloody magic powers. She was probably too scared to . . . no, that's really upset me, that 'as.'

'I'm sorry,' said Strike, 'but I have to ask: did you ever hear that Brenner used prostitutes? Ever hear any rumours about him, locally?'

'Not a word,' said Janice. 'I'd've told someone, if I'd 'eard that. It wouldn't be ethical, not in our catchment area. All the women there were registered to our practice. She'd've been a patient.'

'According to Talbot's notes,' said Strike, 'somebody claimed they saw Brenner in Michael Cliffe House on the evening Margot disappeared. The story Brenner gave the police was that he went straight home.'

'Michael Cliffe 'Ouse . . . that's the tower block on Skinner Street, innit?' said Janice. 'We 'ad patients in there, but otherwise . . .' Janice appeared sickened. 'You've upset me,' she said again. ''Im and that poor Athorn woman . . . and there's me defending 'im to all and sundry, because of 'is experiences in the war. Not two weeks back, I 'ad Dorothy's son sitting exactly where you are now—'

'Carl Oakden was here?' said Strike sharply.

'Yeah,' said Janice, 'and 'e didn't wipe 'is feet, neither. Dog shit all up my 'all carpet.'

'What did he want?' asked Strike.

'Well, 'e *pretended* it was a nice catch-up,' said Janice. 'You'd think I might not recognise 'im after all this time, but actually, 'e don't look that much diff'rent, not really. Anyway, 'e sat in that chair where you are, spouting all sorts of rubbish about old times and 'is mum remembering me fondly – ha! Dorothy Oakden, remember me fondly? Dorothy thought Irene and me were a pair of hussies, skirts above our knees, going out to the pub togevver . . .

''E mentioned *you*,' said Janice, with a beady look. 'Wanted to know if I'd met you, yet. 'E wrote a book about Margot, you know, but it never made it into the shops, which 'e's angry about. 'E told me all about it when 'e was 'ere. 'E's finking of writing another one and it's *you* what's got 'im interested in it. The famous detective solving the case – or the famous detective *not* solving the case. Either one'll do for Carl.'

'What was he saying about Brenner?' asked Strike. There would be time enough later to consider the implications of an amateur biographer tramping all over the case.

'Said Dr Brenner was a sadistic old man, and there I was, sort of sticking up for Dr Brenner . . . but now you're telling me this about Deborah Athorn . . .'

'Oakden said Brenner was sadistic, did he? That's a strong word.'

'I fort so, too. Carl said 'e'd never liked 'im, said Dr Brenner used to go round Dorothy's 'ouse a lot, which I never realised, for Sunday lunch and that. I always fort they were just workmates. You know, Dr Brenner probably told Carl off, that's all. 'E was an 'oly terror when 'e was a kid, Carl, and 'e comes across as the kind of man 'oo 'olds a grudge.'

'If Oakden comes round here again,' said Strike, 'I'd advise you not to let him in. He's done time, you know. For conning . . .' He just stopped himself saying 'old' '. . . single women out of their money.'

'*Oh*,' said Janice, taken aback. 'Blimey. I'd better warn Irene. 'E said 'e was going to try 'er next.'

'And he seemed primarily interested in Brenner, did he, when he came round here?'

'Well, no,' said Janice. ''E seemed mostly interested in *you*, but yeah, we talked about Brenner more'n anyone else at the practice.'

'Mrs Beattie, you wouldn't happen to still have that newspaper obituary of Brenner you mentioned? I think you said you kept it?'

'Oh,' said Janice, glancing towards the drawer at

the base of her china cabinet, 'yeah . . . Carl wanted to see that, too, when 'e 'eard I 'ad it . . .'

She pushed herself out of the sofa and crossed to the china cabinet. Gripping the mantelpiece to steady herself, she knelt down, opened the drawer and began rummaging.

'They're all in a bit of a state, my clippings. Irene finks I'm bonkers, me and my newspapers,' she added, wrist-deep in the contents of the drawer. 'She's never been much for the news or politics or any of that, but I've always saved interesting bits and pieces, you know: medical fings, and I won't lie, I do like a story on the royals and . . .'

She began tugging on what looked like the corner of a cardboard folder.

'. . . and Irene can fink it's strange all she likes, but I don't see what's wrong – with saving – the story of . . .'

The folder came free.

'. . . a life,' said Janice, walking on her knees to the coffee table. 'Why's that morbid? No worse'n keeping a photo.'

She flipped open the folder and began looking through the clippings, some of them yellow with age.

'See? I saved that for 'er, for Irene,' said Janice, holding up an article about holy basil. 'Supposed to 'elp with digestive problems, I fort Eddie could plant some in the garden for 'er. She takes too many pills for 'er bowels, they do as much 'arm as good, but Irene's one of those 'oo, if it doesn't come in a tablet, she don't wanna know . . .

'Princess Diana,' said Janice with a sigh, flashing a commemorative front page at Strike. 'I was a fan . . .'

'May I?' asked Strike, reaching for a couple of pieces of newsprint.

''Elp yourself,' said Janice, looking over her spectacles at the pieces of paper in Strike's hand. 'That article on diabetes is very interesting. Care's changed so much since I retired. My godson's Type One. I like to keep up with it all . . . and that'll be the fing about the kid 'oo died of peritonitis, in your other 'and, is it?'

'Yes,' said Strike, looking at the clipping, which was brown with age.

'Yeah,' said Janice darkly, still turning over bits of newspaper, ''e's the reason I'm a nurse. That's what put the idea in me 'ead. 'E lived two doors down from me when I was a kid. I cut that out an' kept it, only photo I was ever gonna 'ave . . . bawled my bloody eyes out. The doctor,' said Janice, with a hint of steel, 'was called out and 'e never bloody turned up. 'E would've come out for a middle-class kid, we all knew that, but little Johnny Marks from Bethnal Green, 'oo cared . . . and the doctor was criticised, but never struck off . . . If there's one thing I *ate*, it's treating people diff'rent because of where they were born.'

With no apparent sense of irony, she shifted

more pictures of the royals out of the way, looking puzzled.

'Where's Dr Brenner's thing?' she muttered.

Still clutching several clippings, she walked on her knees back towards the open drawer and rummaged in there again.

'No, it *really* isn't 'ere,' said Janice, returning to the coffee table. 'That's very odd . . .'

'You don't think Oakden took it, do you?' Strike suggested.

Janice looked up.

'That cheeky sod,' she said slowly. ''E could of bloody asked.'

She swept her clippings back into their folder, returned it to her drawer, used the mantelpiece to pull herself back up, knees clicking loudly again, then sat back down on the sofa with a sigh of relief and said,

'You know, 'e was always light-fingered, that boy.'

'What makes you say that?'

'Money went missing, back at the practice.'

'Really?' said Strike.

'Yeah. It all come to 'an 'ead after Margot disappeared. Little bits of money kept going missing and they fort it was Wilma, the cleaner – ev'ryone except me. *I* always fort it was Carl. 'E used to drop in after school, and in the school 'olidays. I dropped a word in Dr Gupta's ear, but I dunno, probably 'e didn't want to upset Dorothy, and it was easier to push Wilma out. True, there were ovver issues wiv Wilma . . . she drank,' said Janice, 'and 'er cleaning wasn't the best. She couldn't prove she never nicked it, and after there was a staff meeting about it, she resigned. She could see the way it was going.'

'And did the thefts stop?'

'Yeah,' said Janice, 'but so what? Carl might've thought 'e'd better give it rest, after nearly being found out.'

Strike, who tended to agree, said,

'Just a couple more questions. The first's about a woman called Joanna Hammond.'

'I should know 'oo that is, should I?'

'She was Steve Douthwaite's—'

'—girlfriend, 'oo killed 'erself,' said Janice. 'Oh yeah.'

'Can you remember whether she was registered with the St John's practice?'

'No, she weren't. I fink they lived over in Hoxton.'

'So Margot wouldn't have been involved with the coroner, or had any other professional connection with her death?'

'No, she'll 'ave been same as me: never knew the woman existed till she was already dead and Steve come looking for 'elp. I bet I know why you're asking, though,' said Janice. 'Talbot was dead set on Steve being the Essex Butcher, wasn't 'e? On and on about Steve, in all those interviews I 'ad with 'im. But honestly, Steve Douthwaite was a gentle soul. I grew up wiv a couple of proper violent men. Me father was one. I know the type, and Steve definitely weren't it.'

Remembering how endearing some women had found the apparent vulnerability of Dennis Creed, Strike merely nodded.

'Talbot asked wevver I'd ever visited that Joanna, as a nurse. I told 'im she wasn't a St John's patient, but that didn't put 'im off. Did I think there was anything fishy about 'er death, even so? I kept saying, "I never met the woman. 'Ow do I know?" I was getting worn down wiv it all by then, honestly, being treated like I was Gypsy bloody Rose Lee. I told Talbot, go see what the coroner said!'

'And you don't know whether there *was* a death Margot was worried about?' Strike asked. 'A death that was maybe categorised as natural, or accidental, but where she thought there might have been foul play?'

'What makes you ask that?' said Janice.

'Just trying to clear up something Talbot left in his notes. He seemed to think Margot might've had suspicions about the way somebody died. You were mentioned in connection with the death.'

Janice's round blue eyes widened behind her glasses.

'Mentioned as having witnessed something, or perhaps been present,' Strike elaborated. 'There was no hint of accusation.'

'I should bloody well 'ope not!' said Janice. 'No,

I never *witnessed* nothing. I'd've said if I 'ad, wouldn't I?'

There was a short pause, which Strike judged it prudent not to break, and sure enough, Janice piped up again.

'Look, I can't speak for Margot forty years on. She's gone, i'n't she? It isn't fair on either of us. I don't wanna be casting suspicion round, all these years later.'

'I'm just trying to eliminate possible lines of inquiry,' said Strike.

There was a longer pause. Janice's eyes drifted over the tea tray and on to the picture of her late partner, with his stained teeth and his kind, sleepy eyes. Finally, she sighed and said,

'All right, but I want you to write down that this was *Margot's* idea, not mine, all right? I'm not accusing no one.'

'Fair enough,' said Strike, pen poised over his notebook.

'All right then, well – it was very sensitive, because of us working wiv 'er – Dorothy, I mean.

'Dorothy and Carl lived wiv Dorothy's mother. 'Er name was Maud, though I wouldn't remember that if Carl 'adn't been 'ere the ovver day. We were talking and I mentioned 'is gran, and 'e called 'er "bloody Maud", not "Grandma" or nothing.

'Anyway, Maud 'ad an infection on 'er leg, a sore what was taking its time 'ealing. It needed dressing and looking after, so I was visiting the

208

'ouse a lot. Ev'ry time I was in there, she told me *she* owned the 'ouse, not Dorothy. She was letting 'er daughter and grandson live wiv 'er. She liked saying it, you know. Feeling the power.

'I wouldn't say she'd be much fun to live with. Sour old lady. Nothing ever right for 'er. She moaned a lot about 'er grandson being spoiled – but like I said, 'e was an 'oly terror when 'e was younger, so I can't blame 'er there.

'Anyway,' said Janice, 'before the sore on 'er leg was 'ealed, she died, after falling downstairs. Now, 'er walking wasn't great, because she'd been laid up for a bit with this sore leg, and she needed a stick. People *do* fall downstairs, and if you're elderly, obviously that can 'ave serious consequences, but . . .

'Well, a week afterwards, Margot asked me into 'er consulting room for a word, and . . . well, yeah, I got the impression Margot was maybe a bit uneasy about it. She never said anyfing outright, just asked me what I fort. I knew what she was saying . . . but what could we do? We weren't there when she fell and the family said they was downstairs and just 'eard 'er take the tumble, and there she was at the bottom of the stairs, knocked out cold, and she died two nights later in 'ospital.

'Dorothy never showed no emotion about it, but Dorothy never *did* show much emotion about anything. What could we do?' Janice repeated, her palms turned upwards. 'Obviously I could see the way Margot's mind was working, because she knew Maud owned the 'ouse, and now Dorothy and Carl were sitting pretty, and . . . well, it's the kind of thing doctors consider, of course they do. It'll come back on them, if they've missed anything. But in the end, Margot never done nothing about it and as far as I know there was never any bother.

'There,' Janice concluded, with a slight air of relief at having got this off her chest. 'Now you know.'

'Thank you,' said Strike, making a note. 'That's very helpful. Tell me: did you ever mention this to Talbot?'

'No,' said Janice, 'but someone else mighta done. Ev'ryone knew Maud 'ad died, and 'ow she died, because Dorothy took a day off for the funeral. I'll be honest, by the end of all my interviews wiv Talbot, I just wanted to get out of there. Mostly 'e wanted me to talk about me dreams. It was creepy, honestly. Weird, the 'ole thing.'

'I'm sure it was,' said Strike. 'Well, there's just one more thing I wanted to ask, and then I'm done. My partner managed to track down Paul Satchwell.'

'Oh,' said Janice, with no sign of embarrassment or discomfort. 'Right. That was Margot's old boyfriend, wasn't it?'

'Yes. Well, we were surprised to find out you know each other.'

Janice looked at him blankly.

'What?'

'That you know each other,' Strike repeated.

'Me and Paul Satchwell?' said Janice with a little laugh. 'I've never even met the man!'

'Really?' said Strike, watching her closely. 'When he heard you'd told us about the sighting of Margot in Leamington Spa, he got quite angry. He said words to the effect,' Strike read off his notebook, 'that you were trying to cause trouble for him.'

There was a long silence. A frown line appeared between Janice's round blue eyes. At last she said,

'Did 'e mention me by name?'

'No,' said Strike. 'As a matter of fact, he seemed to have forgotten it. He just remembered you as "the nurse". He also told Robin that you and Margot didn't like each other.'

''E said Margot didn't like *me*?' said Janice, with the emphasis on the last word.

'I'm afraid so,' said Strike, watching her.

'But . . . no, sorry, that's not right,' said Janice. 'We used to get on great! Ovver than that one time wiv Kev and 'is tummy . . . all right, I *did* get shirty wiv 'er then, but I knew she *meant* it kindly. She fort she was doing me a favour, examining 'im . . . I took offence because . . . well, you do get a bit defensive, as a mother, if you fink another woman's judging you for not taking care of your kids properly. I was on me own with Kev and . . . you just feel it more, when you're on your own.'

211

'So why,' Strike asked, 'would Satchwell say he knew you, and that you wanted to get him into trouble?'

The silence that followed was broken by the sound of a train passing beyond the hedge: a great rushing rumble built and subsided, and the quiet of the sitting room closed like a bubble in its wake, holding the detective and the nurse in suspension as they looked at each other.

'I fink you already know,' said Janice at last.

'Know what?'

'Don't give me that. All them fings you've solved – you're not a stupid man. I fink you already know, and all this is to try and scare me into telling you.'

'I'm certainly not trying to *scare*—'

'I know you didn't like 'er,' said Janice abruptly. 'Irene. Don't bovver pretending, I know she annoyed you. If I couldn't read people I wouldn't 'ave been any good at my job, going in and out of strangers' 'ouses all the time, would I? And I was *very* good at my job,' said Janice, and somehow the remark didn't seem arrogant. 'Listen: you saw Irene in one of 'er show-off moods. She was so excited to meet you, she put on a big act.

'It's not easy for women, living alone when they're used to company, you know. Even me, coming back from Dubai, it's been a readjustment. You get used to 'aving family around you and then you're back in the empty 'ouse again, alone . . . Me, I don't mind me own company, but Irene 'ates it.

'She's been a very good friend to me, Irene,' said Janice, with a kind of quiet ferocity. 'Very kind. She 'elped me out financially, after Larry died, back when I 'ad nothing. I've always been welcome in 'er 'ouse. We're company for each other, we go back a long way. So she might 'ave a few airs and graces, so what? So 'ave plenty of people . . .'

There was another brief pause.

'Wait there,' said Janice firmly. 'I need to make a phone call.'

She got up and left the room. Strike waited. Beyond the net curtains, the sun suddenly slid out from behind a bullet-coloured cloud, and turned the glass Cinderella coach on the mantelpiece neon bright.

Janice reappeared with a mobile in her hand.

'She's not picking up,' she said, looking perturbed.

She sat back down on the sofa. There was another pause.

'*Fine*,' said Janice at last, as though Strike had harangued her into speech, 'it wasn't me 'oo knew Satchwell – it was Irene. But don't you go thinking she's done anyfing she shouldn't've! I mean, not in a *criminal* sense. It worried 'er like 'ell, after. I was worried *for* 'er . . . Oh Gawd,' said Janice.

She took a deep breath then said,

'All right, well . . . she was engaged to Eddie at

the time. Eddie was a lot older'n Irene. 'E worshipped the ground she walked on, an' she loved 'im, too. She *did*,' said Janice, though Strike hadn't contradicted her. 'And she was *really* jealous if Eddie so much as looked at anyone else . . .

'But she always liked a drink and a flirt, Irene. It was 'armless. *Mostly* 'armless . . . that bloke Satchwell 'ad a band, didn't 'e?'

'That's right,' said Strike.

'Yeah, well, Irene saw 'em play at some pub. I wasn't wiv 'er the night she met Satchwell. I never knew a fing about it till after Margot 'ad gone missing.

'So she watched Satchwell and – well, she fancied 'im. And after the band 'ad finished, she sees Satchwell come into the bar, and 'e goes right to the back of the room to Margot, 'oo's standing there in a corner, in 'er raincoat. Irene fort Satchwell must've seen 'er from the stage. Irene 'adn't spotted Margot before, because she was up the front, wiv 'er friends. Anyway, she watched 'em, and Satchwell and Margot 'ad a short chat – really short, Irene said – and it looked like it turned into an argument. And then Irene reckoned Margot spotted 'er, and that's when Margot walked out.

'So then, Irene goes up to that Satchwell and tells 'im she loved the band and everything and, well, one thing led to another, and . . . yeah.'

'Why would Satchwell think she was a nurse?' asked Strike.

Janice grimaced.

'Well, to tell you the truth, that's what the silly girl used to tell blokes she was, when they were chatting 'er up. She used to pretend to be a nurse because the fellas liked it. As long as they knew naff all about medical stuff she managed to fool 'em, because she'd 'eard the names of drugs and all that at work, though she got most of 'em wrong, God love 'er,' said Janice, with a small eye roll.

'So was this a one-night stand, or . . .?'

'No. It was a two-, three-week thing. But it didn't last. Margot disappearing . . . well, that put the kibosh on it. You can imagine.

'But for a couple of weeks there, Irene was . . . infatuated, I s'pose you'd say. She *did* love Eddie, you know . . . it was a bit of a feather in 'er cap to 'ave this older man, Eddie, successful business and everything, wanting to marry 'er, but . . . it's funny, isn't it?' said Janice quietly. 'We're all animals, when you take everything else away. She *totally* lost 'er 'ead over Paul Satchwell. Just for a few weeks. Tryin' to see 'im as much as she could, sneaking around . . . I bet she scared the life out of 'im, actually,' said Janice soberly, 'because from what she told me later, I fink 'e only took 'er to bed to spite Margot. Margot was 'oo 'e really wanted . . . and Irene realised that too late. She'd been used.'

'So the story of Irene's sore tooth,' said Strike, 'which then became the story of a shopping trip . . .'

215

'Yeah,' said Janice quietly. 'She was with Satchwell that afternoon. She took that receipt off 'er sister to use with the police. *I* never knew till afterwards. I 'ad her in floods of tears in my flat, pouring 'er 'eart out. Well, 'oo else could she tell? Not Eddie or 'er parents! She was terrified of it coming out, and losing Eddie. She'd woken up by then. All she wanted was Eddie, and she was scared 'e'd drop 'er if 'e found out about Satchwell.

'See, Satchwell as good as told Irene, the last time they met, 'e was using 'er to get back at Margot. 'E'd been angry at Margot for saying she'd only come to watch the band outta curiosity, and for getting shirty when 'e tried to persuade 'er to go back to 'is flat. 'E gave 'er that little wooden Viking thing, you know. 'E'd 'ad it on 'im, 'oping she'd turn up, and I fink 'e thought she'd just *melt* or somefing when 'e did that, and that'd be the end of Roy . . . like that's all it takes, to walk out on a kid and a marriage, a little wooden doll . . . 'E said some nasty stuff about Margot to Irene . . . prick tease was the least of it . . .

'Anyway, after Margot went missing and the police got called in, Satchwell rings Irene up and says not to mention anyfing 'e'd said about being angry at Margot, and she begged 'im never to tell anyone about the both of 'em, and that's 'ow they left it. And I was the only one 'oo knew, and I kept me mouth shut, too, because . . . well, that's what you do when it's a friend, isn't it?'

'So when Charlie Ramage said he'd seen

216

Margot in Leamington Spa,' said Strike, 'were you aware—?'

'—that that's where Satchwell come from? Not then, I wasn't, not when Charlie first told me. But not long after, there was a news story about some old geezer in Leamington Spa what 'ad put up a sign in 'is front garden. "Whites united against coloured invasion" or some such 'orrible thing. Me and Larry was out for dinner with Eddie and Irene, and Eddie's talking about this old racist in the news, and then, when Irene and I went to the loo, she says to me, "Leamington Spa, that's where Paul Satchwell was from." She 'adn't mentioned 'im to me in ages.

'I won't lie, it give me a proper uncomfortable feeling, 'er telling me that, because I thought, oh my Gawd, what if Charlie really did see Margot? What if Margot ran off to be with 'er ex? But then I fort, 'ang on, though: if Margot only went as far as Leamington Spa, 'ow come she 'asn't never been seen since? I mean, it's 'ardly Timbuktu, is it?'

'No,' said Strike. 'It isn't. And is that all Irene's ever told you about Margot and Satchwell?'

'It's enough, innit?' said Janice. Her pink and white complexion seemed more faded than when Strike had arrived, the veins beneath her eyes darker. 'Look, *don't* give Irene an 'ard time. Please. She don't seem it, but she's soft under all that silly stuff. She worries, you know.'

'I can't see why I'd have to give her a hard time,'

said Strike. 'Well, you've been very helpful, Mrs Beattie. Thank you. That clears up quite a few points for me.'

Janice slumped backwards on the sofa, frowning at Strike.

'You smoke, don't you?' she said abruptly. 'I can smell it off you. Didn't they stop you smoking after you 'ad that amputation?'

'They tried,' said Strike.

'Very bad for you,' she said. 'Won't 'elp wiv your mobility, either, as you get older. Bad for your circulation *and* your skin. You should quit.'

'I know I should,' said Strike, smiling at her as he returned his notebook to his pocket.

'Hmm,' said Janice, her eyes narrowed. '"'Appened to be in the area", my Aunt Fanny.'

CHAPTER 51

. . . neuer thinke that so
That Monster can be maistred or destroyd:
He is not, ah, he is not such a foe,
As steele can wound, or strength can
* ouerthroe.*

Edmund Spenser
The Faerie Queene

The domed turrets of the Tower of London
rose behind the wall of dirty yellow brick,
but Robin had no attention to spare for
ancient landmarks. Not only was the meeting she'd
set up without Strike's knowledge supposed to
start in thirty minutes' time, she was miles from
where she'd expected to be at one o'clock, and
completely unfamiliar with this part of London.
She ran with her mobile in her hand, glancing
intermittently at the map on its screen.

Within a few paces, the phone rang. Seeing that
it was Strike, she answered the call.

'Hi. Just seen Janice.'

'Oh good,' said Robin, trying not to pant as she scanned her surroundings for either a Tube sign or a taxi. 'Anything interesting?'

'Plenty,' said Strike, who was strolling back along Nightingale Grove. Notwithstanding his recent exchange with the nurse, he'd just lit a Benson & Hedges. As he walked into the cool breeze, the smoke was snatched from his lips every time he exhaled. 'Where are you at the moment?'

'Tower Bridge Road,' said Robin, still running, still looking around in vain for a Tube sign.

'Thought you were on Shifty's Boss this morning?'

'I was,' said Robin. It was probably best that Strike knew immediately what had just happened. 'I've just left him on Tower Bridge with Barclay.'

'When you say "with" Barclay—'

'They might be talking by now, I don't know,' said Robin. Unable to talk normally while jogging, she slowed to a fast walk. 'Cormoran, SB looked as though he was thinking of jumping.'

'Off Tower Bridge?' asked Strike, surprised.

'Why not Tower Bridge?' said Robin, as she rounded a corner onto a busy junction. 'It was the nearest accessible high structure . . .'

'But his office isn't anywhere near—'

'He got off at Monument as usual but he didn't go into work. He looked up at the office for a bit, then walked away. I thought he was just stretching his legs, but then he headed out onto Tower Bridge and stood there, staring down at the water.'

Robin had spent forty anxious minutes watching SB stare down at the cement-coloured river below, his briefcase hanging limply by his side, while traffic rumbled along the bridge behind him. She doubted that Strike could imagine how nerve-racking she'd found the wait for Barclay to come and relieve her.

There was still no sign of a Tube station. Robin broke into a jog again.

'I thought of approaching him,' she said, 'but I was worried I'd startle him into jumping. You know how big he is, I couldn't have held him back.'

'You really think he was—?'

'Yes,' said Robin, trying not to sound triumphant: she'd just caught sight of a circular red Tube sign through a break in the traffic and started running. 'He looked utterly hopeless.'

'Are you running?' asked Strike, who could now hear her feet hitting the ground even over the growl of traffic.

'Yes,' said Robin, and then, 'I'm late for a dental appointment.'

She'd regretted not coming up with a solid reason earlier for not being able to interview Janice Beattie, and had decided on this story, should Strike ask again.

'Ah,' said Strike. 'Right.'

'Anyway,' Robin said, weaving around passers-by, 'Barclay arrived to take over – he agreed SB looked like he was thinking of jumping – and he said—'

She was developing a stitch in her side now.

'—said – he'd go and try – and talk to him – and that's when I left. At least – Barclay's big enough – to hold him back if he tries anything,' she finished breathlessly.

'But it also means SB will recognise Barclay in future,' Strike pointed out.

'Well, yeah, I know that,' said Robin, slowing to a walk again as she was almost at the Underground steps, and massaging the stitch in her side, 'but given that we thought he might be about to kill himself—'

'Understood,' said Strike, who had paused in the shadow of Hither Green station to finish his cigarette. 'Just thinking logistics. 'Course, if we're lucky, he might spill the beans to Barclay about what Shifty's got on him. Desperate men are sometimes willing to—'

'Cormoran, I'm going to have to go,' said Robin, who'd reached the Underground entrance. 'I'll see you back at the office after my appointment and you can fill me in about Janice.'

'Right you are,' said Strike. 'Hope it doesn't hurt.'

'What doesn't hu—? Oh, the dentist, no, it's just a check-up,' said Robin.

Really convincing, Robin, she thought, angry at herself, as she shoved her mobile back into her pocket and ran down the steps into the Underground.

Once on the train, she stripped off her jacket, because she was sweating from running, and neatened her hair with the aid of her reflection in the dirty dark window opposite her. Between SB and his possibly suicidal ideation, lying to Strike, her feeble cover story and the potential risks of the meeting she was about to have, she felt jittery. There'd been another occasion, a couple of years previously, when Robin had chosen to pursue a line of inquiry while keeping it secret from Strike. It had resulted in Strike sacking her.

This is different, she tried to reassure herself, smoothing sweaty strands of hair off her forehead. *He won't mind, as long as it works. It's what he wants, too.*

She emerged at Tottenham Court Road station twenty minutes later and hurried with her jacket over her shoulder into the heart of Soho.

Only when she was approaching the Star café, and saw the sign over the door, did she register the coincidence of the name. Trying not to think about asteroids, horoscopes or omens, Robin entered the café, where round wooden tables stood on a red-brick floor. The walls were decorated with old-fashioned tin signs, one of which was advertising ROBIN CIGARETTES. Directly beneath this, perhaps deliberately, sat an old man wearing a black windcheater, his face ruddy with broken veins and his thick grey hair oiled into a quiff that had the appearance of not having changed since the fifties. A walking stick was propped against the wall beside him. On his other side sat a teenage girl with long neon-yellow hair, who was texting on her phone and didn't look up until Robin had approached their table.

'Mr Tucker?' said Robin.

'Yeah,' said the man hoarsely, revealing crooked brown teeth. 'Miss Ellacott?'

'Robin,' she said, smiling as they shook hands.

'This is my granddaughter, Lauren,' said Tucker.

'Hiya,' said Lauren, glancing up from her phone, then back down again.

'I'll just get myself a coffee,' said Robin. 'Can I buy either of you anything?'

They declined. While Robin bought herself a flat white, she sensed the eyes of the old man on her. During their only previous conversation, which had been by phone, Brian Tucker had talked for a quarter of an hour, without pause, about the disappearance of his eldest daughter, Louise, in 1972, and his lifelong quest to prove that Dennis Creed had murdered her. Roy Phipps had called Tucker 'half-insane'. While Robin wouldn't have gone that far on the evidence to date, there was no doubt that he seemed utterly consumed by Creed, and with his quest for justice.

When Robin returned to the Tuckers' table and sat down with her coffee, Lauren put her phone away. Her long neon extensions, the unicorn tattoo on her forearm, her blatantly false eyelashes and her chipped nail varnish all stood in contrast to the innocent, dimpled face just discernible beneath her aggressively applied contouring.

'I came to help Grandad,' she told Robin. 'He doesn't walk so well these days.'

'She's a good girl,' said Tucker. 'Very good girl.'

'Well, thanks very much for meeting me,' Robin told both of them. 'I really appreciate it.'

Close to, Tucker's swollen nose had a strawberry-like appearance, flecked as it was with blackheads.

'No, I appreciate it, Miss Ellacott,' he said in his low, hoarse voice. 'I think they're really going to let it happen this time, I do. And like I said on the phone, if they don't, I'm ready to break into the television studio—'

'Well,' said Robin, 'hopefully we won't need to do anything that dras—'

'—and I've told them that, and it's shaken them up. Well, that, and your contact nudging the Ministry of Justice,' he conceded, gazing at Robin through small, bloodshot eyes. 'Mind you, I'm starting to think I should've threatened them with the press years ago. You don't get anywhere with these people playing by the rules, they just fob you off with their bureaucracy and their so-called expert opinions.'

'I can only imagine how difficult it's been for you,' said Robin, 'but given that we might be in with a chance to interview him, we don't want to do anything—'

'I'll have justice for Louise if it kills me,' said Tucker. 'Let them arrest me. It'll just mean more publicity.'

'But we wouldn't want—'

'She don't want you to do nothing silly, Grandad,' said Lauren. 'She don't want you to mess things up.'

'No, I won't, I won't,' said Tucker. His eyes were small, flecked and almost colourless, set in pouches of purple. 'But this might be our one and only chance, so it must be done in the right way *and by the right interrogator.*'

'Is he not coming?' said Lauren. 'Cormoran Strike? Grandad said he might be coming.'

'No,' said Robin, and seeing the Tuckers' faces fall, she added quickly, 'He's on another case just now, but anything you'd say to Cormoran, you can say to me, as his part—'

'It's got to be him who interviews Creed,' Tucker said. 'Not you.'

'I under—'

'No, love, you don't,' said Tucker firmly. 'This has been my whole life. I understand Creed better than any of the morons who've written books about him. I've studied him. He's been cut off from any kind of attention for years, now. Your boss is a famous man. Creed'll want to meet him. Creed'll think he's cleverer, of course he will. He'll want to beat your boss, want to come out of it on top, but the temptation of seeing his name in the papers again? He's always thrived on the publicity. I think he'll be ready to talk, as long as your boss can make him believe it's worth his while . . . he's kosher, your boss, is he?'

226

Under almost any other circumstances, Robin would have said 'he's actually my partner', but today, understanding what she was being asked, she said,

'Yes, he's kosher.'

'Yeah, I thought he seemed it, I thought so,' said Brian Tucker. 'When your contact got in touch, I went online, I looked it all up. Impressive, what he's done. He doesn't give interviews, does he?'

'No,' said Robin.

'I like that,' said Tucker, nodding. 'In it for the right reasons. But the name's known, now, and that'll appeal to Creed, and so will the fact your boss has had contact with famous people. Creed likes all that. I've told the Ministry of Justice and I told your contact, I want this Strike to do it, I don't want the police interviewing him. They've had their go and we all know how well *that* went. And no more bloody *psychiatrists*, thinking they're so smart and they can't even agree on whether the bastard's sane or not.

'I know Creed. I understand Creed. I've made a lifelong study of his psychology. I was there every day in court, during the trial. They didn't ask him about Lou in court, not by name, but he made eye contact with me plenty of times. He'll have recognised me, he'll have known who I was, because Lou was my spitting image.

'When they asked him in court about the jewellery – you know about the pendant, Lou's pendant?'

'Yes,' said Robin.

'She got it a couple of days before she disappeared. Showed it to her sister Liz, Lauren's mother – didn't she?' he asked Lauren, who nodded. 'A butterfly on a chain, nothing expensive, and because it was mass-produced, the police said it could have been anyone's. Liz remembered the pendant differently – that's what threw the police off, she wasn't sure at first that it was Lou's – but she admitted she only saw it briefly. And when they mentioned the jewellery, Creed looked straight at me. He knew who I was. Lou was my spit image,' repeated Tucker. 'You know his explanation for having a stash of jewellery under the floorboards?'

'Yes,' said Robin, 'he said he'd bought it because he liked to cross-dress—'

'That he'd bought it,' said Tucker, talking over Robin, 'to dress up in.'

'Mr Tucker, you said on the phone—'

'Lou nicked it from that shop they all used to go to, what was it—?'

'Biba,' said Lauren.

'Biba,' said Tucker. 'Two days before she disappeared, she played truant and that evening she showed Lauren's mum, Liz, what she'd stolen. She was a handful, Lou. Didn't get on with my second wife. The girls' mum died when Lou was ten. It affected Lou the worst, more than the other two. She never liked my second wife.'

He'd told Robin all of this on the phone, but still, she nodded sympathetically.

'My wife had a row with Lou the morning before she disappeared, and Lou bunked off school again. We didn't realise until she didn't come home that night. Rang round all her friends, none of them had seen her, so we called the cops. We found out later, one of her friends had lied. She'd smuggled Lou upstairs and not told her parents.

'Lou was spotted three times next day, still in her school uniform. Last known sighting was outside a launderette in Kentish Town. She asked some geezer for a light. We knew she'd started smoking. That was partly what she rowed with my wife about.

'Creed picked up Vera Kenny in Kentish Town, too,' said Tucker, hoarsely. 'In 1970, right after he'd moved into the place by Paradise Park. Vera was the first woman he took back to that basement. He chained them up, you know, and kept them alive while he—'

'Grandad,' said Lauren plaintively, 'don't.'

'No,' Tucker muttered, dipping his head, 'sorry, love.'

'Mr Tucker,' said Robin, seizing her chance, 'you said on the phone you had information about Margot Bamborough nobody else knows.'

'Yeah,' said Tucker, groping inside his windcheater for a wad of folded papers, which he unfolded with shaking hands. 'This top one, I got through a warder at Wakefield, back in '79. I used to hang round there every weekend in the late seventies, watch them all coming in and out. Found out where they liked to drink and everything.

'Anyway, this particular warder, I won't say his name, but we got chummy. Creed was on a high-security wing, in a single cell, because all the other cons wanted to take a pop at him. One geezer nearly took out Creed's eye in '82, stole a spoon from the canteen and sharpened the handle to a point in his cell. Tried to stab Creed through the eyeball. Just missed, because Creed dodged. My mate told me he screamed like a little girl,' said Tucker, with relish.

'Anyway, I said to my mate, I said, anything you can find out, anything you can tell me. Things Creed's saying, hints he gives, you know. I paid him for it. He could've lost his job if anyone had found out. And my mate got hold of this and smuggled it out to me. I've never been able to admit to having it, because both of us would be in trouble if it got out, but I called up Margot Bamborough's husband, what was his name—?'

'Roy Phipps.'

'Roy Phipps, yeah. I said, "I've got a bit of Creed's writing here you're going to want to see. It proves he killed your wife."'

A contemptuous smile revealed Tucker's toffee-brown teeth again.

'But he didn't want to know,' said Tucker. 'Phipps thought I was a crank. A year after I called him,

I read in the paper he'd married the nanny. Creed did Dr Phipps a good turn, it seems.'

'Grandad!' said Lauren, shocked.

'All right, all right,' muttered Tucker. 'I never liked that doctor. He could've done us a lot of good, if he'd wanted to. Hospital consultant, he was the kind of man the Home Secretary would've listened to. We could've kept up the pressure if he'd helped us, but he wasn't interested, and when I saw he was off with the nanny I thought, ah, right, everything's explained.'

'Could I—?' Robin began, gesturing towards the paper Tucker was still holding flat to the table, but he ignored her.

'So it was just me and Jerry for years,' said Tucker. 'Jerry Wolfson, Kara's brother. You know who that is?' he shot at Robin.

'Yes, the nightclub hostess—'

'Nightclub hostess, hooker on the side, and a drug habit as well. Jerry had no illusions about her, he wasn't naive, but it was still his sister. She raised him, after their mother left. Kara was all the family he had.

'February 1973, three months after my Lou, Kara disappeared as well. Left her club in Soho in the early hours of the morning. Another girl left at exactly the same time. It wasn't far from here, as a matter of fact,' said Tucker, pointing out of the door. 'The two girls go different ways up the street. The friend looks back and sees Kara bending down and talking to a van driver at the

231

end of the road. The friend assumed that Kara knew the driver. She walks off. Kara's never seen again.

'Jerry spoke to all Kara's friends at the club, after, but nobody knew anything. There was a rumour going round, after Kara disappeared, that she'd been a police informer. That club was run by a couple of gangland figures. Suited them, to say she was an informer, see? Scare the other girls into keeping shtum about anything they'd seen or heard in the club.

'But Jerry never believed Kara was a snitch. He thought it was the Essex Butcher from the start – the van was the giveaway. So we joined forces.

'He tried to get permission to visit Creed, same as me, but the authorities wouldn't let us. Jerry gave up, in the end. Drank himself to death. Something like this happens to someone you love, it marks you. You can't get out from under it. The weight of it crushes some people.

'My marriage broke up. My other two daughters didn't speak to me for years. Wanted me to stop going on about Lou, stop talking about Creed, pretend it never—'

'That's not fair, Grandad,' said Lauren, sternly.

'Yeah, all right,' mumbled Tucker. 'All right, I grant you, Lauren's mum, she's come round lately. I said to Liz, "Think of all the time I should've spent with Lou, like I've spent with you and Lisa. Add it all up. Family meals and holidays. Helping her with her homework. Telling her to clean her

232

room. Arguing with her—" My God, she could be bolshie. Watching her graduate, I expect, because she was clever, Lou, even if she did get in trouble at school with all the bunking off. I said to Liz, "I never got to walk her up the aisle, did I? Never got to visit her in hospital when her kids were born. Add up all the time I would've given her if she'd lived—"'

Tucker faltered. Lauren put a plump hand over her grandfather's, which had swollen, purple joints.

'—add all that time together,' Tucker croaked, his eyes filmy with tears, 'and that's what I owe her, to find out what happened to her. That's all I'm doing. Giving her her due.'

Robin felt tears prickle behind her own eyelids.

'I'm so sorry,' she said quietly.

'Yeah, well,' said Tucker, wiping his eyes and nose roughly on the sleeve of his windcheater. He now took the top sheet of writing and thrust it at Robin. 'There you are. That shows you what we're up against.'

Robin took the paper, on which was written two short paragraphs in clear, slanting writing, every letter separate and distinct, and began to read.

She attempts to control through words and sometimes with flattery. Tells me how clever I am, then talks about 'treatment'. The strategy is laughably transparent. Her 'qualifications' and her 'training' are, compared to my self-knowledge, my self-awareness, the flicker of a damp match beside the light of the sun.

She promises a diagnosis of madness will mean gentler treatment for me. This she tells me between screams, as I whip her face and breasts. Bleeding, she begs me to see that she could be of use to me. Would testify for me. Her arrogance and her thirst for dominance have been fanned by the societal approval she gained from the position of 'doctor'. Even chained, she believes herself superior. This belief will be corrected.

'You see?' said Tucker in a fierce whisper. 'He had Margot Bamborough chained in his basement. He's enjoying writing about it, reliving it. But the psychiatrists didn't think it was an admission, they reckoned Creed was just churning out these bits of writing to try and draw more attention to himself. They said it was all a game to try and get more interviews, because he liked pitting his wits against the police, and reading about himself in the press, seeing himself on the news. They said that was just a bit of fantasy, and that taking it serious would give Creed what he wanted, because talking about it would turn him on.'

'Gross,' said Lauren, under her breath.

'But my warder mate said – because you know, there was three women they thought Creed had done whose bodies were never found: my Lou, Kara Wolfson and Margot Bamborough – and my warder mate said, it was the doctor he really liked being asked about. Creed likes high-status people, see. He thinks he could've been the boss of some multinational, or some professor or something, if he hadn't of turned to killing. My mate told me all this. He said, Creed sees himself on that sort of level, you know, just in a different field.'

Robin said nothing. The impact of what she'd just read wasn't easily dispelled. Margot Bamborough had become real to Robin, and she'd just been forced to imagine her, brutalised and bleeding, attempting to persuade a psychopath to spare her life.

'Creed got transferred to Belmarsh in '83,' Tucker continued, patting the papers still laid in front of him, and Robin forced herself to concentrate, 'and they started drugging him so he couldn't get a – you know, couldn't maintain . . .

'And that's when I got permission to write to him, and have him write back to me. Ever since he was convicted, I'd been lobbying the authorities to let me question him directly, and let him write back. I wore them down in the end. I had to swear I'd never publicise what he wrote me, or give the letter to the press, but I'm the only member of a victim's family he's ever been allowed direct contact with . . . and there,' he said, turning the next two sheets of paper towards Robin. 'That's what I got back.'

The letter was written on prison writing paper. There was no 'Dear Mr Tucker'.

Your letter reached me three weeks ago, but I was placed in solitary confinement shortly afterwards and deprived of writing materials, so have been unable to answer. Ordinarily I'm not permitted to respond to enquiries like yours, but I gather your persistence has worn the authorities down. Unlikely as it may seem, I admire you for this, Mr Tucker. Resilience in the face of adversity is one of my own defining characteristics.

During my three weeks of enforced solitude, I've wondered how I could possibly explain to you what not one man in ten thousand might hope to understand. Although you think I must be able to recall the names, faces and personalities of my various 'victims', my memory shows me only the many-limbed, many-breasted monster with whom I cavorted, a foul-smelling thing that gave tongue to pain and misery. Ultimately, my monster was never much of a companion, though there was fascination in its contortions. Given sufficient stimulus, it could be raised to an ecstasy of pain, and then it knew it lived, and stood tremulously on the edge of the abyss, begging, screaming, pleading for mercy.

How many times did the monster die, then live again? Too few to satisfy me. Even though its face and voice mutated, its reactions never varied. Richard Merridan, my old psychiatrist, gave what possessed me other names,

236

but the truth is that I was in the grip of a divine frenzy.

Colleagues of Merridan's disputed his conclusion that I'm sane. Regrettably, their opinions were dismissed by the judge. In conclusion: I might have killed your daughter, or I might not. Either I did so in the grip of some madness which still occludes my memory, and which a more skilful doctor might yet penetrate, or I never met her, and little Louise is out there somewhere, laughing at her daddy's attempts to find her, or perhaps enduring a different hell to the one in which my monster lived.

Doubtless the additional psychiatric support available at Broadmoor would help me recover as much memory as possible. For their own inscrutable reasons, however, the authorities prefer to keep me here at Belmarsh. Only this morning I was threatened under the noses of warders. Regardless of the obvious fact that a cachet attaches to anyone who attacks me, I'm exposed, daily, to intimidation and physical danger. How anyone expects me to regain sufficient mental health to assist police further is a mystery.

Exceptional people ought to be studied only by those who can appreciate them. Rudimentary analysis, such as I've been subjected to thus far, merely entrenches my inability to recollect all that I did. Maybe you,

Mr Tucker, can help me. Until I'm in a hospital environment where I can be given the assistance I require, what incentive do I have to dredge my fragmented memory for details that may help you discover what happened to your daughter? My safety is being compromised on a daily basis. My mental faculties are being degraded.

You will naturally be disappointed not to receive confirmation of what happened to Louise. Be assured that, when the frenzy is not upon me, I am not devoid of human sympathy. Even my worst critics concede that I actually understand others much more easily than they understand me! For instance, I can appreciate what it would mean to you to recover Louise's body and give her the funeral you so desire. On the other hand, my small store of human empathy is being rapidly depleted by the conditions in which I am currently living. Recovery from the last attack upon me, which nearly removed my eye, was delayed due to the refusal of the authorities to let me attend a civilian hospital. 'Evil men forfeit the right to fair treatment!' Such seems to be the public's view. However, brutality breeds brutality. Even the most dim-witted psychi-atrists agree, there.

Do you have a merciful soul, Mr Tucker? If so, the first letter you'll write upon receiving this will be to the authorities, requesting that the remainder of my sentence will be served in Broadmoor, where the secrets my unruly memory still holds may be coaxed to the surface at last.

Ever yours,
Dennis

Robin finished reading, and looked up.

'You can't see it, can you?' said Tucker, with an oddly hungry expression. 'No, of course you can't. It isn't obvious. I didn't see it myself, at first. Nor did the prison authorities. They were too busy warning me they weren't going to transfer him to Broadmoor, so I needn't ask.'

He jabbed the bottom of the letter with a yellow-nailed finger.

'The clue's there. Last line. *First letter. My sentence.* Put together the first letter of every sentence, and see what you get.'

Robin did as she was bidden.

'Y – O – U – R – D – A – U – G – H – T – E – R . . .' Robin read out loud, until, fearing where the message was going to end, she fell silent, until she reached the last sentence, when the taste of milky coffee seemed to turn rancid in her mouth, and she said, 'Oh God.'

'What's it say?' asked Lauren, frowning and straining to see.

'Never you mind,' said Tucker shortly, taking the letter back. 'There you are,' he told Robin, folding up the papers and shoving them back into his inside pocket. 'Now you see what he is. He killed Lou like he killed your doctor and he's gloating about it.'

Before Robin could say anything, Tucker spun his next bit of paper to face her, and she saw a photocopied map of Islington, with a circle inked around what looked like a large house.

'Now,' he said, 'there are two places nobody's ever looked, where I think he might've hid bodies. I've been back over everywhere what had a connection with him, kid or adult. Police checked all the obvious, flats he'd lived and that, but never bothered with these.

'When Lou disappeared in November '72, he wouldn't've been able to bury her in Epping Forest, because—'

'They'd just found Vera Kenny's body there,' said Robin.

Tucker looked grudgingly impressed.

'You do your homework at that agency, don't you? Yeah, exactly. There was still a police presence in the forest at the time.

'But see that, there?' said Tucker, tapping on the marked building. 'That's a private house, now, but in the seventies it was the Archer Hotel, and guess who used to do their laundry? Creed's dry cleaner's. He used to pick up stuff from them once a week in his van, and bring it back again, sheets and bedspreads and what have you . . .

'Anyway, after he was arrested, the woman who

owned the Archer Hotel gave a quote to the *Mail*, saying he always seemed so nice and polite, always chatty when he saw her . . .

'That isn't marked on modern maps,' said Tucker, now moving his finger to a cross marked in the grounds of the property, 'but it's on the old deeds. There's a well out the back of that property. Just a shaft into the ground that collects rainwater. Predated the current building.

'I tracked the owner down in '89, after she'd sold up. She told me the well was boarded up in her time, and she planted bushes round it, because she didn't want no kid going down it accidental. But Creed used to go through that garden to deliver laundry, right past the place where the well was. He'll have known it was there. She couldn't remember telling him,' said Tucker quickly, forestalling Robin's question, 'but that's neither here nor there, is it? She wasn't going to remember every word they said to her, was she, after all that time?

'Dead of night, Creed could've pulled up a van by the rear entrance, gone in through the back gate . . . but by the time I realised all this,' said Tucker, gritting his brown teeth in frustration, 'the Archer'd gone back to being a private property, and now there's been a bloody conservatory built over the old well.'

'Don't you think,' said Robin cautiously, 'when they built over it, they might have noticed—'

'Why would they?' said Tucker aggressively. 'I

never knew a builder who went looking for work when he could just slap concrete over it. Anyway, Creed's not stupid. He'd've thrown rubbish down there on top of the body, wouldn't he? Cover it up. So *that's* a possibility,' he said firmly. 'And then you've got this.'

Tucker's last piece of paper was a second map.

'That there,' he said, tapping his swollen-knuckled finger on another circled building, 'is Dennis Creed's great-grandmother's house. It's mentioned in *The Demon of Paradise Park*. Creed said, in one of his interviews, the only time he ever saw countryside when he was a kid was when he got taken there.

'And look here,' said Tucker, pointing on a large patch of green. 'The house backs right onto Great Church Wood. Acres of woodland, acres and acres. Creed knew the way there. He had a van. He'd played in those woods as a child.

'We know he chose Epping Forest for most of the bodies, because he had no known connection with the place, but by '75, police were regularly checking Epping Forest by night, weren't they? But here's a different wood he knows, and it's not so far away from London, and Creed's got his van and his spades ready in the back.

'My best guess,' said Tucker, 'is my Lou and your doc are in the well or in the woods. And they've got different technology now to what they had in the seventies. Ground-penetrating radar and what have you. It wouldn't be difficult to see

242

if there was a body in either of those places, not if the will was there.

'But,' said Tucker, sweeping the two maps off the table and folding them up with his shaking hands, 'there's no will, or there hasn't been, not for years. Nobody in authority cares. They think it's all over, they think Creed'll never talk. So that's why it's got to be your boss who interviews him. I wish it could be me,' said Tucker, 'but you've seen what Creed thought I was worth . . .'

As Tucker slid his papers back inside his windcheater, Robin became aware that the café around them had filled up during their conversation. At the nearest table sat three young men, all with amusingly Edwardian beards. So long attuned only to Tucker's low, hoarse voice, Robin's ears seemed suddenly full of noise. She felt as though she'd suddenly been transported from the distant past into a brash and indifferent present. What would Margot Bamborough, Louise Tucker and Kara Wolfson make of the mobile phones in almost every hand, or the sound of Pharrell Williams's 'Happy' now playing somewhere nearby, or the young woman carrying a coffee back from the counter, her hair in high bunches, wearing a T-shirt that read GO F#CK YOUR #SELFIE?

'Don't cry, Grandad,' said yellow-haired Lauren softly, putting her arm around her grandfather as a fat tear rolled down his swollen nose and fell upon the wooden table. Now that he'd stopped talking about Louise and Creed, he seemed to have become smaller.

'It's affected our whole family,' Lauren told Robin. 'Mum and Auntie Lisa are always scared if me and my cousins go out after dark—'

'Quite right!' said Tucker, who was now mopping his eyes on his sleeve again.

'—and all us grew up knowing it's something that can *really happen*, you know?' said the innocent-faced Lauren. 'People *really do* disappear. They *really do* get murdered.'

'Yes,' said Robin. 'I know.'

She reached across the table and briefly gripped the old man's forearm.

'We'll do everything we can, Mr Tucker, I promise. I'll be in touch.'

As she left the café, Robin was aware that she'd just spoken for Strike, who knew absolutely nothing of the plan to interview Creed, let alone to try and find out what had happened to Louise Tucker, but she had no energy left to worry about that just now. Robin drew her jacket more closely around her and walked back to the office, her thoughts consumed by the terrible vacuum left in the wake of the vanished.

CHAPTER 52

Oft Fire is without Smoke.

Edmund Spenser
The Faerie Queene

It was one o'clock in the morning, and Strike was driving towards Stoke Newington to relieve Robin, who was currently keeping watch over the terraced house that Shifty's Boss was again visiting, and where he was almost certainly indulging in another bout of the blackmailable behaviour Shifty had somehow found out about. Even though Shifty's hold on his boss had driven the latter onto Tower Bridge, SB didn't appear able or willing to give up whatever it was he was doing inside the house of Elinor Dean.

The night was crisp and clear, although the stars overhead were only dimly visible from brightly lit Essex Road, and Barclay's voice was currently issuing from the speaker of the BMW. A week had passed since the Scot had managed to persuade

SB to leave Tower Bridge and get a coffee with him.

'He cannae help himself, the poor bastard.'

'Clearly,' said Strike. 'This is his third visit in ten days.'

'He said to me, "Ah cannae stop." Says it relieves his stress.'

'How does he square that with the fact he's suicidal?'

'It's the blackmail that's makin' him suicidal, Strike, no' whatever he gets up tae in Stoke Newington.'

'And he didn't give *any* indication what he does in there?'

'I told ye, he said he doesnae shag her, but that his wife'll leave him if it gets oot. Could be rubber,' added Barclay, thoughtfully.

'What?'

'Rubber,' repeated Barclay. 'Like that guy we had who liked wearin' latex to work under his suit.'

'Oh yeah,' said Strike. 'I forgot about him.'

The various sexual predilections of their clients often blurred in Strike's memory. He could hear the hum of the casino in the background. Shifty had been in there for hours and Barclay had been keeping him company, unnoticed, from across the floor.

'Anyway,' said Barclay, 'ye want me tae stay in here, do ye? Because it's costin' a small fortune and ye said the client's gettin' pissy aboot how much we're chargin'. I could watch when the slimy bastard leaves, from ootside on the street.'

'No, stay on him, keep photographing him, and try and get something incriminating,' said Strike.

'Shifty's coked oot o' his head,' said Barclay.

'Half his colleagues will be cokeheads, as well. We're going to need something worse than that to nail the bastard for blackmailing people onto high bridges . . .'

'You're goin' soft, Strike.'

'Just try and get something on the fucker and don't place large bets.'

'It's no' the gamblin' that'll bankrupt us,' said Barclay, 'it's the drinks.'

He hung up, and Strike wound down the window and lit a cigarette, trying to ignore the pain in his stiff neck and shoulders.

Like SB, Strike could have used a respite from life's problems and challenges, but such outlets were currently non-existent. Over the past year, Joan's illness had taken from him that small sliver of time that wasn't given over to work. Since his amputation, he no longer played any kind of sport. He saw friends infrequently due to the demands of the agency, and derived many more headaches than pleasures from his relatives, who were being particularly troublesome just now.

Tomorrow was Easter Sunday, meaning that Joan's family would be gathering together in St Mawes to scatter her ashes at sea. Quite apart from the mournful event itself, Strike wasn't looking forward to yet another long journey to Cornwall, or to further enforced contact with Lucy, who'd made it clear over the course of several phone calls that she was dreading this final farewell. Again and again she returned to her sadness at not having a grave to visit, and Strike detected an undertone of blame, as though she thought Strike ought to have overruled Joan's dying wishes. Lucy had also expressed disappointment that Strike wasn't coming down for the whole weekend, as she and Greg were, and added bluntly that he'd better remember to bring Easter eggs for all three of his nephews, not just Jack. Strike could have done without transporting three fragile chocolate eggs all the way to Truro on the train, with a holdall to manage and his leg sore from days and weeks of non-stop work.

To compound his stress, both his unknown half-sister, Prudence, and his half-brother Al had started texting him again. His half-siblings seemed to imagine that Strike, having enjoyed a moment of necessary catharsis by shouting at Rokeby over the phone, was probably regretting his outburst, and more amenable to attending his father's party to make up. Strike hadn't answered any of their texts, but he'd experienced them as insect bites: determined not to scratch, they were nevertheless the source of a niggling aggravation.

Overhanging every other worry was the Bamborough case which, for all the hours he and

Robin were putting into it, was proving as opaque as it had when first they'd agreed to tackle the forty-year-old mystery. The year's deadline was coming ever closer, and nothing resembling a breakthrough had yet occurred. If he was honest, Strike had low hopes of the interview with Wilma Bayliss's daughters, which he and Robin would be conducting later that morning, before Strike boarded the train to Truro.

All in all, as he drove towards the house of the middle-aged woman for whom SB seemed to feel such an attraction, Strike had to admit he felt a glimmer of sympathy for any man in desperate search of what the detective was certain was some form of sexual release. Recently it had been brought home to Strike that the relationships he'd had since leaving Charlotte, casual though they'd been, had been his only unalloyed refuge from the job. His sex life had been moribund since Joan's diagnosis of cancer: all those lengthy trips to Cornwall had eaten up time that might have been given to dates.

Which wasn't to say he hadn't had opportunities. Ever since the agency had become successful, a few of the rich and unhappy women who'd formed a staple of the agency's work had shown a tendency to size up Strike as a potential palliative for their own emotional pain or emptiness. Strike had taken on a new client of exactly this type the previous day, Good Friday. As she'd replaced Mrs Smith, who'd already initiated divorce proceedings against

249

her husband on the basis of Morris's pictures of him with their nanny, they'd nicknamed the thirty-two-year-old brunette Miss Jones.

She was undeniably beautiful, with long legs, full lips and skin of expensive smoothness. She was of interest to the gossip columns partly because she was an heiress, and partly because she was involved in a bitter custody battle with her estranged boyfriend, on whom she was seeking dirt to use in court. Miss Jones had crossed and re-crossed her long legs while she told Strike about her hypocritical ex-partner's drug use, the fact that he was feeding stories about her to the papers, and that he had no interest in his six-month-old daughter other than as a means to make Miss Jones unhappy. While he was seeing her to the door, their interview concluded, she'd repeatedly touched his arm and laughed longer than necessary at his mild pleas- antries. Trying to usher her politely out of the door under Pat's censorious eye, Strike had had the sensation of trying to prise chewing gum off his fingers.

Strike could well imagine Dave Polworth's comments had he been privy to the scene, because Polworth had trenchant theories about the sort of women who found his oldest friend attractive, and of whom Charlotte was the purest example of the type. The women most readily drawn to Strike were, in Polworth's view, neurotic, chaotic and occasionally dangerous, and their fondness for the bent-nosed ex-boxer indicated a subconscious desire for something rocklike to which they could attach themselves like limpets.

Driving through the deserted streets of Stoke Newington, Strike's thoughts turned naturally to his ex-fiancée. He hadn't responded to the desperate text messages she'd sent him from what he knew, having Googled the place, to be a private psychiatric clinic. Not only had they arrived on the eve of his departure for Joan's deathbed, he hadn't wanted to fuel her vain hopes that he would appear to rescue her. Was she still there? If so, it would be her longest ever period of hospitalisation. Her one-year-old twins were doubtless in the care of a nanny, or the mother-in-law Charlotte had once assured him was ready and willing to take over maternal duties.

A short distance away from Elinor Dean's street, Strike called Robin.

'Is he still inside?'

'Yes. You'll be able to park right behind me, there's a space. I think number 14 must've gone away for Easter with the kids. Both cars are gone.'

'See you in five.'

When Strike turned into the street, he saw the old Land Rover parked a few houses down from Elinor's front door, and was able to park without difficulty in the space directly behind it. As he turned off his engine, Robin jumped down out of her Land Rover, closed the door quietly, and walked around the BMW to the passenger's side, a messenger bag over her shoulder.

'Morning,' she said, sliding into the seat beside him.

'Morning. Aren't you keen to get away?'

As he said it, the screen of the mobile in her hand lit up: somebody had texted her. Robin didn't even look at the message, but turned the phone over on her knee, to hide its light.

'Got a few things to tell you. I've spoken to C. B. Oakden.'

'Ah,' said Strike.

Given that Oakden seemed primarily interested in Strike, and that Strike suspected Oakden was recording his calls, the two detectives had agreed that it should be Robin who warned him away from the case.

'He didn't like it,' said Robin. 'There was a lot of "it's a free country", and "I'm entitled to talk to anyone I like". I said to him, "Trying to get in ahead of us and talk to witnesses could hamper our investigation." He said, as an experienced biographer—'

'Oh, fuck off,' said Strike under his breath.

'—he knows how to question people to get information out of them, and it might be a good idea for the three of us to pool our resources.'

'Yeah,' said Strike. 'That's exactly what this agency needs, a convicted con man on the payroll. How did you leave it?'

'Well, I can tell he *really* wants to meet you

and I think he's determined to withhold everything he knows about Brenner until he comes
face to face with you. He wants to keep Brenner
as bait.'

Strike reached for another cigarette.

'I'm not sure Brenner's worth C. B. Oakden.'

'Even after what Janice said?'

Strike took a drag on the cigarette, then blew
smoke out of the window, away from Robin. 'I
grant you, Brenner looks a lot fishier now than he
did when we started digging, but what are the
odds Oakden's actually got useful information?
He was a kid when all this happened and nicking
that obituary smacks of a man trying to scrape up
things to say, rather than—'

He heard a rustling beside him and turned to
see Robin opening her messenger bag. Slightly
to his surprise, Robin was pulling out Talbot's
notebook again.

'Still carrying that around with you, are you?'
said Strike, trying not to sound exasperated.

'Apparently I am,' she said, moving her mobile
onto the dashboard so that she could open the
book in her lap. Watching the phone, Strike saw
a second text arrive, lighting up the screen, and
this time, he caught sight of the name: Morris.

'What's Morris texting you about?' Strike said,
and even to his ears, the question sounded
critical.

'Nothing. He's just bored, sitting outside Miss
Jones's boyfriend's house,' said Robin, who was

flicking through Talbot's notebook. 'I want to show you something. There, look at that.'

She passed him the book, open to a page Strike remembered from his own perusal of the notes. It was close to the end of the notebook, where the pages were most heavily embellished with strange drawings. In the middle of this page danced a black skeleton holding a scythe.

'Ignore all the weird tarot drawings,' said Robin. 'Look there, though. That sentence between the skeleton's legs. The little symbol, the circle with the cross in it, stands for the Part of Fortune . . .'

'What's that?' asked Strike.

'It's a point in the horoscope that's supposed to be about worldly success. "Part of Fortune in Second, MONEY AND POSSESSIONS." And "Mother's House", underlined. The Oakdens lived on Fortune Street, remember? And the Part of Fortune was in the house of money and posses-sions when Margot disappeared, and he's connecting that with the fact that Dorothy inher-ited her mother's house, and saying that wasn't a tragedy, but a stroke of luck for Dorothy.'

'You think?' said Strike, rubbing his tired eyes.

'Yes, because look, he then starts rambling about Virgo – which is Dorothy's sign under both systems – being petty and having an axe to grind, which from what we know about her fits. Anyway,' said Robin, 'I've been looking at dates of birth, and guess what? Under both the traditional and Schmidt's systems, Dorothy's mother was a Scorpio.'

♀ holds SECRETS - ♀ primitive instincts, dark side personality, SECRETS ♀ not maternal but SEXUAL, yes, crude sensation, unfaithful, dishonest, was in 11th when ♀ disappeared, house of FRIENDSHIPS yet claims with family?? 11th house also House of ♏, what did she do there? Blood on floor – a ritual? Obeah? THERE THE GOAT DEMONS WILL GREET EACH OTHER AND THERE THE LILIT WILL FIND REST 'Nine drops of impure blood' Question FAMILY of ♀ also neighbours

Contrast ♀ and ☽ black moon/ white moon

BAPHOMET HERMAPHRODITE

'She lives in the world of Romance, in the perpetual dream of Rapture'
- 'Silently and effortlessly she goes about her work'
'Her image is of extreme purity and beauty, with infinite subtlety; to see the truth of her is hardly possible, for she reflects the nature of the observer in great perfection'
TRUSTED ♀ didn't want to dismiss ♀ IN LOVE WITH ♑?

⊗ in 2nd MONEY and POSSESSIONS. Mother's House

21° ♊   20° ♋

Lévi: St John agrees
sulphur = Ether
mercury = Water
salt = Dragon's blood
or MENSTRUUM OF THE EARTH
'The things of transcendent symbolism can only be understood rightly by the true children of science.'

ADAMS: ♍ 'outlook is apt to be petty' 'difficult to conceal the fact that she has an axe to grind' TRUE ⊗ says ♀♀♂ ♄ are SCARLET WOMEN who RIDE UPON THE BEAST

'I am the Snake that Knowledge and and bright beasts of men with drunkenness. strange drugs'

giveth Delight glory, and stir the To worship me take wine and A CROWLEY

'Christ's sake, how many more Scorpios are we going to find?'

'I know what you mean,' said Robin, unfazed, 'but from what I've read, Scorpio's one of the most common birth signs. Anyway, this is the important bit: Carl Oakden was born on the sixth of April. That means he's Aries under the traditional system, but Pisces under Schmidt's.'

A short silence followed.

'How old was Oakden when his grandmother fell downstairs?' asked Strike.

'Fourteen,' said Robin.

Strike turned his face away from Robin to blow smoke out of the window again.

'You think he pushed his grandmother, do you?'

'It might not have been deliberate,' said Robin. 'He could've pushed past her and she lost her balance.'

'"Margot confronted Pisces." It'd be a hell of a thing to accuse a child of—'

'Maybe she never confronted him at all. The confrontation might have been something Talbot suspected, or imagined. Either way—'

'—it's suggestive, yeah. It *is* suggestive . . .' Strike let out a slight groan. 'We're going to *have* to interview bloody Oakden, aren't we? There's a bit of a hotspot developing around that little grouping, isn't there? Brenner and the Oakdens, outward respectability—'

'—inward poison. Remember? That's what Oonagh Kennedy said about Dorothy.'

The detectives sat for a moment or two, watching Elinor Dean's front door, which remained closed, her dark garden silent and still.

'How many murders,' Robin asked, 'd'you think go undetected?'

'Clue's in the question, isn't it? "Undetected" – impossible to know. But yeah, it's those quiet, domestic deaths you wonder about. Vulnerable people picked off by their own families, and everyone thinking it was ill health—'

'—or a mercy that they've gone,' said Robin.

'Some deaths *are* a mercy,' said Strike.

And with these words, in both of their mind's eyes rose an image of horror. Strike was remembering the corpse of Sergeant Gary Topley, lying on the dusty road in Afghanistan, eyes wide open, his body missing from the waist down. The vision had recurred in Strike's nightmares ever since he'd seen it, and occasionally, in these dreams, Gary talked to him, lying in the dust. It was always a comfort to remember, on waking, that Gary's consciousness had been snuffed out instantly, that his wide-open eyes and puzzled expression showed that death had claimed him before his brain could register agony or terror.

But in Robin's mind there was a picture of something she wasn't sure had ever happened. She was imagining Margot Bamborough chained to a radiator (*I whip her face and breasts*), pleading for her life (*the strategy is laughably transparent*), and suffering torments (*it could be raised to an ecstasy*

*of pain, and then it knew it lived, and stood tremu-
lously on the edge of the abyss, begging, screaming,
begging for mercy).*

'You know,' said Robin, talking partly to break
the silence and dispel that mental image, 'I'd
quite like to find a picture of Dorothy's mother,
Maud.'

'Why?'

'For confirmation, because – I don't think I told
you, look . . .'

She flicked backwards in the notebook to the
page littered with water signs. In small writing
beneath a picture of a scorpion were the words
'MOLE (Adams).'

'Is that a new sign?' asked Strike. 'The Mole?'

'No,' said Robin, smiling, 'Talbot's alluding to
the fact that the astrologer Evangeline Adams
said the true Scorpio often has a birthmark, or
a prominent mole. I've read her book, got it
second hand.'

There was a pause.

'What?' said Strike, because Robin was looking
at him expectantly.

'I was waiting for you to jeer.'

'I lost the will to jeer some way back,' said Strike.
'You realise we're supposed to have solved this
case in approximately fourteen weeks' time?'

'I know,' sighed Robin. She picked up her mobile
to check the time, and out of the corner of his
eye, Strike saw yet another text from Morris. 'Well,
we're meeting the Bayliss sisters later. Maybe

they'll have something useful to tell us . . . are you sure you want to interview them with me? I'd be fine to do it alone. You're going to be really tired after sitting here all night.'

'I'll sleep on the train to Truro afterwards,' said Strike. 'You got any plans for Easter Sunday?'

'No,' said Robin. 'Mum wanted me to go home but . . .'

Strike wondered what the silent sequel to the sentence was, and whether she'd made plans with someone else, and didn't want to tell him about it. Morris, for instance.

'OK, I swear this is the last thing I'm going to bring up from Talbot's notebook,' Robin said, 'but I want to flag something up before we meet the Baylisses.'

'Go on.'

'You said yourself, he seemed racist, from his notes.'

'"Black phantom",' Strike quoted, 'yeah.'

'And "Black Moon Lilith—"'

'—and wondering whether she was a witch.'

'Exactly. I think he really harassed her, and probably the family, too,' Robin said. 'The language he uses for Wilma – "crude", "dishonest" . . .' Robin flicked back to the page featuring the three horned signs, 'and "woman as she is now in this aeon . . . armed and militant".'

'A radical feminist witch.'

'Which sounds quite cool when you say it,' said Robin, 'but I don't think Talbot meant it that way.'

'You think this is why the daughters didn't want to talk to us?'

'Maybe,' said Robin. 'So I think we need to be . . . you know. Sensitive to what might have gone on. Definitely not go in there looking as though we suspect Wilma of anything.'

'Point well made, and taken,' said Strike.

'Right then,' said Robin with a sigh, as she put the notebook back into her messenger bag. 'I'd better get going . . . What *is* he doing in there?' Robin asked quietly, looking at Elinor Dean's front door.

'Barclay thinks it might be a rubber fetish.'

'He'd need a lot of talcum powder to wriggle himself into anything made of rubber, the size of that belly.'

Strike laughed.

'Well, I'll see you in . . .' Robin checked the time on her mobile, 'seven hours, forty-five minutes.'

'Sleep well,' said Strike.

As she walked away from the BMW, Strike saw her looking at her mobile again, doubtless reading Morris's texts. He watched as she got into the ancient Land Rover, then turned the tank-like vehicle in a three-point turn, raising a hand in farewell as she passed him, heading back to Earl's Court.

As Strike reached for the Thermos of tea under his seat, he remembered the supposed dental appointment of the other day, about which Robin had sounded strangely flustered, and which had taken place (though Strike hadn't previously made the connection) on Morris's afternoon off. A most unwelcome possibility crossed his mind: had Robin lied, like Irene Hickson, and for the same reason? His mind darted to what Robin had said a few months previously, when she'd mentioned her ex-husband having a new partner: 'Oh, I didn't tell you, did I? I told Morris.'

As he unscrewed his Thermos, Strike mentally reviewed Robin's behaviour around Morris in the last few months. She'd never seemed to particularly like him, but might that have been an act, designed to deflect attention? Were his partner and his subcontractor actually in a relationship which he, busy with his own troubles, had failed to spot?

Strike poured himself tea, settled back in his seat, and glowered at Elinor Dean's closed door through the steam rising from plastic-tasting tea the colour of mud. He was angry, he told himself, because he should have established a work rule that partners weren't allowed to date subcontractors, and for another reason which he preferred not to examine, because he knew perfectly well what it was, and no good could come of brooding upon it.

CHAPTER 53

Like three faire branches budding farre and
*   wide,*
That from one roote deriu'd their vitall sap:
And like that roote that doth her life diuide,
Their mother was . . .

Edmund Spenser
The Faerie Queene

Seven hours later, in the cool, flat daylight of an overcast morning, Robin, who was back in her Land Rover, took a detour on her way to the café where she and Strike would be meeting the three Bayliss sisters.

When Maya, the middle sister, had suggested meeting in Belgique in Wanstead, Robin had realised how close she'd have to drive to the Flats where Dennis Creed had disposed of his second-to-last known victim, twenty-seven-year-old hairdresser Susan Meyer.

Half an hour ahead of the planned interview, Robin parked the Land Rover beside a stretch of shops on Aldersbrook Road, then crossed the street and headed up a short footpath, which led her to the reedy bank of the man-made Alexandra Lake, a wide stretch of water on which various wildfowl were bobbing. A couple of ducks came paddling hopefully towards Robin, but when she failed to produce bread or other treats, they glided away again, compact, self-sufficient, their onyx eyes scanning both water and bank for other possibilities.

Thirty-nine years ago, Dennis Creed had driven to this lake under cover of night, and rolled the headless, handless corpse of Susan Meyer into it, bound up in black plastic and rope. Susan Meyer's distinctive wedge cut and shy smile had earned her a prominent place on the cover of *The Demon of Paradise Park*.

The milky sky looked as opaque as the shallow lake, which resembled jade silk in which the gliding wildfowl made rippling creases. Hands in her pockets, Robin looked out over the water and the rustling weeds, trying to imagine the scene when a park worker had spotted the black object in the water, which he'd assumed initially was a tarpaulin swollen with air, until he hooked it with a long pole, felt the grisly weight and made an instant connection (or so he told the television crew who arrived shortly after the police and ambulance) with the bodies that kept turning up in Epping Forest, barely ten miles away.

Creed had abducted Susan exactly a month

before Margot disappeared. Had they overlapped in Creed's basement? If so, Creed had, for a brief period, held three women there simultaneously. Robin preferred not to think about what Andrea, or Margot, if she'd been there, must have felt on being dragged into Creed's basement, seeing a fellow woman chained there, and knowing that she, too, would be reduced to that emaciated and broken-boned state before she died.

Andrea Hooton was the last woman Creed was known to have killed, and he'd varied the pattern when it came to disposing of her body, driving eighty miles from his house in Liverpool Road to throw the corpse off Beachy Head. Both Epping Forest and Wanstead Flats had become too heavily patrolled by then, and in spite of Creed's evident wish to make sure the Essex Butcher was credited with every kill, as evidenced by the secret store of press clippings he kept beneath the floorboards in his basement flat, he'd never wanted to be caught.

Robin checked her watch: it was time to head to the interview with the Bayliss sisters. Walking back to the Land Rover, she pondered the divide between normalcy and insanity. On the surface, Creed had been far saner than Bill Talbot. Creed had left no half-crazed scribblings behind him to explain his thought processes; he'd never plotted the course of asteroids to guide him: his interviews with psychiatrists and police had been entirely lucid. Not for Creed the belief in signs and symbols, a secret language decipherable only by initiates, a refuge in mystery or magic. Dennis Creed had been a meticulous planner, a genius of misdirection in his neat little white van, dressed in the pink coat he'd stolen from Vi Cooper, and sometimes wearing a wig that, from a distance, to a drunk victim, gave his hazy form a feminine appearance just long enough for his large hands to close over a gasping mouth.

When Robin arrived in the street where the café stood, she spotted Strike getting out of his BMW a short distance away from the entrance. Noticing the Land Rover in turn, Strike raised a hand in greeting and headed up the street towards her, while finishing what looked like a bacon and egg McMuffin, his chin stubbly, the shadows beneath his eyes purple.

'Have I got time for a fag?' were the first words he spoke, checking his watch as Robin got down out of the car and slammed the door. 'No,' he answered himself, with a sigh. 'Ah well . . .'

'You can take the lead on this interview,' he told Robin, as they headed together towards the café. 'You've done all the legwork. I'll take notes. Remind me what their names are?'

'Eden's the eldest. She's a Labour councillor from Lewisham. Maya's the middle one, and she's deputy headmistress of a primary school. The youngest is Porschia Dagley, and she's a social worker—'

'—like her mother—'

'Exactly, and she lives just up the road from here. I think we've come to her neck of the woods because she's been ill, so the others didn't want her to have to travel.'

Robin pushed open the door of the café and led the way inside. The interior was sleekly modern, with a curved counter, a wooden floor and a bright orange feature wall. Close to the door at a table for six sat three black women. Robin found it easy to identify which sister was which, because of the photographs she'd seen on the family's Facebook pages, and on the Lewisham Council website.

Eden, the councillor, sat with her arms folded, a wavy bob casting a shadow over most of her face, so that only a carefully lipsticked, unsmiling plum mouth was clearly visible. She wore a well-tailored black jacket and her demeanour was suggestive of a businesswoman who'd been inter-rupted during an important meeting.

Maya, the deputy headmistress, wore a corn-flower blue sweater and jeans. A small silver cross hung around her neck. She was smaller in build than Eden, the darkest skinned and, in Robin's opinion, the prettiest of the sisters. Her long, braided hair was tied back in a thick ponytail, she wore square-framed glasses over her large, wide-set eyes and her full mouth, with its naturally up-tilted corners, conveyed warmth. A leather handbag sat in Maya's lap, and she was gripping it with both hands as though afraid it might other-wise escape.

Porschia, the youngest sister and the social worker, was also the heaviest. Her hair had been cropped almost to her skull, doubtless because of her recent chemotherapy. She'd pencilled in the eyebrows that were just beginning to grow back; they arched over hazel eyes that shone gold against her skin. Porschia was wearing a purple smock top with jeans and long beaded earrings, which swung like miniature chandeliers as she looked around at Strike and Robin. As they approached the table Robin spotted a small tattoo on the back of Porschia's neck: the trident from the Barbadian flag. Robin knew that Eden and Maya were both well into their fifties, and that Porschia was forty-nine, but all three sisters could have passed for at least ten years younger than their real ages.

Robin introduced herself and Strike. Hands were shaken, Eden unsmiling throughout, and the detectives sat down, Strike at the head of the table, Robin between him and Porschia, facing Maya and Eden. Everyone but Eden made laboured small talk about the local area and the weather, until the waiter came to take their order. Once he'd left, Robin said,

'Thanks very much for meeting us, we really do appreciate it. Would you mind if Cormoran takes notes?'

Maya and Porschia shook their heads. Strike tugged his notebook out of his coat pocket and opened it.

'As I said on the phone,' Robin began, 'we're really after background, building up a complete picture of Margot Bamborough's life in the months—'

'Could *I* ask a couple of questions?' interrupted Eden.

'Of course,' said Robin politely, though expecting trouble.

Eden swept her hair back out of her face, revealing ebony-dark eyes.

'Did you two know there's a guy phoning around everyone who was connected to St John's, saying he's going to write a book about you investigating Bamborough's disappearance?'

Shit, thought Robin.

'Would this be a man called Oakden?' asked Strike.

'No, Carl Brice.'

'It's the same bloke,' said Strike.

'Are you connected to him or—?'

'No,' said Strike, 'and I'd strongly advise you not to talk to him.'

'Yeah, we worked that out for ourselves,' said Eden, coolly. 'But this means there'll be publicity, won't there?'

Robin looked at Strike, who said,

'If we solve the case, there'll be publicity even without Oakden – or Brice, or whatever he's calling himself these days – but that's a big "if". To be frank, the odds are we're not going to solve it, in which case I think Oakden's going to find it very hard to sell any books, and whatever you tell us will never go any further.'

'What if we know something that might help you solve the case, though?' asked Porschia, leaning forwards, so that she could look past Robin at Strike.

There was an infinitesimal pause in which Robin could almost feel Strike's interest sharpening, along with her own.

'Depends what that information is,' Strike answered slowly. 'It *might* be possible not to divulge where we got it, but if the source is important to getting a conviction . . .'

There was a long pause. The air between the sisters seemed charged with silent communications.

'Well?' said Porschia at last, on an interrogative note.

'We *did* decide to,' Maya mumbled to Eden, who continued to sit in silence, arms folded.

'OK, *fine*,' said Eden, with a don't-blame-me-later inflection.

The deputy headmistress reached absently for the little silver cross around her neck, and held it as she began to talk.

'I need to explain a bit of background, first,' she said. 'When we were kids – Eden and I were already teenagers, but Porschia was only nine—'

'Eight,' Porschia corrected her.

'Eight,' Maya said obediently, 'our dad was convicted of – of rape and sent to prison.'

'He didn't do it, though,' said Eden.

Robin reached automatically for her coffee cup and took a sip, so as to hide her face.

'He didn't, OK?' said Eden, watching Robin. 'He had a white girlfriend for a couple of months. The whole of Clerkenwell knew. They'd been seen together in bars all over the place. He tried to end it, and she cried rape.'

Robin's stomach lurched as though the floor had tilted. She very much wanted this story to be untrue. The idea of any woman lying about rape was repugnant to her. She'd had to talk through every moment of her own assault in court. Her soft-spoken fifty-three-year-old rapist and would-be murderer had taken the stand afterwards to explain to the jury how the twenty-year-old Robin had invited him into the stairwell of her hall of residence for sex. In his account, everything had been consensual: she'd whispered that she liked it rough, which had accounted for the heavy bruising around her neck, she'd enjoyed it so much she'd asked him back the following night, and yes (with a little laugh in the dock), of course he'd been surprised, nicely spoken young girl like her, coming on to him like that, out of nowhere . . .

'Easy thing for a white woman to do to a black man,' said Eden, ''specially in 1972. Dad already had a record, because he'd got into a fight a few years before that. He went down for five years.'

'Must've been hard on the family,' said Strike, not looking at Robin.

'It was,' said Maya. 'Very hard. The other kids at school . . . well, you know what kids are like . . .'

'Dad had been bringing in most of the money,' said Porschia. 'There were five of us, and Mum had never had much schooling. Before Dad got arrested, she'd been studying, trying to pass some exams, better herself. We were just about making ends meet while Dad was bringing in a wage, but once he was gone, we struggled.'

'Our mum and her sister married two brothers,' said Maya. 'Nine children between them. The families were really close, right up until Dad got arrested – but then everything changed. My Uncle Marcus went to court every day while Dad was on trial, but Mum wouldn't go and Uncle Marcus was really angry at her.'

'Well, he knew it would've made a big difference, if the judge had seen Dad had the family united behind him,' snapped Eden. '*I* went. I bunked off school to go. I knew he was innocent.'

'Well, good for you,' said Porschia, though her tone was far from congratulatory, 'but Mum didn't want to sit in open court listening to her husband talk about how often he had sex with his girlfriend—'

'That woman was trash,' said Eden curtly.

'*Dirty water does cool hot iron,*' said Porschia, with a Bajan inflection. 'His choice.'

'So, anyway,' said Maya hastily, 'the judge believed the woman, and Dad got put away. Mum never went to visit him inside, and she wouldn't take me or Porschia or our brothers, either.'

'I went,' piped up Eden again. 'I got Uncle

271

Marcus to take me. He was still our dad. Mum had no right to stop us seeing him.'

'Yeah, so,' continued Maya, before Porschia could say anything, 'Mum wanted a divorce, but she had no money for legal advice. So Dr Bamborough put her in touch with this feminist lawyer, who'd give legal help to women in difficult circumstances, for a reduced fee. When Uncle Marcus told Dad that Mum had managed to get herself a lawyer, Dad wrote to her from prison, begging her to change her mind. He said he'd found God, that he loved her and he'd learned his lesson and all he wanted was his family.'

Maya took a sip of her coffee.

'About a week after Mum got Dad's letter, she was cleaning Dr Bamborough's consulting room one evening after everyone had left, and she noticed something in the bin.'

Maya unfastened the handbag she'd been holding on her lap, and took out a pale blue piece of heavily creased paper, which had clearly been crumpled up into a ball at some point in the past. She held it out to Robin, who laid it flat on the table so that Strike could read it, too.

The faded handwriting was a distinctive mix of capitals and lower-case letters.

LEAVE MY GIRL ALONE YOU CUNT
OR I'LL MAKE SURE YOU GO TO
HELL SLOW AND PAINFUL.

Robin glanced sideways at Strike and saw her own, barely disguised astonishment mirrored there. Before either of them could say anything, a group of young women passed their table, forcing Strike to push his chair in. Chatting and giggling, the women sat down at the table behind Maya and Eden.

'When Mum read that,' said Maya, speaking more quietly so that the newcomers couldn't hear her, 'she thought Dad had sent it. Not *literally*, because the prison censor would never have let that go out – she thought someone had done it for him.'

'Specifically, Uncle Marcus,' said Eden, arms folded and expression pinched. 'Uncle Marcus, who was a lay preacher and never used the c-word in his life.'

'Mum took the note over to Uncle Marcus and Auntie Carmen's,' said Maya, ignoring this interjection, 'and asked Marcus straight out if he was behind it. He denied it, but Mum didn't believe him. It was the mention of hell: Marcus was a fire-and-brimstone kind of preacher back then—'

'—and he didn't believe Mum really wanted a divorce,' said Porschia. 'He blamed Dr Bamborough for persuading Mum to leave Dad, because, you know, Mum *really* needed a white woman to point out her life was shit. She'd never have noticed otherwise.'

'Going for a cigarette, OK?' said Eden abruptly.

She pushed herself up and walked out, her heels rapping on the wooden floorboards.

Both younger sisters seemed to exhale in relief with her departure.

'She was Dad's favourite,' Maya told Strike and Robin quietly, watching through the window as Eden took out a packet of Silk Cut, shook her hair out of her face and lit herself a cigarette. 'She really loved him, even if he was a womaniser.'

'And she never got on with Mum,' said Porschia. 'Their rows would've woken the dead.'

'In fairness,' said Maya, 'them splitting up hit Eden hardest. She left school at sixteen, got herself a job at Marks & Spencer to help support—'

'Mum never wanted her to drop out of school,' said Porschia. 'That was Eden's choice. Eden likes to claim it was a sacrifice she made for the family, but come on. She couldn't *wait* to get out of school, because Mum put so much pressure on her to get good grades. She likes to claim she was a second mother to all of us, but that's not how I remember it. *I* mostly remember her whacking merry hell out of me if I so much as looked at her wrong.'

On the other side of the window, Eden stood smoking with her back to them.

'The whole situation was a nightmare,' said Maya sadly. 'Mum and Uncle Marcus never made it up, and with Mum and Carmen being sisters . . .'

'Let's just tell them now, while she can't stick her oar in,' Porschia urged Maya, and turning to

Strike and Robin, she said, 'Auntie Carmen was helping Mum get the divorce, behind Uncle Marcus's back.'

'How?' asked Robin, as a waiter passed their table on the way to the group of women at the next table.

'See, when the lawyer Dr Bamborough had recommended told Mum what she charged, Mum knew she'd never be able to afford her, not even at the reduced rates,' said Porschia.

'Mum came home afterwards and cried,' said Maya, 'because she was desperate to have the divorce done and dusted before Dad got out of jail. She knew otherwise he'd just move right back in and she'd be trapped. Anyway, a few days later, Dr Bamborough asked her how things had gone with the lawyer, and Mum admitted she wasn't going to go through with the divorce, for lack of funds, so,' Maya sighed, 'Dr Bamborough offered to pay the lawyer, in exchange for Mum doing a few hours a week cleaning the house out in Ham.'

The women at the table behind theirs were now flirting with the young waiter, wondering whether it was too early for a cream cake, giggling about breaking their diets.

'Mum didn't feel she could refuse,' said Maya. 'But what with the costs of getting all the way out to Ham, and the time it would take her to get out there, when she already had two other jobs and exams coming up . . .'

'Your Aunt Carmen agreed to do the cleaning

for her,' guessed Robin, and out of the corner of her eye she saw Strike glance at her.

'Yeah,' said Maya, eyes widening in surprise. 'Exactly. It seemed like a good solution. Auntie Carmen was a housewife and Uncle Marcus and Dr Bamborough were both out at work all day, so Mum thought neither of them would ever know the wrong woman was turning up.'

'There was one sticky moment,' said Porschia, 'remember, M? When Dr Bamborough asked us all over to a barbecue at her house?' She turned to Robin. 'We couldn't go, because Dr Bamborough's nanny would've realised Mum wasn't the woman turning up once a week to clean. My Auntie Carmen didn't like that nanny,' Porschia added. 'Didn't like her at all.'

'Why was that?' asked Strike.

'She thought the girl was after Dr Bamborough's husband. Went red every time she said his name, apparently.'

The door of the café opened and Eden walked back inside. As she sat down, Robin caught a whiff of smoke mingling with her perfume.

'Where've you got to?' she asked, looking cold.

'Auntie Carmen cleaning instead of Mum,' said Maya.

Eden re-folded her arms, ignoring her coffee.

'So the statement your mother gave the police, about the blood and Dr Phipps walking across the garden—' said Strike.

'—was really her telling him everything Carmen

276

had told *her*, yeah,' said Maya, feeling again for the cross around her neck. 'She couldn't own up that her sister had been going there instead of her, because my Uncle Marcus would've gone *crazy* if he'd found out. Auntie Carmen *begged* Mum not to tell the police and Mum agreed.

'So she had to pretend she was the one who'd seen the blood on the carpet and Dr Phipps walking across the lawn.'

'Only,' interrupted Porschia, with a humourless laugh, 'Carmen changed her mind about Dr Phipps, after. Mum went back to her after her first police interview and said, "They're asking whether I couldn't have got confused and mistaken one of the workmen for Dr Phipps." Carmen said, "Oh. Yeah. I forgot there were workmen round the back. Maybe I did."'

Porschia let out a short laugh, but Robin knew she wasn't truly amused. It was the same kind of laughter Robin had taken refuge in, the night she'd discussed rape with Max over the kitchen table.

'I know it isn't funny,' said Porschia, catching Maya's eye, 'but come on. Carmen was always ditzy as hell, but you'd think she might've made sure of her facts *then*, wouldn't you? Mum was literally sick with stress, like, *retching* if she ate anything. And then that old bitch of a secretary at work found her having a dizzy spell . . .'

'Yeah,' said Eden, suddenly coming to life. 'Next thing was, Mum was accused of being a thief and a drunk and the practice fired her. The old secretary claimed she'd had a secret sniff of Mum's Thermos and smelled booze in it. Total fabrication.'

'That was a few months after Margot Bamborough disappeared, wasn't it?' asked Strike, his pen poised over his notebook.

'Oh, I'm sorry,' Eden said with icy sarcasm, 'did I go off topic? Back to the missing white lady, everyone. Never mind what the black woman went through, who gives a shit?'

'Sorry, I didn't—' began Strike.

'D'you know who Tiana Medaini is?' Eden shot at him.

'No,' he admitted.

'*No*,' said Eden, 'of course you bloody don't. Forty years after Margot Bamborough went missing, here we all are, fussing over her and where she went. Tiana Medaini's a black teenager from Lewisham. She went missing last year. How many front pages has Tiana been on? Why wasn't she top of the news, like Bamborough was? Because we're not worth the same, are we, to the press or to the bloody police?'

Strike appeared unable to find an adequate response; doubtless, Robin thought, because Eden's point was unarguable. The picture of Dennis Creed's only black victim, Jackie Aylett, a secretary and mother of one, was the smallest and the least distinct of the ghostly black and white images of Creed's victims on the cover of *The Demon of*

Paradise Park. Jackie's dark skin showed up worst on the gloomy cover. The greatest prominence had been given to sixteen-year-old Geraldine Christie and twenty-seven-year-old Susan Meyer, both of them pale and blonde.

'When Margot Bamborough went missing,' Eden said fiercely, 'the white women at her practice were treated like bone china by the police, OK? Practically mopping their bloody tears for them – but not our mum. They treated her like a hardened con. That policeman in charge, what was his name—?'

'Talbot?' suggested Robin.

'"What are you hiding? Come on, I know you're hiding something."'

The mysterious figure of the Hierophant rose up in Robin's mind. The keeper of secrets and mysteries in the Thoth tarot wore saffron robes and sat upon a bull ('the card is referred to Taurus') and in front of him, half his size, stood a black priestess, her hair braided like Maya's ('Before him is the woman girt with a sword; she represents the Scarlet Woman . . .'). Which had come first, the laying out of tarot cards signifying secrecy and concealment, or the policeman's instinct that the terrified Wilma was lying to him?

'When he interviewed me—' began Eden.

'Talbot interviewed *you*?' asked Strike sharply.

'Yeah, he came to Marks & Spencer unannounced, to my work,' said Eden, and Robin realised that Eden's eyes were suddenly bright with tears.

'Someone else at the practice had seen that anonymous note Bamborough got. Talbot found out Dad was inside and he'd heard Mum was cleaning for the doctor. He went to every man in our family, accusing them of writing the threatening letters, and then he came to me, asking me really strange questions about all my male relatives, wanting to know what they'd been up to on different dates, asking whether Uncle Marcus often stayed out overnight. He even asked me about Dad and Uncle Marcus's—'

'—star signs?' asked Robin.

Eden looked astounded.

'The hell did you know that?'

'Talbot left a notebook. It's full of occult writing. He was trying to solve the case using tarot cards and astrology.'

'Astrology?' repeated Eden. 'Effing *astrology*?'

'Talbot shouldn't have been interviewing you without an adult present,' Strike told Eden. 'What were you, sixteen?'

Eden laughed in the detective's face.

'That might be how it works for white girls, but we're different, aren't you listening? We're hardy. We're *tough*. That occult stuff,' Eden said, turning back to Robin, 'yeah, that makes sense, because he asked me about *obeah*. You know what that is?'

Robin shook her head.

'Kind of magic they used to practise in the Caribbean. Originated in West Africa. We were all born in Southwark, but, you know, we were all black pagans to Inspector Talbot. He had me alone in the back room and he was asking me stuff about rituals using blood, about black magic. I was terrified, I didn't know what he was on about. I thought he meant Mum and the blood on the carpet, hinting she'd done away with Dr Bamborough.'

'He was having a psychotic breakdown,' said Robin. 'That's why they took him off the case. He thought he was hunting a devil. Your mum wasn't the only woman he thought might have supernatural power – but he was definitely racist,' Robin added quietly. 'That's clear from his notes.'

'You never told us about the police coming to Marks & Spencer,' said Porschia. 'Why didn't you tell us?'

'Why would I?' said Eden, angrily blotting her damp eyes. 'Mum was already ill with the stress of it all, I had Uncle Marcus shouting at me that Mum had put the police onto him and his boys, and I was really scared, if Uncle Marcus found out about the officer coming to my work, he'd report him, which was the last thing we needed. God, it was a mess,' said Eden, pressing her hands briefly against her wet eyes, 'such a bloody mess.'

Porschia looked as though she'd like to say something comforting to her elder sister, but Robin had the impression that this would be such a departure from their usual relationship, she didn't know quite how to set about it. After a moment or two, Porschia muttered,

'Need the loo,' pushed her chair away from the table and disappeared into the bathroom.

'I didn't want Porsh to come today,' said Maya, as soon as the bathroom door swung shut behind her younger sister. She was tactfully not looking at her elder sister, who was trying to pretend she wasn't crying, while surreptitiously wiping more tears from her eyes. 'She doesn't need this stress. She's only just finished chemo.'

'How's she doing?' asked Strike.

'She was given the all-clear last week, thank God. She's talking about going back to work on reduced hours. I think it's too early.'

'She's a social worker, isn't she?' asked Robin.

'Yeah,' sighed Maya. 'A backlog of a hundred desperate messages every morning, and you know you're in the firing line if anything goes wrong with a family you haven't been able to reach. I don't know how she does it. But she's like Mum. Two peas in a pod. She was always Mum's baby, and Mum was her hero.'

Eden let out a soft 'huh', which might have been agreement or disparagement. Maya ignored it. There was a short pause, in which Robin reflected on the tangled ties of family. A proxy war between Jules and Wilma Bayliss seemed still to be playing out in the next generation.

The bathroom door swung open again and Porschia reappeared. Instead of taking her seat beside Robin, she swivelled her wide hips around Strike at the end of the table, and edged in behind a startled Maya, who pulled her chair in hastily, until she reached Eden. After thrusting a handful of toilet roll into her elder sister's hand, Porschia slid her plump arms around Eden's neck and dropped a kiss on the top of her head.

'What are you doing?' said Eden huskily, reaching up to clasp her youngest sister's arms, not to remove them, but to hold them there. Strike, Robin saw out of the corner of her eye, was pretending to examine his notebook.

'Thanking you,' said Porschia softly, dropping another kiss on the top of her eldest sister's head before letting her go. 'For agreeing to do this. I know you didn't want to.'

Everyone sat in slightly startled silence while Porschia squeezed her way back around the table and resumed her seat next to Robin.

'Have you told them the last bit?' Porschia asked Maya, while Eden blew her nose. 'About Mum and Betty Fuller?'

'No,' said Maya, who appeared shell-shocked by the act of reconciliation she'd just witnessed. 'You're the one Mum told it to, I thought you should.'

'Right,' said Porschia, turning to look at Strike and Robin. 'This really is the last thing we know, and there might be nothing in it, but you might as well have it, now you know the other stuff.'

Strike waited, pen poised.

'Mum told me this not long after she retired. She shouldn't have, really, because it was about a client, but when you hear what it was, you'll understand.

'Mum kept working in Clerkenwell after she'd qualified as a social worker. It was where all her friends were; she didn't want to move. So she really got to know the local community.

'One of the families she was working with lived in Skinner Street, not that far from the St John's practice—'

'Skinner Street?' repeated Strike. The name rang a bell, but, exhausted as he was, he couldn't immediately remember why that was. Robin, on the other hand, knew immediately why Skinner Street sounded familiar.

'Yeah. The family was called Fuller. They had just about every problem you can think of, Mum said: addiction, domestic abuse, criminality, the lot. The sort of head of the family was a grandmother who was only in her forties, and this woman's main source of income was prostitution. Betty was her name, and Mum said she was like a local news service, if you wanted to know about the underworld, anyway. The family had been in the area for generations.

'Anyway, one day, Betty says to Mum, bit sly, to see her reaction: "Marcus never sent no threatening notes to that doctor, you know."

'Mum was gobsmacked,' said Porschia. 'Her first thought was that Marcus was visiting the woman, you know, as a client – *I know he wasn't,*' said Porschia quickly, holding up a hand to forestall

Eden, who'd opened her mouth. 'Mum and Marcus hadn't spoken for years at this point. Anyway, it was all innocent: Betty had met Marcus because the church was doing a bit of outreach in the local area. He'd brought round some Harvest Festival stuff for the family, and tried to persuade Betty to come along to a church service.

'Betty had worked out Marcus's connection with Mum, because Mum was still going by "Bayliss", and Betty claimed she knew who *really* wrote the threatening notes to Margot Bamborough, and that the person who wrote the notes was the same person who killed her. Mum said, "Who was it?" And Betty said if she ever told, Margot's killer would kill her, too.'

There was a short silence. The café clattered around them, and one of the women at the next table, who was eating a cream slice, said loudly, with unctuous pleasure,

'*God* that's good.'

'Did your mother believe Betty?' asked Robin.

'She didn't know what to think,' said Porschia. 'Betty knew some very rough people, so it was possible she'd heard something on the grapevine, but who knows? People talk, don't they, and they like making themselves important,' and Robin remembered Janice Beattie saying exactly this, as she passed on the rumour of Margot Bamborough appearing in a graveyard. 'But if there was anything in it, a woman like Betty, she'd go to the moon before she went to the cops.

'She might well be dead by now,' said Porschia, 'given her lifestyle, but for what it's worth, there it is. Shouldn't be hard to find out whether she's still alive.'

'Thanks very much for telling us,' said Strike. 'That's definitely worth following up.'

Having told all they knew, the three sisters now lapsed into a pained silence. It wasn't the first time that Robin had had cause to consider how much collateral damage each act of violence left in its wake. The disappearance of Margot Bamborough had evidently wreaked havoc in the lives of the Bayliss girls, and now she knew the full extent of the grief it had brought them, and the painful nature of the memories associated with it, she perfectly understood Eden's initial refusal to talk to detectives. If anything, she had to ask herself why the sisters had changed their minds.

'Thank you so much for this,' she said sincerely. 'I know Margot's daughter will be incredibly grateful that you agreed to talk to us.'

'Oh, it's the daughter who's hired you, is it?' said Maya. 'Well, you can tell her from me, Mum felt guilty all her life that she didn't come clean with the police. She liked Dr Bamborough, you know. I mean, they weren't close friends or anything, but she thought she was a decent person.'

'It weighed on her,' said Porschia. 'Right up until her death, it weighed on her. That's why she kept that note. She'd have wanted us to do this. There's always handwriting analysis and stuff, isn't there?'

Strike agreed that there was. He went to pay the bill and Robin waited at the table with the sisters, who she could tell wanted the detectives gone, and as quickly as possible. They'd disclosed their personal trauma and their family's secrets, and now a thin layer of polite small talk was too onerous to sustain, and any other form of conversation impossible. Robin was relieved when Strike re-joined her, and after brief farewells, the two of them left the café.

The moment he hit clean air, Strike paused to pull his Benson & Hedges out of his pocket and lit one.

'Needed that,' he muttered, as they walked on. 'So . . . Skinner Street . . .'

'. . . is where Joseph Brenner was seen on the night Margot Bamborough disappeared,' said Robin.

'Ah,' muttered Strike, briefly closing his eyes. 'I *knew* there was something.'

'I'll look into Betty Fuller as soon as I get home,' said Robin. 'What did you think of the rest of it?'

'The Bayliss family really went through it, didn't they?' said Strike, pausing beside the Land Rover and glancing back at the café. His BMW lay another fifty yards ahead. He took another drag on his cigarette, frowning. 'Y'know . . . it gives us another angle on Talbot's bloody notebook,' he admitted. 'Strip away all the occult shit, and he was right, wasn't he? Wilma *was* hiding stuff from him. A lot of stuff, actually.'

'I thought that, too,' said Robin.

'You realise that threatening note's the first piece of physical evidence we've found?'

'Yes,' said Robin, checking her watch. 'What time are you heading to Truro?'

Strike didn't answer. Looking up, Robin saw that he was staring so fixedly across the open park on the other side of the road that she turned, too, to see what had captured his attention, but saw nothing except a couple of gambolling West Highland terriers and their male owner, who was walking along, swinging a pair of leads.

'Cormoran?'

Strike appeared to recall his attention from a long way away.

'What?' he said, and then, 'Yeah. No, I was just . . .'

He turned to look back at the café, frowning.

'Just thinking. But it's nothing, I think I'm doing a Talbot. Seeing meaning in total coincidence.'

'What coincidence?'

But Strike didn't answer until the café doors opened, and the three Bayliss sisters emerged in their coats.

'We should get going,' he said. 'They must be sick of the sight of us by now. I'll see you Monday. Let me know if you find out anything interesting on Betty Fuller.'

CHAPTER 54

But nothing new to him was that same pain;
Nor pain at all; for he so oft had tried
The power thereof, and lov'd so oft in vain.

Edmund Spenser
The Faerie Queene

The train gave a lurch: the sleeping Strike's head rolled sideways and hit the cold window. He woke, feeling drool on his chin. Wiping it on his coat sleeve, he peered around. The elderly couple opposite him were politely immersed in their reading material, but across the aisle, four teenagers were enjoying paroxysms of silent laughter, carefully not looking at him, their shoulders shaking as they feigned interest in the fields out of the window. Apparently he'd been snoring with his mouth wide open, because it was now unpleasantly dry. Checking his watch, he saw that he'd been asleep at least two hours.

Strike reached for the tartan Thermos sitting on the table in front of him, which he'd rinsed out and refilled in McDonald's earlier, and poured himself a black coffee while the teenagers continued to gasp and snort with laughter. Doubtless they thought him comically odd and old, with his snores and his tartan Thermos, but a year of navigating swaying train carriages had taught him that his prosthetic leg appreciated as few trips to the catering car as possible. He drank a cup of plastic-tainted coffee, then re-settled himself comfortably, arms folded, looking out at the fields gliding past, bestridden with power pylons, the flat white cloud given a glaucous glow by the dust on the glass. The landscape registered only incidentally: Strike's attention was focused inwards on the odd idea that had occurred to him after the interview with the Bayliss sisters.

Of course, the idea might be nothing but the product of an overburdened mind making spurious connections between simple coincidences. He mentally turned it this way and that, examining it from different angles, until finally, yawning, he inched sideways over into the empty seat beside him, and laboriously pulled himself up into a standing position in the aisle, so he could access the holdall in the luggage rack overhead. Beside his holdall sat a Waitrose bag, because he'd made a detour into the supermarket on the way to Paddington station, where he'd grabbed three Easter eggs for his nephews, or rather, three choc-olate hedgehogs ('Woodland Friends') because they were relatively compact. Now, groping in his holdall for *The Demon of Paradise Park*, he accidentally knocked over the carrier bag containing the chocolate. The uppermost hedgehog fell out: in his attempt to catch it, he accidentally batted it up into the air; the box bounced off the back of the elderly woman's seat, causing her to squeak in surprise, and the box hit the floor.

The teenagers for whom Strike was unintentionally mounting a one-man comedy show were now openly gasping and crying with laughter. Only when Strike bent down awkwardly to pick up the now cracked chocolate hedgehog, one hand on the teenagers' table to steady himself, did one of the young women spot the metal rod that served as his right ankle. He knew what she'd seen by the abrupt cessation of her laughter, and the frantic, whispered shushing of her friends. Panting, sweating and now aware of half the carriage's eyes on him, he shoved the damaged hedgehog back into its bag, found *The Demon of Paradise Park* in his holdall and then, sweating slightly, but taking malicious pleasure in the po-faced shock of the teenagers beside him, sidled back into his window seat.

After flicking through the book in search of the part he wanted to re-read, Strike finally found the chapter two-thirds of the way through the book, entitled 'Capture'.

Thus far, Creed's relationship with landlady Violet Cooper had been key to his continuing safety. Violet herself admits that for the first five years of his tenancy, she'd never have believed harm of 'Den', who she saw as a lonely and gentle soul, fond of their singalong evenings, and probably gay.

However, the pains he'd once taken to keep Violet happy had begun to irk Creed. Where once he'd drugged her because he was planning to pound bones to dust in the basement, or needed to load a corpse into the van by night, he now began lacing her gin-and-oranges with barbiturates purely to avoid the tedium of her company.

Creed's manner towards Violet also changed. He became 'mean' to her, 'taking the Mickey when there was no need, saying nasty things, laughing at me for using the wrong words and stuff, treating me like I was stupid, which he'd never done before.

'I remember one time, I was telling him about the place my brother bought when he retired, cottage in the country, every-thing lovely, and I said, "You should've seen the garden, his roses and a gazebo," and he laughed at me, Dennis, well, jeered, really, because I'd said it wrong. *Gazzy*bo, I said, and I've never forgotten it, he said, "Don't use words if you can't say 'em, you just look thick."

'It hurt my feelings. I hadn't seen that

nasty side of him. I knew he was clever, he used to do the *Times* crossword every day. Knew all the answers on *Mastermind*, when we watched it together, but he'd never put me down before.

'Then, one night, he starts going on about my will. He wants to know who I'm going to leave the house to. He as good as asked me to leave it to him.

'I didn't like that. I wasn't an old woman, I wasn't planning to die any time soon. I changed the subject, but he started on it again a few nights later. I said, "Look, how d'you think that makes me feel, Dennis, you going on like this, like I'm on my last legs? You're making me feel like you're going to do away with me."

'He got uppity and said it was all right for me, but he had nothing, no security or nothing, and what if he got turfed out on the street by whoever I left the house to? And he flounced out. We made it up, later, but it left a nasty taste.'

It would seem the height of foolhardiness for Creed to persuade Violet into changing her will and then kill her. Quite apart from having an obvious motive, he'd be risking the ingression of police into the basement where he was concealing the remains and belongings of at least five women. However, Creed's arrogance and sense of inviolability seem to have known no bounds by this time. He was also stockpiling pills in larger quantities than ever, which brought him into contact with more than one street dealer. This made him more widely recognisable.

One of his new drugs contacts was Michael Cleat, who sold barbiturates stolen from a contact at a pharmaceutical company. Cleat would later cut a deal with police in exchange for his testimony at the killer's trial. Creed, he testified, had asked Cleat whether he or his contact could procure a doctor's prescription pad. Police suspected that Creed was hoping to fake a prescription for Violet, to explain her possession of the means to overdose . . .

In spite of the coffee, Strike's eyelids began to droop again. After another couple of minutes, his head sank sideways and the book slipped out of his slack grasp.

When he woke up again, the sky outside had turned coral pink, the laughing teenagers were gone, and he found himself ten minutes from Truro station. Stiffer than ever and in no mood for the family reunion, he wished he was heading back to his attic flat for a shower and some peace. Nevertheless, his heart lifted slightly when he saw Dave Polworth waiting for him on the platform. The bag of chocolate hedgehogs rattled slightly as

Strike clambered laboriously off the train. He'd have to remember to give the broken one to Luke.

'All right, Diddy?' said Polworth, as they shook hands and patted each other on the back, Strike's Waitrose bag impeding a hug.

'Thanks for picking me up, Chum, really appreciate it.'

They drove to St Mawes in Polworth's Dacia Duster, discussing plans for the following day. Polworth and his family had been invited to the scattering of the ashes, along with Kerenza the Macmillan nurse.

'. . . except it's not going to be a scattering,' said Polworth, driving through country lanes, as the sun turned into a burning coal on the horizon, 'more like a floating.'

'How's that?'

'Lucy's got an urn,' said Polworth. 'Water soluble, cotton and clay. She was showing me last night. It's supposed to look like a flower. You put the ashes inside and the whole thing bobs away and dissolves.'

'Nice idea,' said Strike.

'Prevents stupid accidents,' said Polworth, pragmatically. 'Remember Ian Restarick, from school? His grandad wanted his ashes thrown off Land's End. The dozy fuckers chucked them off in a high wind and ended up with their mouths full of the old boy. Restarick told me he was blowing ash out of his nose for a week after.'

Laughing, Strike felt his phone buzz in his

pocket, and pulled it out. He was hoping the text might be Robin, perhaps telling him she'd already located Betty Fuller. Instead, he saw an unknown number.

I hated you as much as I did because I loved you so much. My love never ended but yours did. It wore out. I wore it out

Polworth was still talking, but Strike was no longer listening. He read the text through several times, frowning slightly, then put the phone back in his pocket and tried to concentrate on his old friend's anecdotes.

At Ted's house there were cries of welcome, and hugs from his uncle, Lucy and Jack. Strike tried to look delighted to be there, in spite of his fatigue, and knowing he'd have to wait to sleep until everyone else had gone to bed. Lucy had made pasta for everyone, and when she wasn't tending to everybody else's needs, telling Luke off for kicking Adam or picking at her own plate, she teetered on the verge of tears.

'It's so strange, isn't it?' she whispered to her brother after dinner, while Greg and the boys, at Greg's insistence, were clearing the table, 'Being here without her?' And without a pause she hurried on, 'We've decided we're going to do the ashes in the morning, because the weather looks good, and then come back here for Easter lunch.'

'Sounds great,' said Strike.

He knew how much importance Lucy placed on arrangements and plans, on having everything done in the right way. She fetched the urn and admired the stylised white lily. Ted had already placed Joan's ashes inside.

'That's great. Joan would have loved it,' he said, with no idea whether that was true or not.

'And I've bought pink roses for all of us to throw into the water with it,' said Lucy, tears welling again.

'Nice touch,' said Strike, suppressing a yawn. He really did just want to shower, then lie down and sleep. 'Thanks for sorting all this out, Luce. Oh, and I brought Easter eggs for the boys, where do you want them?'

'We can put them in the kitchen. Did you remember to get some for Roz and Mel, too?'

'Who?'

'Dave and Penny's girls, they'll be coming tomorrow, too.'

Fuck's sake.

'I didn't think—'

'Oh, Stick,' said Lucy, 'aren't you their godfather?'

'No, I'm not,' said Strike, doing his very best not to sound short tempered, 'but fine, yeah, I'll nip down the shops tomorrow morning and buy some more.'

Later, when he was at last alone in the dark sitting room, lying on the sofa with which he'd become so unwillingly familiar over the past year, his prosthetic leg propped against the coffee table, he checked his phone again. There were, he was pleased to see, no more messages from the unknown number, and, exhausted as he was, he managed to fall asleep quickly.

However, at shortly before four in the morning, the phone rang. Jerked out of a profound sleep, Strike groped for it, registered the time then raised it to his ear.

'Hello?'

There was a long silence, although he could hear breathing on the end of the line.

'Who is this?' he said, suspecting the answer.

'Bluey,' came a tiny whisper. 'It's me.'

'It's four in the morning, Charlotte.'

'I know,' she whispered, and gave what might have been a giggle or a sob. She sounded strange; possibly manic. Strike stared up at the dark ceiling, his aunt's ashes a mere twelve feet away.

'Where are you?'

'In hell.'

'Charlotte—'

She hung up.

Strike could hear his own heart beating with ominous force, like a kettle drum deep inside a cave. Red-hot threads of panic and dread darted through him.

How many more burdens was he supposed to bear? Had he not paid enough, given enough, sacrificed enough – loved enough? Joan seemed very close just now, in the darkness of her own sitting room, with her ornamental plates and her dried flowers, closer even than her dusty remains, in that vaguely ludicrous white lily, which would look so puny and insignificant bobbing away on the wide sea, like a discarded paper plate. He seemed to hear her last words as he lay there: 'You're a good man . . . helping people . . . I'm proud of you . . .'

Charlotte had called him from the same unknown number she'd texted from earlier. Strike's exhausted mind now eddied around the known facts, which were that Charlotte had suicide attempts in her past, that she was married with children, and that she'd recently been committed to a mental facility. He remembered his resolution of weeks ago, to phone her husband if she sent him any more self-destructive messages, but Jago Ross wouldn't be at his merchant bank at 4 a.m. on an Easter weekend. He wondered whether it would be cruelty or kindness to ignore the call, and how he'd bear the knowledge that she'd overdosed, if he didn't respond. After a very long ten minutes, during which he half expected her to call him back, Strike sat up to compose a text.

I'm in Cornwall. My aunt's just died. I think you need help, but I'm the wrong person to give it to you. If you're alone, you need to get hold of someone and tell them how you're feeling.

The terrible thing was how well he and Charlotte knew each other. Strike knew just how pusillanimous, how disingenuous, Charlotte would find this bland response. She'd know that some small part of him (shrunken by determined abstinence, though never eradicated) felt a pull back towards her, especially in this extremity, not only because he'd assumed responsibility for her happiness for years, but because he could never forget that she'd come to him when he was at his lowest ebb, lying in a hospital bed with a freshly amputated leg, wondering what possible life there was for him now. He could still remember her appearing in the doorway, the most beautiful woman he'd ever seen, and how she'd walked down the ward towards him and kissed him wordlessly on the mouth, and that moment, more than any other, had told him that life would continue, would contain glorious moments of beauty and pleasure, that he wasn't alone any more, and that his missing leg didn't matter to the woman he couldn't forget.

Sitting in the darkness, atypically cold because of his exhaustion, Strike typed four more words –

It will get better

– and sent the message. Then he lay back down and waited for the phone to vibrate again, but it remained silent, and eventually he fell asleep.

He was woken, inevitably, by Luke bursting into the sitting room. While he listened to Luke clattering around the kitchen, Strike reached for his phone and looked at it. Charlotte had sent two more texts, one an hour previously, the next half an hour later.

Bluey I'm sorry about your aunt. is it the one I met?

And then, when Strike hadn't answered:

Am I evil? Jago says I am. I used to think I couldn't be, because you loved me

At least she wasn't dead. With a vice-like sensation in his belly, Strike sat up, put on his prosthesis and attempted to shut Charlotte out of his mind.

Breakfast wasn't a particularly relaxing affair. The table was so crowded with Easter eggs, it was like being in some cartoonish nest. Strike ate off a plate on his lap. Lucy had bought Strike and Ted an egg each, and the detective now gathered that he should have bought his sister one, as well. All three boys had tottering piles.

'What's a hedgehog got to do with Easter?' Adam asked Strike, holding up his uncle's offering.

'Eastertime's spring, isn't it?' said Ted, from the end of the table. 'It's when hibernating animals wake up.'

'Mine's all broken,' said Luke, shaking the box.

'That's a shame,' said Strike, and Lucy shot him a sharp look.

She was tense, telling off her sons for looking at their phones during the meal, glaring at Strike when he checked his own, constantly glancing out of the window, to check the state of the weather. The detective was glad of an excuse to get out of the house to buy Polworth's daughters Easter eggs, but he'd walked barely ten yards down the sloping road, cigarette in hand, when the family pulled up in their Dacia. When Strike confided his errand in an undertone, Polworth said,

'Fuck that, they've got enough chocolate for a year at home. Leave it.'

At eleven o'clock, with a leg of lamb left in the oven and the timer set, after Luke had been told that no, he couldn't take his iPad on the boat, and one false start, due to the need to return to the house for the Polworths' younger daughter to have the pee she'd insisted she didn't need before they left, the party made its way successfully down to the harbour, where they met Kerenza the nurse, and boarded Ted's old sailing boat, *Jowanet*.

Strike, who'd once been his uncle's proud help-meet, no longer had the balance to work either sails or rudder. He sat with the women and children, spared the necessity of making conversation by the noise of wind against canvas. Ted shouted commands to Polworth and Jack. Luke was eating chocolate, his eyes screwed up against the cold breeze; Polworth's daughters were huddled, shivering, beside their mother, who had her arms around them. Tears were already trickling down Lucy's cheeks as she cradled the flat white urn in her lap. Beside her, Kerenza held a bunch of dark pink roses loosely wrapped in cellophane, and it was left to Greg and Polworth to shout at the children to watch out for the boom as they tacked around the peninsula where St Mawes Castle stood sentinel.

The surface of the sea changed from second to second, from rippling plain of sage and grey, to mesh of diamond-bright sparkles. The smell of ozone was as familiar and comforting to Strike as that of beer. He was just thinking how glad he was that Joan had chosen this, and not a grave, when he felt his phone vibrate against his chest. Unable to resist the temptation to read what he knew would be a text from Charlotte, he pulled it out and read it.

I thought you'd come back I thought you'd stop me marrying him I didn't think you'd let me do it

He put the phone back into his pocket. Luke was watching him and Strike thought he saw the idea occur of asking why Uncle Cormoran could look at his phone, whereas he was banned from bringing his iPad, but the look his uncle gave him seemed to make him think better of the idea, and he merely stuffed more chocolate in his mouth.

A feeling of constraint seemed to fall over everyone, even Luke, as Ted turned the boat into the wind and brought the boat slowly to a halt, the sail flapping loudly in the wind, St Mawes Castle now the size of a sandcastle in the distance. Kerenza handed around the roses, one for everyone except Ted, who took the remainder of the bouquet between the hands that were forever sunburned. Nobody spoke, and yet the moment didn't feel anticlimactic. While the sails flapped angrily overhead, Ted bent low over the side of the boat and dropped the urn gently into the sea, murmuring his farewell, and the object Strike had imagined would look inadequate and tawdry became, precisely because of its smallness as it bobbed gallantly on the ocean, affecting, and strangely noble. Soon, the last earthly remains of Joan Nancarrow would dissolve into the sea, and only the pink roses, tossed one by one into the sea by each of them, would remain to show the place where she'd disappeared.

Strike put his arm around Lucy, who rested her head on his shoulder, as they sailed back to shore. Rozwyn, the elder of Polworth's daughters, broke into sobs initially provoked by the sight of the urn vanishing in the distance, but sustained by her enjoyment of her own grief and the sympathy of her mother. Strike watched until he could no longer see the white dot, then turned his eyes towards shore, thinking of the leg of lamb waiting for them back at the house.

His phone vibrated yet again, minutes after he'd regained firm ground. While Polworth helped Ted tie up the boat, Strike lit a cigarette and turned away from the group to read the new text.

I want to die speaking the truth people are such liars everyone I know lies in such if them swant to stop pretending

'I'll walk back,' he told Lucy.

'You can't,' she said at once, 'lunch'll be ready for us—'

'I'm going to want another one of these,' Strike said firmly, holding up his cigarette in her disapproving face. 'I'll meet you up there.'

'Want company, Diddy?' asked Polworth. 'Penny can take the girls back up to the house.'

'No, you're all right, mate,' said Strike. 'Need to make a work call,' he added quietly, so that Lucy couldn't hear. As he said it, he felt his mobile vibrate again.

'Goodbye, Corm,' said Kerenza, her freckled face kindly as ever. 'I'm not coming for lunch.'

'Great,' said Strike, 'no, sorry, I mean – thanks for coming, Kerenza, Joan was so fond of you.'

When Kerenza had finally got into her Mini, and the family's cars were driving away, Strike pulled out his phone again.

Never forget that I loved you goodbye blues x

Strike called the number. After a few rings, it went to voicemail.

'Charlotte, it's me,' said Strike. 'I'm going to keep ringing till you pick up.'

He hung up and dialled again. The number went to voicemail for a second time.

Strike began to walk, because his anxiety required action. The streets around the harbour weren't busy. Most people would be sitting down to Easter lunch. Over and again he dialled Charlotte's number, but she didn't answer.

It was as though a wire was tightening around his skull. His neck was rigid with tension. From second to second his feelings fluctuated between rage, resentment, frustration and fear. She'd always been an expert manipulator. She'd also narrowly escaped death by her own hand, twice.

The phone might be going unanswered because she was already dead. There could be sporting guns at the Castle of Croy, where her husband's family had lived for generations. There'd be heavy-duty medications at the clinic: she might have stockpiled them. She might even have taken a razor blade to herself, as she'd once tried to do during one of her and Strike's more vicious rows.

After calling the number for the tenth time, Strike came to a halt, looking out over the railings at the pitiless sea, which breathed no consolation as it rushed to and then retreated from the shore. Memories of Joan, and the way she'd clung so fiercely to life, flooded his mind: his anxiety about Charlotte was laced with fury, for throwing life away.

And then his phone rang.

'Where are you?' he almost shouted.

'Bluey?'

She sounded drunk, or very stoned.

'*Where are you?*'

'. . . told you,' she mumbled. 'Bluey, d'you 'member . . .'

'Charlotte, WHERE ARE YOU?'

'Told you, S'monds . . .'

He turned and began to half-run, half-hobble back the way he'd come: there was an old-fashioned red telephone box twenty yards back, and with his free hand he was already pulling coins from his trouser pocket.

'Are you in your room? *Where are you?*'

The telephone box smelled urinous, of cigarette butts and dirt from a thousand silt-clogged soles.

'C'n see sky . . . Bluey, I'm so . . .'

She was still mumbling, her breathing slow.

'One one eight, one one eight?' said a cheery voice through the receiver in his left hand.

'Symonds House, it's a residential psychiatric clinic in Kent.'

'Shall I connect—?'

'Yes, connect me . . . Charlotte, are you still there? Talk to me. Where are you?'

But she didn't answer. Her breathing was loud and becoming guttural.

'Symonds House,' said a bright female voice in his other ear.

'Have you got an in-patient there called Charlotte Ross?'

'I'm sorry, sir,' said the receptionist, 'we don't disclose—'

'She's overdosed. She's just called me from your facility, and she's overdosed. You need to find her – she might be outside, have you got grounds there?'

'Sir, can I ask you—?'

'*Check Charlotte Ross's whereabouts, now, I've got her on another line and she's overdosed.*'

He heard the woman speaking to someone away from the phone.

'. . . Mrs Ross . . . first floor, just to make . . .'

The voice spoke in his ear again, still professionally bright, but anxious now.

'Sir, what number is Mrs Ross calling from? She – in-patients don't have their own mobiles.'

'She's got one from somewhere,' said Strike, 'as well as a shitload of drugs.'

Somewhere in the background of the call he heard shouting, then loud footsteps. He tried to insert another coin into the slot, but it fell straight through and came out at the bottom.

'Fuck—'

'Sir, I'm going to ask you not to talk to me like that—'

'No, I just—'

The line went dead. Charlotte's breath was now barely audible.

Strike slammed as much change as he had in his pockets into the slot, then redialled telephone enquiries. Within a minute, he was again connected to the female voice at Symonds House.

'Symonds House—'

'Have you found her? I got cut off. Have you found her?'

'I'm afraid I can't disclose—' said the harassed-sounding woman.

'She got hold of a mobile and the means to kill herself on your watch,' said Strike, 'so you can bloody well disclose whether she's dead—'

'Sir, I'd appreciate you not shouting at me—'

But then Strike heard distant male voices through the mobile clamped to his other ear. There was no point hanging up and ringing: Charlotte hadn't heard his ten previous calls. She must have the mobile on silent.

'SHE'S HERE!' he bellowed, and the woman on the payphone line shrieked in shock. 'FOLLOW MY VOICE, SHE'S HERE!'

Strike was bellowing into the phone, well aware of the almost impossible odds of searchers hearing him: he could hear swishing and cracking, and knew that Charlotte was outside, probably in undergrowth.

Then, through the mobile, he heard a man shout.

'Shit, she's here – SHE'S HERE! Fuck . . . get an ambulance!'

'Sir,' said the shell-shocked woman, now that Strike had stopped yelling, 'could I have your name?'

But Strike hung up. Over the sound of his change clattering into the returned coin box, he continued to listen to the two men who'd found Charlotte, one of them shouting details of her overdose to the emergency services, the other repeatedly calling Charlotte's name, until somebody noticed that the mobile beside her was active, and turned it off.

CHAPTER 55

Of louers sad calamities of old,
Full many piteous stories doe remaine . . .

Edmund Spenser
The Faerie Queene

As a noted beauty and socialite with a tantalising number of celebrity connections and a rebellious, self-destructive past, Charlotte was an old staple of the gossip columns. Naturally, her emergency hospitalisation out of a private psychiatric clinic made news.

The tabloids ran photo-heavy stories, showing Charlotte at the ages of fourteen (when she'd first run away from her private school and sparked a police hunt), eighteen (arm in arm with her well-known broadcaster father, a thrice-married heavy drinker), twenty-one (with her model-turned-socialite mother, at a cocktail party) and thirty-eight, where, as beautiful as ever, she smiled blankly alongside her white-blond husband, twin babies in her arms, an exquisite drawing room in the background. Nobody had been able to find a picture of her with Cormoran Strike, but the fact that they'd once dated, which Charlotte herself had been careful to mention to the press when she got engaged to Jago, ensured that his name appeared in print alongside hers. 'Emergency hospitalisation', 'history of addiction issues', 'troubled past': though the tabloids didn't say so explicitly, only the most naive reader could be left in doubt that Charlotte had attempted to take her own life. The story gained a second wind when an unnamed 'inside source' at Symonds House confided that the future Viscountess Ross had 'allegedly' been found face down in a shrubbery, right behind an old summer house.

The broadsheets' stories led with the questionable practices of the exorbitantly priced Symonds House, 'which' (said the *Telegraph*) 'has a reputation for being the last resort of the wealthy and well-connected. Controversial treatments include transcranial magnetic stimulation and the hallucinogen psilocybin (more commonly known as magic mushrooms).' They, too, used large photographs of Charlotte to embellish their stories, so Robin, who furtively read all of them and felt guilty afterwards, was reminded constantly how very beautiful Strike's ex had always been.

Strike hadn't mentioned a word of the business to Robin, and she hadn't asked. A moratorium had lain over Charlotte's name ever since that night, four years previously, when Robin had still been the temp, and an extremely drunk Strike confided in her that Charlotte had lied about being pregnant with his child. All Robin knew right now was that Strike had returned from Cornwall in a particularly buttoned-up mood, and while she knew that the disposal of his aunt's ashes must have been a sad occasion, she couldn't help suspecting this other source for his moodiness.

Out of loyalty to Strike, she refused to gossip about his ex, even though everyone around her seemed to want to talk about it. A week after Strike returned from Cornwall, Robin entered the office, already in a bad mood because Matthew had again postponed mediation. On seeing the door open, Pat the secretary hastily tried to hide a copy of the *Daily Mail* she'd been poring over with Morris. On realising that the new arrival was Robin rather than Strike, Pat had given her raven's caw of laughter and slapped the paper back onto her desk.

'Caught red-handed,' said Morris with a wink at Robin. 'Seen all this about the boss's ex?'

He's not my boss, he's my partner, thought Robin, but she merely said, 'Yes.'

'Talk about punching above his bloody weight,' said Morris, examining a picture of Charlotte at twenty-one in a beaded mini-dress. 'The fuck did a bloke who looks like him end up with that?'

Robin wasn't even safe from it at home. Max, whose floppy hair had been cropped short to play the ex-army officer, had begun shooting his TV series, and was more cheerful than she'd ever known him. Max was also thoroughly intrigued to know that Strike had been involved with Charlotte for sixteen years.

'I met her once,' he told Robin, who'd come upstairs after several hours in her room, combing online records for Betty Fuller. The one-time prostitute was proving harder to find than she'd anticipated.

'Really?' said Robin, who both wanted and didn't want to hear the story.

'Yeah, I was in a play years ago with her half-brother. Simon Legard? He starred in that mini-series about the financial crash, what was it called? She came to watch our play and took us all out for dinner afterwards. I liked her, actually, she was a real laugh. Some of those posh girls are a lot funnier than you'd think.'

'Mm,' said Robin noncommittally, and she returned immediately to her room with her cup of tea.

'I bet she tried to call Corm before she did it,' was Ilsa's cool comment on the phone, two weeks after Easter, by which time Robin had succeeded, through patient cross-referencing, in identifying the woman she thought was most likely to be the Betty Fuller who'd lived in Skinner Street at the time of Margot Bamborough's disappearance. Betty was now living in sheltered housing in Sans Walk, not far from her original flat, and Robin planned to pay her a visit the following afternoon, after the mediation with Matthew which seemed at last to be going ahead.

Ilsa had rung to wish Robin good luck. Robin had been trying not to think about having to see Matthew, telling herself that the ordeal would be over in a couple of hours, but it had become progressively harder to focus on her list of questions for Betty Fuller as the evening progressed, and she'd been glad, initially, to be interrupted by Ilsa.

'What's Corm saying about the whole Charlotte thing?' Ilsa asked.

'Nothing,' said Robin truthfully.

'No, he never talks about her any more,' said Ilsa. 'I wonder how much longer her marriage is going to last. Must be hanging by a thread. I'm quite surprised it's limped on this long, actually. She only did it to get back at Corm.'

'Well, she's had children with Jago,' Robin pointed out, then instantly regretted it. Ilsa had already told her that she and Nick had decided not to try a fourth round of IVF.

'She never wanted kids,' said Ilsa. 'That was something she and Corm had in common. That, and having really similar mothers. Drink, drugs and a million men each, except Charlotte's is still alive. So, you haven't spoken to him about it all?'

'No,' said Robin, who was feeling marginally worse for this conversation, in spite of Ilsa's kind intentions. 'Ilsa, sorry, but I'd better go. I've got work to do for tomorrow.'

315

'Can't you take the afternoon off? We could meet for a coffee, you'll probably need some R&R afterwards. Corm wouldn't mind, would he?'

'I'm sure he wouldn't,' said Robin, 'but we're so busy, and I'm following up a lead. Anyway, work gives me something to think about other than Matthew. Let's catch up at the weekend, if you're free.'

Robin slept badly that night. It wasn't Charlotte who wove her way in and out of her dreams, but Miss Jones, the agency's client who, as everyone had now noticed, had taken such a shine to Strike that he'd had to ask Pat to stop putting her calls through. Robin woke before her alarm went off, glad to escape a complicated dream in which it was revealed that Miss Jones had been Matthew's wife all along, and that Robin was defending herself against a charge of fraud at the end of a long, polished table in a dark boardroom.

Wanting to look professional and confident, she dressed in black trousers and jacket, even though Matthew knew perfectly well that she spent most of her investigative life in jeans. Casting one last look in her mirror before leaving her room, she thought she looked washed-out. Trying not to think about all those pictures of Charlotte Ross, who rarely dressed in anything but black, but whose porcelain beauty merely shone brighter in contrast, Robin grabbed her handbag and left her room.

While waiting for the Tube, Robin tried to

distract herself from the squirming feeling of nerves in her stomach by checking her emails.

Dear Miss Ellacott,

As previously stated I'm not prepared to talk to anyone except Mr Strike. This is not intended as any slight on you but I would feel more comfortable speaking man to man. Unfortunately, I will be unavailable from the end of next week due to work commitments which will be taking me out of the country. However I can make space on the evening of the 24th. If this is agreeable to Mr Strike, I suggest the American Bar in the Stafford hotel as a discreet meeting place. Kindly let me know if this is acceptable.

Sincerely,

CB Oakden

Twenty minutes later, when she'd emerged from Holborn Tube station and had reception again, Robin forwarded this message to Strike. She had a comfortable quarter of an hour to spare before her appointment and there were plenty of places to grab a coffee in her vicinity, but before she could do so, her mobile rang: it was Pat, at the office.

'Robin?' said the familiar croaking voice. 'D'you

know where Cormoran is? I've tried his phone but he's not picking up. I've got his brother Al here in the office, wanting to see him.'

'Really?' said Robin, startled. She'd met Al a couple of years previously, but knew that he and Strike weren't close. 'No, I don't know where he is, Pat. Have you left a message? He's probably somewhere he can't pick up.'

'Yeah, I've left a voicemail,' said Pat. 'All right, I'll keep trying him. Bye.'

Robin walked on, her desire for a coffee forgotten in her curiosity about Al turning up at the office. She'd quite liked Al when she'd met him; he seemed in slight awe of his older half-brother, which Robin had found endearing. Al didn't look much like Strike, being shorter, with straight hair, a narrow jaw and the slight divergent squint he'd inherited from their famous father.

Thinking about Strike's family, she turned the corner and saw, with a thrill of dread that brought her to a halt, Matthew climbing out of a taxi, wearing an unfamiliar dark overcoat over his suit. His head turned, and for a moment they were looking at each other, fifty yards apart like gunslingers ready to fire. Then Robin's mobile rang; she reached for it automatically, and when she'd put it to her ear and looked up, Matthew had disappeared into the building.

'Hello?'

'Hi,' said Strike, 'just got the email from Oakden. "Out of the country", my arse.'

Robin glanced at her watch. She still had five minutes, and her lawyer, Judith, was nowhere in sight. She drew back against the cold stone wall and said,

'Yeah, I thought that, too. Have you rung Pat back?'

'No, why?'

'Al's at the office.'

'Al who?'

'Your brother, Al,' said Robin.

There was a brief pause.

'Fuck's sake,' said Strike under his breath.

'Where are you?' asked Robin.

'At a B&Q in Chingford. Our blonde friend in Stoke Newington's shopping.'

'What for?'

'Rubber foam and MDF, for starters,' said Strike. 'That bloke from Shifty's gym's helping her. Where are you?'

'Waiting outside Matthew's lawyers. It's mediation morning,' said Robin.

'Shit,' said Strike, 'I forgot. Best of luck. Listen – take the rest of the day off, if you'd—'

'I don't want time off,' said Robin. She'd just spotted Judith in the distance, walking briskly towards her in a red coat. 'I'm planning to go and see Betty Fuller afterwards. I'd better go, Cormoran. Speak later.'

She hung up and walked forwards to meet Judith, who smiled broadly.

'All right?' she asked, patting Robin on the arm

with the hand not holding her briefcase. 'Should be fine. You let me do the talking.'

'Right,' said Robin, smiling back with as much warmth as she could muster.

They walked up the steps together into a small lobby area, where a stocky, suited man with a haircut like Caesar's came forward with a perfunctory smile, his hand outstretched to Judith.

'Ms Cobbs? Andrew Shenstone. Ms Ellacott? How d'you do?'

His handshake left Robin's hand throbbing. He and Judith walked ahead of Robin through double doors, chatting about London traffic, and Robin followed, dry-mouthed and feeling like a child trailing its parents. After a short walk up a dark corridor, they turned left into a small meeting room with an oval table and a shabby blue carpet. Matthew was sitting there alone, still wearing his overcoat. He readjusted himself in his chair when they entered. Robin looked directly into his face as she sat down, diagonally opposite him. To her surprise, Matthew looked instantly away. She'd imagined him glaring across the table, with that strange muzzle-like whitening around his mouth he'd worn during arguments towards the end of their marriage.

'Right then,' said Andrew Shenstone, with another smile, as Judith Cobbs opened the file she'd brought with her. He had a leather document holder sitting, closed, in front of him. 'Your client's position remains as stated in your letter of the fourteenth, Judith, is that correct?'

'That's right,' said Judith, her thick black glasses perched on the end of her nose as she scanned a copy of said letter. 'Ms Ellacott's perfectly happy to forgo any claim on your client, except in respect of the proceeds from the sale of the flat in – um—'

Hastings Road, thought Robin. She remembered moving into the cramped conversion with Matthew, excitedly carrying boxes of pot plants and books up the short path, Matthew plugging in the coffee machine that had been one of their first joint purchases, the fluffy elephant he'd given her so long ago, sitting on the bed.

'—Hastings Road, yes,' said Judith, scanning her letter, 'from which she'd like the ten thousand pounds her parents contributed to the deposit, upon purchase.'

'Ten thousand,' repeated Andrew Shenstone. He and Matthew looked at each other. 'In that case, we're agreeable.'

'You're . . . agreeable?' said Judith Cobbs, as surprised as Robin herself.

'My client's circumstances have changed,' said Shenstone. 'His priority now is securing the divorce as speedily as possible, which I think your client has indicated is also preferable to her, excepting the ten thousand pounds? Of course,' added Shenstone, 'we're almost at the requisite two years, so . . .'

Judith looked at Robin, who nodded, her mouth still dry.

'Then I think we can conclude things today. Very good indeed,' said Andrew Shenstone complacently, and it was impossible to escape the suspicion that he was addressing himself. 'I've taken the liberty of drawing up . . .'

He opened his document holder, spun it around on the polished table top and pushed it towards Judith, who read the document inside carefully.

'Yes,' she said finally, sliding the document sideways to Robin, who learned that Matthew was promising to transfer the money to Robin's account within seven days of signature. 'Happy?' Judith added in an undertone to Robin.

'Yes,' said Robin, slightly dazed.

What, she wondered, had been the point of dragging her here? Had it been one last demonstration of power, or had Matthew only decided that morning to give in? She reached into her handbag, but Judith was already holding out her own fountain pen, so Robin took it and signed. Judith passed the document back to Andrew Shenstone, who slid it over to Matthew, who scrawled a hasty signature. He glanced up at Robin when he'd done so, then looked quickly away again, and in that moment, Robin knew what had happened, and why he'd given her what she wanted.

'Very good,' said Andrew Shenstone again, and he slapped the table with his thick hand and laughed. 'Well, short and sweet, eh? I think we're . . .?'

'Yes,' said Judith, with a little laugh, 'I think we are!'

Matthew and Robin rose and watched their lawyers gathering up their things and, in Judith's case, pulling her coat back on. Disorientated by what had just happened, Robin again had the sensation of being a child with its parents, unsure how to quit the situation, waiting for the lawyers to release her.

Andrew Shenstone held the door open for Robin and she passed back into the corridor, heading towards the lobby. Behind her, the lawyers were talking about traffic again. When they paused in the lobby to take leave of each other, Matthew, after a brief word of thanks to Shenstone, walked straight out past Robin, into the street.

Robin waited for Andrew Shenstone to disappear inside the building again before addressing Judith.

'Thanks so much,' she said.

'Well, I didn't really do much, did I?' said Judith, laughing. 'But mediation often brings people to their senses, I've seen it happen before. Much harder to justify yourself in a room with objective observers.'

They shook hands, and Robin headed out into a spring breeze that blew her hair into her mouth. She felt slightly unsettled. Ten thousand pounds. She'd offered to give it back to her parents, knowing that they'd struggled to match Matthew's parents' contribution, but they'd told her to keep it. She'd have to settle her bill with Judith, of course, but the remainder would give her a buffer, maybe even help her back towards her own place.

She turned a corner and there, right in front of her, standing at the kerb, his arm raised in his attempt to hail a taxi, was Matthew.

Catching sight of her, he stood frozen for a moment, his hand still raised, and the taxi he'd been trying to hail slowed ten yards away, and picked up a couple instead.

'Sarah's pregnant, isn't she?' said Robin.

He looked down at her, not quite as tall as Strike, but as good-looking as he'd been at seventeen, on the day he'd asked her out.

'Yeah.' He hesitated. 'It was an accident.'

Was it hell, thought Robin. Sarah had always known how to get what she wanted. Robin realised at last how long a game Sarah had played: always present, giggling, flirting, prepared to settle for Matthew's best friend to keep him close. Then, as her clutch tightened, but Matthew threatened to slip through it, there'd been the diamond earring she'd left in Robin's bed and now, still more valuable, a pregnancy to make sure of him, before he could enter a dangerous state of singledom. Robin had a strong suspicion that this was what had lain behind the two postponements of mediation. Had a newly hormonal and insecure Sarah made scenes, frightened of Matthew coming face to face with Robin while he hadn't yet decided whether he wanted either the baby or its mother?

'And she wants to be married before she has it?'

'Yeah,' said Matthew. 'Well, so do I.'

Did the image of their own wedding flash across his mind, as it flashed across Robin's? The church in Masham that both of them had attended since primary school, the reception in that beautiful hotel, with the swans in the lake that refused to swim together, and the disastrous reception, during which Robin had known, for a few terrifying seconds, that if Strike had asked her to leave with him, she'd have gone.

'How're things with you?'

'Great,' said Robin.

She put up a good front. What you do, when you meet the ex, isn't it? Pretend you think you did the right thing. No regrets.

'Well,' he said, as the traffic rolled past, 'I need to . . .'

He began to walk away.

'Matt.'

He turned back.

'What?'

'I'll never forget . . . how you were, when I really needed you. Whatever else . . . I'll never forget that part.'

For a fraction of a second, his face worked slightly, like a small boy's. Then he walked back to her, bent down, and before she knew what was happening, he'd hugged her quickly, then let go as though she was red hot.

'G'luck, Robs,' he said thickly, and walked away for good.

CHAPTER 56

Whereas this Lady, like a sheepe astray,
Now drowned in the depth of sleepe all
*   fearlesse lay.*

Edmund Spenser
The Faerie Queene

At the precise moment Matthew turned to
walk away from Robin in Holborn, Strike,
who was sitting in his parked car three
miles away, outside the familiar terraced house in
Stoke Newington, decided to call his brother, lest
Al sit in wait for him at the office all day. The
detective's anger was shot through with other, less
easily identifiable feelings, of which the least
painful to acknowledge was grudging admiration
for Al's persistence. Strike didn't doubt that Al
had come to the office for a last-ditch attempt to
persuade Strike into some form of reconciliation
with his father, preferably before or during the
party to celebrate his father's new album. Having
always considered Al a fairly weak and sybaritic

326

character, Strike had to admit he was showing guts, risking his older brother's fury.

Strike waited until Elinor Dean had unloaded the foam and the cheap wood from her car and carried it all inside with the aid of her friend from Shifty's gym, watched the front door close, then called Al's number.

'Hi,' said Al, picking up after a single ring.

'Why are you in my office?' asked Strike.

'Wanted to see you, bruv. Talk face to face.'

'Well, I won't be back there today,' lied Strike. 'So I suggest you say whatever it is you've got to say now.'

'Bruv—'

'Who's there with you?'

'Er – your secretary – Pat, is it?' Strike heard Al turn away from his mobile to check, and heard Pat's caw of agreement, 'and a bloke called—'

'Barclay,' said the Scot loudly, in the background.

'Right, well, go into my office for some privacy,' said Strike. He listened while Al told Pat what Strike had asked him to do, heard the familiar sound of his own office door closing, then said,

'If this is about what I think it's about—'

'Cormoran, we didn't want to tell you this, but Dad's got cancer.'

Oh, for fuck's sake.

Strike leaned forwards momentarily and rested his forehead on the steering wheel of his car, before he sat up again.

'Prostate,' Al continued. 'They reckon they've caught it early. But we thought you should know, because this party isn't just about celebrating the band's anniversary, and the new album. It's about giving him something to look forward to.'

There was a silence.

'We thought you should know,' Al repeated.

Why should I fucking know? thought Strike, eyes on the closed door of Elinor Dean's house. He had no relationship with Rokeby. Did Al expect him to weep, to rush to Rokeby's side, to express compassion or pity? Rokeby was a multimillionaire. Doubtless he'd enjoy the very best treatment. The memory of Joan's lily urn bobbing away on the sea recurred as Strike said,

'OK, well, I don't really know how to respond to that. I'm sure it's a bugger for everyone who cares about him.'

Another long silence followed.

'We thought this might make a difference,' said Al quietly.

'To what?'

'To your attitude.'

'As long as they've caught it early, he'll be fine,' said Strike bracingly. 'Probably live to father another couple of kids he never sees.'

'Jesus Christ!' said Al, really angry now. 'You might not give a shit, but he happens to be my dad—'

'I give a shit about people who've ever given a shit about me,' said Strike, 'and keep your fucking voice down, those are my employees you're airing my private business in front of.'

'*That's* your priority?'

Strike thought of Charlotte who, according to the papers, remained in hospital, and of Lucy, who was agitating to know whether Strike would be able to take the weekend off, to join Ted at her house in Bromley for the weekend. He thought of the clients in the Shifty case, who were hinting they'd terminate payment in a week's time unless the agency found out what hold Shifty had on his boss. He thought of Margot Bamborough, and the rapidly vanishing year they'd been allotted to find out what had happened to her. Inexplicably, he thought of Robin, and the fact that he'd forgotten that today was her mediation session with Matthew.

'I've got a life,' said Strike, keeping a curb on his temper only by exercising maximum self-control, 'which is hard and complicated, just like everyone else's. Rokeby's got a wife and half a dozen kids and I'm at maximum capacity for people who need me. I'm not coming to his fucking party, I'm not interested in hearing from him, I don't want a relationship with him. I don't know how much clearer I can make this, Al, but I'm—'

The line went dead. Without regretting anything he'd said, but nevertheless breathing heavily, Strike threw his mobile onto the passenger seat, lit a cigarette and watched Elinor Dean's front door for another fifteen minutes until, on a sudden whim, he snatched up the phone from beside him again, and called Barclay.

'What are you doing right now?'

'Filin' my expenses,' said the Scot laconically. 'That casino cost ye a fortune.'

'Is my brother still there?'

'No, he left.'

'Good. I need you to come and take over in Stoke Newington.'

'I havenae got my car wi' me.'

'OK, well, fuck it, then,' said Strike angrily.

'I'm sorry, Strike,' said Barclay, 'but I'm s'posed tae have this afternoon off—'

'No, *I'm* sorry,' said Strike, closing his eyes. He had the same sensation of a wire tightening around his forehead that he'd experienced in St Mawes. 'Getting frustrated. Enjoy your afternoon off. Seriously,' he added, in case Barclay thought he was being sarcastic.

Having hung up on Barclay, Strike rang Robin.

'How did mediation go?'

'Fine,' said Robin, though she sounded strangely flat. 'We've settled.'

'Great!'

'Yeah. It's a relief.'

'Did you say you're going to Betty Fuller's?'

'Yes, I was just about to head into the Tube.'

'Remind me where she lives?'

'Sheltered housing on Sans Walk in Clerkenwell.'

'OK, I'll meet you there,' said Strike.

'Really? I'm fine to—'

'I know, but I want to be there,' Strike cut across her.

He pulled away from Elinor Dean's house knowing that he'd just been abrasive towards his two favourite colleagues. If he was going to vent his temper, it could at least have been at Pat and Morris's expense.

Twenty minutes later, Strike entered Clerkenwell via Percival Street. To his right were the nondescript red-brick flats where Janice Beattie and Steve Douthwaite had once lived, and he wondered yet again what had become of Margot's one-time patient, whose whereabouts, in spite of his and Robin's best efforts, remained unknown.

Sans Walk was a narrow pedestrianised one-way street. Strike parked his BMW as close to it as possible. The day was surprisingly warm, in spite of a good amount of cloud. As he approached Sans Walk, he saw Robin waiting for him at the entrance.

'Hi,' she said. 'It's up the other end, that red-brick modern building with the circular tower thing on top.'

'Great,' said Strike, as they set off together. 'Sorry for earlier, I—'

'No, it's fine,' said Robin, 'I know we really need results soon.'

But Strike thought he detected a slight coolness.

'Al pissed me off,' he explained. 'So I might've been a bit—'

'Cormoran, it's fine,' repeated Robin, but with a smile that reassured Strike.

'Great news about the mediation,' he said.

'Yes,' said Robin, though she didn't look particularly pleased. 'So, what d'you think's the best tack to take with Betty Fuller?'

'Be honest and direct about who we are and what we're investigating,' said Strike, 'and then play it by ear, I think. And hope to Christ she's not demented . . .'

Priory House was a modern, multi-level building with a shared garden at the back. As they approached the front doors, a middle-aged couple came out; they had the relieved look of people who'd just done their duty, and, smiling at Strike and Robin, they held open the door to let them walk inside.

'Thanks very much,' said Robin, smiling at them, and as the couple walked on, she heard the woman say,

'At least she remembered who we are, this time . . .'

Had it not been for the mobility scooters, the place would have resembled a hall of residence, with its hardy dark grey carpet underfoot, its bulletin board bristling with pamphlets and a depressing smell of communal cooking hanging in the air.

'She's on the ground floor,' said Robin, pointing towards a corridor. 'I checked the names on the buzzer.'

They passed a number of identical pine doors until they reached the one with 'Elizabeth Fuller' printed on a card in a metal holder. Through the wood came the muffled sounds of voices. Just as it had been when he'd visited Janice Beattie, the TV was turned up very high inside. Strike rapped hard on the door.

After a lengthy wait, the door opened very slowly to reveal a panting old lady wearing a nasal cannula, who'd pulled her oxygen tank to the door with her. Over her shoulder, Strike saw a TV blaring the reality show *The Only Way is Essex*.

'*I'm fine. You just upset me, Arg,*' a heavily made-up girl in bright blue was saying onscreen.

Betty Fuller looked as though she'd been subject to heavier gravity than the rest of humankind. Everything about her had sagged and drooped: the corners of her lipless mouth, her papery eyelids, her loose jowls, the tip of her thin nose. It appeared that the flesh had been sucked down out of her upper body into her lower: Betty had almost no bust, but her hips were broad and her poor bare legs were immensely swollen, both ankles thicker than her neck. She wore what looked like a pair of men's slippers and a dark green knitted dress on which there were several stains. A yellowish scalp was clearly visible through the sparse grey hair slicked back off her face and a hearing aid was prominent in her left ear.

'Who're you?' she wheezed, looking from Robin to Strike.

'Afternoon, Mrs Fuller,' said Strike loudly and clearly, 'my name's Cormoran Strike and this is Robin Ellacott.'

He pulled his driver's licence out of his pocket and showed it to her, with his card. She made an impatient gesture, to show she couldn't read them; her eyes were milky with glaucoma.

'We're private detectives,' said Strike, voice still raised over the arguing pair on-screen ('*At the end of the day, Lucy, she slept, on a one-night stand, wiv a boy*—' '*Arg – Arg – Arg – this is irrelevant*—').

'We've been hired to try and find out what happened to Margot Bamborough. She was a doctor who—'

''Oo?'

'Dr Margot Bamborough,' Strike repeated, still more loudly. 'She went missing from Clerkenwell in 1974. We heard you—'

'Oh yeah . . .' said Betty Fuller, who appeared to need to draw breath every few words. 'Dr Bamborough . . . yeah.'

'Well, we wondered whether we could talk to you about her?'

Betty Fuller stood there for what seemed a very long twenty seconds, thinking this over, while onscreen a young man in a maroon suit said to the over-made-up girl, '*I didn't wanna bring it up but you come over to me*—'

Betty Fuller made an impatient gesture, turned and shuffled back inside. Strike and Robin glanced at each other.

'Is it all right to come in, Mrs Fuller?' asked Strike loudly.

She nodded. Having carefully positioned her oxygen tank, she fell back into her armchair, then tugged the knitted dress in an effort to make it cover her knees. Strike and Robin entered the room and Strike closed the door. Watching the old lady struggle to pull her dress down, Robin had an urge to take a blanket off the unmade bed, and place it decorously over her lap.

Robin had discovered during her research that Betty was eighty-four. The old lady's physical state shocked her. The small room smelled of BO and urine. A door showed a small toilet leading off the single bedroom. Through the open wardrobe door, Robin saw crumpled clothes which had been thrown there, and two empty wine bottles, half hidden in underwear. There was nothing on the walls except a cat calendar: the month of May showed a pair of ginger kittens peeking out from between pink geranium blossoms.

'Would it be all right to turn this down?' Strike shouted over the TV, where the couple onscreen continued to argue, the woman's eyelashes as thick as woolly bear caterpillars.

'Turn it . . . off,' said Betty Fuller. ''S a recording.'

The Essex voices were suddenly extinguished. The two detectives looked around. There were only two choices for seats: the unmade bed and a hard, upright chair, so Robin took the former,

335

Strike the latter. Removing his notebook from his pocket, Strike said,

'We've been hired by Dr Bamborough's daughter, Mrs Fuller, to try and find out what happened to her.'

Betty Fuller made a noise like 'hurhm', which sounded disparaging, although Strike thought it might also have been an attempt to clear phlegm out of her throat. She rocked slightly to one side in her chair and pulled ineffectually at the back of her dress. Her swollen lower legs were knotted with varicose veins.

'So, you remember Dr Bamborough disappearing, do you, Mrs Fuller?'

'. . . 'es,' she grunted, still breathing heavily. In spite of her incapacity and unpromising manner, Strike had the impression of somebody both more alert than they might appear at first glance, and happier to have company and attention than the unprepossessing exterior might suggest.

'You were living in Skinner Street then, weren't you?'

She coughed, which seemed to clear her lungs, and in a slightly steadier voice, she said,

'Was there till . . . last year. Michael Cliffe . . . 'Ouse. Top floor. Couldn't manage, no more.'

Strike glanced at Robin; he'd expected her to lead the interrogation, assumed Betty would respond better to a woman, but Robin seemed oddly passive, sitting on the bed, her gaze wandering over the small room.

'Were you one of Dr Bamborough's patients?' Strike asked Betty.

'Yeah,' wheezed Betty. 'I was.'

Robin was thinking, is this where single people end up, people without children to look out for them, without double incomes? In small boxes, living vicariously through reality stars?

Next Christmas, no doubt, she'd run into Matthew, Sarah and their new baby in Masham. She could just imagine Sarah's proud strut through the streets, pushing a top-of-the-range pushchair, Matthew beside her, and a baby with Sarah's white-blonde hair peeking over the top of the blankets. Now, when Jenny and Stephen ran into them, there'd be common ground, the shared language of parenthood. Robin decided there and then, sitting on Betty Fuller's bed, to make sure she didn't go home next Christmas. She'd offer to work through it, if necessary.

'Did you like Dr Bamborough?' Strike was asking Betty.

'She were . . . all right,' said Betty.

'Did you ever meet any of the other doctors at the practice?' asked Strike.

Betty Fuller's chest rose and fell with her laboured breathing. Though it was hard to tell with the nasal cannula in the way, Strike thought he saw a thin smile.

'Yeah,' she said.

'Which ones?'

'Brenner,' she said hoarsely, and coughed again.

'Needed an 'ouse call . . . 'mergency . . . she weren't available.'

'So Dr Brenner came out to see you?'

'Hurhm,' said Betty Fuller. 'Yeah.'

There were a few small, cheaply framed photographs on the windowsill, Robin noticed. Two of them showed a fat tabby cat, presumably a lamented pet, but there were also a couple showing toddlers, and one of two big-haired teenaged girls, wearing puff-sleeved dresses from the eighties. So you could end up alone, in near squalor, even if you had children? Was it solely money, then, that made the difference? She thought of the ten thousand pounds she'd be receiving into her bank account later that week, which would be reduced immediately by legal bills and council tax. She'd need to be careful not to fritter it away. She really needed to start saving, to start paying into a pension.

'You must have been seriously unwell, were you?' Strike was asking Betty. 'To need a house call?'

He had no particular reason for asking, except to establish a friendly conversational atmosphere. In his experience of old ladies, there was little they enjoyed more than discussing their health.

Betty Fuller suddenly grinned at him, showing chipped yellow teeth.

'You ever taken it . . . up the shitter . . . with a nine-inch cock?'

Only by exercising the utmost restraint did Robin prevent herself letting out a shocked laugh.

She had to hand it to Strike: he didn't so much as grin as he said,

'Can't say I have.'

'Well,' wheezed Betty Fuller, 'you can . . . take it from me . . . fuckin' . . . agony . . . geezer went at me . . . like a fucking power drill . . . split my arsehole open.'

She gasped for air, half-laughing.

'My Cindy 'ears me moanin' . . . blood . . . says "Mum, you gotta . . . get that seen to . . ." called . . . doctor.'

'Cindy's your—?'

'Daughter,' said Betty Fuller. 'Yeah . . . got two. Cindy and Cathy . . .'

'And Dr Brenner came out to see you, did he?' asked Strike, trying not to dwell on the mental image Betty had conjured.

'Yeah . . . takes a look . . . sends me to A&E, yeah . . . nineteen stitches,' said Betty Fuller. 'And I sat on . . . an ice pack . . . for a week . . . and no fuckin' money . . . comin' in . . . After that,' she panted, 'no anal . . . unless they was . . . payin' double and nuthin' over . . . six inches . . . neither.'

She let out a cackle of laughter, which ended in coughs. Strike and Robin were carefully avoiding looking at each other.

'Was that the only time you met Dr Brenner?' asked Strike, when the coughing had subsided.

'No,' croaked Betty Fuller, thumping her chest. 'I seen 'im regular . . . ev'ry Friday night . . . for monfs . . . after.'

She didn't seem to feel any qualms about telling Strike this. On the contrary, Strike thought she seemed to be enjoying herself.

'When did that arrangement start?' asked Strike.

'Couple o' weeks . . . after 'e seen me . . . for me arse,' said Betty Fuller. 'Knocked on me door . . . wiv 'is doctor's bag . . . pretendin' 'e'd . . . come to check . . . then 'e says . . . wants a regular 'pointment. Friday night . . . 'alf past six . . . tell the neighbours . . . medical . . . if they ask . . .'

Betty paused to cough noisily. When she'd quelled her rattling chest, she went on,

'. . . and if I told anyone . . . 'e'd go to the cops . . . say I was . . . extorting 'im . . .'

'Threatened you, did he?'

'Yeah,' panted Betty Fuller, though without rancour, 'but 'e wasn't . . . try'na get it . . . free . . . so I kep' . . . me mouf shut.'

'You never told Dr Bamborough what was going on?' asked Robin.

Betty looked sideways at Robin who, in Strike's view, had rarely looked as out of place as she did sitting on Betty's bed: young, clean and healthy, and perhaps Betty's drooping, occluded eyes saw his partner the same way, because she seemed to resent both question and questioner.

''Course I fuckin' . . . didn't. She tried ta get me to . . . stop working . . . Brenner . . . easiest job of the week.'

'Why was that?' asked Strike.

Betty laughed wheezily again.

''E liked me . . . lyin' still, like I was . . . coma . . . playin' dead. 'E fucked me . . . sayin' 'is dirty words . . . I pretended . . . couldn't 'ear . . . except once,' said Betty, with a half-chuckle, half-cough, 'the bleedin' fire alarm . . . went off 'alfway . . . I said . . . in 'is ear . . . "I'm not stayin' dead . . . if we're on fuckin' fire . . . I've got kids . . . next room . . ." 'E was livid . . . turned out it was . . . false alarm . . .'

She cackled, then coughed again.

'D'you think Dr Bamborough suspected Dr Brenner of visiting you?' asked Robin.

'No,' said Betty, testily, with another sideways glance. ''Course she fuckin' didn't . . . was eivver of us gonna tell 'er?'

'Was Brenner with you,' asked Strike, 'the night she went missing?'

'Yeah,' said Betty Fuller indifferently.

'He arrived and left at the usual times?'

'Yeah,' said Betty again.

'Did he keep visiting you, after Dr Bamborough disappeared?'

'No,' said Betty. 'Police . . . all over the surgery . . . no, 'e stopped comin' . . . I 'eard . . . 'e retired, not long after . . . Dead now, I s'pose?'

'Yes,' said Strike, 'he is.'

The ruined face bore witness to past violence. Strike, whose own nose had been broken, was sure Betty's hadn't originally been the shape it was now, with its crooked tip.

'Was Brenner ever violent to you?'

'Never.'

'While your – arrangement was going on,' said Strike, 'did you ever mention it to anyone?'

'Nope,' said Betty.

'What about after Brenner retired?' asked Strike. 'Did you happen to tell a man called Tudor Athorn?'

'Clever, aincha?' said Betty, with a cackle of mild surprise. 'Yeah, I told Tudor . . . 'e's long gawn, 's well . . . used to drink . . . wiv Tudor. 'Is nephew's . . . still round 'ere . . . grown up . . . I seen 'im . . . about. Retarded,' said Betty Fuller.

'In your opinion,' said Strike, 'given what you know about Brenner, d'you think he'd have taken advantage of a patient?'

There was a pause. Betty's milky eyes surveyed Strike.

'On'y . . . if she was out cold.'

'Not otherwise?' said Strike.

Taking a deep breath of oxygen through her crooked nose, Betty said,

'Man like that . . . when there's one fing . . . what really . . . gets 'im off . . . that's all 'e wants . . .'

'Did he ever want to drug you?' asked Strike.

'No,' said Betty, 'didn't need to . . .'

'D'you remember,' asked Strike, turning a page in his notebook, 'a social worker called Wilma Bayliss?'

'Coloured girl?' said Betty. 'Yeah . . . you smoke, dontcha?' she added. 'Can smell it . . . give us

342

one,' she said, and out of the wrecked old body came a whiff of flirtatiousness.

'I don't think that's a good idea,' said Strike, smiling. 'Seeing as you're on oxygen.'

'Oh fuck off, then,' said Betty.

'Did you like Wilma?'

''Oo?'

'Wilma Bayliss, your social worker.'

'She were . . . like they all are,' said Betty, with a shrug.

'We spoke to Mrs Bayliss's daughters recently,' said Strike. 'They were telling us about the threatening notes that were sent to Dr Bamborough, before she disappeared.'

Betty breathed in and out, her collapsed chest doing its valiant best for her, and a small squeak issued from her ruined lungs.

'Do you know anything about those notes?'

'No,' said Betty. 'I 'eard . . . they'd bin sent. Everyone 'eard, round 'ere.'

'Who did they hear it from?'

'Probably that Irene Bull . . .'

'You remember Irene, do you?'

With many more pauses to catch her breath, Betty Fuller explained that her youngest sister had been in the same year as Irene at school. Irene's family had lived in a road off Skinner Street: Corporation Row.

'Thought . . . 'er shit . . . smelled of roses . . . that one,' said Betty. She laughed, but then broke yet again into a volley of hoarse coughs. When she'd recovered, she said, 'The police . . . asked 'em all . . . not to talk . . . but the mouth on . . . that girl . . . everyone knew . . . there'd been threats made.'

'According to Wilma's daughters,' said Strike, watching for Betty's reaction, 'you knew who sent those notes.'

'No, I never,' said Betty Fuller, no longer smiling.

'You were sure Marcus Bayliss hadn't sent them, though?'

'Marcus never . . . 'e was a lovely . . . y'know, I always liked . . . a darkie, me,' said Betty Fuller, and Robin, hoping Betty hadn't seen her wince, looked down at her hands. 'Very 'andsome . . . I'd've given it . . . 'im for free . . . hahaha . . . big, tall man,' said Betty wistfully, '. . . kind man . . . no, 'e never freatened no doctor.'

'So who d'you think—?'

'My second girl . . . my Cathy . . .' continued Betty, determinedly deaf, 'er dad was a darkie . . . dunno 'oo 'e was . . . condom split . . . I kept 'er 'cause . . . I like kids, but . . . she don't give a shit . . . about me. Smackhead!' said Betty fiercely. '*I* never touched it . . . seen too many . . . go that way . . . stole from me . . . I told 'er . . . keep the fuck . . . my 'ouse . . .

'Cindy's good,' gasped Betty. She was fighting her breathlessness now, though still relishing Strike's captive attention. 'Cindy . . . drops by. Earning . . . decent money . . .'

'Really?' said Strike, playing along, waiting for his opportunity. 'What does Cindy do?'

'Escort,' wheezed Betty. 'Lovely figure . . . up West . . . makin' more'n I ever . . . Arabs an' whatnot . . . but she says . . . "Ma, you wouldn't . . . like it these days . . . all they want . . . is anal."' Betty cackled, coughed and then, without warning, turned her head to look at Robin perched on the bed and said with vitriol: '*She* don't find it . . . funny, this one . . . do you?' she demanded of Robin, who was taken aback. ''S'pect . . . you give it away . . . for meals an' jewellery . . . an' fink it's . . . fink it's free . . . look at 'er face,' wheezed Betty, eyeing Robin with dislike, 'you're the same as . . . the sniffy fuckin' . . . social worker . . . we 'ad round . . . when I . . . minding Cathy's kids . . . gorn now,' said Betty, angrily. 'Took into care . . .

'"*New*, Mrs Fuller",' said Betty, adopting a grotesquely genteel accent, '"*new*, it meks . . . *new* diff'rence to *me* . . . 'ow yew ladies mek . . . ends meet . . . *sex work is work*" . . . they'll tell yer that . . . patronisin' . . . fuckin' . . . but would they . . . want *their* daughters . . . doin' it? *Would they fuck*,' said Betty Fuller, and she paid for her longest speech yet with her most severe spate of coughing.

'Cindy does . . . too much coke,' Betty wheezed, her eyes watering, when she could talk again. '. . . keeps the weight off . . . Cathy, it was smack . . . boyfriend . . . workin' for 'im . . . beat 'er blue . . . pregnant and lost it . . .'

'I'm sorry to hear that,' said Strike.

'It's all kids . . . on the street . . . these days,' said Betty, and a glimmer of what Strike thought was real distress showed through the determinedly tough exterior. 'Firteen, fourteen . . . children . . . my day . . . we'd've marched 'em . . . right back 'ome . . . it's all right, grown women, but kids – whatchew fucking starin' at?' she barked to Robin.

'Cormoran, I might—' said Robin, standing up and gesturing towards the door.

'Yeah, off you fuck,' said Betty Fuller, watching with satisfaction as Robin left her room. 'You doin' 'er, are you?' she wheezed at Strike, once the door had clicked shut behind Robin.

'No,' he said.

'What the fuck's . . . point, then?'

'She's very good at the job,' said Strike. 'When she's not up against someone like you, that is,' and Betty Fuller grinned, displaying her Cheddar-yellow teeth.

'Hahaha . . . I know . . . 'er type . . . knows fuckin' nothing . . . 'bout real life . . .'

'There was a man living in Leather Lane, back in Margot Bamborough's day,' said Strike. 'Name of Niccolo Ricci? "Mucky", they used to call him.'

Betty Fuller said nothing, but the milky eyes narrowed.

'What d'you know about Ricci?' asked Strike.

'Same as . . . ev'ryone,' said Betty.

Out of the corner of his eye, Strike saw Robin emerge into the daylight. She lifted her hair briefly off her neck, as though needing to remove weight from herself, then walked out of sight with her hands in her jacket pockets.

'It warn't Mucky . . . what freatened 'er,' said Betty. ''E wouldn't . . . write notes. Not 'is . . . style.'

'Ricci turned up at the St John's practice Christmas party,' said Strike. 'Which seemed odd.'

'Don't know . . . nuffin' 'bout that . . .'

'Some of the people at the party assumed he was Gloria Conti's father.'

'Never 'eard of 'er,' wheezed Betty.

'According to Wilma Bayliss's daughters,' said Strike, 'you told their mother you were scared of the person who wrote the notes. You said the writer of the notes killed Margot Bamborough. You told Wilma he'd kill you, too, if you said who he was.'

Betty's milky eyes were expressionless. Her thin chest laboured to get enough oxygen into her lungs. Strike had just concluded that she definitely wasn't going to talk, when she opened her mouth.

'Local girl I knew,' she said, 'friend o' mine . . . *she* met Mucky . . . 'e come cruisin' . . . our corner . . . 'e says to Jen . . . "You're better'n this . . . workin' the street . . . body like yours . . . I could get you . . . five times what . . . you're earnin' 'ere . . ." so off Jen goes,' said Betty, 'up West . . .

Soho . . . strippin' for punters . . . sex wiv 'is mates . . .'

'I met 'er . . . coupla years later . . . visitin' 'er mum . . . and she tole me a story.

'Girl at their club . . . gorgeous girl, Jen said . . . got raped . . . knifepoint. Cut . . .' said Betty Fuller, indicating her own sagging torso, 'right down the ribs . . . by a mate . . . of Ricci's . . .

'Some people,' said the old woman, 'fink a hooker . . . being raped . . . it just means she never . . . got paid . . . 'spect your Miss Stick-Up-'Er-Arse,' said Betty, glancing at the window, 'finks that . . . but it ain't that . . .

'This girl . . . angry . . . wants revenge . . . get back . . . at Ricci . . . so the silly bitch . . . turns police informer . . .

'And Mucky found out,' wheezed Betty Fuller, 'and 'e filmed it . . . as they killed 'er. My mate Jen was told . . . by someone . . . what 'ad seen . . . the film . . . Ricci kept it . . . in the safe . . . show people . . . if they needed . . . scaring . . .

'Jen's dead now,' said Betty Fuller. 'Overdosed . . . firty-odd years ago . . . fort she'd be better . . . up West . . . and 'ere's me . . . workin' the streets . . . still alive.

'I ain't got nuffing . . . to say . . . about no notes . . . it warn't Marcus . . . that's all . . . That's my meals on wheels,' said Betty, her head turning, and Strike saw a man heading towards the outside door, with a pile of foil trays in his arms.

'I'm done,' Betty said, who seemed suddenly

tired and cross. 'You can turn . . . telly back on . . . and move . . . that table over . . . pass me that knife and fork . . . in the loo . . .'

She'd rinsed them off in the bathroom sink, but they were still dirty. Strike washed them again before taking them to her. After arranging the table in front of her armchair, and turning *The Only Way is Essex* back on, he opened the door to the meals-on-wheels man, who was grey-haired and cheery.

'Oh hello,' said the newcomer in a loud voice. 'This your son, Betty?'

'Is he fuck,' wheezed Betty Fuller. 'Whatchew got?'

'Chicken casserole and jelly and custard, love . . .'

'Thanks very much for talking to me, Mrs Fuller,' said Strike, but Betty's stock of goodwill had plainly been exhausted, and she was now far more interested in her food.

Robin was leaning against a nearby wall, reading something off her phone, when Strike emerged from the building.

'I thought it was best to clear out,' she said, in a flat voice. 'How did it go?'

'She won't talk about the notes,' said Strike, as the pair of them headed back down Sans Walk, 'and if you ask me why, I'd say it's because she thinks Mucky Ricci wrote them. I've found out a bit more about that girl in the snuff movie.'

'You're joking?' said Robin, looking worried.

'Apparently she was a police informer in one of Ricci's—'

Robin gasped.

'Kara Wolfson!'

'What?'

'Kara Wolfson. One of the women they thought Creed might have killed. Kara worked at a night-club in Soho – the owners put it about after she disappeared that she'd been a police informer!'

'How did you know that?' asked Strike, taken aback. He couldn't remember this information from *The Demon of Paradise Park*.

Robin suddenly remembered that she'd heard this from Brian Tucker, back at the Star Café. She hadn't yet heard back from the Ministry of Justice about the possibility of interviewing Creed, and as Strike still had no inkling what she was up to, she said,

'Think I read it online . . .'

But with a new heaviness pressing on her heart, Robin remembered that Kara's only remaining close relative, the brother she'd raised, had drunk himself to death. Hutchins had said the police weren't able to do anything about that film. Kara Wolfson's body might be anywhere. Some stories didn't have neat endings: there was nowhere to lay flowers for Kara Wolfson, unless it was on the corner near the strip joint where she'd last been seen.

Fighting the depression now threatening to overwhelm her, Robin raised her phone to show

Strike what she'd been looking up, and said in a determinedly matter-of-fact voice,

'I was just reading about somnophilia, otherwise known as sleeping princess syndrome.'

'Which, I take it—?'

'Was Brenner's kink,' said Robin, and reading off her phone, she said, '"Somnophilia is a paraphilia in which the individual is sexually aroused by someone non-responsive . . . some psychologists have linked somnophilia with necrophilia." Cormoran . . . you know how he had barbiturates stocked up in his office?'

'Yeah,' said Strike slowly, as they walked back towards his car. 'Well, this is going to give us something to talk to Dorothy's son about, isn't it? I wonder whether she was game for playing dead? Or whether she found herself sleeping a long time, after Brenner had been round for lunch?'

Robin gave a small shudder.

'I know,' Strike continued, as he lit up, 'I said he'd be a last resort, but we've only got three months left. I'm starting to think I'm going to have to pay Mucky Ricci a visit.'

CHAPTER 57

But all his mind is set on mucky pelfe,
To hoord vp heapes of euill gotten masse,
For which he others wrongs, and wreckes
*   himself.*

Edmund Spenser
The Faerie Queene

Adding daytime surveillance of St Peter's Roman Catholic Nursing Home to the rota meant that as May progressed, the agency was again struggling to cover all open cases. Strike wanted to know how many visitors were going in and out, and at what times, so that he might ascertain when he'd have the best chance of entering the building without running into one of the old gangster's relatives.

The nursing home lay in a quiet Georgian street on the very edge of Clerkenwell, in a quiet, leafy enclave where dun-coloured brick houses sported neo-classical pediments and glossy black front doors. A dark wood plaque on the exterior wall

352

of the nursing home was embellished with a cross, and a biblical quotation, in gold:

For you know that it was not with perishable things such as silver or gold that you were redeemed from the empty way of life handed down to you from your ancestors, but with the precious blood of Christ, a lamb without blemish or defect.

Peter 1:18–19

'Nice sentiment,' as Strike commented to Robin, on one of their handovers, 'but nobody's getting in there without a good bit of cash.'

The private nursing home was small and clearly expensive. The staff, all of whom the agency quickly grew to know by sight, wore dark blue scrubs and hailed mostly from abroad. There was a black male nurse who sounded as though he'd come from Trinidad, and two blondes who talked Polish to each other every morning as they passed whichever agency member happened to be loitering in the area at the time, feigning a call on their mobile, reading a newspaper or appearing to wait, slightly impatiently, for a friend who never showed up.

A podiatrist and a hairdresser went regularly in and out of the home, but after two weeks' daytime surveillance, the agency tentatively concluded that Ricci only received visits on Sundays, when his two sons appeared, wearing the resigned looks of people for whom this was an unwelcome chore. It was easy to identify which brother was which from pictures that had appeared in the press. Luca looked, in Barclay's phrase, 'like a piano fell oan his heid', having a bald, flat, noticeably scarred skull. Marco was smaller, slighter and hairier, but gave off an air of barely contained violence, slamming his hand repeatedly on the nursing home's doorbell if the door wasn't opened immediately, and slapping a grandson around the back of the head for dropping a chocolate bar on the pavement. Both the brothers' wives had a hard-boiled look about them, and none of the family had the good looks Robin associated with Italians. The great-grandfather sitting mutely behind the doors of the nursing home might have been a true Latin, but his descendants were disappointingly pallid and Saxon in appearance, right down to the little ginger-haired boy who dropped his chocolate.

It was Robin who first laid eyes on Ricci himself, on the third Saturday the agency was watching the home. Beneath her raincoat, Robin was wearing a dress, because she was meeting Strike later at the Stafford hotel in Mayfair, to interview C. B. Oakden. Robin, who'd never been to the hotel, had looked it up and learned that the five-star establishment, with its bowler-hatted doormen, was one of the oldest and smartest hotels in London, hence her atypical choice of surveillance wear. As she'd previously disguised herself while lurking outside St Peter's (alternately beanie hat, hair up, dark contact lenses and sunglasses), she felt safe to look like herself for once as she strolled up and down the street, pretending to talk on the phone, although she'd added clear-lensed glasses she'd remove for the Stafford.

The elderly residents of St Peter's were occasionally escorted or wheeled down the street in the afternoon to the nearby square, which had a central private garden enclosed by railings, open only to keyholders, there to doze or enjoy the lilac and pansies while well wrapped up against the cold. Hitherto, the agency had seen only elderly women taken on the outings, but today, for the first time, an old man was among the group coming down a ramp at the side of the building.

Robin recognised Ricci instantly, not by his lion ring, which, if he was wearing it, was well hidden beneath a tartan rug, but by the profile that time might have exaggerated, but could not disguise. His thick black hair was now dark grey and his nose and earlobes enormous. The large eyes that reminded Strike of a Basset hound had an even more pronounced droop these days. Ricci's mouth hung slightly open as one of the Polish nurses pushed him towards the square, talking to him brightly, but receiving no response.

'You all right, Enid, love?' the black male nurse called ahead to a frail-looking old lady wearing a sheepskin hat, and she laughed and nodded.

Robin gave the group a head start, then followed, watching as one of the nurses unlocked the gate to the garden, and the party disappeared inside. Walking around the square with her phone clamped to her ear, pretending to be in conversation, Robin thought how typical it was that today, of all days, she'd worn heels, never imagining that there might have been a possibility of approaching Ricci and chatting to him.

The group from the nursing home had come to a halt beside flower-beds of purple and yellow, Ricci parked in his wheelchair beside an empty park bench. The nurses chatted amongst themselves, and to those old ladies capable of doing so, while the old man stared vacantly across the lawns.

If she'd been wearing her usual trainers, Robin thought, she might possibly have been able to scale the railings and get into the garden unseen: there was a clump of trees that would provide cover from the nurses, and she could have sidled over to Ricci and found out, at the very least, whether he had dementia. Unfortunately, she had absolutely no chance of managing that feat in her dress and high heels.

As she completed her walk around the square, Robin spotted Saul Morris walking towards her. Morris was early, as he always tended to be, whenever it was Robin from whom he was taking over.

He's going to mention either the glasses or the heels first, Robin thought.

'High heels,' said Morris, as soon as he was

within earshot, his bright blue eyes sweeping over her. 'Don't think I've ever seen you in heels before. Funny, I never think of you as tall, but you are, aren't you? Sexy specs, too.'

Before Robin could stop him, he'd stooped and kissed her on the cheek.

'I'm the guy you're meeting on a blind date,' he told her, straightening up again and winking.

'How do we account for the fact that I'm about to leave you standing here?' Robin asked, unsmiling, and Morris laughed too hard, just as he did at Strike's mildest jokes.

'Dunno – what would it take to make you walk out on a blind date?' asked Morris.

You turning up, thought Robin, but ignoring the question she checked her watch and said,

'If you're OK to take over now, I'll head—'

'Here they come,' said Morris quietly. 'Oh, the old fella's outside this time, is he? I wondered why you'd abandoned the front door.'

The comment aggravated Robin almost as much as his flirtatious manner. Why did he think she'd leave the front door, unless the target had moved? Nevertheless, she waited beside him while the small group of nurses and residents, having decided that twenty minutes was enough fresh air, passed them on the other side of the street, heading back to the home.

'My kids were taken out like that at nursery,' said Morris quietly, watching the group pass. 'All bundled up in pushchairs, the helpers wheeling them out. Some of that lot are probably wearing nappies, too,' he said, his bright blue eyes following the St Peter's party. 'Christ, I hope I never end up like that. Ricci's the only man, too, poor sod.'

'I think they're very well looked after,' Robin said, as the Trinidadian nurse shouted,

'Up we go, Enid!'

'Like being a kid again, though, isn't it?' said Morris, as they watched the wheelchairs rolling along in procession. 'But with none of the perks.'

'S'pose so,' said Robin. 'I'll head off, then, if you're ready to take over.'

'Yeah, no problem,' said Morris, but he immediately added, 'where're you going, all dressed up like that?'

'I'm meeting Strike.'

'*Oh*,' said Morris, eyebrows raised, 'I see—'

'No,' said Robin, 'you don't. We're interviewing someone at a really smart hotel.'

'Ah,' said Morris. 'Sorry.'

But there was a strange complacency, bordering on complicity, about the way Morris bade her goodbye, and it wasn't until Robin had reached the end of the street that the unwelcome thought occurred to her that Morris had entirely misread the sharpness of her denial that she was going on a date with Strike; that he might, in fact, have interpreted it as Robin wanting to make it quite clear that her affections weren't engaged elsewhere.

Was Morris – *could* he be – so deluded as to

358

think that Robin was secretly hoping that his un-subtle flirtation might lead to something happening between them? Even after what had happened on Boxing Day, when she'd shouted at him for sending her that dick pic? Little though she wanted to believe it, she was afraid that the answer was 'yes'. Morris had been extremely drunk when she'd shouted at him, and possibly incapable of judging just how truly angry and disgusted she'd been. He'd seemed sincerely ashamed of himself in the immediate aftermath, so she'd forced herself to be friendlier than she wanted to be, purely out of a desire to foster team cohesion. The result had been that Morris had returned to his pre-dick pic ways. She only answered his late-night texts, mostly containing jokes and attempts at banter, to stop him pestering her with 'have I offended you?' follow-ups. Now it occurred to her that what she considered professionalism Morris took as encour-agement. Everything he said to her about work suggested that he saw her as less able and less experienced than the rest of the agency: perhaps he also thought her naive enough to be flattered by the attentions of a man she actually found condescending and slimy.

Morris, Robin thought, as she headed towards the Tube, didn't actually like women. He desired them, but that, of course, was an entirely different matter: Robin, who was forever marked by the ineradicable memory of the man in the gorilla mask, knew better than most that desire and liking were different, and sometimes mutually exclusive, things. Morris gave himself away constantly, not only in the way he spoke to Robin, but in his desire to call Mrs Smith 'Rich Bitch', his attribution of venal or provocative motives to every woman under surveillance, in the barely disguised disgust with which he noted that Mucky Ricci was now forced to live in a houseful of females. *Christ, I hope I never end up like that.*

Robin walked another few steps, and suddenly stopped dead, earning herself a curious glance from a passing traffic warden. She'd had an idea, triggered by what Morris had just said to her: or rather, the idea had slammed its way into the forefront of her mind and she knew that it had been there in her subconscious all along, waiting for her to admit it.

Moving aside so as not to get in the way of passers-by, Robin pulled out her phone and checked the list of paraphilias she'd last consulted when looking up sleeping princess syndrome.

Autonepiophilia.

'Oh God,' Robin muttered. 'That's it. That's got to be it.'

Robin called Strike, but his number went to voicemail; he was doubtless already on the Tube, heading for the Stafford. After a moment or two's thought, she called Barclay.

'Hiya,' said the Scot.

'Are you still outside Elinor Dean's?'

'Yeah.'

'Is there anyone in there with her?'

'No.'

'Sam, I think I know what she's doing for those men.'

'Whut?'

Robin told him. The only answer was a long silence. Finally, Barclay said,

'You're aff yer heid, Robin.'

'Maybe,' said Robin, 'but the only way to know for sure is to knock on her door and ask if she'll do it for you. Say you were recommended to her by SB.'

'Will I fuck,' said Barclay. 'Does Strike know ye're asking me tae do this?'

'Sam, we've got a week left before the client pulls the plug. The worst that can happen is that she denies it. We're not going to have many more chances.'

She heard Barclay exhale, hard.

'All right, but it's on ye if ye're wrong.'

Robin hurried onwards towards the Tube station, second-guessing herself as she went. Would Strike think she was wrong to tell Barclay to go in, on her hunch? But they had a week left before the client withdrew funding: what was there, now, to lose?

It was Saturday evening, and Robin arrived on the crowded Tube platform to find she'd just missed a train. By the time she exited at Green Park station, she'd lost the chance of arriving at the American Bar early, which she'd hoped to do, so that she and Strike could have a few words together before Oakden arrived. Worse still, when she hurried down St James's Street, she saw, with a sense of déjà vu, a large crowd blocking the bottom of the road, being marshalled by police. As Robin slowed down, wondering whether she'd be able to get through the dense mass of people to the Stafford, a couple of sprinting paparazzi overtook her, in pursuit of a series of black Mercedeses. As Robin watched them pressing their lenses against windows, she became aware that the crowd in the distance was chanting '*Jonn-ny! Jonn-ny!*' Through the windows of one of the cars heading towards the event, Robin glimpsed a woman in a Marie Antoinette wig. Only when she was nearly knocked sideways by a sprinting pair of autograph hunters, both of them holding Deadbeats posters, did Robin realise with a thrill of shock that Strike's father was the Jonny whose name was being chanted.

'Shit,' she said aloud, wheeling around and hurrying back up the road, pulling out her mobile as she went. She knew there was another entrance to the Stafford via Green Park. Not only was she going to be late, but a horrible suspicion had just hit her. Why had Oakden been so determined to meet on this specific evening? And why had it had to be this bar, so close to what she was afraid was an event involving Strike's father? Did Strike know, had he realised, what was happening close by?

She called him, but he didn't pick up. Still walking, she typed out a text:

Cormoran I don't know whether you know this, but Jonny Rokeby's having an event around the corner. I think it's possible Oakden's trying to set you up.

Breaking into a jog, because she was already five minutes late, she knew she'd just told Strike, for the very first time, that she knew who his father was.

On her arrival in Green Park, she saw from a distance a policeman at the rear entrance, who, with one of the hotel's bowler-hatted attendants, was politely but firmly turning away two men with long-lensed cameras.

'Not this way, sorry,' said the policeman. 'Only for tonight. If it's the hotel you want, you'll have to go round the front.'

'What's going on?' demanded a suited man hand in hand with a beautiful Asian woman in a cheongsam. 'We've got a dinner booking! Why can't we go through?'

'Very sorry, sir, but there's an event on at Spencer House,' explained the doorman, 'and police want us to stop people using this as a short cut.'

The two men with cameras swore and turned away, jogging back the way Robin had come. She lowered her head as they passed her, glad that she was still wearing her unneeded glasses, because her picture had appeared in the press during a court case a couple of years back. Maybe she was being paranoid, but Robin was worried the pressmen had been trying to use the Stafford not as a short cut to Rokeby and his guests, but as a means of getting to his estranged son.

Now that the photographers had gone, the bowler-hatted attendant permitted the woman in the cheongsam and her companion to enter, and after giving Robin a shrewd up-and-down glance, evidently decided she wasn't a photographer and allowed her to proceed through the gate into a courtyard, where well-dressed drinkers were smoking beneath exterior heaters. After checking her mobile and seeing that Strike hadn't answered her text, she hurried up the steps into the American Bar.

It was a comfortable, elegant space of dark wood and leather, with pennants and baseball caps from many American states and universities hanging from the ceiling. Robin immediately spotted Strike standing in a suit at the bar, his surly expression lit by the rows of illuminated bottles on the wall.

'Cormoran, I just—'

'If you're about to tell me my father's just round the corner,' said Strike tersely, 'I know. This arsehole doesn't realise I'm wise to his attempted set-up, yet.'

Robin glanced into the far corner. Carl Oakden was sitting there, legs spread wide, an arm along the back of the leather bench. He was wearing a suit, but no tie, and his attitude was clearly meant to suggest a man at ease in these cosmopolitan surroundings. With his slightly too-close-together eyes and his narrow forehead, he still resembled the boy who'd smashed Roy's mother's crystal bowl all those years ago.

'Go and talk to him. He wants some food, I'm getting menus,' muttered Strike. 'We'd just got started on Steve Douthwaite. Apparently, Dorothy always thought the bloke was suspicious.'

Heading towards Oakden, Robin prayed that Strike was going to keep his temper. She'd only once seen him lose his cool with a witness, and had no desire to see it happen again.

'Mr Oakden?' she said, smiling as she reached him and extending her hand. 'I'm Robin Ellacott, we've emailed—'

'I know,' said Oakden, turning his head slowly to look her up and down with a smirk. He ignored her outstretched hand and Robin could tell he did so deliberately. Refusing to show that she realised that he was trying to be offensive, she shrugged off her raincoat.

'Nice bar,' she said pleasantly, sitting down opposite him. 'I've never been here before.'

'Normally takes you cheaper places, does he?' asked Oakden.

'Cormoran was just telling me you remember your mother talking about Steve Douth—'

'Love,' said Oakden, legs still wide apart, arm

along the back of the leather bench, 'I told you all along, I'm not interested in being palmed off with assistants or secretaries. I'll talk to him, or nobody.'

'I'm actually Cormoran's—'

'I'll bet you are,' said Oakden, with a snigger. 'Don't suppose he can get rid of you now, can he?'

'Sorry?'

'Not now you've been knifed, trying to do a man's job,' said Oakden, with a glance towards her forearm as he raised his cocktail to his lips. 'You'd probably sue the shit out of him, if he tried.'

Oakden, who'd evidently done his homework on the detectives, was clearly revelling in his rudeness. Robin could only suppose that the con man assumed she was too desperate for his information to take offence at his manner. He seemed determined to derive maximum pleasure from this encounter: to enjoy free alcohol and food, and bait a woman who was unlikely to walk away. Robin wondered which paper or picture agency he'd contacted, to propose luring Strike within a few hundred yards of his father's party, and how much Oakden stood to gain, if they could get a picture of Strike apparently publicly snubbing his father, or catch the detective on record saying something angry and quotable.

'There you go,' said Strike, throwing a couple of leather-bound menus onto the table and sitting down. He hadn't thought to bring Robin anything to drink. Oakden picked up a menu and perused it slowly, and he seemed to enjoy keeping them waiting.

'I'll have the club sandwich,' he said at last, and Strike hailed a waiter. The order given, Strike turned back to Oakden and said,

'Yeah, so you were saying, your mother found Douthwaite—'

'Oh, she definitely thought he was a charmer,' said Oakden. His eyes, Robin noted, kept moving to the entrance of the bar, and she was sure Oakden was waiting for photographers to burst in. 'Wide boy, you know the type. Chatting up the slags on reception. The old woman said he tried it on with everyone. The nurse got all giggly when he was around and all.'

Robin remembered the gambolling black skeleton of Talbot's notebook, and the words written beside Crowley's figure of death: *Fortuna says Pallas Athena, Ceres, Vesta and Cetus are SCARLET WOMEN who RIDE UPON THE BEAST . . .*

'And did your mother think he fancied Dr Bamborough?'

Oakden took a sip of his cocktail and smacked his lips.

'Well, I mean, Margot,' he said, with a small snort of laughter, and Robin found herself irrationally resentful of Oakden using the missing doctor's first name, 'you know, she was the classic wanted-it-all-ways, wasn't she?'

'What ways were those?' said Strike.

'Bunny Girl,' said Oakden, taking another sip of his drink, 'legs out, tits out. Then, quick, get the white coat on—'

'Don't think GPs wear white coats,' said Strike.

'I'm talking metaphorically,' said Oakden airily. 'Child of her time, wasn't she?'

'How's that?'

'The rise of gynocentric society,' said Oakden, with a slight bow towards Robin, who suddenly thought his narrow head resembled a stoat's. 'Late sixties, early seventies, it's when it all started changing, isn't it? You've got the pill: consequence-free fucking. Looks like it benefits the male, but by enabling women to avoid or subvert the reproductive function, you're repressing natural and healthy patterns of sex behaviour. You've got a gynocentric court system, which favours the female even if she didn't want the kids in the first place. You've got misandrist authoritarianism masquerading as a campaign for equal rights, policing men's thoughts and speech and natural behaviour. And you've got widespread sexual exploitation of men. Playboy Club, that's all bullshit. Look, but don't touch. It's the old courtly love lie. The woman's there to be worshipped, the man's there to spew cash, but never get satisfaction. Suckers, the men who hang round those places.

'Bamborough didn't look after her own kid,' said Oakden, his eyes again darting to the entrance and back to Strike, 'didn't fuck her own husband, from what I heard, he was nearly always too ill to perform. He had plenty of cash though, so she gets a nanny and goes lording it over men at work.'

'Who, specifically, did she lord it over?' asked Strike.

'Well, Douthwaite ran out of there practically crying last time he saw her, my old woman said. But that's been our culture since the sixties, hasn't it? Male suffering, nobody gives a shit. People whine when men break, when they can't handle it any more, when they lash out. If Douthwaite did her in – I don't *personally* think he did,' said Oakden with an expansive gesture, and Robin reminded herself that Carl Oakden had almost certainly never laid eyes on Steven Douthwaite, and that he'd been fourteen years old when Margot disappeared, 'but *if* he did, I'd lay odds it's because she kicked his pain back in his teeth. Only women bleed,' said Oakden, with a contemptuous little laugh, 'isn't that right?' he shot at Robin. 'Ah, there's my sandwich.'

While the waiter served him, Robin got up and headed to the bar, where the beautiful woman in the cheongsam, whose hair hung like black silk in the light of the banked bottles of spirits, was standing with her partner. Both were ordering cocktails and looked delighted to be in each other's company. For a few seconds Robin suddenly wondered whether she'd ever again feel as they did. Her job reminded her almost daily of the many ways in which men and women could hurt each other.

As she ordered herself a tonic water, Robin's phone rang. Hoping it was Barclay, she instead saw her mother's name. Perhaps Linda had got wind of Sarah's pregnancy. Matthew might have taken his wife-to-be back to Masham by now, to share the good news. Robin muted the phone, paid for her drink, wishing it was alcoholic, and carried it back to the table in time to hear Oakden say to Strike,

'No, that didn't happen.'

'You didn't add vodka to the punch at Dr Bamborough's barbecue?'

Oakden took a large bite of his free sandwich, and chewed it insolently. In spite of his thin hair and the many wrinkles around his eyes, Robin could clearly see the spoiled teenager inside the fifty-four-year-old.

'Nicked some,' said Oakden thickly, 'then drank it in the shed. Surprised they missed it, but the rich are tight. How they stay minted, isn't it?'

'We heard the punch made someone sick.'

'Not my fault,' said Oakden.

'Dr Phipps was pretty annoyed, I hear.'

'Him,' said Oakden, with a smirk. 'Things worked out all right for old Phipps, didn't they?'

'In what way?' asked Strike.

'Wife out the way, marrying the nanny. All very convenient.'

'Didn't like Phipps, did you?' said Strike. 'That came across in your book.'

'You've read it?' said Oakden, momentarily startled. 'How come?'

'Managed to track down an advance copy,' said Strike. 'It should've come out in '85, right?'

'Yeah,' said Oakden.

'D'you remember the gazebo that was under construction in the garden when the barbecue happened?'

One of Oakden's eyelids flickered. He raised a hand quickly to his face and made a sweep of his forehead, as though he felt a hair tickling him.

'No,' he said.

'It's in the background of one of your photos. They'd just started building the columns. I expect they'd already put down the floor.'

'I can't remember that,' said Oakden.

'The shed where you took the vodka wasn't near there, then?'

'Can't've been,' said Oakden.

'While we're on the subject of nicking things,' said Strike, 'would you happen to have the obituary of Dr Brenner you took from Janice Beattie's house?'

'I never stole no obituary from her house,' said Oakden, with a display of disdain. 'What would I want that for?'

'To get some information you could try and pass off as your own?'

'I don't need to look up old Joe Brenner, I know

371

plenty about him. He came round our house for his dinner every other Sunday. My old woman used to cook better than his sister, apparently.'

'Go on, then,' said Strike, his tone becoming combative, 'amaze us.'

Oakden raised his sparse eyebrows. He chewed another bite of sandwich and swallowed it, before saying,

'Hey, this was all your idea. You don't want the information, I'm happy to go.'

'Unless you've got more than you put in your book—'

'Brenner wanted Margot Bamborough struck off the bloody medical register. Come round our house one Sunday full of it. Couple of weeks before she disappeared. There,' said Oakden pugnaciously, 'I kept that out of the book, because my mother didn't want it in there.'

'Why was that?'

'Still loyal to him,' said Oakden, with a little snort of laughter. 'And I wanted to keep the old dear happy at the time, because noises had been made about writing me out of the will. Old women,' said the convicted con man, 'are a bit too persuadable if you don't keep an eye on them. She'd got chummy with the local vicar by the eighties. I was worried it was all going to go to rebuild the bloody church steeple unless I kept an eye on her.'

'Why did Brenner want Bamborough struck off?'

'She examined some kid without parental permission.'

'Was this Janice's son?' asked Robin.

'Was I talking to you?' Oakden shot at her.

'You,' growled Strike, 'want to keep a civil tongue in your bloody head. Was it Janice's son, yes or no?'

'Maybe,' said Oakden, and Robin concluded that he couldn't remember. 'Point is, that's unethical behaviour, looking at a kid without a parent there, and old Joe was all worked up about it. "I'll have her struck off for this," he kept saying. There. Didn't get *that* from no obituary, did I?'

Oakden drank the rest of his cocktail straight off, then said,

'I'll have another one of those.'

Strike ignored this, saying,

'And this was two weeks before Bamborough disappeared?'

'About that, yeah. Never seen the old bastard so excited. He loved disciplining people, old Joe. Vicious old bastard, actually.'

'In what way?'

'Told my old woman in front of me she wasn't hitting me enough,' said Oakden. 'She bloody listened, too. Tried to lay about me with a slipper a couple of days later, silly cow. She learned not to do that again.'

'Yeah? Hit her back, did you?'

Oakden's too-close-together eyes raked Strike, as though trying to ascertain whether he was worth educating.

'If my father had lived, he'd've had the right to punish me, but her trying to humiliate me because Brenner told her to? I wasn't taking that.'

'Exactly how close were your mother and Brenner?'

Oakden's thin brows contracted.

'Doctor and secretary, that's all. There wasn't anything else between them, if that's what you're implying.'

'They didn't have a little lie down after lunch, then?' said Strike. 'She didn't come over sleepy, after Brenner had come over?'

'You don't want to judge everyone's mother by yours,' said Oakden.

Strike acknowledged the jibe with a dark smile and said,

'Did your mother ask Brenner to sign the death certificate for your grandmother?'

'The hell's that got to do with anything?'

'Did she?'

'I dunno,' said Oakden, his eyes darting once again towards the bar's entrance. 'Where did you get that idea? What're you even asking that for?'

'Your grandmother's doctor was Margot Bamborough, right?'

'I dunno,' said Oakden.

'You can remember every word your mother told you about Steve Douthwaite, right down to him flirting with receptionists and looking tearful the last time he left the surgery, but you can't remember details of your own grandmother falling downstairs and killing herself?'

'I wasn't there,' said Oakden. 'I was out at a mate's house when it happened. Come home and seen the ambulance.'

'Just your mother at home, then?'

'The hell's this relevant to—?'

'What's the name of the mate whose house you were at?' asked Strike, for the first time taking out his notebook.

'What're you doing?' said Oakden, with an attempt at a laugh, dropping the last portion of his sandwich on his plate. 'What are you fucking implying?'

'You don't want to give us his name?'

'Why the fuck should – he was a schoolmate—'

'Convenient for you and your mother, old Maud falling downstairs,' said Strike. 'My information is she shouldn't have been trying to navigate stairs alone, in her condition. Inherited the house, didn't you?'

Oakden began to shake his head very slowly, as though marvelling at the unexpected stupidity of Cormoran Strike.

'Seriously? You're trying to . . . wow. *Wow.*'

'Not going to tell me the name of your school-friend, then?'

'*Wow,*' said Oakden, attempting a laugh. 'You think you can—'

'—drop a word in a friendly journalist's ear, to the effect that your long career of screwing over old ladies started with a good hard push in the small of your grandmother's back? Oh yeah, I definitely can.'

'Now you wait a fucking—'

'I know you think it's me being set up tonight,' said Strike, leaning in. His body language was unmistakeably menacing, and out of the corner of her eye, Robin saw the black-haired woman in the cheongsam and her partner watching warily, both with their drinks at their lips. 'But the police have still got a note written to them in 1985, telling them to dig beneath the cross of St John. DNA techniques have moved on a lot since then. I expect they'll be able to get a good match from the saliva under the envelope flap.'

Oakden's eyelid twitched again.

'You thought you were going to stir up a bit of press interest in the Bamborough case, to get people interested in your shitty book, didn't you?'

'I never—'

'I'm warning you. You go talking to the papers about me and my father, or about me working the Bamborough case, and I'll make sure you get nailed for that note. And if by chance that doesn't work, I'll put my whole agency onto turning over every part of your miserable fucking life, until I've got something else on you to take to the police. Understand?'

Oakden, who looked momentarily unnerved, recovered himself quickly. He even managed another little laugh.

'You can't stop me writing about whatever I want. That's freedom of—'

'I'm warning you,' repeated Strike, a little more loudly, 'what'll happen if you get in the way of this case. And you can pay for your own fucking sandwich.'

Strike stood up and Robin, caught off guard, hastened to grab her raincoat and get up, too.

'Cormoran, let's go out the back,' she said, thinking of the two photographers lurking at the front of the building, but they hadn't gone more than two steps when they heard Oakden call after them.

'You think I'm scared of your fucking agency? Some fucking detective you are!' he said, and now most of the heads in their vicinity turned. Glancing back, Robin saw that Oakden had got up, too: he'd come out from behind the table and was planted in the middle of the bar, clearly set on making a scene.

'Strike, please, let's just go,' said Robin, who now had a presentiment of real trouble. Oakden was clearly determined to come out of the encounter with something sellable, or at the very least, a narrative in which he'd come out on top. But Strike had already turned back towards their interviewee.

'You didn't even know your own fucking father's having a party round the corner,' said Oakden loudly, pointing in the direction of Spencer House. 'Not going to pop in, thank him for fucking your mother on a pile of beanbags while fifty people watched?'

Robin watched what she had dreaded unfold in apparent slow motion: Strike lunged for Oakden. She made a grab for the arm Strike had drawn back for a punch, but too late: his elbow slammed into Robin's forehead, breaking her glasses in two. Dark spots popped in front of Robin's eyes and the next thing she knew, she'd fallen backwards onto the floor.

Robin's attempted intervention had given the con man a few seconds in which to dodge, and instead of receiving what might have been a knockout punch, he suffered no worse than a glancing blow to the ear. Meanwhile the enraged Strike, who'd barely registered his arm being impeded, realised what he'd done only when he saw drinkers all over the bar jumping to their feet, their eyes on the floor behind him. Turning, he saw Robin lying there, her hands over her face, a trickle of blood issuing from her nose.

'Shit!' Strike bellowed.

The young barman had run out from behind the bar. Oakden was shouting something about assault. Still slightly dizzy, tears of pain streaming from her eyes, the humiliated Robin was assisted back onto her feet by a couple of affluent-looking grey-haired Americans, who were fussing about getting her a doctor.

'I'm absolutely fine,' she heard herself saying. She'd taken the full force of Strike's elbow between her eyebrows, and she realised her nose was bleeding only when she accidentally sprayed blood onto the kind American's white shirt front.

'Robin, shit—' Strike was saying.

'Sir, I'm going to have to—'

'Yes, we're *absolutely* going to leave,' Robin told the waiter, absurdly polite, while her eyes watered and she tried to stem the bleeding from her nostrils. 'I just need – oh, thank you so much,' she said to the American woman, who'd handed Robin her raincoat.

'Call the police!' Oakden was shouting. Thanks to Robin's intervention, he was entirely unmarked. 'Someone call the bloody police!'

'I won't be pressing charges,' Robin said to nobody in particular.

'Robin – I'm so—'

Grabbing a handful of Strike's sleeve, warm blood still trickling down onto her chin, Robin muttered,

'Let's just go.'

She trod on the cracked lens of her glasses as they headed out of the silent bar, the drinkers staring after them.

CHAPTER 58

His louely words her seemd due recompence
Of all her passed paines: one louing howre
For many yeares of sorrow can dispence:
A dram of sweete is worth a pound of sowre:
Shee has forgott, how many, a woeful stowre
For him she late endurd; she speakes no more
Of past . . .
Before her stands her knight, for whom she
    toyld so sore.

Edmund Spenser
The Faerie Queene

'Robin—'
'*Don't* tell me I shouldn't have tried to stop you,' she said through gritted teeth, as they hurried through the outside courtyard. Her vision was blurred with tears of pain. Smokers turned to gape as she passed, trying to staunch her bleeding nose. 'If that punch had connected, we'd be back there waiting for the police.'

To Robin's relief, there were no paparazzi waiting

for them as they headed into Green Park, but she was scared that it wouldn't take long, after the scene Strike had just made, for them to come hunting again.

'We'll get a cab,' said Strike, who was currently consumed with a mixture of total mortification and rage against Oakden, his father, the press and himself. 'Listen, you're right—'

'I know I'm right, thanks!' she said, a little wildly.

Not only was her face throbbing, she was now wondering why Strike hadn't warned her about Rokeby's party; why, in fact, he'd let himself get lured there by a second-rate chancer like Oakden, careless of consequences for their case and for the agency.

'TAXI!' bellowed Strike, so loudly that Robin jumped. Somewhere nearby, she heard running footsteps.

A black cab pulled up and Strike pushed Robin inside.

'Denmark Street,' he yelled at the cabbie, and Robin heard the shouts of photographers as the taxi sped up again.

'It's all right,' said Strike, twisting to look out of the back window, 'they're on foot. Robin . . . I'm so fucking sorry.'

She'd pulled a mirror out of her bag to try and clean up her smarting face, wiping blood from her upper lip and chin. It looked as though she was going to have two black eyes: both were rapidly swelling.

'D'you want me to take you home?' said Strike.

Furious at him, fighting the urge to cry out of pain, Robin imagined Max's surprise and curiosity at seeing her in this state; imagined having to make light, again, of the injuries she'd sustained while working for the agency. She also remembered that she hadn't gone food shopping in days.

'No, I want you to give me something to eat and a strong drink.'

'You've got it,' said Strike, glad to have a chance to make reparations. 'Will a takeaway do?'

'No,' said Robin sarcastically, pointing at her rapidly blackening eyes, 'I'd like to go to the Ritz, please.'

Strike started to laugh but cut himself off, appalled at the state of her face.

'Maybe we should go to casualty.'

'Don't be ridiculous.'

'Robin—'

'You're sorry. I know. You said.'

Strike's phone rang. He glanced down: Barclay could wait, he decided, and muted it.

Three-quarters of an hour later, the taxi dropped them at the end of Denmark Street, with a takeaway curry and a couple of clinking bottles. Once upstairs, Robin repaired to the toilet on the landing, where she washed dried blood from her nostrils and chin with a wad of wet toilet paper. Two increasingly swollen, red-purplish mounds containing her eyes looked back at her out of the cracked mirror. A blue bruise was spreading over her forehead.

Inside the office, Strike, who'd normally have eaten the curry straight out of the foil tray it had come in, had brought out mis-matched plates, knives and forks, then, because Robin wanted a strong drink, went upstairs to his flat where he had a bottle of his favourite whisky. There was a small freezer compartment in his fridge, where he kept ice packs for his stump in addition to an ice tray. The cubes within this had been there for over a year, because although Strike enjoyed the odd drink of spirits, he generally preferred beer. About to leave the flat with the ice tray, he had second thoughts, and doubled back for one of the ice packs, as well.

'Thank you,' muttered Robin, when Strike reappeared, accepting the proffered ice pack. She was sitting in Pat's seat, behind the desk where she'd once answered the phone, where Strike had laid out the curry and plates. 'And you'd better re-do next week's rota,' she added, applying the ice pack gingerly to her left eye first, 'because there isn't a concealer in the world that's going to cover up this mess. I'm not going to have much chance of going unnoticed on surveillance with two black eyes.'

'Robin,' said Strike yet again, 'I'm so fucking sorry. I was a tit, I just . . . What d'you want, vodka, whisky—?'

'Whisky,' she said. 'On the rocks.'

Strike poured both of them a triple measure.

'I'm sorry,' he said, yet again, while Robin took a welcome gulp of Scotch, then began helping herself to curry. Strike sat down on the fake leather sofa opposite the desk. 'Hurting you's the last thing – there's no excuse for – I saw red, I lost it. My father's other kids have been pestering me for months to go to that fucking party,' said Strike, running his hand through the thick, curly hair that never looked disarranged. He felt she was owed the whole story now: the reason, if not the excuse, that he'd fucked up so badly. 'They wanted us to get a group photo taken together for a present. Then Al tells me Rokeby's got prostate cancer – which doesn't seem to have prevented him having four hundred mates over for a good old knees-up . . . I ripped up the invitation without registering where the thing was being held. I should've realised Oakden was up to something, I took my eye off the ball, and—'

He downed half his drink in one.

'There's no excuse for trying to punch him, but everything – these last few months – Rokeby rang me in February. First time ever. Tried to bribe me into meeting him.'

'He tried to *bribe* you?' said Robin, pressing the ice pack to her other eye, remembering the shouted 'go fuck yourself' from the inner office, on Valentine's Day.

'As good as,' said Strike. 'He said he was open

to suggestions for helping me out . . . well, it's forty years too fucking late for that.'

Strike downed the rest of his whisky, reached for the bottle and poured the same again into his glass.

'When did you last see him?' Robin asked.

'When I was eighteen. I've met him twice,' Strike said. 'First time was when I was a kid. My mother tried to ambush him with me, outside a recording studio.'

He'd only ever told Charlotte this. Her family was at least as dysfunctional and peculiar as his own, riven with scenes that to other people might've been epoch defining – 'it was a month before Daddy torched Mummy's portrait in the hall, and the panelling caught fire, and the fire brigade came, and we all had to be evacuated via the upstairs windows' – but to the Campbells were so normalised they seemed routine.

'I thought he wanted to see me,' said Strike. The shock of what he'd done to Robin, and the whisky scorching his throat, had liberated memories he usually kept locked up tight inside him. 'I was seven. I was so fucking excited. I wanted to look smart, so he'd be – so he'd be proud of me. Told my mum to put me in my best trousers. We got outside this studio – my mother had music industry contacts, someone had tipped her off he was going to be there – and they wouldn't let us in. I thought there'd been some mistake. The bloke on the door obviously didn't realise my dad wanted to see me.'

Strike drank again. The curry lay cooling between them.

'My mother kicked off. They were threatening her when the band's manager got out of his car behind us. He knew who my mother was and he didn't want a public scene. He took us inside, into a room away from the studio.

'The manager tried to tell her it was a dumb move, turning up. If she wanted more money, she should go through lawyers. That's when I realised my father hadn't invited us at all. She was just trying to force her way in. I started crying,' said Strike roughly. 'Just wanted to go . . .

'And then, while my mother and Rokeby's manager are going at it hammer and tongs, Rokeby walks in. He heard shouting on the way back from the bathroom. Probably just done a line; I realised that later. He was already wound up when he came in the room.

'And I tried to smile,' said Strike. 'Snot all over my face. I didn't want him to think I was a whiner. I'd been imagining a hug. "There you are, at last." But he looked at me like I was nothing. Some fan's kid, in too-short trousers. My trousers were always too fucking short . . . I grew too fast . . .

'Then he clocked my mother, and he twigged. They started rowing. I can't remember everything they said. I was a kid. The gist was how dare she butt in, she had his lawyer's contact details, he was paying enough, it was her problem if she pissed it all away, and then he said, "This was a fucking accident." I thought he meant, he'd come to the studio accidentally or something. But then he looked at me, and I realised, he meant me. *I* was the accident.'

'Oh God, Cormoran,' said Robin quietly.

'Well,' said Strike, 'you've got to give him points for honesty. He walked out. We went home.

'For a while afterwards, I held out a bit of hope he'd regretted what he'd said. It was hard to let go of the idea he wanted to see me, deep down. But nothing.'

While the sun was far from setting, the room was becoming steadily darker. The high buildings of Denmark Street cast the outer office into shadow at this time of the evening, and neither detective had turned on the interior lights.

'Second time we met,' said Strike, 'I made an appointment with his management. I was eighteen. Just got into Oxford. We hadn't touched any of Rokeby's money for years. They'd been back to court to put restrictions on what my mother could do with it, because she was a nightmare with cash, just threw it away. Anyway, unbeknownst to me, my aunt and uncle had informed Rokeby I'd got into Oxford. My mother got a letter saying he had no obligations to me now I'd turned eighteen, but reminding her I could use the money that had been accumulating in the bank account.

'I arranged to see him at his manager's office.

He was there with his long-time lawyer, Peter Gillespie. Got a smile off Rokeby this time. Well, I was off his hands financially now, but old enough to talk to the press. Oxford had clearly been a bit of a shock to him. He'd probably hoped, with a background like mine, I'd slide quietly out of sight for ever.

'He congratulated me on getting into Oxford and said I had a nice little nest egg all built up now, because my mother hadn't spent any of it for six, seven years.

'I told him,' said Strike, 'to stick his fucking money up his arse and set fire to it. Then I walked out.

'Self-righteous little prick, I was. Didn't occur to me that Ted and Joan were going to have to stump up if Rokeby didn't, which is what they did . . . I only realised that later. But I didn't take their money long. After my mother died, midway through my second year, I left Oxford and enlisted.'

'Didn't he contact you after your mum died?' asked Robin quietly.

'No,' said Strike, 'or if he did, I never got it. He sent me a note when my leg got blown off. I'll bet that put the fear of God into him, hearing I'd been blown up. Probably worried sick about what the press might make of it all.

'Once I was out of Selly Oak, he tried to give me the money again. He'd found out I was trying to start the agency. Charlotte's friends knew a couple of his kids, which is how he got wind of it.'

Robin felt something flip in her stomach at the sound of Charlotte's name. Strike so rarely acknowledged her existence.

'I said no, at first. I didn't want to take the money, but no other fucker wanted to lend a one-legged ex-soldier without a house or any savings enough money to set up a detective agency. I told his prick of a lawyer I'd take just enough money to start the agency and pay it back in instalments. Which I did.'

'That money was yours all along?' said Robin, who could remember Gillespie pressing Strike for repayment every few weeks, when she'd first joined the agency.

'Yeah, but I didn't want it. Resented even having to borrow a bit of it.'

'Gillespie acted as though—'

'You get people like Gillespie round the rich and famous,' said Strike. 'His whole ego was invested in being my father's enforcer. The bastard was half in love with my old man, or with his fame, I dunno. I was pretty blunt on the phone about what I thought about Rokeby, and Gillespie couldn't forgive it. I'd insisted on a loan agreement between us, and Gillespie was going to hold me to it, to punish me for telling him exactly what I thought of the pair of them.'

Strike pushed himself off the sofa, which made its usual farting noises as he did so, and began helping himself to curry. When they both had full plates, he went to fetch two glasses of water. He'd already got through a third of the whisky.

'Cormoran,' said Robin, once he was settled back on the sofa and had started eating. 'You do realise, I'm never going to gossip about your father to other people? I'm not going to talk to *you* about him if you don't want to, but . . . we're partners. You could have told me he was hassling you, and let off steam that way, instead of punching a witness.'

Strike chewed some of his chicken jalfrezi, swallowed, then said quietly,

'Yeah, I know.'

Robin ate a bit of naan. Her bruised face was aching less now: the ice pack and the whisky had both numbed her, in different ways. Nevertheless, it took a minute to marshal the courage to say,

'I saw Charlotte's been hospitalised.'

Strike looked up at her. He knew, of course, that Robin was well aware who Charlotte was. Four years previously, he'd got almost too drunk to walk, and told her a lot more than he'd ever meant to, about the alleged pregnancy Charlotte had insisted was his, which had broken them apart for ever.

'Yeah,' said Strike.

And he told Robin the story of the farewell text messages, and his dash to the public payphone, and how he'd listened until they'd found Charlotte lying in undergrowth in the grounds of her expensive clinic.

'Oh my Christ,' said Robin, setting down her fork. 'When did you know she was alive?'

'Knew for sure two days later, when the press reported it,' said Strike. He heaved himself back out of his chair, topped up Robin's whisky, then poured himself more before sitting back down again. 'But I'd concluded she must be alive before that. Bad news travels faster than good.'

There was a long silence, in which Robin hoped to hear more about how being drawn into Charlotte's suicide attempt, and by the sounds of it, saving her life, had made him feel, but Strike said nothing, merely eating his curry.

'Well,' said Robin at last, 'again, in future, maybe we could try that talking thing, before you die of a stress-induced heart attack or, you know, end up killing someone we need to question?'

Strike grinned ruefully.

'Yeah. We could try that, I s'pose . . .'

Silence closed around them again, a silence that seemed to the slightly drunk Strike to thicken like honey, comforting and sweet, but slightly dangerous if you sank too far into it. Full of whisky, contrition and a powerful feeling he preferred at all times not to dwell upon, he wanted to make some kind of statement about Robin's kindness and her tact, but all the words that occurred to him seemed clumsy and unserviceable: he wanted to express something of the truth, but the truth was dangerous.

How could he say, look, I've tried not to fancy you since you first took off your coat in this office. I try not to give names to what I feel for you, because I already know it's too much, and I want peace from the shit that love brings in its wake. I want to be alone, and unburdened, and free.

But I don't want you to be with anyone else. I don't want some other bastard to persuade you into a second marriage. I like knowing the possibility's there, for us to, maybe . . .

Except it'll go wrong, of course, because it always goes wrong, because if I were the type for permanence, I'd already be married. And when it goes wrong, I'll lose you for good, and this thing we've built together, which is literally the only good part of my life, my vocation, my pride, my greatest achievement, will be forever fucked, because I won't find anyone I enjoy running things with, the way I enjoy running them with you, and everything afterwards will be tainted by the memory of you.

If only she could come inside his head and see what was there, Strike thought, she'd understand that she occupied a unique place in his thoughts and in his affections. He felt he owed her that information, but was afraid that saying it might move this conversation into territory from which it would be difficult to retreat.

But, from second to second, sitting here, now with more than half a bottle of neat whisky inside him, a different spirit seemed to move inside him, asking himself for the first time whether determined solitude was what he really wanted, for evermore.

Joanie reckons you're gonna end up with your business partner. That Robin girl.

All or nothing. See what happens. Except that the stakes involved in making any kind of move would be the highest of his life; higher by far than when he'd staggered across a student party to chat up Charlotte Campbell, when, however much agony he'd endured for her later, he'd risked nothing more than minor humiliation, and a good story to tell.

Robin, who'd eaten as much curry as she could handle, had now resigned herself to not hearing what Strike felt for Charlotte. She supposed it had been a forlorn hope, but it was something she was very keen to know. The neat whisky she'd drunk had given the night a slight fuzziness, like a rain haze, and she felt slightly wistful. She knew that if it hadn't been for the alcohol, she might feel simply unhappy.

'I suppose,' said Strike, with the fatalistic daring of a trapeze artist, swinging out into the spotlight, only black air beneath him, 'Ilsa's been trying to matchmake, your end, as well?'

Across the room, sitting in shadow, Robin experienced something like an electric shock through her body. That Strike would even allude to a third party's idea of them being romantically involved was unprecedented. Didn't they always act as though nothing of the sort could be further from anyone's mind? Hadn't they always pretended certain dangerous moments had never happened, such as when she'd modelled that green dress for him, and hugged him while wearing her wedding dress, and felt the idea of running away together pass through his mind, as well as hers?

'Yes,' she said, at last. 'I've been worried . . . well, embarrassed about it, because I haven't . . .'

'No,' said Strike quickly, 'I never thought *you* were . . .'

She waited for him to say something else, suddenly acutely aware, as she'd never been before, that a bed lay directly above them, barely two minutes from where they sat. And, like Strike, she thought, everything I've worked and sacrificed for is in jeopardy if I take this conversation to the wrong place. Our relationship will be forever marred by awkwardness and embarrassment.

But worse than that, by far: she was scared of giving herself away. The feelings she'd been denying to Matthew, to her mother, to Ilsa and to herself must remain hidden.

'Well, sorry,' said Strike.

What did that mean, Robin wondered, her heart thumping very hard: she took another large gulp of whisky before she said,

'Why are you apologising? You're not—'

'She's *my* friend.'

'She's mine, too, now,' said Robin. 'I . . . don't think she can help herself. She sees two friends of the opposite sex getting on . . .'

'Yeah,' said Strike, all antennae now: was that all they were? Friends of the opposite sex? Not wanting to leave the subject of men and women, he said,

'You never told me how mediation went. How come he settled, after dragging it out all this time?'

'Sarah's pregnant. They want to get married before she has it . . . or before she gets too big for a designer dress, knowing Sarah.'

'Shit,' said Strike quietly, wondering how upset she was. He couldn't read her tone or see her clearly: the office was now full of shadow, but he didn't want to turn on the lights. 'Is he – did you expect that?'

'S'pose I should have,' said Robin, with a smile Strike couldn't see, but which hurt her bruised face. 'She was probably getting annoyed with the way he was dragging out our divorce. When he was about to end their affair, she left an earring in our bed for me to find. Probably getting worried he wasn't going to propose, so she forgot to take her pill. It's the one way women can control men, isn't it?' she said, momentarily forgetting Charlotte, and the baby she claimed to have lost. 'I've got a feeling she'd just told him she was pregnant when he cancelled mediation the first time. Matthew said it was an accident

. . . maybe he didn't want to have it, when she first told him . . .'

'Do you want kids?' Strike asked Robin.

'I used to think so,' said Robin slowly. 'Back when I thought Matthew and I were . . . you know. For ever.'

As she said it, memories of old imaginings came to her: of a family group that had never existed, but which had once seemed quite vivid to her. The night that Matthew had proposed, she'd formed a clear mental picture of the pair of them with three children (a compromise between his family, where there had been two children, and her own, which had had four). She'd seen it all quite clearly: Matthew cheering on a young son who was learning to play rugby, as he'd done himself; Matthew watching his own little girl onstage, playing Mary in the school nativity play. It struck her now how very conventional her imaginings had been, and how much Matthew's expectations had become her own.

Sitting here in the darkness with Strike, Robin thought that Matthew would, in fact, be a very good father to the kind of child he'd be expecting: in other words, a little boy who wanted to play rugby, or a little girl who wanted to dance in a tutu. He'd carry their pictures around in his wallet, he'd get involved at their schools, he'd hug them when they needed it, he'd care about their homework. He wasn't devoid of kindness: he felt guilty when he did wrong. It was simply that what

Matthew considered right was so heavily coloured by what other people did, what other people considered acceptable and desirable.

'But I don't know, any more,' said Robin, after a short pause. 'I can't see myself having kids while doing this job. I think I'd be torn . . . and I don't ever want to be torn again. Matthew was always trying to guilt me out of this career: I didn't earn enough, I worked too many hours, I took too many risks . . . but I love it,' said Robin, with a trace of fierceness, 'and I don't want to apologise for that any more . . .

'What about you?' she asked Strike. 'Do *you* want children?'

'No,' said Strike.

Robin laughed.

'What's funny?'

'I give a whole soul-searching speech on the subject and you're just: *no.*'

'I shouldn't be here, should I?' said Strike, out of the darkness. 'I'm an accident. I'm not inclined to perpetuate the mistake.'

There was a pause, then Robin said, with asperity,

'Strike, that's just bloody self-indulgent.'

'Why?' said Strike, startled into a laugh. When he'd said the same to Charlotte, she'd both understood and agreed with him. Early in her teens, her drunken mother had told Charlotte she'd considered aborting her.

'Because . . . for God's sake, you can't let your

whole life be coloured by the circumstances of your conception! If everyone who was conceived accidentally stopped having kids—'

'We'd all be better off, wouldn't we?' said Strike robustly. 'The world's overpopulated as it is. Anyway, none of the kids I know make me particularly keen to have my own.'

'You like Jack.'

'I do, but that's one kid out of God knows how many. Dave Polworth's kids – you know who Polworth is?'

'Your best mate,' said Robin.

'He's my oldest mate,' Strike corrected her. 'My best mate . . .'

For a split-second he wondered whether he was going to say it, but the whisky had lifted the guard he usually kept upon himself: why not say it, why not let go?

'. . . is you.'

Robin was so amazed, she couldn't speak. Never, in four years, had Strike come close to telling her what she was to him. Fondness had had to be deduced from offhand comments, small kindnesses, awkward silences or gestures forced from him under stress. She'd only once before felt as she did now, and the unexpected gift that had engendered the feeling had been a sapphire and diamond ring, which she'd left behind when she walked out on the man who'd given it to her.

She wanted to make some kind of return, but for a moment or two, her throat felt too constricted.

'I . . . well, the feeling's mutual,' she said, trying not to sound too happy.

Over on the sofa, Strike dimly registered that somebody was on the metal staircase below their floor. Sometimes the graphic designer in the office beneath worked late. Mostly Strike was savouring the pleasure it had given him to hear Robin return his declaration of affection.

And now, full of whisky, he remembered holding her on the stairs at her wedding. This was the closest they'd come to that moment in nearly two years, and the air seemed thick with unspoken things, and again, he felt as though he stood on a small platform, ready to swing out into the unknown. *Leave it there*, said the surly self that coveted a solitary attic space, and freedom, and peace. *Now*, breathed the flickering demon the whisky had unleashed, and like Robin a few minutes previously, Strike was conscious that they were sitting mere feet from a double bed.

Footsteps reached the landing outside the glass outer door. Before either Strike or Robin could react, it had opened.

'Is the power oot?' said Barclay, and he flicked on the light. After a moment in which the three blinked at each other in surprise, Barclay said,

'You're a friggin' genius, R – the fuck happened tae yer face?'

CHAPTER 59

The warlike Britonesse . . .
. . . with such vncouth welcome did receaue
Her fayned Paramour, her forced guest,
That being forst his saddle soone to leaue,
Him selfe he did of his new loue deceaue:
And made him selfe then ample of his follie.
Which done, she passed forth not taking
  leaue,
And left him now as sad, as whilome iollie,
Well warned to beware with whom he dar'd
  to dallie.

Edmund Spenser
The Faerie Queene

Blinking in the bright light, Robin reached again for the ice pack.

'Strike hit me. Accidentally.'

'Jesus,' said Barclay. 'Wouldnae wanna see what he can do deliberately. How'd that happen?'

'My face got in the way of his elbow,' said Robin.

'Huh,' said Barclay, hungrily eyeing the almost

empty curry cartons, 'what wus that? Compensation?'

'Exactly,' said Robin.

'Tha' why neither of yiz have been answerin' yer phones fer the last three hours?'

'Shit, sorry, Sam,' said Robin, pulling out her mobile and looking at it. She'd had fifteen missed calls from Barclay since muting her mother in the American Bar. She was also pleased to see that she'd missed a couple of texts from Morris, one of which seemed to have a picture attached.

'Beyond the call of duty to come in person,' said the slightly drunk Strike. He wasn't sure whether he was more glad or annoyed that Barclay had interrupted, but on balance, he thought annoyance was uppermost.

'The wife's at her mother's wi' the bairn over-night,' said Barclay. 'So I thought I'd come deliver the good news in person.'

He helped himself to a poppadum and sat down on the arm of the sofa at the other end to Strike.

'I've found oot what SB gets up tae in Stoke Newington. All down tae Robin. You ready for this?'

'What?' said Strike, looking between Barclay and Robin. 'When—?'

'Earlier,' said Robin, 'before I met you.'

'Rang the doorbell,' said Barclay, 'said I'd bin recommended by SB, wondered whether she could help me oot. She didnae believe me. I had to get a foot in the door to stop her slammin' it on me.

Then she says SB told her a Scottish guy talked him doon off Tower Bridge the other day.

'So I decide it's cut our losses time,' said Barclay. 'I said, yeah, that wuz me. I'm a friend. We know what ye're up to in here. You're gonnae wanna talk to me, if ye care aboot your client.

'So she let me in.'

Barclay ate a bit of poppadum.

'Sorry, starvin'. Anyway, she takes me in the back room, and there it all is.'

'There what all is?'

'Giant playpen she's knocked up, out o' some foam an' MDF,' said Barclay, grinning. 'Big old changin' mat. Stack of adult nappies. Johnson's baby powder.'

Strike appeared to have been struck momentarily speechless. Robin began to laugh, but stopped quickly, because it made her face hurt.

'Poor old SB gets aff on bein' a baby. She's only got one other client, that guy at the gym. Doesnae need any more, because SB pays her so much. She dresses 'em up. Changes 'em. Powders their fucking arses—'

'You're having a laugh,' said Strike. 'This can't be real.'

'It is real,' said Robin, with the ice pack pressed to her face. 'It's called . . . hang on . . .'

She brought up the list of paraphilias on her phone again.

'Autonepiophilia. "Being aroused by the thought of oneself as an infant."'

402

'How the hell did you—?'

'I was watching the old people being wheeled out of the nursing home,' said Robin. 'Morris said they were like kids, that some of them were probably wearing nappies and it just . . . *clicked.* I saw her buying a ton of baby powder and dummies in the supermarket, but we've never once seen a child go in or out of that house. Then there was that patting on the head business, like the men were little kids . . .'

Strike remembered following the gym manager home, the man's hand over his lower face as he left Elinor Dean's house, as though he'd had something protruding from his mouth that he wanted to conceal.

'. . . and big boxes being delivered, of something really light,' Robin was saying.

'That'll be the adult nappies,' said Barclay. 'Anyway . . . she's no' a bad woman. Made me a cup of tea. She kens aboot the blackmail, but here's something interestin': she and SB don't think Shifty knows what's really goin' on inside that hoose.'

'How come?'

'The gym manager let it slip tae Shifty he knew a big man at Shifty's company. SB and the gym guy sometimes go in the playpen together, see. Like it's a nurs – like it's a nurser—'

Barclay suddenly broke into peals of laughter and Strike followed suit. Robin pressed the ice pack to her face and joined in. For a minute, all three of them roared with laughter at the mental image of the two men in nappies, sitting in their MDF playpen.

'—like it's a nursery,' said Barclay in a falsetto, wiping tears out of his eyes. 'Fuck me, it takes all sorts, eh? Anyway, the tit at the gym lets this slip, an' Shifty, knowin' old SB never went tae a gym in his life, an' that he lives on the other side o' London, probes a wee bit, and notices the other guy gettin' uncomfortable. So Shifty follows SB. Watches him going in and oot Elinor's place. Draws the obvious conclusion: she's a hooker.

'Shifty then walks intae SB's office, closes the door, gives him Elinor's address, and says he kens what's goin' on in there. SB was shittin' himself, but he's no fool. He reckons Shifty thinks it's just straight sex, but he's worried Shifty might do more diggin'. See, SB found Elinor online, advertisin' her services in some dark corner o' the net. SB's scared Shifty'll go looking for whut she really does if he denies it's sex, an' if anyone finds oot whut really goes on in there, SB's gonna be straight back up Tower Bridge.

'So, that bit's no' so funny,' said Barclay, more soberly. 'The guy at the gym only came clean tae SB and Elinor a coupla months ago, about talking tae Shifty. He's aboot ready tae kill himself, for what he's done. Elinor's taken her ad down, but the internet never forgets, so that's no bloody use . . .

'The worst thing, Elinor says, is Shifty himself

is a right cock. SB's told her all aboot him. Apparently Shifty takes his coke habit tae work and he's always feelin' up his PA, but SB cannae do anything about it, for fear of retribution. So,' said Barclay, 'what are we gonnae do, eh? Tell the board SB's suit troosers dinnae fit him properly because he's wearin' a nappy underneath?'

Strike didn't smile. The amount of whisky he'd consumed didn't particularly help his mental processes. It was Robin who spoke first.

'Well, we can tell the board everything, and accept that's going to ruin a few lives . . . or we can let them terminate our contract without telling them what's going on, and accept that Shifty's going to keep blackmailing SB . . . or . . .'

'Yeah,' said Strike heavily, 'that's the question, isn't it? Where's the third option, where Shifty gets his comeuppance and SB doesn't end up in the Thames?'

'It sounds,' said Robin to Barclay, 'as though Elinor would back SB up, if he claimed it was just an affair? Of course, SB's wife mightn't be happy.'

'Aye, Elinor'd back him up,' said Barclay. 'It's in her interests.'

'I'd like to nail Shifty,' said Strike. 'That'd please the client no end, if we helped them get rid of Shifty without the company's name getting splashed all over the papers . . . which it definitely will if it gets out their CEO likes having his arse powdered . . .

'If that PA's being sexually harassed,' Strike said, 'and watching him do coke at work, why isn't she complaining?'

'Fear of not being believed?' Robin suggested. 'Of losing her job?'

'Could you,' Strike said to Robin, 'ring Morris for me? He'll still have the girl's contact details. And, Barclay,' Strike added, getting up from the sofa on the third attempt, and heading for the inner office, 'come in here, we're going to have to change next week's rota. Robin can't follow people looking like she just did three rounds with Tyson Fury.'

The other two went into Strike's office. Robin stayed sitting at Pat's desk for a moment, thinking not about what Barclay had just told them, but about the moments before he'd arrived, when she and Strike had been sitting in semi-darkness. The memory of Strike telling her she was his best friend made her heart feel immeasurably lightened, as though something she hadn't realised was weighing on it had been removed for ever.

After a moment's pleasurable savouring of this feeling, she pulled out her mobile, and opened the texts Morris had sent her earlier. The first, which had the picture attached, said '**lol**'. The image was of a sign reading: 'Viagra Shipment Stolen. Cops Looking For Gang of Hardened Criminals.' The second text said, '**Not funny?**'

'No,' Robin muttered. 'Not funny.'

Getting to her feet, she pressed Morris's number,

and began to clear up the curry one-handed, while she held the phone to her ear.

'Evening,' said Morris, after a couple of rings. 'Calling to tell me you've found a hardened criminal?'

'Are you driving?' asked Robin, ignoring the witticism.

'On foot. Just seen the old folks' home locked up for the night. I'm actually right by the office, I'm on my way to relieve Hutchins. He's outside the Ivy, keeping an eye on Miss Jones's boyfriend.'

'Well, we need the details of Shifty's PA,' said Robin.

'What? Why?'

'We've found out what he's blackmailing SB about, but,' she hesitated, imagining the jokes she'd have to hear at SB's expense, if she told Morris what Elinor Dean was doing for him, 'it's nothing illegal and he's not hurting anyone. We want to talk to Shifty's PA again, so we need her contact details.'

'No, I don't think we should go back to her,' said Morris. 'Bad idea.'

'Why?' Robin asked, as she dropped the foil tins into the pedal bin, suppressing her frown because it made her bruised face ache.

'Because . . . fuck's sake,' said Morris, who usually avoided swearing to Robin. 'You were the one who said we shouldn't use her.'

Behind Robin, in the inner office, Barclay laughed at something Strike had said. For the third time that evening, Robin had a feeling of impending trouble.

'Saul,' she said, 'you aren't still seeing her, are you?'

He didn't answer immediately. Robin picked up the plates from the desk and put them in the sink, waiting for his answer.

'No, of course I'm not,' he said, with an attempt at a laugh. 'I just think this is a bad idea. You were the one who said, before, that she had too much to lose—'

'But we wouldn't be asking her to entrap him or set him up this time—'

'I'll need to think about this,' said Morris.

Robin put the knives and forks into the sink, too.

'Saul, this isn't up for debate. We need her contact details.'

'I don't know whether I kept them,' said Morris, and Robin knew he was lying. 'Where's Strike right now?'

'Denmark Street,' said Robin. Not wanting another sly joke about her and Strike being together after dark, she purposely didn't say she was there, too.

'OK, I'll ring him,' said Morris, and before Robin could say anything else, he'd hung up.

The whisky she'd drunk was still having a slightly anaesthetic effect. Robin knew that if she were entirely sober, she'd be feeling still more incensed at yet another example of Morris treating her not as a partner in the firm, but as Strike's secretary.

Turning on the taps in the cramped kitchen area, she began rinsing off the plates and forks, and as curry sauce dripped down the drain, her thoughts drifted again to those moments before Barclay had arrived, while she and Strike had still been sitting in semi-darkness.

Out on Charing Cross Road, a car passed, blaring Rita Ora's 'I Will Never Let You Down', and softly, under her breath, Robin sang along:

> *'Tell me baby what we gonna do*
> *I'll make it easy, got a lot to lose . . .'*

Putting the plug into the sink, she began to fill it, squirting washing-up liquid on top of the cutlery. Singing, her eyes fell on the unopened vodka Strike had bought, but which neither of them had touched. She thought of Oakden stealing vodka at Margot's barbecue . . .

> *'You've been tired of watching me*
> *forgot to have a good time . . .'*

. . . and claiming that he hadn't spiked the punch. Yet Gloria had vomited . . . At the very moment Robin drew breath into her lungs to call to Strike, and tell him her new idea, two hands closed on her waist.

Twice in Robin's life, a man had attacked her

from behind: without conscious thought, she simultaneously stamped down hard with her high heel on the foot of the man behind her, threw back her head, smashing it into his face, grabbed a knife in the sink and spun around as the grip at her waist disappeared.

'FUCK!' bellowed Morris.

She hadn't heard him coming up the stairs over the noise of water splashing into the sink and her own singing. Morris was now doubled up, hands clamped over his nose.

'FUCK!' he shouted again, taking his hands away from his face, to reveal that his nose was bleeding. He hopped backwards, the imprint of her stiletto imprinted in his shoe, and collapsed onto the sofa.

'What's going on?' said Strike, emerging at speed from the inner office and looking from Morris on the sofa to Robin, who was still holding the knife. She turned off the taps, breathing hard.

'He grabbed me,' she said, as Barclay emerged from the inner room behind Strike. 'I didn't hear him coming.'

'It – was – a – fucking – *joke*,' said Morris, examining the blood smeared on his hands. 'I only meant to make you jump – fuck's *sake*—'

But adrenalin and whisky had suddenly unleashed an anger in Robin such as she hadn't felt since the night she'd left Matthew. Light-headed, she advanced on Morris.

'Would you sneak up on Strike and grab him

round the waist? D'you creep up on Barclay and hug him? *D'you send either of them pictures of your dick?'*

There was a silence.

'You bitch,' said Morris, the back of his hand pressed to his nostrils. 'You said you wouldn't—'

'He did what?' said Strike.

'Sent me a dick pic,' snapped the furious Robin, and turning back to Morris, she said, 'I'm not some sixteen-year-old work experience girl who's scared of telling you to stop. I don't want your hands on me, OK? I don't want you kissing me—'

'He sent you—?' began Strike.

'I didn't tell you because you were so stressed,' said Robin. 'Joan was dying, you were up and down to Cornwall, you didn't need the grief, but I'm done. I'm not working with him any more. I want him gone.'

'Christ's sake,' said Morris again, dabbing at his nose, 'it was a *joke*—'

'Ye need tae learn tae read the fuckin' room, mate,' said Barclay, who was standing against the wall, arms folded, and seemed to be enjoying himself.

'You can't fucking fire me over—'

'You're a subcontractor,' said Strike. 'We're not renewing your contract. Your non-disclosure agreement remains in operation. One word of anything you've found out working here, and I'll make sure you never get another detective job. Now get the fuck out of this office.'

Wild-eyed, Morris stood up, still bleeding from his left nostril.

'Fine. You want to keep her on because you've got a hard-on for her, fine.'

Strike took a step forwards; Morris nearly fell over the sofa, backing away.

'Fine,' he said again.

He turned and walked straight out of the office, slamming the glass door behind him. While the door vibrated, and Morris's footsteps clanged away down the metal stairs, Barclay pushed himself off the wall, plucked the knife Robin was still holding out of her hand and went to drop it into the sink with the dirty crockery.

'Never liked that tosser,' he said.

Strike and Robin looked at each other, then at the worn carpet, where a couple of drops of Morris's blood still glistened.

'One all, then,' said Strike, clapping his hands together. 'What say, first to break Barclay's nose wins the night?'

PART VI

So past the twelue Months forth, and their dew places found.

Edmund Spenser
The Faerie Queene

CHAPTER 60

Fortune, the foe of famous cheuisaunce
Seldome (said Guyon) yields to vertue aide,
But in her way throwes mischiefe and
*   mischaunce,*
Whereby her course is stopt, and passage
*   staid.*

Edmund Spenser
The Faerie Queene

What would have happened had Sam Barclay not opened the door that evening and switched on the light was a question that preoccupied both detective partners over the weekend, each of them re-running the conversation in their head, wondering what the other was thinking, and whether too much had been said, or given away.

Sober now, Strike had to be glad he hadn't done what whisky had been urging him to do. Had he acted on that alcohol-fuelled impulse, he might now be in a state of bitter remorse, with no way back to the friendship that was unique in his life. Yet in his free moments, he wondered whether Robin had known how dangerously close he'd come to pushing the conversation into territory that had previously been fenced around with barbed wire, or that, seconds before Barclay flicked the light switch, Strike had been trying to remember when he'd last changed his sheets.

Robin, meanwhile, had woken on Sunday morning with her face aching as though it had been trodden on, a slight hangover, and a volatile mixture of pleasure and anxiety. She went back over everything she'd said to Strike, hoping she hadn't betrayed any of those feelings she habitually denied, even to herself. The memory of him telling her she was his best friend caused a little spurt of happiness every time she returned to it, but as the day wore on, and her bruising worsened, she wished she'd been brave enough to ask him directly how he now felt about Charlotte Campbell.

An image of Charlotte hung permanently in Robin's head these days, like a shadowy portrait she'd never wanted hung. The picture had acquired shape and form in the four years since they'd passed on the stairs in the Denmark Street office, because of the many details Ilsa had given her, and the snippets she'd read in the press. Last night, though, that image had become stark and fixed: a darkly romantic vision of a lost and dying love, breathing her final words in Strike's ear as she lay among trees.

And this was, however you looked at it, an extraordinarily powerful image. Strike had once, when extremely drunk, told Robin that Charlotte was the most beautiful woman he'd ever seen, and as she hovered between life and death, that beautiful woman had chosen to contact Strike, to tell him she loved him still. What did prosaic Robin Ellacott have to offer that was in any way equal to such high-stakes drama, such extremity of emotion? An up-to-date rota, nearly docketed invoices and cups of strong tea? Doubtless because of the pain in her face, Robin's mood vacillated between diminishing cheerfulness and a tendency to brood. Finally, she gave herself a stern talking to: Strike had given her an unprecedented assurance of affection, and she'd never have to see Saul Morris again, and she should be delighted about both.

Predictably, it was Pat who took the sudden firing of Saul Morris hardest. Strike delivered the news on Monday morning, as he and the secretary narrowly missed colliding in the doorway onto Denmark Street, Strike on his way out, Pat on her way in. Both of them were preparing for the ingestion of nicotine, Pat having just taken out the electronic cigarette she used during work hours, Strike already holding the Benson & Hedges he rarely smoked in the office.

'Morning,' said Strike. 'I've left a note on your desk, couple of things I'd like you to do while I'm out. Robin'll be in at ten. Oh—'

He'd taken a couple of steps before turning back.

'—and can you calculate Morris's pay up to Friday and transfer it into his account right away? He's not coming back.'

He didn't wait for a reaction, so it was Robin who took the brunt of their secretary's disappointment when she arrived at ten to ten. Pat had Radio Two playing, but turned it off the moment the door handle turned.

'Morning. Why – what 'appened to you?' said Pat.

Robin's face looked worse, two days on, than it had on Saturday. While the swelling had subsided, both eyes were ringed in dark grey tinged with red.

'It was an accident. I bumped into something,' said Robin, stripping off her coat and hanging it on a peg. 'So I won't be on surveillance this week.'

She took a book out of her handbag and crossed to the kettle, holding it. She hadn't particularly enjoyed the covert staring on the Tube that morning, but wasn't going to mention Strike's elbow to Pat, because she tried, wherever possible, not to fuel Pat's antipathy for her partner.

'Why won't Saul be coming back?' Pat demanded.

'He didn't work out,' said Robin, her back to Pat as she took down two mugs.

'What d'you mean?' said Pat indignantly. 'He

418

caught that man who was having it away with the nanny. He always kept his paperwork up to date, which is more'n you can say for that Scottish nutter.'

'I know,' said Robin. 'But he wasn't a great team player, Pat.'

Pat took a deep drag of nicotine vapour, frowning.

'He,' she nodded towards the empty chair where Strike usually sat, 'could take a few lessons from Morris!'

Robin knew perfectly well that it wasn't Pat's decision who the partners hired and fired, but unlike Strike, she also thought that in such a small team, Pat deserved the truth.

'It wasn't Cormoran who wanted him gone,' she said, turning to face the secretary, 'it was me.'

'You!' said Pat, astounded. 'I thought the pair of you were keen on each other!'

'No. I didn't like him. Apart from anything else, he sent me a picture of his erect penis at Christmas.'

Pat's deeply lined face registered an almost comical dismay.

'In . . . in the post?'

Robin laughed.

'What, tucked inside a Christmas card? No. By text.'

'You didn't—?'

'Ask for it? No,' said Robin, no longer smiling. 'He's a creep, Pat.'

She turned back to the kettle. The untouched bottle of vodka was still standing beside the sink. As Robin's eyes fell on it, she remembered the idea that had occurred to her on Saturday night, shortly before Morris's hands closed around her waist. After giving the secretary her coffee, she carried her own into the inner office, along with the book she'd taken from her bag. Pat called after her,

'Shall I update the rota, or will you?'

'I'll do it,' said Robin, closing the door, but instead, she called Strike.

'Morning,' he said, answering on the second ring.

'Hi. I forgot to tell you an idea I had on Saturday night.'

'Go on.'

'It's about Gloria Conti. Why did she vomit in the bathroom at Margot's barbecue, if Oakden didn't spike the punch?'

'Because he's a liar, and he *did* spike the punch?' suggested Strike. He was currently in the same Islington square that Robin had patrolled on Friday, but he paused now and reached for his cigarettes, eyes on the central garden, which today was deserted. Beds densely planted with purple pansies looked like velvet cloaks spread upon the glistening grass.

'Or did she throw up because she was pregnant?' said Robin.

'I thought,' said Strike, after a pause while

lighting a cigarette, 'that only happens in the mornings? Isn't that why it's called—'

On the point of saying 'morning sickness', Strike remembered the expectant wife of an old army friend, who'd been hospitalised for persistent, round-the-clock vomiting.

'My cousin threw up any time of the day when she was pregnant,' said Robin. 'She couldn't stand certain food smells. And Gloria was at a barbecue.'

'Right,' said Strike, who was suddenly remembering the odd notion that had occurred to him after talking to the Bayliss sisters. Robin's theory struck him as stronger than his. In fact, his idea was weakened if Robin's was true.

'So,' he said, 'you're thinking it might've been Gloria who—'

'—had the abortion at the Bride Street clinic? Yes,' said Robin. 'And that Margot helped her arrange it. Irene mentioned Gloria being closeted in Margot's consulting room, remember? While Irene was left on reception?'

The lilac bush in the central garden was casting out such a heavy scent that Strike could smell it even over the smoke of his cigarette.

'I think you could be on to something here,' said Strike slowly.

'I also thought this might explain—'

'Why Gloria doesn't want to talk to us?'

'Well, yes. Apart from it being a traumatic memory, her husband might not know what happened,' said Robin. 'Where are you just now?'

'Islington,' said Strike. 'I'm about to have a crack at Mucky Ricci.'

'What?' said Robin, startled.

'Been thinking about it over the weekend,' said Strike, who, unlike Robin, had had no time off, but had run surveillance on Shifty and Miss Jones's boyfriend. 'We're nearly ten months into our year, and we've got virtually nothing. If he's demented, obviously it'll be no-go, but you never know, I could be able to get something out of him. He might even,' said Strike, 'get a kick out of reliving the good old days . . .'

'And what if his sons find out?'

'He can't talk, or not properly. I'm banking on him being unable to tell them I've been in. Look,' said Strike, in no particular hurry to hang up, because he wanted to finish his cigarette, and would rather do it talking to Robin, 'Betty Fuller thinks Ricci killed her, I could tell. So did Tudor Athorn; he told his nephew so, and they were the kind of people who were plugged into local gossip and knew about local low life.

'I keep going back to the thing Shanker said, when I told him about Margot vanishing without a trace. "Professional job." When you take a step back and look at it,' said Strike, now down to the last centimetre of his cigarette, 'it seems borderline impossible for every trace of her to have disappeared, unless someone with plenty of practice handled it.'

'Creed had practice,' said Robin quietly.

'D'you know what I did last night?' said Strike,

422

ignoring this interjection. 'Looked up Kara Wolfson's birth certificate online.'

'Why? Oh,' said Robin, and Strike could hear her smiling, 'star sign?'

'Yeah. I know it breaks the means before motive rule,' he added, before Robin could point it out, 'but it struck me that someone might've told Margot about Kara's murder. Doctors know things, don't they? In and out of people's houses, having confidential consultations. They're like priests. They hear secrets.'

'You were checking whether Kara was a Scorpio,' said Robin. It was a statement rather than a question.

'Exactly. And wondering whether Ricci looked into that party to show his goons which woman they were going to pick off.'

'Well?'

'Well what?'

'*Was* Kara a Scorpio?'

'Oh. No. Taurus – seventeenth of May.'

Strike now heard pages turning at Robin's end of the call.

'Which means, according to Schmidt . . .' said Robin, and there was a brief pause, '. . . she was Cetus.'

'Huh,' said Strike, who'd now finished his cigarette. 'Well, wish me luck. I'm going in.'

'Good l—'

'*Cormoran Strike!*' said somebody gleefully, behind him.

As Strike hung up on Robin, a slender black woman in a cream coat came alongside him, beaming.

'You don't remember me, do you?' she said. 'Selly Oak. I'm—'

'Marjorie!' said Strike, the memory coming back to him. 'Marjorie the physiotherapist. How are you? What're you—?'

'I do a few hours in the old folks' home up the road!' said Marjorie. 'And look at *you*, all famous . . .'

Fuck.

It took Strike twenty-five minutes to extricate himself from her.

'. . . so that's bloody that,' he told Robin later at the office. 'I pretended I was in the area to visit my accountant, but if she's working at St Peter's, there's no chance of us getting in to see Ricci.'

'No chance of *you* getting in there—'

'I've already told you,' said Strike sharply. The state of Robin's face was a visible warning against recklessness, of the perils of failing to think through consequences. 'You're not going anywhere near him.'

'I've got Miss Jones on the line,' Pat called from the outer office.

'Put her through to me,' said Robin, as Strike mouthed 'thanks'.

Robin talked to Miss Jones while continuing to readjust the rota on her computer, which, given Robin's own temporary unavailability for surveillance, and Morris's permanent absence, was like trying to balance a particularly tricky linear equation. She spent the next forty minutes making vague sounds of agreement whenever Miss Jones paused to draw breath. Their client's objective, Robin could tell, was staying on the line long enough for Strike to come back to the office. Finally, Robin got rid of her by pretending to get a message from Pat saying Strike would be out all day.

It was her only lie of the day, Robin thought, while Strike and Pat discussed Barclay's expenses in the outer office. Given that Strike was adept himself at avoiding pledging his own word when he didn't want to, he really ought to have noticed that Robin had made no promises whatsoever about staying away from Mucky Ricci.

CHAPTER 61

Then when the second watch was almost past,
That brasen dore flew open, and in went Bold Britomart . . .

Edmund Spenser
The Faerie Queene

In the first week of June, a blind item appeared in the *Metro*, concerning Strike's presence in the American Bar on the night of his father's party.

Which famous son of a famous father preferred to spend the night of his old man's celebrations brawling in a bar five hundred yards from the party, rather than hobnobbing with his family? Our spies tell us a punch was thrown, and his faithful assistant was unable to *Hold it Back*. A father-son competition for publicity? Dad definitely won this round.

426

As *Hold it Back* was the name of one of Jonny Rokeby's albums, nobody could really be in much doubt which father and son were in question. A couple of journalists called Strike's office, but as neither he nor Rokeby were disposed to comment, the story fizzled out for lack of details. 'Could've been worse,' was Strike's only comment. 'No photos, no mention of Bamborough. Looks like Oakden's been frightened out of the idea of selling stories about us.'

Feeling slightly guilty, Robin had already scrolled through the pictures of Jonny Rokeby's party on her phone, while on surveillance outside Miss Jones's boyfriend's house. Rokeby's guests, who included celebrities from both Hollywood and the world of rock 'n' roll, had all attended in eighteenth-century costumes. Buried in the middle of all the famous people was a single picture of Rokeby surrounded by six of his seven adult children. Robin recognised Al, grinning from beneath a crooked powdered wig. She could no more imagine Strike there, trussed up in brocade, with patches on his face, than she could imagine him pole-vaulting.

Relieved as she was that Oakden appeared to have given up the idea of discussing the agency with the press, Robin's anxiety mounted as June progressed. The Bamborough case, which mattered to her more than almost anything else, had come to a complete standstill. Gloria Conti had met Anna's request for her cooperation with silence,

Steve Douthwaite remained as elusive as ever, Robin had heard no news about the possibility of interviewing Dennis Creed, and Mucky Ricci remained cloistered inside his nursing home, which, owing to the agency's reduced manpower, nobody was watching any more.

Even temporary replacements for Morris were proving impossible to find. Strike had contacted everyone he knew in the Special Investigation Branch, Hutchins had asked his Met contacts, and Robin had canvassed Vanessa, but nobody was showing any interest in joining the agency.

'Summer, isn't it?' said Barclay, as he and Robin crossed paths in the office one Saturday afternoon. 'People don't want tae start a new job, they want a holiday. I ken how they feel.'

Both Barclay and Hutchins had booked weeks off with their wives and children months in advance, and neither partner could begrudge their subcontractors a break. The result was that by mid-July, Strike and Robin were the only two left working at the agency.

While Strike devoted himself to following Miss Jones's boyfriend, still trying to find out anything that might prove that he was an unsuitable person to have custody of his daughter, Robin was trying to kindle an acquaintance with Shifty's PA, which wasn't proving easy. So far that month, wearing a different wig and coloured contacts each time, Robin had tried to engage her in conversation in a bar, deliberately tripped over her in a nightclub, and followed her into the ladies in Harvey Nichols. While the PA didn't seem to have the slightest idea that it was the same woman opportuning or inconveniencing her, she showed no inclination to chat, let alone confess that her boss was a lech or a coke user.

Having tried and failed to sit next to the PA in a sandwich bar in Holborn one lunchtime, Robin, who today had dark hair and dark brown eyes courtesy of hair chalk and contact lenses, decided the moment had come to try and wheedle information out of a very old man, instead of a pretty young woman.

She hadn't reached this decision lightly, nor did she approach it in any casual spirit. While Robin was vaguely fond of Strike's old friend Shanker, she was under no illusions about how evil a person would have to be to scare a man who'd been steeped in criminal violence since the age of nine. Accordingly, she'd worked out a plan, of which the first step was to have a full and effective disguise. Today's happened to be particularly good: she'd learned a lot about make-up since starting the job with Strike, and she'd sometimes had the satisfaction of seeing her partner double-take before he realised who she was. After checking her reflection carefully in the mirror of a McDonald's bathroom, and reassuring herself that she not only looked utterly unlike Robin Ellacott, but that nobody would guess she'd recently had two black eyes, she set off for the

Tube, and just under twenty minutes later, arrived at Angel station.

The garden where the old residents of St Peter's sometimes sat was empty as she passed it, in spite of the warm weather. The pansies were gone, replaced by pink asters and the broad, sunny street where the nursing home lay was almost deserted.

The quotation from St Peter gleamed gold in the sunshine as Robin approached the front door.

. . . it was not with perishable things such as silver or gold that you were redeemed . . . but with the precious blood of Christ . . .

Robin rang the bell. After a few moments, a chubby black-haired woman in the familiar blue uniform opened it.

'Afternoon,' she said, sounding Spanish.

'Hi,' said Robin, her North London accent copied from her friend Vanessa. 'I'm here to visit Enid? I'm her great-granddaughter.'

She'd stored up the only first name she'd heard for any of the old ladies in the home. Her great fear had been that Enid might have died before she got to use it, or that Enid had no family.

'Oh, that's nice,' said the nurse, smiling and gesturing towards a visitors' book just inside the door. 'Sign in, please, and don't forget to sign out when you leave. She's in her room. Might be asleep!'

Robin stepped into a dark, wood-panelled hall. She deliberately hadn't asked which number

430

Enid's room was, because she intended to get lost finding it.

A number of walking frames and a couple of collapsible wheelchairs were lined up against the wall. The hall was dominated by an enormous crucifix facing the door, on which a pallid plaster Jesus hung, his six-pack rendered with startling precision, scarlet blood dripping from hands, feet and the punctures left by his crown of thorns. The home smelled better than Betty Fuller's sheltered accommodation: though there was a definite undertone of old cooking smells, it mingled with that of furniture wax.

Sunlight poured through the fan window behind Robin as she bent over the visitors' book and wrote in the date, the time she'd entered the building and the fake name she'd decided on: *Vanessa Jones.* Over the table where the visitors' book lay hung a board showing the name of each resident. Beside each was a little sliding door, which could be adjusted to show whether the occupant was 'in' or 'out'. Niccolo Ricci was currently – and, Robin suspected, almost permanently – 'in'.

There was a lift, but she chose to take the red-carpeted and wooden-banistered stairs, passing the Trinidadian nurse she'd often seen while on surveillance, who was descending. He smiled and wished her a good afternoon, his arms laden with packs of incontinence pads.

A doorway led off the first landing, a small sign beside it announcing that this way lay bedrooms

1 to 10. Robin set off along the corridor, reading names off doors. Unfortunately, 'Mrs Enid Billings' lived behind door number 2 and, as Robin swiftly discovered, Ricci wasn't on her floor. Aware that this was going to make any claim of having got lost on the way to Enid's room implausible in the extreme, Robin doubled back, and climbed up to the second floor.

A few steps along an identical corridor to the one below, she heard a woman with a strong Polish accent in the distance, and backed hastily into an alcove where a sink and cupboard had been placed.

'D'you need the bathroom? *Do – you – need – the – bathroom, Mister – Ricci?*'

A low moan answered.

'*Yes?*' said the voice. '*Or no?*'

There was a second, answering moan.

'*No?* All right then . . .'

Footsteps grew louder: the nurse was about to pass the alcove, so Robin stepped boldly out from it, smiling.

'Just washing my hands,' she told the approaching nurse, who was blonde and flat-footed and merely nodded as she passed, apparently preoccupied with other matters.

Once the nurse had disappeared, Robin proceeded down the corridor, until she reached the door of number 15, which bore the name 'Mr Nico Ricci'.

Unconsciously holding her breath, Robin

knocked gently, and pushed. There was no lock on the inside of the door; it swung open at once.

The room inside, while small, faced south, getting plenty of sun. A great effort had been made to make the room homely: watercolour pictures hung on the walls, including one of the Bay of Naples. The mantelpiece was covered in family photographs, and a number of children's paintings had been taped up on the wardrobe door, including one captioned 'Grandpa and Me and a Kite'.

The elderly occupant was bent almost double in an armchair beside the window. In the minute that had elapsed since the nurse left him, he'd fallen fast asleep. Robin let the door close quietly behind her, crept across to Ricci and sat down on the end of his single bed, facing the one-time pimp, pornographer and orchestrator of gang-rape and murder.

There was no doubt that the staff looked after their charges well. Ricci's dark grey hair and his fingernails were as clean as his bright white shirt collar. In spite of the warmth of the room, they'd dressed him in a pale blue sweater. On one of the veiny hands lying limp on the chair beside him glistened the gold lion's head ring. The fingers were curled up in a way that made Robin wonder whether he could still use them. Perhaps he'd had a stroke, which would account for his inability to talk.

'Mr Ricci?' said Robin quietly.

He made a little snorting snuffle, and slowly

raised his head, his mouth hanging open. His enormous, drooping eyes, though not as filmy as Betty Fuller's, nevertheless looked dull, and like his ears and nose seemed to have grown while the rest of him shrank, leaving loose folds of dark skin.

'I've come to ask you some questions,' said Robin quietly. 'About a woman called Margot Bamborough.'

He gaped at her, open-mouthed. Could he hear her? Could he understand? There was no hearing aid in either of his overlarge ears. The loudest noise in the room was the thumping of Robin's heart.

'Do you remember Margot Bamborough?' she asked.

To her surprise, Ricci made his low moan. Did that mean yes or no?

'You do?' said Robin.

He moaned again.

'She disappeared. D'you know—?'

Footsteps were coming along the corridor outside. Robin got up hastily and smoothed away the impression she'd left on the bedspread.

Please God, don't let them be coming in here.

But God, it seemed, wasn't listening to Robin Ellacott. The footsteps grew louder, and then the door opened to reveal a very tall man whose face was pitted with acne scars and whose knobbly bald head looked, as Barclay had said, as though something heavy had been dropped on it: Luca Ricci.

'Who're you?' he said. His voice, which was far softer and higher than she'd imagined, made the hairs on the back of her neck prickle. For a second or two, Robin's terror threatened to derail her carefully worked out contingency plan. The very worst she'd expected to have to deal with was a nurse. None of the Riccis should have been here; it wasn't Sunday. And of all the Riccis she would have wanted to meet, Luca was the last.

'You his relative?' Robin asked in her North London accent. 'Oh, fank Gawd! He was making a weird moaning noise. I've just been visiting my gran, I fort he was ill or somefing.'

Still standing in the doorway, Luca looked Robin up and down.

'He doesthn't mean anything by it,' said Luca, who had a lisp. 'He moanth a bit, but it don't mean nothing, do it, eh, Dad?' he said loudly to the old man, who merely blinked at his eldest son.

Luca laughed.

'What'th your name?' he asked Robin.

'Vanessa,' she said promptly. 'Vanessa Jones.'

She took half a step forwards, hoping he'd move aside, but he remained planted exactly where he was, though smiling a little more widely. She knew he'd understood that she wanted to leave, but couldn't tell whether his evident determination to keep her inside was done for the simple pleasure of keeping her momentarily trapped, or because he hadn't believed her reason for being in his father's room. Robin could feel sweat under her armpits and over her scalp, and hoped to God that her hair chalk wouldn't come off.

'Never theen you around here before,' said Luca.

'No, it's my first time,' said Robin, forcing herself to smile. 'They look after 'em well, don't they?'

'Yeah,' said Luca, 'not bad. I usually come Thundayth, but we're off to Florida tomorrow. Gonna mith hith birthday. Not that he knowth it'th hith birthday – do you, eh?' he said, addressing his father, whose mouth continued to hang open, his eyes fixed vacantly on his son.

Luca took a small wrapped package from under his jacket, leaned over to the chest of drawers and laid it on top without moving his large feet so much as an inch.

'Aw, that's nice,' said Robin.

She could feel the sweat on her breastbone now, where it would be visible to Luca. The room was as warm as a greenhouse. Even had she not known who Luca was, she'd have known *what* he was. She could feel the potential for violence coming off him like radiation. It was in the greedy smile he was giving her, in the way he was now leaning up against the door jamb, revelling in the silent exercise of power.

'It'th only chocolateth,' said Luca. 'Who'th your granny?'

'Great-granny, really, but I call her "Gran",'

Robin said, playing for time, trying to remember any of the names she'd passed on the way to Ricci's room. 'Sadie.'

'Where'th she?'

'Couple of rooms that way,' said Robin, pointing left. She hoped he couldn't hear how dry her mouth was. 'Promised my mum I'd pop in and visit her while she's on holiday.'

'Yeah?' said Luca. 'Where'th your Mum gone?'

'Florence,' Robin invented wildly. 'Art galleries.'

'Yeah?' said Luca again. 'Our family'th from Napleth, originally. Innit, Dad?' he called over Robin's head at the gaping old man, before looking Robin up and down again. 'Know what my old man uthed to be?'

'No,' said Robin, trying to maintain her smile.

'He owned thtrip clubth,' said Luca Ricci. 'Back in the old dayth, he'd've had your pantieth right off you.'

She tried to laugh, but couldn't, and saw that Luca was delighted to see her discomfort.

'Oh yeah. Girl like you? He'd've offered you a hothtess job. It wath good money, too, even if you did have to blow thome of Dad'th mateth, hahaha.'

His laugh was as high-pitched as a woman's. Robin couldn't join in. She was remembering Kara Wolfson.

'Well,' she said, feeling the sweat trickling down her neck, 'I really need—'

'Don't worry,' said Luca, smiling, still standing

firmly between her and the door, '*I'm* not in that game.'

'What do you do?' asked Robin, who'd been on the verge of asking him to move aside, but lost her nerve.

'I'm in inthuranthe,' said Luca, smiling broadly. 'What about you?'

'Nursery nurse,' said Robin, taking the idea from the children's daubs on the wardrobe door.

'Yeah? Like kidth, do you?'

'I love them,' said Robin.

'Yeah,' said Luca. 'Me too. I got thix.'

'Wow,' said Robin. 'Six!'

'Yeah. And I'm not like him,' said Luca, looking over Robin's head again, at his gaping father. 'He wathn't interethted in uth until we were grown up. I like the littl'unth.'

'Oh, me too,' said Robin fervently.

'You needed to get knocked down by a car to get *hith* attention, when we were kidth,' said Luca. 'Happened to my brother Marco, when he wath twelve.'

'Oh no,' said Robin politely.

He was playing with her, demanding that she give him appropriate responses, while both of them were equally aware that she was too scared to ask him to move aside, afraid of what he might do. Now he smiled at her feigned concern for his brother Marco's long-ago car accident.

'Yeah, Dad thtayed at the hothpital with Marco for three weekth tholid, till Marco wath out of danger,' said Luca. 'At leatht, I think it wath Marco he wath thtaying for. Might've been the nurtheth. In the old dayth,' said Luca, looking Robin up and down again, 'they wore black thtockingth.'

Robin could hear footsteps again, and this time she prayed, *please be coming in here*, and her prayer was answered. The door behind Luca opened, hitting him in the back. The flat-footed blonde nurse was back.

'Oh, sorry, Mr Ricci,' she said, as Luca stepped aside. 'Oh,' she repeated, becoming aware of Robin's presence.

''E was moaning,' Robin said again, pointing at Mucky, in his chair. 'Sorry, I shouldn't've – I fort he might be in pain or something.'

And right on cue, Mucky Ricci moaned, almost certainly to contradict her.

'Yeah, he does a bit of that, if he wants something,' said the nurse. 'Probably ready for the bathroom now, are you, Mr Ricci?'

'I'm not thtaying to watch him crap,' said Luca Ricci, with a little laugh. 'I only came to drop off hith prethent for Thurthday.'

Robin was already halfway out of the door, but to her horror, she'd walked barely three steps when Luca appeared behind her, taking one stride to her every two.

'Not going to thay goodbye to Thadie?' he asked, as they passed the door of Mrs Sadie O'Keefe.

'Oh, she fell asleep while I was in there, bless her,' said Robin. 'Flat out.'

They walked down the stairs, Luca slightly behind her all the way. She could feel his eyes, like lasers, on the nape of her neck, on her legs and her backside.

After what felt like ten minutes, though it was barely three, they reached the ground floor. The almost life-size plaster Jesus looked sadly down upon the killer and the impostor as they headed towards the door. Robin had just placed her hand on the handle when Luca said,

'Hang on a moment, Vanetha.'

Robin turned, a pulse thrumming in her neck.

'You've got to thign out,' said Luca, holding out a pen to her.

'Oh, I forgot,' said Robin, with a breathless giggle. 'I told you – it's my first time here.'

She bent over the visitors' book. Directly below the signature she'd written on entering the building was Luca's.

LUCA RICCI

In the space left for 'Comments' he'd written,

BROUGHT HIM SOME CHOCOLATES FOR HIS BIRTHDAY ON THURSDAY, PLEASE GIVE HIM THEM ON THE MORNING OF THE 25TH JULY.

Robin scrawled the time beside her signature, then turned back to the door. He was holding it open for her.

'Fanks very much,' she said breathlessly, sidling past him into the fresh air.

'Give you a lift anywhere?' Luca asked her, pausing at the top of the steps to the street. 'My car'th round the corner. Athton Martin.'

'Oh, no, fanks very much, though,' said Robin. 'I'm meeting my boyfriend.'

'Be good, then,' said Luca Ricci. 'And if you can't be good, be thafe, hahaha.'

'Yes,' said Robin, a little wildly. 'Oh, and enjoy Florida!'

He raised a hand to her and began to walk away, whistling 'Begin the Beguine'. Light-headed with relief, Robin walked off in the opposite direction. It took the utmost restraint to stop herself breaking into a run.

Once she'd reached the square, she slid behind the lilac bush and watched the front of the nursing home for a full half an hour. Once she was certain that Luca Ricci had genuinely left, she doubled back.

CHAPTER 62

Oftimes it haps, that sorrowes of the mynd
Find remedie vnsought, which seeking cannot
fynd.

Edmund Spenser
The Faerie Queene

The row, for which Robin was braced, was one of the worst she and Strike had ever had. His fury that she'd approached Mucky Ricci, after his clear warnings and instructions not to, remained unabated even after a solid hour's argument in the office that evening, which culminated in Robin seizing her bag and walking out while Strike was mid-sentence, leaving him facing the vibrating glass door, wishing it had shattered, so he could bill her.

A night's sleep only slightly mitigated Strike's anger. Yes, there were major differences between Robin's actions this time, and those that had seen him sack her three years previously: she hadn't, for instance, spooked a suspect into hiding. Nor was there any indication, at least in the first twenty-four hours following her visit, that either the Ricci family or the nursing home suspected 'Vanessa Jones' of being anyone other than she'd claimed to be. Above all (but this fact rankled, rather than soothed), Robin was now a partner in the firm, rather than a lowly subcontractor. For the first time, Strike was brought up against the hard fact that if they ever parted ways, a legal and financial tangle would engulf him. It would, in fact, be akin to a divorce.

He didn't want to split from Robin, but his newly awakened awareness that he'd made it very difficult to do so increased his ire. The atmosphere between them remained strained for a fortnight after her visit to St Peter's until, on the first morning in August, Robin received a terse text from Strike asking her to abandon her fresh attempt to befriend Shifty's PA, and come back to the office.

When she entered the inner room, she found Strike sitting at the partners' desk, with bits and pieces of the Bamborough police file laid out in front of him. He glanced up at her, noted that her eye and hair colour were her own, then said brusquely,

'The Shifty clients have just rung up. They've terminated the job, for lack of results.'

'Oh no,' said Robin, sinking into the chair opposite him. 'I'm sorry, I really tried with Shifty's PA—'

'And Anna and Kim want to talk to us. I've set up a conference call at four o'clock.'

'They aren't—?'

'Winding things up?' said Strike unemotionally. 'Probably. Apparently they've had a spur-of-the-moment invitation from a friend to join them on holiday in Tuscany. They want to talk to us before they go, because they'll still be away on the fifteenth.'

There was a long silence. Strike didn't appear to have anything else to say, but resumed his perusal of various bits of the case file.

'Cormoran,' said Robin.

'What?'

'Can we please talk about St Peter's?'

'I've said everything I've got to say,' said Strike, picking up Ruby Elliot's statement about the two women struggling together in the rain, and pretending to read it again.

'I don't mean about me *going* there. I've already said—'

'You said you wouldn't approach Ricci—'

'I "agreed" not to go near Ricci,' said Robin, sketching quotation marks in the air, 'just like you "agreed" with Gregory Talbot not to tell the police where you got that roll of film.' Hyperaware of Pat typing away in the outer office, Robin was speaking quietly. 'I didn't set out to *defy* you; I left him up to you, remember? But it needed doing, and you couldn't. In case you hadn't noticed, I'm a damn sight better than you are at disguising my appearance.'

'That's not in question,' said Strike, throwing aside Ruby Elliot's statement and picking up

Gloria's description of Theo, instead. 'What bugs me, as you *bloody well know*, is that you didn't tell me you were going to—'

'D'you ring *me* every three seconds and tell me what you're going to do next? You're happy enough for me to work on my own initiative when it suits—'

'Luca Ricci's done time for putting electrodes on people's genitals, Robin!' said Strike, dropping the pretence that the description of Theo had his attention.

'How many times are we going to go over this? D'you think I was *pleased* when he walked in the room? I'd *never* have gone in there if I'd known he was about to make a surprise appearance! The fact remains—'

'—it's not a fact—'

'—if I hadn't—'

'—this theory—'

'*It isn't a bloody theory, Strike, it's reality, and you're just being pig-headed about it.*' Robin pulled her mobile out of her back pocket and brought up the photo she'd taken on her second visit to the nursing home, which had lasted barely two minutes, and involved her taking a quick, unwitnessed photograph of Luca Ricci's handwriting in the visitors' book.

'Give me the anonymous note,' she ordered Strike, holding out her hand for the piece of crumpled blue paper they'd taken away from their meeting with the Bayliss sisters. '*There.*'

She set them side by side, facing Strike. To Robin, the similarities were undeniable: the same odd mixture of capital and lower-case letters, all distinct and separate, but with odd and unnecessary little flourishes, rather like the incongruous lisp of a tall, dangerous-looking man whose skin was as pitted as a partly peeled orange.

'You can't prove it's the same writing from a photograph,' said Strike. He knew he was being ungracious, but his anger wasn't yet fully spent. 'Expert analysis relies on pen pressure, apart from anything else.'

'OK, fine,' said Robin, who now had a hard, angry lump in her throat. She got up and walked out, leaving the door slightly ajar. Through the gap, Strike heard her talking to Pat, followed by the tinkle of mugs. Annoyed though he was, he still hoped she was going to get him a cup of tea, as well.

Frowning slightly, he pulled Robin's mobile and the anonymous note towards him and looked again from one to the other. She was right, and he'd known, though not acknowledged it, from the moment she'd shown him the picture on her phone, on her return from St Peter's. Though he hadn't told Robin so, Strike had forwarded a picture of both the anonymous note and Luca Ricci's visitors' book message to an expert handwriting analyst he'd reached through his police contacts. The woman had expressed caution about reaching a hard and fast conclusion without having the original samples in front of her, but said that, on the evidence, she was 'seventy to eighty per cent certain' that both had been written by the same person.

'Does handwriting remain that consistent, forty years apart?' Strike asked.

'Not always,' the expert replied. 'You expect changes, typically. Mostly, people's handwriting deteriorates with age because of physical factors. Mood can have an influence, too. My research tends to show that handwriting alters least in people who write infrequently, compared with those who write a lot. Occasional writers seem to stick with the style they adopted early, possibly in school. In the case of these two samples, there are certainly distinctive features that seem to have hung around from youth.'

'I think it's fair to say this guy doesn't write a lot in his line of work,' said Strike.

Luca's last spell in jail, as Shanker had told him, had been for ordering and overseeing a stabbing. The victim had been knifed in the balls. By a miracle, he'd survived, 'but 'e won't be 'avin' any more kids, poor cunt,' Shanker had informed Strike, two nights previously. 'Can't get a fuckin' 'ard-on wivvout agony. Not worf living, is it, after that? The knife sliced straight through the right bollock, I 'eard – course, they 'ad him pinned down—'

'No need for details,' Strike had said. He'd just experienced a nasty sensation radiating out of his own balls up to his chest.

Strike had called Shanker on some slight pretext, purely to see whether any rumour had reached his old friend of Luca Ricci being concerned that a female detective had turned up in his father's nursing home. As Shanker hadn't mentioned anything, Strike had to conclude that no such whispers were abroad.

While this was a relief, it wasn't really a surprise. Once he'd calmed down, Strike had been forced to admit to himself that he was sure Robin had got away with it. Everything Strike knew about Luca Ricci suggested he'd never have let her walk away unscathed if he'd believed she was there to investigate any member of his family. The kinds of people whose darkest impulses were kept in check by their own consciences, the dictates of the law, by social norms and common sense might find it hard to believe anyone would be so foolish or reckless as to hurt Robin inside a nursing home bedroom, or march her out of the building with a knife to her back. *He wouldn't do it in broad daylight*, they'd say. *He wouldn't dare, with witnesses all around!* But Luca's fearsome reputation rested on his propensity for brazen violence, no matter where he was, or who was watching. He operated on an assumption of impunity, for which he had much justification. For every prison term he'd served, there'd been many incidents that should have seen him convicted, but which he'd managed to escape by intimidating witnesses, or terrifying others into taking the rap.

Robin returned to the inner office, stony-faced, but carrying two mugs of tea. She pushed the door closed with her foot, then set down the darker of the two teas in front of Strike.

'Thanks,' muttered Strike.

'You're welcome,' she replied stiffly, checking her watch as she sat down again. They had twenty minutes to go, before the conference call with Anna and Kim.

'We can't,' said Strike, 'tell Anna we think Luca Ricci wrote the anonymous notes.'

Robin simply looked at him.

'We can't have two nice middle-class women walking around telling people Ricci threatened Margot, and maybe killed her,' said Strike. 'We'd be putting them in danger, quite apart from ourselves.'

'Can't we at least show the samples to an expert?'

'I have,' said Strike, and he explained what the woman had said.

'Why didn't you tell—?'

'Because I was still bloody angry,' said Strike, sipping his tea. It was exactly the way he liked it, strong, sweet and the colour of creosote. 'Robin, the reality is, if we take the photo and the note to the police, whether or not anything comes of it, you'll have painted a giant target on your back. Ricci'll start digging around on who could have photographed his handwriting in that visitors' book. It won't take him long to find us.'

'He was twenty-two when Margot went missing,'

said Robin quietly. 'Old enough and big enough to abduct a woman. He had contacts to help with the disposal of a body. Betty Fuller thought the person who wrote the notes was the killer, and she's still scared of telling us who it was. That could imply the son, just as well as the father.'

'I grant you all that,' said Strike, 'but it's time for a reality check. We haven't got the resources to go up against organised criminals. You going to St Peter's was reckless enough—'

'Could you explain to me why it was reckless when I did it, but not when you were planning to do it?' said Robin.

Strike was momentarily stymied.

'Because I'm less experienced?' said Robin. 'Because you think I'll mess it up, or panic? Or that I can't think on my feet?'

'None of those,' said Strike, though it cost him some pain to admit it.

'Well then—'

'Because my chances of surviving if Luca Ricci comes at me with a baseball bat are superior to yours, OK?'

'But Luca doesn't come at people with baseball bats,' said Robin reasonably. 'He comes at them with knives, electrodes and acid, and I don't see how you'd withstand any of them better than I would. The truth is, you're happy to take risks you don't want me to take. I don't know whether it's lack of confidence in me, or chivalry, or one dressed up as the other—'

'Look—'

'No, *you* look,' said Robin. 'If you'd been recognised in there, the whole agency would have paid the price. I've read up on Ricci, I'm not stupid. He goes for people's families and associates and even their *pets* as often as he goes for them personally. Like it or not, there are places I can go more easily than you. I'm less distinctive-looking, I'm easier to disguise, and people trust women more than men, especially around kids and old people. We wouldn't know *any* of this if I hadn't gone to St Peter's—'

'We'd be better off not knowing it,' Strike snapped back. 'Shanker said to me months back, "If Mucky's the answer, you need to stop asking the question." Same goes for Luca, in spades.'

'You don't mean that,' said Robin. 'I know you don't. You'd never choose not to know.'

She was right, but Strike didn't want to admit it. Indeed, one of the things that had kept his anger simmering for the past two weeks was that he knew there was a fundamental lack of logic in his own position. If trying to get information on the Ricci family had been worth doing at all, it should have been done, and as Robin had proven, she'd been the best person for the job. While he resented the fact that she hadn't warned him what she was about to do, he knew perfectly well that if she'd done so, he'd have vetoed it, out of a fundamentally indefensible desire to keep her out of harm's way, when the logical conclusion of that line of thinking was that she oughtn't to be doing this job at all. He wanted her to be open and direct with him, but knew that his own incoherent position on her taking physical risks was the reason she hadn't been honest about her intentions. The long scar on her forearm reproached him every time he looked at it, even though the mistake that had led to the attack had been entirely her own. He knew too much about her past; the relationship had become too personal: he didn't want to visit her in hospital again. He felt precisely that irksome sense of responsibility that kept him determinedly single, but without any of the compensatory pleasures. None of this was her fault, but it had taken a fortnight for him to look these facts clearly in the face.

'OK,' he muttered at last. 'I wouldn't choose not to know.' He made a supreme effort. 'You did bloody well.'

'Thank you,' said Robin, as startled as she was gratified.

'Can we agree, though – please? That in future, we talk these things through?'

'If I'd asked you—'

'Yeah, I might've said no, and I'd've been wrong, and I'll bear that in mind next time, OK? But as you keep reminding me, we're partners, so I'd be grateful—'

'All right,' said Robin. 'Yes. We'll discuss it. I'm sorry I didn't.'

At that moment, Pat knocked on the door and opened it a few inches.

'I've got a Ms Phipps and a Ms Sullivan on the line for you.'

'Put them through, please,' said Strike.

Feeling as though she was sitting in on the announcement of bad medical news, Robin let Strike do the talking to Anna and Kim. He took the couple systematically through every interview the agency had conducted over the past eleven and a half months, telling them the secrets he and Robin had unearthed, and the tentative conclusions they'd drawn.

He revealed that Irene Hickson had been briefly involved with Margot's ex-boyfriend, and that both had lied about it, and explained that Satchwell might have been worried that Margot would tell the authorities about the way his sister died; that Wilma the cleaner had never set foot in Broom House, and that the story of Roy walking was almost certainly false; that the threatening notes had been real, but (with a glance at Robin) that they hadn't managed to identify the writer; that Joseph Brenner had been a more unsavoury character than anyone had realised, but that there was nothing to tie him to Margot's disappearance; that Gloria Conti, the last person to see Margot alive, was living in France, and didn't want to talk to them; and that Steve Douthwaite, Margot's suspicious patient, had vanished without trace. Lastly, he told them that they believed they'd identified the van seen speeding away from Clerkenwell Green on the night that Margot disappeared, and were confident that it hadn't been Dennis Creed's.

The only sound to break the silence when Strike first stopped talking was the soft buzzing emitted by the speaker on his desk, which proved the line was still open. Waiting for Anna to speak, Robin suddenly realised that her eyes were full of tears. She'd so very much wanted to find out what had happened to Margot Bamborough.

'Well . . . we knew it would be difficult,' said Anna at last. 'If not impossible.'

Robin could tell that Anna was crying, too. She felt wretched.

'I'm sorry,' said Strike formally. 'Very sorry, not to have better news for you. However, Douthwaite remains of real interest, and—'

'No.'

Robin recognised Kim's firm negative.

'No, I'm sorry,' said the psychologist. 'We agreed a year.'

'We're actually two weeks short,' said Strike, 'and if—'

'Have you got any reason to believe you can find Steve Douthwaite in the next two weeks?'

Strike's slightly bloodshot eyes met Robin's wet ones.

'No,' he admitted.

'As I said in my email, we're about to go on holiday,' said Kim. 'In the absence of actually finding Margot's body, there was always bound to be another angle you could try, one more person who might know something, and as I said at the start of this, we haven't got the money, or, frankly, the emotional stamina, to keep this going for ever. I think it's better – cleaner – if we accept that you've done your best, and thank you for the trouble you've clearly taken. This has been a worthwhile exercise, even if – I mean, Anna and Roy's relationship's better than it's been in years, thanks to your visit. He'll be glad to hear that the cleaner accepted he wasn't able to walk that day.'

'Well, that's good,' said Strike. 'I'm only sorry—'

'I knew,' said Anna, her voice wavering, 'that it was going to be . . . almost impossible. At least I know I tried.'

After Anna had hung up, there was a silence in the room. Finally Strike said 'Need a pee', pulled himself up and left the room.

Robin got up, too, and began to gather together the photocopied pages from the police file. She couldn't believe it was all over. Having put the records into a neat pile, she sat down and began to flick through them one more time, knowing that she was hoping to see something – anything – they'd overlooked.

From Gloria Conti's statement to Lawson:

She was a short, dark, stocky woman who looked like a gypsy. I judged her to be in her teens. She came in alone and said she was in a lot of pain. She said her name was Theo. I didn't catch her surname and I didn't ask her to repeat it because I thought she needed urgent attention. She was clutching her abdomen. I told her to wait and I went to ask Dr Brenner if he'd see her, because Dr Bamborough was still with patients.

From Ruby Elliot's statement to Talbot:

I saw them beside a telephone box, two women sort of struggling together. The tall one in the raincoat was leaning on the short one, who wore a plastic rain hood. They looked like women to me, but I didn't see their faces. It looked to me like one was trying to make the other walk quicker.

From Janice Beattie's statement to Lawson:

I've been on speaking terms with Mr Douthwaite since he was assaulted at the flats, but I wouldn't call him a friend. He did tell me how upset he was his friend had killed herself. He told me he had headaches. I thought it was tension. I know he grew up in foster care, but he never told me the names of any of his foster mothers. He never talked to me about Dr Bamborough except to say he'd gone to her about his headaches. He didn't tell me he was leaving Percival House. I don't know where he's gone.

From Irene Hickson's second statement to Lawson:

The attached receipt proves that I was in Oxford Street on the afternoon in question. I deeply regret not being honest about my whereabouts, but I was ashamed of lying to get the afternoon off.

And beneath the statement was the photocopy of Irene's receipt: Marks & Spencer, three items, which came to a total of £4.73.

From Joseph Brenner's statement to Talbot:

I left the practice at my usual time, having promised my sister that I'd be home in time for dinner. Dr Bamborough kindly agreed to see the emergency patient, as she had a later appointment with a friend in the area. I have no idea whether Dr Bamborough had personal troubles. Our relationship was entirely professional. I have no knowledge of anyone who wanted to do her harm. I remember one of her patients sending her a small box of chocolates, although I can't say for certain that it was from Steven Douthwaite. I don't know Mr Douthwaite. I remember Dr Bamborough seemed displeased when Dorothy handed the chocolates to her, and asked Gloria, the receptionist, to throw them straight in the bin, although she later took them back out of the bin. She had a very sweet tooth.

Strike re-entered the office and dropped a five-pound note onto the table in front of Robin.

'What's that for?'

'We had a bet,' he said, 'about whether they'd extend the year if we had any outstanding leads. I said they would. You said they wouldn't.'

'I'm not taking that,' said Robin, leaving the fiver where it lay. 'There are still two more weeks.'

'They've just—'

'They've paid till the end of the month. I'm not stopping.'

'Did I not make myself clear just now?' said Strike, frowning down at her. 'We're leaving Ricci.'

'I know,' said Robin.

She checked her watch again.

'I'm supposed to be taking over from Andy in an hour. I'd better go.'

After Robin had left, Strike returned the photocopied papers to the boxes of old police records that still lay underneath the desk, then went out into the office where Pat sat, electronic cigarette between her teeth as always.

'We've lost two clients,' he told her. 'Who's next on the waiting list?'

'That footballer,' said Pat, bringing up the encrypted file on her monitor to show Strike a well-known name. 'And if you want to replace both of them, there's that posh woman who's got the chihuahua.'

Strike hesitated.

'We'll just take the footballer for now. Can you ring his assistant and say I'm available to take details any time tomorrow?'

'It's Saturday,' said Pat.

'I know,' said Strike. 'I work weekends and I doubt he'll want anyone to see him coming in here. Say I'm happy to go to his place.'

He returned to the inner office and pushed up the window, allowing the afternoon air, heavy with exhaust fumes and London's particular smell of warm brick, soot and, today, a faint trace of leaves, trees and grass, to permeate the office. Tempted to light up, he restrained himself out of deference to Pat, because he'd asked her not to smoke in the office. Clients these days were nearly all non-smokers and he felt it gave a poor impression to have the place reeking like an ashtray. He leaned on the windowsill and watched the Friday-night drinkers and shoppers walking up and down Denmark Street, half-listening to Pat's conversation with the Premier League footballer's assistant, but mostly thinking about Margot Bamborough.

He'd known all along there was only the remotest chance of finding out what had happened to her, but where had fifty weeks gone? He remembered all the time spent with Joan in Cornwall, and the other clients who'd come and gone, and asked himself if they might have found out what had happened to Margot Bamborough if none of these things had got in the way. Tempting though it was to blame distractions, he believed the outcome would have been the same. Perhaps Luca Ricci was the answer they weren't ever going to be able to admit. A plausible answer, in many ways: a professional hit, done for some inscrutable underworld reason, because Margot had got too close to a secret, or interfered in the gangsters' business. *Leave my girl alone* . . . she'd been the type to advise a stripper, or a hooker, or a porn actress, or an addict, to choose a different life, to give evidence against men who abused her . . .

'Eleven tomorrow,' rasped Pat, from behind Strike. 'At 'is place. I've left his address on the desk for you.'

'Thanks very much,' he said, turning to see her already in her coat. It was five o'clock. She looked vaguely surprised to hear his thanks, but ever since Robin had shouted at him for being rude to Pat, Strike had been consciously trying to be politer to the secretary. For a moment she hesitated, electronic cigarette between her yellow teeth, then removed it to say,

460

'Robin told me what that Morris did. What he sent her.'

'Yeah,' said Strike. 'Sleazy bastard.'

'Yeah,' said Pat. She was scrutinising him closely, as though seeing things she hadn't ever expected to find. ''Orrible. And 'e always reminded me,' she said surprisingly, 'of a young Mel Gibson.'

'Really?' said Strike.

'Funny fing, looks,' she said. 'You make assumptions.'

'I s'pose,' said Strike.

'You've got a real look of my first 'usband,' Pat told him.

'Is that right?' said Strike, startled.

'Yeah. Well . . . I'll be off. 'Ave a good weekend.'

'You too,' said Strike.

He waited until her footsteps had died away on the metal staircase, before pulling out his cigarettes, lighting one and returning to the inner office, where the window was still open. Here, he took an old ashtray out of the desk drawer and Talbot's leather notebook out of the top drawer of the filing cabinet, and settled down in his usual chair to flick through it once more, stopping at the final page.

Strike had never given Talbot's final jottings more than cursory attention, partly because his patience had run out by the time he got there, partly they were among the most shambolic and incoherent parts of the notes. Tonight, though, he

461

had a melancholy reason for examining the last page of Talbot's notebook, because Strike, too, had come to the end of the case. So he examined Talbot's drawing of the demon he believed he'd conjured before the ambulance came to take him away: the spirit of Margot Bamborough, returned from some astral plane to haunt him in the form of Babalon, the Mother of Abominations.

There was no pressure to understand any more. Strike defocused his mind as he'd have relaxed his eyes, the better to spot one of those apparently three-dimensional images hidden in what appeared to be a flat pattern. His eyes glided over the phrases and fragments Talbot had half-remembered from Crowley's writings, and of consultation of the Thoth tarot. As he scrutinised the picture of the heavy-breasted demon, on whose belly the penitent Talbot had subsequently inscribed a Christian cross, he remembered Robin's words all those months previously in Hampton Court Palace, about the allure of myth and symbol, and the idea of the collective unconscious, where archetypes lurked. This demon, and the disconnected phrases that had seemed pertinent to Talbot in his psychotic state, had sprung from the policeman's own subconscious: it was too easy, too simplistic, to blame Crowley and Lévi for what Talbot's own mind had chosen to retain. This was what it generated, in a last spasm of madness, in a final attempt at resolution. *Seven veils, seven heads, seven streams. Lust and strange drugs. Seven around her neck. The poisoned darkness of the BLACK MOON. Blood and sin. She rides upon the lion serpent.*

Strike bent the lamp closer to the page, so that he could scrutinise the drawing more closely. Was he deluding himself, or did some of these crazy jottings indicate that Talbot had noticed the odd coincidences that Strike had, after talking to the Bayliss sisters? As his gaze moved from one fragment of mystic writing to another, Strike thought he saw, not just a penitent churchgoer trying to make amends for his descent into witchcraft, but the last desperate effort of a good detective, trying to salvage clues from chaos, sense from madness.

CHAPTER 63

At last resoluing forward still to fare,
Till that some end they finde or in or out,
That path they take, that beaten seemd most
  bare,
And like to lead the labyrinth about . . .

Edmund Spenser
The Faerie Queene

Over the next couple of weeks, Robin noticed that *Astrology 14* by Steven Schmidt, the second-hand book she'd left at the office, kept changing position. One morning it was on top of the filing cabinet where she'd left it, a few days later on Strike's half of the desk, and the following evening lying beside the kettle. Similarly, various bits of the Bamborough police records kept appearing, then disappearing again, while Bill Talbot's leather-bound notebook had vanished from the filing cabinet and, she suspected, made its way upstairs to Strike's attic flat.

The agency was once again very busy. The new

client, a Premier League footballer, had sunk two million pounds into a proposed nightclub which had failed to materialise. His partner in the venture had now disappeared, along with all the money. The footballer, nicknamed Dopey by an unsympathetic Barclay, feared press exposure almost as much as not getting his cash back.

Meanwhile, Miss Jones's boyfriend continued to live a frustratingly law-abiding life, but she appeared happy to keep paying the agency's bills, as long as Strike endured twice-weekly phone calls with her. During these supposed catch-ups, she told Strike all her problems, and hinted broadly that a dinner invitation would be happily accepted.

In addition to these clients, and leapfrogging those on the waiting list, was Shifty's Boss, who'd been forced into early retirement by the board. SB walked in off Denmark Street one morning looking for Barclay, who'd left his contact details with Elinor Dean. To Strike's surprise, early retirement seemed not to have spurred SB into despair, but liberated him.

'If you can believe it, I was genuinely thinking of killing myself, just a few months back,' he told Strike. 'But I'm out from under that bastard's thumb now. Now I've told my wife about Elinor—'

'Told her, have you?' said Strike, surprised.

'And she's been very understanding,' said SB. 'In my previous marriage, my – well, my needs – were taken care of by my ex-wife, but since we split . . . anyway, Portia and I have talked it all through, and she's perfectly happy for my arrangement with Elinor to continue, as long as there's no infidelity.'

Strike hid his expression behind his mug. He could well imagine that Portia, with her inch-long nails and her professional blow-dries, her thrice-yearly holidays, her black American Express card and her six-bedroomed house with swimming pool in West Brompton, preferred someone else to change SB's nappy.

'No, all I want *now*,' said SB, his satisfied smile replaced by a hard glare, 'is to make sure that shifty bastard gets what's coming to him. And I'm prepared to pay.'

So the agency had resumed surveillance on both Shifty and his PA.

The upshot of three demanding cases meant that most of the communication between the two partners was done by phone for the rest of the month. Their paths finally crossed one Thursday afternoon in late August, when Strike entered the office as Robin was about to leave it.

Pat, who was listening to the radio while paying a slew of bills, offered to turn it off on seeing Strike, whose attention had just been caught by the figure-hugging blue dress Robin was wearing.

'No, it's fine,' he said. 'Nice to hear some music.'

'Cormoran, can I have a quick word before I go?' Robin asked, beckoning him into the inner office.

'. . . next up, in our hundred hits of the

seventies, an oldie but goodie from one-hit-wonder Middle of the Road: "Chirpy Chirpy Cheep Cheep . . ."'

'Where're you off to?' said Strike, closing the internal door on Pat. He'd spent most of the previous night on his feet, watching Shifty get drunk and coked up in a nightclub, and today driving between the various addresses Dopey's business partner had used over the previous two years. Unshaven and aching all over, he grunted in relief as he sank into his usual chair.

'The Vintry. Wine bar in the City,' said Robin. 'Gemma's going to be there later, Andy heard her arranging it. I'm hoping she's with girlfriends. I'm going to try and infiltrate the group somehow.'

Gemma was Shifty's PA. Through the closed door they now heard strains of a jaunty song playing on the radio, with its incongruous lyric,

'*Where's your mamma gone?*'

'You're still working on Bamborough, aren't you?' Robin asked.

'Just going back over a few things,' Strike admitted.

'And?'

'And nothing. It's like a maze. Moment I start thinking I'm getting somewhere, I turn a corner and come up against a dead end. Or find myself back where I started. Why are you looking so pleased?'

'I'm just glad you haven't given up,' said Robin.

'You won't say that when they cart me off to the

same asylum as Bill Talbot. If I never see another fucking star sign, it'll be too soon . . . Where the *hell* is Douthwaite? What happened to him?'

'You think—?'

'I think he's bloody fishy, I always did. His alibi amounts to fuck all. Then he changes his name. Then, as you found out, another young woman dies in his vicinity – that drowned Redcoat. Then he vanishes again.

'If I could just speak to Douthwaite,' said Strike, drumming his fingers on the desk, 'I'd give it up.'

'Really?' said Robin.

He glanced at her, then, frowning, looked away. She was looking particularly sexy in that blue dress, which he'd never seen before.

'Yeah, if I could speak to Douthwaite, that'd do me.'

'*Last night I heard my mamma singing a song . . .*'

'And maybe Gloria Conti,' said Strike.

'*Woke up this morning, and my mamma was gone . . .*'

'And Creed,' said Strike. 'I'd like to talk to Dennis Creed.'

Robin felt a little skip of excitement. She'd received an email earlier, telling her to expect a decision by the end of the day on whether or not Creed could be re-interviewed.

'I'd better get going,' she said. 'Gemma's supposed to be there at six. It was nice of you,' she added, as she reached for the door handle, 'to let Pat keep the radio on.'

'Yeah, well,' said Strike, with a shrug. 'Trying to be friendly.'

As Robin was putting on her coat in the outer office, Pat said,

'That's a very good colour on you.'

'Thanks. It's quite old. Miracle it still fits, all the chocolate I've been eating lately.'

'Would he like a cuppa, d'you think?'

'I'm sure he would,' said Robin, surprised. Apparently Strike wasn't the only one who was trying to be friendly.

'Oooh, I used to love this,' said Pat, as the opening bars of 'Play That Funky Music' filled the office, and as Robin walked down the stairs, she heard Pat singing along, in her raspy baritone:

> *Once I was a funky singer,*
> *Playin' in a rock and roll band . . .*

The Vintry, which Robin reached twenty minutes later, lay near Cannon Street Tube station in the heart of the financial district, and was precisely the kind of place her ex-husband had most enjoyed. Undemandingly modern in a conventional, high-spec manner, with its sleek mixture of steel beams, large windows and wooden floors, it had a hint of open-plan office about it, in spite of the long bar with padded stools. There was the odd quirky touch, such as the two stuffed rabbits on a window-sill, which carried model guns and wore shooting caps, but in the main the clientele, which consisted

470

overwhelmingly of men in suits, were cocooned in an atmosphere of tasteful beige blandness. They stood in cliques, fresh from the day's work, drinking, laughing together, reading newspapers or their phones, or eyeing up the few female customers – to Robin they seemed to exude not just confidence, but self-satisfaction. She received a number of appreciative looks as she sidled between stockbrokers, bankers and traders on her way to the bar.

Looking carefully around the large open-plan area, Robin gathered that Gemma hadn't yet arrived, so she took a free bar stool, ordered a tonic water and pretended to be reading the day's news off her phone, purely to avoid the open staring of the two young men to her right, one of whom seemed determined to make Robin look up, if only to ascertain where the annoying, braying laugh was coming from. To her left, a pair of older men were discussing the imminent Scottish independence referendum.

'Polls are looking shaky,' said the first man. 'Hope Cameron knows what he's doing.'

'They'd be bloody mad to do it. Mad.'

'There's opportunity in madness – for a few, anyway,' said the first man. 'I remember, when I was in Hong Kong – oh, I think that's our table free . . .'

The two speakers departed for their dinner. Robin glanced around again, carefully avoiding meeting the eyes of the young man with the braying laugh, and a patch of scarlet at the far end of the bar caught her eye. Gemma had arrived, and was standing alone, trying to catch the barman's eye. Robin slid off her bar stool, and carried her drink over to Gemma, whose long dark hair fell in gypsyish curls to the middle of her back.

'Hi – Linda?'

'What?' said Gemma, startled. 'No, sorry.'

'Oh,' said Robin, looking crestfallen. 'Maybe I've got the wrong bar. Has this place got other branches?'

'I've no idea, sorry,' said Gemma, still with her hand raised, trying to attract the barman's attention.

'She said she'd be wearing red,' said Robin, looking around at the sea of suits.

Gemma glanced at Robin, mildly interested.

'Blind date?'

'I wish,' said Robin, rolling her eyes. 'No, it's a friend of a friend who thinks there might be an opening at Winfrey and Hughes. The woman said she'd meet me for a quick drink.'

'Winfrey and Hughes? That's where I work.'

'You're kidding!' said Robin, with a laugh. 'Hey – you're not really Linda, are you? And pretending to be someone different, because you don't like the look of me or something?'

'No,' said the other woman, smiling. 'I'm Gemma.'

'Oh. Are you meeting someone, or—?'

'S'posed to be,' said Gemma, 'yeah.'

'D'you mind me sitting here with you? Just till they arrive? I was getting some properly lechy looks over there.'

'Tell me about it,' said Gemma, as Robin climbed up onto the barstool beside her. The barman now approached a pinstriped, grey-haired man who'd just arrived.

'Oi,' Robin called, and half a dozen businessmen's heads turned, as well as the barman's. 'She was here first,' said Robin, pointing sideways at Gemma, who laughed again.

'Wow. *You* don't mess around, do you?'

'No point, is there?' said Robin, taking a sip of her water. She'd subtly broadened her Yorkshire accent, as she often did when pretending to be a bolder, brasher character than she really felt herself to be. 'Gotta take charge, or they'll walk all bloody over you.'

'You're not wrong there,' sighed Gemma.

'Winfrey and Hughes isn't like that, is it?' said Robin. 'Full of tossers?'

'Well . . .'

The barman arrived at that moment to take Gemma's order. Once the PA had her large glass of red wine, she took a swig and said,

'It's OK, actually. Depends which bit you're working in. I'm PA to one of the high-ups. The work's interesting.'

'Nice guy?' asked Robin casually.

Gemma drank several mouthfuls of wine before saying,

'He's . . . all right. Devil you know, isn't it? I like the job and the company. I've got a great salary and a ton of friends there . . . oh damn—'

Her handbag had slipped off the barstool. As Gemma bent to retrieve it, Robin, whose eyes had roamed across the vista of cream, grey and beige in front of her, suddenly spotted Saul Morris.

He'd just walked into the bar, wearing a suit, an open-necked shirt and a remarkably smug smile. He glanced around, picked out Gemma and Robin by the bright colours of their dresses, and froze. For a second or two, he and Robin simply stared at each other; then Morris turned abruptly and hurried back out of the bar.

Gemma settled herself back onto her barstool, bag safely on her lap. The mobile phone she'd left lying on the counter now lit up.

'Andy?' said Gemma, answering quickly. 'Yeah . . . no, I'm here already . . .'

There was a long silence. Robin could hear Morris's voice. He was using the same wheedling tone in which he'd tried to talk her into bed, with all those puerile jokes and have-I-upset-yous.

'Fine,' said Gemma, her expression hardening. 'Fine. I just . . . I'm going to take your number off my phone now and I'd like you . . . no, actually, I . . . oh just *fuck off*!'

She hung up, flushed, her lips trembling.

'Why,' she said, 'do they always want to be told they're still nice guys, after they've been total shits?'

'Often wondered that meself,' said Yorkshire Robin. 'Boyfriend?'

'Yeah,' said the shaken Gemma. 'For six months. Then he just stands me up one night, with no explanation. *Then* he comes back a couple of times – booty calls, basically,' she said, taking another big swig of wine. 'And finally he just ghosts me. I texted him yesterday, I said, look, I just wanna meet, just want an explanation—'

'Sounds like a right twat,' said Robin, whose heart was racing with excitement at this perfect opportunity to have a heart-to-heart. 'Hey,' she called to the barman, 'can we have a couple more wines and a menu, please?'

And after that, Robin found getting confidences out of Gemma as easy as shelling peas. With three large glasses of wine inside her, and her new friend from Yorkshire being so funny, supportive and understanding, a plate of chicken and polenta to eat, and a bottle of wine ('Yeah, why the hell not?'), she moved seamlessly from the misdemeanours of 'Andy' to the inappropriate and unsolicited groping by her boss that had escalated until she was on the verge of quitting.

'Can't you go to HR?' asked Robin.

'He says nobody'll believe me because of what happened when we were on a course last year . . . although . . . To tell you the truth, I don't really know *what* happened,' said Gemma, and looking away from Robin she mumbled, 'I mean . . . we had sex . . . but I was so out of it . . . so

475

drunk . . . I mean, it wasn't, you know . . . it wasn't *rape* . . . I'm not saying *that* . . .'

'Were you in a fit state to give consent?' said Robin, no longer laughing. She'd only drunk half a glass of wine.

'Well, not . . . but . . . no, I'm not putting myself through *that*,' said Gemma, flushed and tearful. 'Not the police and everything, God no . . . he's a big shot, he could afford great lawyers . . . an' if I didn't win, how'm I gonna get another job in the City? . . . Court, and the papers . . . anyway, it's too late now . . . people saw me . . . coming out of his room. I pretended it was all OK. I had to, I was so embarrassed . . . rumour mill's been in overdrive since. We both denied anything happened, so how would it look if I . . .

'Andy told me I shouldn't report it,' said Gemma, pouring the last of the bottle into her glass.

'Did he?'

'Yeah . . . I told him about it, firs' time we had sex . . . see, it was the firs' time I'd slept with anyone since . . . and he said, "Yeah, you'll want to keep that quiet . . . be loads of grief for you, an' he'll probably get off" . . . He was ex-police, Andy, he knew all about that kind of thing.'

You total shit, Morris.

'No, if I was going to tell about *anything*,' said Gemma, hazily, 'it'd be the insider bloody trading . . . Oh yeah . . . nobody knows 'cept me . . .'

One hour later, Robin and Gemma emerged into the darkening street, Robin almost holding

476

Gemma up, because she showed a tendency to sag if unsupported. After a ten-minute wait, she succeeded in flagging down a taxi, and loaded the very drunk Gemma into it.

'Le's go out Saturday!' Gemma called to Robin, trying to stop her closing the door.

'Fantastic!' said Robin, who'd given the PA a fake number. 'Ring me!'

'Yeah, I will . . . thanks so much for dinner!'

'No problem!' said Robin, and she succeeded at last in slamming the door on Gemma, who waved at her until the cab turned the corner.

Robin turned away and walked quickly back past the Vintry. A young man in a suit wolf-whistled as she passed.

'Oh bugger off,' muttered Robin, pulling out her phone to call Strike.

To her surprise, she saw she'd missed seven calls from him. She'd also received an email whose subject line read: Creed.

'Oh my God,' said Robin out loud.

She sped up, wanting to get away from the hordes of suited men still walking the streets, to be alone and able to concentrate. Retreating at last into the dark doorway of a grey stone office block, she opened the email. After reading it through three times, to make absolutely sure her eyes weren't deceiving her, she called Strike back.

'There you are!' he said, answering on the first ring. 'Guess what?'

'What?'

'I've found Douthwaite!'

'You've *what?*' gasped Robin, attracting the startled attention of a sober-looking City gent shuffling past in the dark, holding a tightly furled umbrella. '*How?*'

'Names,' said Strike, who sounded elated. 'And Pat listening to hits of the seventies.'

'I don't—'

'He called himself Jacks first time, right? Well, Terry Jacks had a massive hit with a song called "Seasons in the Sun" in '74. They played it this afternoon. We know Douthwaite fancied himself a singer, so I thought, bet that's where he got the idea for "Jacks" . . .'

Robin could hear Strike pacing. He was evidently as excited as she felt.

'So then I went back to Oakden's book. He said Douthwaite's "Longfellow Serenade" was a particular hit with the ladies. I looked it up. That was one of Neil Diamond's. So then,' said Strike, 'I start Googling Steve Diamond . . .

'I'm about to text you a picture,' said Strike. 'Stand by.'

Robin took the phone away from her ear and waited. Within a few seconds, the text arrived, and she opened the accompanying picture.

A sweaty, red-faced, balding man in his sixties was singing into a microphone. He wore a turquoise T-shirt stretched over a sizeable belly. A chain still hung around his neck, but the only other resemblance to the picture of the spiky-haired, cheeky chap in his kipper tie were the eyes, which were as dark and bright as ever.

'It's him,' Robin said.

'That picture came off the website of a pub in Skegness,' said Strike. 'He's still a karaoke king and he co-owns and runs a bed and breakfast up there, with his wife Donna. I wonder,' said Strike, 'whether she realises his name hasn't always been Diamond?'

'This is *amazing*!' said Robin, so jubilant that she began to walk down the street again, purely to use the energy now surging through her. 'You're brilliant!'

'I know,' said Strike, with a trace of smugness. 'So, we're going to Skegness. Tomorrow.'

'I'm supposed to be—'

'I've changed the rota,' said Strike. 'Can you pick me up early? Say, eight o'clock? I'll come out to Earl's Court.'

'Definitely,' said Robin.

'Then I'll see you—'

'Wait,' said Robin.

'Oh, shit, yeah,' said Strike politely. 'Should've asked. How'd it go with Gemma?'

'Great,' said Robin. 'Shifty's insider trading, but never mind that now.'

'He's—?'

'Strike, I don't want to upstage you or anything,' she said, failing to suppress the note of triumph in her voice, 'because finding Douthwaite's incredible, but I think you ought to know . . . you're going to be allowed to interview Dennis Creed in Broadmoor, on September the nineteenth.'

CHAPTER 64

. . . his hand did quake,
And tremble like a leafe of Aspin greene,
And troubled blood through his pale face was
  seene
To come, and goe with tidings from the heart,
As it a ronning messenger had beene.

Edmund Spenser
The Faerie Queene

'Well,' said Strike, getting into the Land Rover next morning.

They beamed at each other: for a moment, Robin thought she saw the idea of hugging her cross Strike's mind, but instead he held out his hand, and shook hers.

'My Christ, you wait a year for a breakthrough . . .'

Robin laughed, put the Land Rover into gear and pulled out onto the road. The day was unusually hot: she was driving in sunglasses, yet Strike noted a scarf protruding from the bag behind her seat.

'Don't think you're going to need that. Proper summer weather,' he said, looking out at the clear sky.

'We'll see,' said Robin sceptically. 'We used to visit Skegness when we were kids. Mum's sister used to live in Boston, up the road. There's usually a bracing breeze off the North Sea.'

'So, I read the email,' said Strike, referring to the message Robin had forwarded him, which laid out both the terms and conditions of him interviewing Dennis Creed, and the reasoning which had led the authorities to permit Strike to do it.

'What did you think?' Robin asked.

'Other than being bloody astounded you pulled this off—'

'It took ages.'

'I'm not surprised. Other than that, I won't lie . . . I'm feeling the pressure.'

'You mean, because of the Tuckers?'

'Yeah,' said Strike, opening the window so he could light a cigarette. 'Anna doesn't know I'm getting this shot, so she won't get their hopes up, but that poor bastard Tucker . . .'

Absolute secrecy about the interview, including signing a non-disclosure agreement that guaranteed Strike would never talk to the press about it, had been the first precondition set by the authorities.

'He really wants it to be you,' said Robin. 'Tucker. He says Creed's got a big ego and he'll

482

want to meet you. And the psychiatrists must agree, mustn't they, or they wouldn't be allowing it? Brian Tucker says Creed always saw himself as high status, and deserving of associating with famous, successful people.'

'It isn't a psychiatrist's job to decide whether I'll be able to get anything out of him,' said Strike. 'I'd imagine all they'll care about is whether I'm going to rile him up. You don't get put in Broadmoor for being mildly eccentric.'

Strike was silent for a long time, looking out of the window, and Robin too remained quiet, not wanting to interrupt his train of thought. When at last Strike spoke again, he sounded matter of fact, and focused on the plan for Skegness.

'I looked up the B&B on TripAdvisor. It's called the Allardice, which is his wife's maiden name. We won't walk in there cold, because if he isn't there and the wife smells a rat, she can call him and warn him not to come back, so we'll park, get ourselves into a position where we can see the building, and ring him. If he's there, we walk straight in before he's got a chance to run – or catch him as he leaves, as the case might be. And if he isn't in, we wait.'

'For how long?' said Robin.

'I'd like to say "as long as it takes",' said Strike, 'but we're not actually being paid for this, so I've got to be back in town on Monday.'

'I could stay behind,' suggested Robin.

'I don't think so,' said Strike.

'Sorry,' said Robin, immediately regretting the suggestion, afraid that Strike might think she was simply after another weekend away in a hotel. 'I know we're short-staffed—'

'It isn't that. You were the one who pointed out women have a habit of dying or disappearing around Steve Douthwaite. Could be a case of bad luck, but on the other hand . . . three different surnames is a lot for a man with nothing to hide. I'm taking the lead on this one.'

They arrived in the small seaside town at eleven, leaving the Land Rover in a car park beside Skegness Bowl, an enormous red-walled seafront bowling alley. Strike could smell and taste the sea as he got out of the car, and turned instinctively towards it, but the ocean was invisible from where he stood. Instead he found himself looking at a manmade waterway of a murky green, along which a laughing young woman and her boyfriend were pedalling a dinghy-sized boat. The driver's door slammed and Strike turned to see Robin, still in sunglasses, wrapping the scarf around her neck.

'Told you,' she said to the mystified Strike, to whom the day felt unequivocally hot. Not for the first time wondering what it was about women and their bizarre ability to feel non-existent chills, Strike lit up, waited beside the Land Rover while Robin bought a parking permit, then walked with her up to Grand Parade, a wide street that ran along the seafront.

'"The Savoy",' said Strike, smirking as he read the names of the larger hotels, whose upper windows could surely see the distant sea. '"The Quorn". "The Chatsworth".'

'Don't jeer,' said Robin. 'I used to love coming to Skegness when I was a kid.'

'The Allardice should be up there,' Strike said, as they crossed the road, pointing up broad Scarbrough Avenue. 'Yeah, that's it, the one with the blue awning.'

They paused on the corner, beside an enormous mock Tudor hotel which boasted the Jubilee Carvery and Café. Early-morning drinkers of both beer and coffee were sitting at outside tables, enjoying the sunshine.

'Perfect place to keep an eye out,' said Strike, pointing at one of these pavement tables. 'I could use a cup of tea.'

'OK, I'll order,' said Robin. 'I need the loo, anyway. Are you going to call him or d'you want me to do it?'

'I will,' said Strike, already sinking onto one of the chairs, and taking out his mobile.

As Robin disappeared into the bar, Strike lit a cigarette, then keyed in the Allardice's number, his eyes on the front of the B&B. It stood in a row of eight tall red buildings, several of which had been converted into small boarding houses and had similar scalloped PVC awnings over the entrances. Spotless white net curtains hung at almost every window.

'Morning, the Allardice,' said a Scottish woman, who sounded on the irritable side of brisk.

'Steve there?' said Strike, faking casualness and confidence.

'That you, Barry love?'

'Yeah,' said Strike.

'He's on his way now,' she said. 'We only had a small, sorry. But do me a favour, Barry, and don't hold him up, because there are four beds to change here and he's supposed to be getting me more milk.'

'Righto,' said Strike, and not wanting to speak another syllable that might reveal him to be anyone other than Barry, he hung up.

'Is he there?' asked Robin anxiously, dropping into the seat opposite Strike. She'd washed her hands in the bathroom, but they were still damp, because she'd been in such a hurry to get back to Strike.

'No,' said Strike, knocking his cigarette ash into the small pink metal bucket placed on the table for that purpose. 'He's delivering something to a bloke up the road and will be back shortly, bringing milk.'

'Oh,' said Robin quietly, turning to look over her shoulder at the Allardice's royal blue awning, on which the name was inscribed in curly white lettering.

The barman brought out two metal pots and china teacups, and the detectives drank their tea in silence, Strike keeping a watchful eye on the

Allardice, Robin on Grand Parade. The sea was blocked from her view by the wide, multicoloured frontage of the entrance to Skegness Pier, which advertised, among other attractions, the optimistically named Hollywood Bar and Diner. Elderly people rode mobility scooters up and down Grand Parade. Families strolled past, eating ice cream. Plume-tailed Maltese, fat pugs and panting chihuahuas trotted over the hot pavements alongside their owners.

'Cormoran,' muttered Robin suddenly.

A man had just turned the corner into Scarbrough Avenue, a heavy carrier bag dangling from his hand. His grey hair was close cropped around the ears, but a few strands had been combed over a wide expanse of sweaty forehead. His round shoulders and hangdog look gave him the air of a man whom life had ground down to a sullen obedience. The same turquoise T-shirt he'd worn in the karaoke picture was stretched tightly over his beer belly. Douthwaite crossed the road, climbed the three steps leading to the Allardice's front door and, with a flash of sun on glass, disappeared from view.

'Have you paid for this?' Strike asked, downing the rest of his tea and putting his empty cup back onto the saucer.

'Yes.'

'Then let's go,' said Strike, dropping his cigarette into the metal bucket and pulling himself to his feet, 'before he can disappear upstairs and start changing beds.'

They crossed the road as fast as Strike could walk and headed up the front steps, which had been painted pale blue. Baskets of purple petunias hung beneath the ground-floor windows and an assortment of stickers adorned the glass portion of the front door, one of which announced that this was a three-star residence, another asking guests to wipe their feet.

A tinkling bell announced their arrival. The deserted hall was narrow, its stairs carpeted in dark blue and green tartan. They waited beside a table laden with leaflets about local attractions, breathing in a combination of fried food and a powerful rose-scented air-freshener.

'. . . and Paula's got new tubes in her sunbeds,' said a Scottish voice, and a woman with short hair dyed canary yellow emerged through a door to the right. A deep vertical line was graven down the middle of her forehead. Barelegged, she wore an apron decorated with a Highland cow over her T-shirt and denim skirt, and a pair of Dr Scholl's sandals.

'We've no vacancies, sorry,' she said.

'Are you Donna?' asked Strike. 'We were hoping for a word with Steve.'

'What about?'

'We're private detectives,' said Strike, pulling out his wallet to hand her a card, 'and we're investigating—'

A hugely obese old lady came into view on the landing above them. She was clad in shocking-pink

488

leggings and a T-shirt bearing the slogan 'The More People I Meet, The More I Like My Dog'. Panting audibly, she began a sideways descent, both hands clutching the banister.

'—a missing person case,' Strike finished quietly, as he handed Donna his card.

At that moment, Steve Douthwaite emerged from behind his wife, a pile of towels in his arms. Close up, his dark eyes were bloodshot and puffy. Every feature had coarsened with age and, possibly, drink. His wife's demeanour, the card in her hand and the presence of the two strangers now looking at him brought him to a halt, the dark eyes frightened above his pile of towels.

'Cormoran Strike?' murmured Donna, reading the card. 'Aren't you the one . . .?'

The old lady, who was barely halfway down the stairs, was now audibly wheezing.

'Get in here,' muttered Donna, pointing Strike and Robin towards the room from which she'd just emerged. 'And you,' she snapped at her husband.

They entered a small public sitting room, with a wall-mounted TV, a sparsely stocked bookcase and a miserable-looking spider plant sitting in a pedestalled urn. Through an arch was a breakfast room, where five tightly packed dining tables were being wiped down by a discontented-looking young woman in glasses, who sped up appreciably when she realised Donna had returned. Robin guessed that they were mother and daughter.

Though the younger woman was dark rather than blonde, life had carved an identical groove of dissatisfaction in her forehead.

'Leave that, Kirsty,' said Donna abruptly. 'Take these towels upstairs, will you? And close the door.'

Kirsty relieved Douthwaite silently of his pile of towels and left the room, her slides slapping the bottoms of her sockless feet. The door clicked shut behind her.

'Sit down,' Donna instructed Strike and Robin, who did so, on a small sofa.

Douthwaite took up a standing position, arms folded, with his back to the TV. Frowning slightly, his eyes flickered over Strike and Robin and back to his wife. The sunlight filtering through the net curtains cast an unforgiving light over his hair, which looked like wispy strands of steel wool.

'He's the one who caught that Shacklewell Ripper,' Donna said to her husband, jerking her head at Strike. 'Why's he after you?' Her voice rose in both pitch and volume. 'Been dicking around with the wrong woman again, have you? *Have you?*'

'What?' said Douthwaite, but it was obvious this was a stalling tactic: he had understood well enough. His right forearm was tattooed with an hourglass, and around it was wrapped a ribbon with the words 'Never Enough'.

'Mr Douthwaite,' Strike began, but Douthwaite said quickly,

'Diamond! It's Diamond!'

'Why're you calling him Douthwaite?' asked Donna.

'I'm sorry,' said Strike insincerely. 'My mistake. Your husband was born Steven Douthwaite, as I'm sure you—'

But Donna clearly hadn't known this. She turned, astonished, from Strike to Douthwaite, who'd frozen, mouth slightly open.

'*Douthwaite?*' repeated Donna. She turned on her husband. 'You told me your name used to be Jacks!'

'I—'

'When were you *Douthwaite?*'

'—ages—'

'Why didn't you tell me?'

'I – what's it matter?'

The bell tinkled again and a group of people was heard out in the hall. Still looking shocked and angry, Donna strode outside to see what was needed, her wooden-soled sandals banging over the tiles. The moment she'd disappeared, Douthwaite addressed Strike.

'What d'you want?'

'We've been hired by Dr Margot Bamborough's daughter, to look into her disappearance,' said Strike.

The parts of Douthwaite's face that weren't ruddy with broken veins blanched.

The enormous old lady who'd been descending the stairs now walked into the room, her wide, innocent face demonstrating total immunity to the atmosphere within.

'Which way's the seal sanctuary?'

'End of the road,' said Douthwaite hoarsely. 'Turn left.'

She sidled out of the room again. The bell outside tinkled.

'Listen,' said Douthwaite quickly, as the sound of his wife's footsteps grew louder again. 'You're wasting your time. I don't know anything about Margot Bamborough.'

'Perhaps you could have a look over your old police statement, at least,' asked Strike, taking a copy out of his inside pocket.

'What?' said Donna, now back in the room. 'What police statement? Oh, for *Christ's* sake,' she said, as the bell tinkled again, and she clunked back out of the room and bellowed up the stairs, 'Kirsty! *KIRSTY!*'

'That doctor,' Douthwaite said, looking at Strike through bloodshot eyes, his forehead sweaty, 'it all happened forty-odd years ago, I don't know anything about what happened, I never did.'

The harried Donna reappeared.

'Kirsty'll mind the front door,' she said, glaring at her husband. 'We'll go upstairs. Lochnagar's empty. We can't go in ours,' she added to Strike and Robin, pointing towards the basement, 'me grandkids are down there, playing computer games.'

Douthwaite hitched up his waistband and threw a wild look outside the net curtains, as though contemplating flight.

'Come on,' said Donna fiercely, and with a return to his hangdog look, he followed his wife out of the door.

Kirsty passed them, heading for the ground floor, as they climbed the steep tartan stairs, Strike making liberal use of the banister to haul himself up. He'd hoped Lochnagar might be on the first floor, but he was disappointed. It lay, as the name might have suggested, right at the top of the B&B, and faced out of the rear of the building.

The furniture inside was made of cheap pine. Kirsty had arranged towels in the shape of kissing swans on the maroon bedspread, which matched the patterned wallpaper of maroon and deep purple. Leads dangled from behind the wall-mounted TV. A plastic kettle sat in the corner on a low table, beside the Corby trouser press. Through the window Strike glimpsed the sea at last: a gleaming golden bar lying low between buildings, in the misty haze created by the net curtains.

Donna crossed the room and took the only chair. Her hands were gripping her own upper arms so tightly that the flesh showed white.

'You can sit down,' she told Strike and Robin.

Having nowhere else to do it, both sat down on the end of the double bed, with its slippery maroon cover. Douthwaite remained at the door, back against it, arms folded, displaying the hourglass tattoo.

'Diamond, Jacks, Douthwaite,' Donna recited. 'How many other names have you had?'

'None,' said Douthwaite, trying for a laugh, but failing.

'Why'd you change your name from Douthwaite to Jacks?' she demanded. 'Why were the police after you?'

'They weren't after me,' croaked Douthwaite. 'This was ages ago. I wanted a fresh start, that's all.'

'How many fresh starts does one man need?' said Donna. 'What did you do? Why'd you have to give a police statement?'

'A doctor went missing,' said Douthwaite, with a glance at Strike.

'What doctor? When?'

'Her name was Margot Bamborough.'

'Bamborough?' repeated Donna, her forehead bifurcated by that deep frown line, 'But that . . . that was all over the news . . .'

'They interviewed all the patients she'd seen before she disappeared,' Douthwaite said quickly. 'It was routine! They didn't have anything on me.'

'You must think I was born bloody yesterday,' said Donna. '*They*,' she pointed at Strike and Robin, 'haven't tracked you down because it was *routine enquiries*, have they? You didn't change your bloody name because it was *routine enquiries*! Screwing her, were you?'

'No, I wasn't bloody screwing her!' said Douthwaite, with his first sign of fight.

'Mr Douthwaite,' began Strike.

'Diamond!' said Douthwaite, more in desperation than in anger.

'I'd be grateful if you'd read through your police statement, see whether you've got anything to add.'

Douthwaite looked as though he'd have liked to refuse, but after a slight hesitation he took the pieces of paper and began to read. The statement was a long one, covering as it did the suicide of Joanna Hammond, his married ex-lover, the beating he'd endured at the hands of her husband, the anxiety and depression which had led to so many visits to the St John's surgery, his assertion that he'd felt nothing more for Margot Bamborough than mild gratitude for her clinical expertise, his denial that he'd ever brought or sent her gifts and his feeble alibi for the time of her disappearance.

'Yeah, I've got nothing to add to that,' Douthwaite said at last, holding the pieces of paper back out to Strike.

'I want to read it,' said Donna at once.

'It's got nothing to do with – it's forty years ago, it's nothing,' said Douthwaite.

'Your real name's Douthwaite and I never knew till five minutes ago! I've got a right to know who you are,' she said fiercely, 'I've got a right to know, so I can decide whether I was a bloody mug to stay with you, after the last—'

'Fine, read it, go on,' said Douthwaite with unconvincing bravado, and Strike handed the statement over to Donna.

She'd read for barely a minute when she burst out,

'You were sleeping with a married – and she *killed* herself?'

'I wasn't – we weren't – once, it happened, once! Nobody kills themselves over that!'

'Why'd she do it, then? Why?'

'Her husband was a bastard.'

'*My* husband's a bastard. I haven't topped myself!'

'Christ's sake, Donna—'

'*What happened?*'

'It was nothing!' said Douthwaite. 'We used to hang out together, few of the lads at work and their wives and whatever, and one night I was out with some other mates and ran into Joanna, who was with some girlfriends and . . . some cunt tipped off her husband we'd left the pub together and—'

'And then this doctor disappeared and all, and the police came calling?'

Donna got to her feet, Douthwaite's crumpled statement quivering in her hand. Still sitting on the slippery maroon coverlet, Robin remembered the day she'd found Sarah Shadlock's diamond earring in her bed, and thought she knew a little, a very little, of what Donna was experiencing.

'I knew you were a bloody cheat and a liar, but

three girlfriends dead? One's a tragedy,' said Donna furiously, and Strike wondered whether they were about to hear a Wildean epigram, 'but *three*? How bloody unlucky can one man get?'

'I never had anything going on with that doctor!'

'You'll try it on with anyone!' shrieked Donna, and addressing Robin, she said, 'Year before last, I catch him in a guest bedroom with one of my best friends—'

'Christ's sake, Donna!' whimpered Douthwaite.

'—and six months ago—'

'*Donna*—'

'—I find out he's been sneaking around with one of our regulars – and now—' said Donna, advancing on Douthwaite, his statements clutched in her fist. 'You creepy bastard, *what happened to all these women?*'

'I had nothing to do with any of them *dying*, fuck's sake!' said Douthwaite, trying for an incredulous laugh and merely looking terrified. 'Donna, come on – you think I'm some kind of *murderer?*'

'You expect me to believe—'

To Strike's surprise, Robin suddenly jumped to her feet. Taking Donna by the shoulders, she guided her back into her chair.

'Put your head down,' Robin was saying, 'head down.'

When Robin moved to untie Donna's apron, which was tight around her waist, and Strike saw that Donna's forehead, which was all he could see

497

now she had sunk her face into her hands, was as white as the net curtain behind her.

'Donna?' said Douthwaite feebly, but his wife whispered,

'You stay away from me, you bastard.'

'Breathe,' Robin was saying, crouching beside Donna's chair. 'Get her some water,' she told Strike, who got up and went into the tiny shower room, where a plastic beaker sat in a holder over the sink.

Almost as pale as his wife, Douthwaite watched as Robin persuaded Donna to drink.

'Stay there, now,' Robin told the landlady, one hand resting on her shoulder. 'Don't get up.'

'Did he have something to do with them dying?' Donna whispered, looking sideways at Robin, her pupils enormous with shock.

'That's what we're here to find out,' Robin murmured back.

She turned and looked meaningfully at Strike, who silently agreed that the best thing he could do for the stricken Donna was to get information out of Douthwaite.

'We've got a number of questions we'd like to ask you,' Strike told him. 'Obviously you're not obliged to answer them, but I'd put it to you that it would be in the best interests of everyone, yourself included, to cooperate.'

'What questions?' said Douthwaite, still flat against the door. Then, in a torrent of words, he said, 'I've never hurt anyone, never, I'm not a violent man. Donna will tell you, I've never laid a finger on her in anger, that's not who I am.'

But when Strike merely continued to look at him, Douthwaite said pleadingly,

'Look, I've told you – with Joanna – it was a one-night stand. I was just a kid,' he said, and in an echo of Irene Hickson, he said, 'You do those kinds of things when you're young, don't you?'

'And when you're old,' whispered Donna. 'And all the bloody years in between . . .'

'Where were you,' Strike asked Douthwaite, 'when Joanna killed herself?'

'In Brent,' said Douthwaite. 'Miles away! And I had witnesses to prove it. We used to work in pairs, selling, each do one side of the street, and I was out with a bloke called Tadger,' and he tried to laugh again. Nobody smiled. 'Tadger, you can imagine the grief he . . . well, he was with me all day . . .

'Got back to the office late in the afternoon, and there was a group of lads in there, and they told us Hammond had just got the message his wife had topped herself . . .

'Terrible,' said the pale and sweating Douthwaite, 'but except for that one night together, I had nothing to do with it. But her old man – well, it was easier to blame me,' said Douthwaite, 'wasn't it, than think about his own bloody behaviour?

'I got home a couple of nights later and he was lying in wait. Ambush. He beat the shit out of me.'

'Good!' said Donna, on a half-sob.

'And your neighbour, Janice the nurse, looked after—'

'Straight off with the neighbour, were you, Steve?' said Donna, with a hollow laugh. 'Get the nurse to mop you up?'

'It wasn't like that!' said Douthwaite with surprising vehemence.

'It's his little trick,' the white-faced Donna told Robin, who was still kneeling by her chair. 'Always got a sob story on the go. Fell for it myself. Heartbroken after the love of his life drowned . . . oh my God,' Donna whispered, slowly shaking her head. 'And she was the third.' With a hysterical little laugh, she said, 'As far as we know. Maybe there are others. Who knows?'

'Christ's sake, Donna!' said Douthwaite, yet again. Patches of underarm sweat were visible through his thin turquoise T-shirt: Strike could literally smell his fear. 'Come on, you know me, you know I'd never hurt anyone!'

'Janice says she advised you to see the doctor about your symp—'

'*She* never told me to go to the doctor!' snapped Douthwaite, one eye on his wife. 'I didn't need telling, I went off my own bat because I was just getting worried about the . . . headaches and . . . mostly headaches. I felt really bad.'

'You visited Margot six times in one two-week period,' said Strike.

'I felt ill, stomach pains and what have you . . .

I mean, it obviously affected me, Joanna dying, and then people talking about me . . .'

'Oh, poor you, poor you,' murmured Donna. 'Jesus effing Christ. You hate going to the doctor. Six times in two weeks?'

'Donna, come on,' said Douthwaite imploringly, 'I was feeling like shit! And then the bloody police come and make out like I was stalking her or something. It was all my health!'

'Did you buy her—?' began Strike.

'—chocolates? No!' said Douthwaite, who suddenly seemed very agitated. 'If someone sent her chocolates, maybe you should find *them*. But it wasn't me! I told the police I never bought her anything, it weren't like that—'

'Witnesses said you seemed distressed and possibly angry, the last time you left Dr Bamborough's surgery,' said Strike. 'What happened during that last visit?'

Douthwaite's breath was coming fast now. Suddenly, almost aggressively, he looked directly into Strike's eyes.

Experienced in the body language of suspects who yearn for the release and relief of unburdening themselves, no matter the consequences, Strike suddenly knew that Douthwaite was teetering on the brink of a disclosure. He'd have given almost anything to spirit the man away now, to a quiet interrogation room, but exactly as he'd feared, the precious moment was snatched away by Donna.

'Turned you down, did she? What did you think,

Steve – a scrubby little failed salesman had a chance with a doctor?'

'*I wasn't bloody looking for a chance!*' said Douthwaite, rounding on his wife, 'I was there for my health, I was in a state!'

'He's like a bloody tomcat,' Donna told Robin, 'slinking around behind everyone's backs. He'll use anything to get his end away, anything. His girlfriend's topped herself and he's using it to chat up nurses and doctors—'

'I wasn't, I was ill!'

'That last meeting—' Strike began again.

'I don't know what you're on about, it was nothing,' Douthwaite said, now avoiding looking Strike in the face. 'The doc was just telling me to take it easy.'

'Like you ever needed telling that, you lazy bastard,' spat Donna.

'Perhaps,' said Strike, 'as you're feeling unwell, Mrs Diamond, I could speak to Steve somewhere sep—'

'Oh no you don't!' said Donna. 'No way! I want—'

She exploded into tears, shoulders sagging, face in her hands.

'I'm going to hear it all now . . . last chance . . .'

'Donna—' said Douthwaite plaintively.

'Don't,' she sobbed into her fingers. 'Don't you dare.'

'Perhaps,' said Strike, hoping to return to the last visit with Margot in due course, 'we could go over your alibi for the time Dr Bamborough disappeared?'

Donna was sobbing, tears and mucus flowing freely now. Robin grabbed a paper napkin off the tray beside the kettle and handed it to her.

Cowed by his wife's distress, Douthwaite allowed Strike to lead him back over his shaky alibi for the evening in question, sticking to the story that he'd been sitting unnoticed in a café, scanning the newspapers for flats to rent.

'I wanted to clear out, get away from all the gossip about Joanna. I just wanted to get away.'

'So the desire to move wasn't triggered by anything that passed between you and Dr Bamborough during your last visit?' Strike asked.

'No,' said Douthwaite, still not looking at Strike. 'How could it be?'

'Given up on her?' Donna asked from behind the wet napkin with which she was blotting her eyes. 'Knew he'd made a fool of himself. Same as with that young lassie from Leeds, eh, Steve?'

'Donna, for *fuck's* sake—'

'He forgets,' Donna said to Robin, 'he's not that cocky little sod in his twenties any more. Deluded, b – baldy bastard,' she sobbed.

'*Donna*—'

'So you moved to Waltham Forest . . .' prompted Strike.

'Yeah. Police. Press. It was a nightmare,' said Douthwaite. 'I thought of ending it, to tell you the—'

'Shame you didn't,' said Donna savagely. 'Save us all a lot of time and trouble.'

As though he hadn't heard this, and ignoring Douthwaite's look of outrage, Strike asked,

'What made you go to Clacton-on-Sea? Did you have family there?'

'I haven't got family, I grew up in care—'

'Oh, someone pass him a bloody violin,' said Donna.

'Well, it's true, isn't it?' said Douthwaite, displaying unvarnished anger for the first time. 'And I'm allowed to tell the truth about my own bloody life, aren't I? I just wanted to be a Redcoat, because I sing a bit and it looked like a fun way to earn a living—'

'Fun,' muttered Donna, 'oh yeah, as long as *you're* having fun, Steve—'

'—get away from people treating me like I'd killed someone—'

'And *whoops*!' said Donna. 'There's another one gone, in the pool—'

'You know *bloody well* I had nothing to do with Julie drowning!'

'How could I know?' said Donna, 'I wasn't there! It was before we even met!'

'I showed you the story in the paper!' said Douthwaite. 'I *showed* you, Donna, come on!' He turned to Strike. 'A bunch of us were drinking in our chalet. Me and some mates were playing poker. Julie was tired. She left before we finished our game, walked back to her chalet. She walked round

504

the pool, slipped in the dark, knocked herself out and—'

For the first time, Douthwaite showed real distress.

'—she drowned. I won't ever forget it. Never. I ran outside in me underpants next morning, when I heard the shouting. I saw her body when they were taking her out of the pool. You don't forget something like that. She was a kid. Twenty-two or something. Her parents came and . . . it was a horrible thing. Horrible. I never . . . that someone can go like that. A slip and a trip . . .

'Yeah, so . . . that's when I applied for a job at the Ingoldmells Butlin's up the road from here. And that's where I met Donna,' he said, with an apprehensive glance at his wife.

'So you leaving Clacton-on-Sea and changing your name again had nothing to do with a man called Oakden coming to question you about Margot Bamborough?' asked Strike.

Donna's head jerked up.

'Oh my God,' she said, 'so even the *Julie* bit's a lie?'

'It's not a lie!' said Douthwaite loudly. 'I *told* you Julie and I had an argument a couple of days before she died, I *told* you that, because I felt so guilty after! This man, this – what did you say his name was? Oakden? – yeah, he turned up, saying he was writing a book about Dr Bamborough disappearing. Went round all the other Redcoats talking to them about me, telling them all I'd been a suspect and how I'd changed my name afterwards, making me sound dodgy as hell. And Julie was really pissed off with me because I hadn't told her—'

'Well, you really learned *that* lesson, didn't you, Steve?' said Donna. 'Run and hide, that's all you know, and when you're found out, you just sneak off and find some other woman to whine to, until she finds you out, and then—'

'Mr Douthwaite,' said Strike, cutting across Donna, 'I want to thank you for your time. I know it's been a shock, having all this raked up again.'

Robin looked up at Strike, astonished. He couldn't be leaving the interview here, surely? The Douthwaites (or Diamonds, as they thought of themselves), looked similarly taken aback. Strike extracted a second card from his pocket and held it out to Douthwaite.

'If you remember anything,' the detective said, 'you know where to find me. It's never too late.'

The hourglass tattoo on Douthwaite's forearm rippled as he held out his hand for the card.

'Who else've you talked to?' Douthwaite asked Strike.

Now that his ordeal was over, he seemed curiously averse to it ending. Perhaps, thought Robin, he feared being alone with his wife.

'Margot's husband and family,' said Strike, watching Douthwaite's reactions. 'The co-workers

who're still alive – Dr Gupta. One of the receptionists, Irene Hickson. Janice Beattie, the nur—'

'That's nice,' piped up Donna, 'the nurse is still
available, Steve—'

'—an ex-boyfriend of Margot's, her best friend,
and a few other people.'

Douthwaite, who'd flushed at his wife's interjection, said,

'Not Dennis Creed?'

'Not yet,' said Strike. 'Well,' he looked from
husband to wife, 'thanks for your time. We appreciate it.'

Robin got to her feet.

'I'm sorry,' she said quietly to Donna. 'I hope
you feel better.'

'Thanks,' mumbled Donna.

As Strike and Robin reached the top of the stairs,
they heard shouting break out again behind the
door of Lochnagar.

'Donna, babes—'

'*Don't you dare call me babes, you fucking bastard!*'

'No point carrying on,' said Strike quietly, setting
off down the steep tartaned stairs as slowly as the
obese old lady had moved. 'He's not going to say
it with her there.'

'Say what?'

'Well, that,' said Strike, as the Douthwaites'
shouts echoed down the stairs, 'is the question,
isn't it?'

CHAPTER 65

Like as a ship, that through the Ocean
  wyde
Directs her course vnto one certaine cost,
Is met of many a counter winde and tyde,
With which her winged speed is let and crost,
And she her selfe in stormie surges tost;
Yet making many a borde, and many a bay,
Still winneth way, ne hath her compasse lost:
Right so it fares with me in this long way,
Whose course is often stayd, yet neuer is
  astray.

Edmund Spenser
The Faerie Queene

'I'm hungry,' Strike announced, once they stepped down onto the sunny pavement outside the Allardice.

'Let's get some fish and chips,' said Robin.

'Now you're talking,' said Strike enthusiastically, as they headed off towards the end of Scarbrough Avenue.

'Cormoran, what makes you think Douthwaite knows something?'

'Didn't you see the way he looked at me, when I asked him about his last appointment with Margot?'

'I must've been looking at Donna. I was seriously worried she was going to pass out.'

'Wish she had,' said Strike.

'Strike!'

'He was definitely thinking about telling me something, then she bloody ruined it.' As they reached the end of the road, he said, 'That was a scared man, and I don't think he's only scared of his wife . . . Do we go left or right?'

'Right,' said Robin, so they headed off along Grand Parade, passing a long open-fronted building called Funland, which was full of beeping and flashing video games, claw machines and coin-operated mechanical horses for children to ride. 'Are you saying Douthwaite's guilty?'

'I think he feels it,' Strike said, as they wove their way in and out of cheerful, T-shirted families and couples. 'He looked at me back there as though he was bursting to tell me something that's weighing on him.'

'If he had actual evidence, why didn't he tell the police? It would've got them off his back.'

'I can think of one reason.'

'He was scared of the person he thought had killed her?'

'Exactly.'

'So . . . Luca Ricci?' said Robin.

At that moment, a male voice from the depths of Funland called, 'White seven and four, *seventy-four.*'

'Possibly,' said Strike, though he didn't sound entirely convinced. 'Douthwaite and Ricci were living in the same area at the time. Maybe going to the same pubs. I suppose he might've heard a rumour about Ricci being out to get her. But that doesn't fit with the eye-witness accounts, does it? If Douthwaite was issuing the warning, you'd think it'd be Margot looking distressed afterwards, whereas we know *he* was the one who came running out of there looking scared and worried . . . but my gut feeling is that Douthwaite thinks whatever happened between them at that last appointment is relevant to her disappearance.'

The entrance to a well-maintained park on their right was ablaze with petunias. Ahead, on an island in the middle of a traffic island, stood a sixty-foot-high clock tower of brick and stone, with a faintly Gothic appearance, and faces like a miniature Big Ben.

'Exactly how many chippies has Skegness got?' Strike asked, as they came to a halt on the busy intersection beside the clock tower. They were standing right beside two establishments which had tables spilling out onto the pavement, and he could see a further two fish and chip shops on the other side of the junction.

'I never counted,' said Robin. 'I was always more

interested in the donkeys. Shall we try here?' she asked, pointing at the nearest free table, which was pistachio green and belonged to Tony's Chippy ('We Sell on Quality not Price').

'Donkeys?' repeated Strike, grinning, as he sat down on the bench.

'That's right,' said Robin. 'Cod or haddock?'

'Haddock, please,' said Strike, and Robin headed into the chip shop to order.

After a minute or so, looking forward to his chips and enjoying the feeling of sun on his back, Strike became aware that he was still watching Robin, and fixed his eyes instead on a fluttering mass just above him. Even though the top of the yellow railings separating Tony's from Harry Ramsbottom's had been fitted with fine spikes to stop birds landing on them, a handful of speckled starlings were doing just that, delicately poised between the needles, and balanced in the iron circles just below them, waiting for the chance to swoop on an abandoned chip.

Watching the birds, Strike wondered what the chances were of Douthwaite ringing the number on his card. He was a man with a long track record of hiding from his past, but Strike had definitely read in his face a desperation he'd only ever seen in the faces of men who could no longer bear the pressure of a terrible secret. Idly rubbing his chin, Strike decided to give the man a short period of grace, then either call him again, or even return, unannounced, to Skegness, where he might waylay

Douthwaite in the street or a pub, where Donna couldn't interfere.

Strike was still watching the starlings when Robin set down two polystyrene trays, two small wooden forks and two cans of Coke on the table.

'Mushy peas,' said Strike, looking at Robin's tray, where a hefty dollop of what looked like green porridge sat alongside her fish and chips.

'Yorkshire caviar,' said Robin, sitting down. 'I didn't think you'd want any.'

'You were right,' said Strike, picking up a sachet of tomato sauce while watching with something like revulsion as Robin dipped a chip into the green sludge and ate it.

'Soft Southerner, you are,' she said, and Strike laughed.

'Don't ever let Polworth hear you say that,' he said, breaking off a bit of fish with his fingers, dipping it in ketchup and eating it. He then, without warning, broke into song:

> *A good sword and a trusty hand!*
> *A merry heart and true!*
> *King James's men shall understand,*
> *What Cornish lads can do.*

'What on earth's that?' asked Robin, laughing.

'First verse of "The Song of the Western Men",' said Strike. 'The gist is that Cornishmen are the antithesis of soft bastards. Bloody hell, this is good.'

'I know. You don't get fish and chips like this in London,' said Robin.

For a few minutes they ate in silence. The greaseproof paper in which the trays of chips were wrapped was printed with old pages of the *Mirror* newspaper. *Paul Quits the Beatles*. There were cartoons too, of the dirty postcard type: a busty blonde in bed with her elderly boss was saying 'Business must be booming. You've never given me so much overtime.' It reminded her of Gemma the PA, who'd perhaps already called the fake number Robin had given her, and realised that it wasn't only her ex, 'Andy', who wasn't all he appeared to be. But Robin had a recording on her phone of everything Gemma knew about Shifty's insider trading and Pat, at that moment, was transcribing it into a document shorn of anything that might identify the informant. Shifty, Robin hoped, would soon be jobless and, with any luck, in court.

A long stretch of fairground rides on the other side of the road hid the sea from her sight. The seats of the distant Ferris wheel were enclosed in casings shaped like pastel-coloured hot-air balloons. Nearby stood a gigantic climbing frame for adults, with ropes and swinging tyres, a hundred feet up in the air. Watching the harnessed people navigating the obstacles, Robin felt a strange mixture of contentment and melancholy: the possibility of an unknown development in the Bamborough case, the delicious chips and peas, the companionship of Strike and the sunshine were all cheering, but she was also remembering chasing along the out-of-sight beach as a small child, trying to outrun her brother Stephen to reach the donkeys and have first pick. Why did the memory of innocence sting so much, as you got older? Why did the memory of the child who'd thought she was invulnerable, who'd never known cruelty, give her more pain than pleasure?

Her childhood had been happy, unlike Strike's; it ought not to hurt. Over the space of summer weekends spread years apart, Robin and her brothers had competed to ride the black donkey called Noddy, who was doubtless long gone. Was it mortality, then, which turned cheerful memories bittersweet? Maybe, Robin thought, she'd bring Annabel here when she was old enough, and treat her to her first donkey ride. It was a nice idea, but she doubted Stephen and Jenny would see Skegness as a desirable weekend destination. Annabel's great-aunt had moved away from Boston: there was no longer any family connection to the area. Times changed, and so did childhoods.

'You all right?' said Strike, watching Robin's face.

'Fine,' she said. 'Just thinking . . . I'm going to be thirty in a few weeks.'

Strike snorted.

'Well, you're getting no sympathy from me,' he said. 'I'll be forty the month after.'

He snapped open his can of Coke and drank.

514

Robin watched a family pass, all four eating ice creams, accompanied by a waddling dachshund that was nosing the Union Jack carrier bag which swung from the father's hand.

'D'you think Scotland's going to leave?'

'Go for independence? Maybe,' said Strike. 'The polls are close. Barclay thinks it could happen. He was telling me about some old mates of his at home. They sound just like Polworth. Same hate figures, same promises everything'll be rainbows and unicorns if only they cut themselves free of London. Anyone pointing out pitfalls or difficulties is scaremongering. Experts don't know anything. Facts lie. "Things can't be any worse than they are."'

Strike put several chips in his mouth, chewed, swallowed, then said,

'But life's taught me things can always get worse than they are. I thought I had it hard, then they wheeled a bloke onto the ward who'd had both his legs and his genitals blown off.'

He'd never before talked to Robin about the aftermath of his life-changing injury. Indeed, he rarely mentioned his missing leg. A barrier had definitely fallen, Robin thought, since their whisky-fuelled talk in the dark office.

'Everyone wants a single, simple solution,' he said, now finishing his last few chips. '*One weird trick to lose belly fat.* I've never clicked on it, but I understand the appeal.'

'Well, reinvention's such an inviting idea, isn't

it?' said Robin, her eyes on the fake hot-air balloons, circling on their prescribed course. 'Look at Douthwaite, changing his name and finding a new woman every few years. Reinventing a whole country would feel amazing. Being part of that.'

'Yeah,' said Strike. 'Of course, people think if they subsume themselves in something bigger, and that changes, they'll change too.'

'Well, there's nothing wrong with wanting to be better, or different, is there?' asked Robin. 'Nothing wrong with wanting to improve things?'

'Not at all,' said Strike. 'But *people* who fundamentally change are rare, in my experience, because it's bloody hard work compared to going on a march or waving a flag. Have we met a single person on this case who's radically different to the person they were forty years ago?'

'I don't know . . . I think *I've* changed,' said Robin, then felt embarrassed to have said it out loud.

Strike looked at her without smiling for the space it took him to chew and swallow a chip, then said,

'Yeah. But you're exceptional, aren't you?'

And before Robin had time for anything other than a slight blush, Strike said,

'Are you not finishing those chips?'

'Help yourself,' said Robin, shoving the tray towards him. She pulled her phone out of her pocket. 'I'll look up that one weird tip to lose belly fat.'

Strike smirked. After wiping her hands on her paper napkin, Robin checked her emails.

'Have you seen this from Vanessa Ekwensi? She's copied you in.'

'What?'

'She might know someone who could replace Morris . . . woman called Michelle Greenstreet . . . she wants to leave the police. She's been in eight years,' said Robin, scrolling slowly down the email, 'not enjoying response policing . . . she's in Manchester . . . wants to relocate to London, very keen on the detective side . . .'

'Sounds promising,' said Strike. 'Let's schedule an interview. She's already cleared the first hurdle with flying colours.'

'What hurdle?' said Robin, looking up.

'Doubt she's ever sent a dick pic.'

He patted his pockets, pulled out his packet of Benson & Hedges but found it empty.

'I need more fags, let's—'

'Wait,' said Robin, who was still staring down at her mobile. 'Oh my God. Cormoran – Gloria Conti's emailed me.'

'You're kidding,' said Strike. Having partly risen, he now let himself fall back onto the bench.

'"Dear Miss Ellacott,"' Robin read aloud, '"I'm sorry I haven't answered your emails. I wasn't aware you were trying to contact me and have only just found out. If convenient, I'd be available to talk to you tomorrow evening at 7pm. Yours sincerely . . ." and she's given her phone number,' said Robin, looking up at Strike, astonished. 'How can she only just have found out? It's been *months* of me emailing her without any response . . . unless Anna's prompted her?'

'Could be,' said Strike. 'Which doesn't suggest someone who wants the investigation over.'

'Of *course* she doesn't,' said Robin. 'But for sanity's sake, you'd have to draw the line somewhere.'

'So what does that make us?'

Robin smiled and shook her head.

'Dedicated?'

'Conti: last person to see Margot alive. Closest person to Margot at the practice . . .'

'I'm thanking her,' said Robin, who was typing fast onto her mobile, 'and agreeing to the call tomorrow.'

'We could do it from the office, together,' said Strike. 'Maybe FaceTime her, if she's agreeable?'

'I'll ask,' said Robin, still typing.

They set off a few minutes later in search of cigarettes, Robin reflecting on how casually she'd just agreed to go into work on a Saturday evening, so she could conduct Gloria's interview with Strike. There was no angry Matthew at home any more, furious about her committing herself to long hours, suspicious about what she and Strike were up to, alone in the office in the evening. And she thought back to Matthew's refusal to look her in the eye across the table at the mediation. He'd changed his partner, and his firm; he'd soon be a father. His life had changed, but had he?

They turned the corner to find themselves facing what Strike mentally categorised as 'acres of tat'. As far as the eye could see were racks of merchandise laid out on the pavement: beach balls, keyrings, cheap jewellery, sunglasses, buckets of candyfloss, fudge and plush toys.

'Look at that,' said Robin suddenly, pointing to her right. A bright yellow sign read: *Your Life Within Your Hands*. On the dark glass of the door below was written: *Palm Reader. Clairvoyant*, along with a circular chart, all twelve signs of the zodiac represented by the glyphs around a central sun.

'What?' said Strike.

'Well, you've had your chart done. Maybe I'd like mine.'

'Fuck's sake,' muttered Strike, and they walked on, Robin smiling to herself.

She waited outside, examining postcards, while Strike entered the newsagent's to buy cigarettes.

Waiting to be served, Strike was seized by a sudden, quixotic impulse (stimulated no doubt by the gaudy colour all around him, by the sunshine and sticks of rock, the rattle and clang of amusement arcades and a stomach full of some of the best fish and chips he'd ever eaten) to buy Robin a toy donkey. He came to his senses almost before the idea had formed: what was he, a kid on a daytime date with his first girlfriend? Emerging again into the sunlight as he left the shop, he noted that he couldn't have bought a donkey if he'd wanted to. There wasn't a single one in sight: the bins full of plushes held only unicorns.

'Back to the car, then?' said Robin.

'Yeah,' said Strike, ripping the cellophane off his cigarettes, but then he said, 'we'll go down to the sea before we head off, shall we?'

'OK,' said Robin, surprised. 'Er – why?'

'Just fancy it. It's wrong, being by the sea without actually laying eyes on it.'

'Is this a Cornish thing?' asked Robin, as they headed back to Grand Parade.

'Maybe,' said Strike, lighting the cigarette between his teeth. He took a drag on his cigarette, exhaled then sang,

> *And when we come to London Wall,*
> *A pleasant sight to view,*
> *Come forth! come forth! ye cowards all:*
> *Here's men as good as you.*

'"The Song of the Western Men?"'

'That's the one.'

'Why d'you think they feel the need to tell Londoners they're just as good? Isn't that a given?'

'Just London, isn't it?' said Strike, as they crossed the road. 'Pisses everyone off.'

'I love London.'

'Me too. But I can see why it pisses everyone off.'

They passed a fountain with a statue in the middle of the Jolly Fisherman, that rotund, bearded sailor skipping along in high wind, who'd been used on posters advertising Skegness for nearly a century, and progressed across a smooth paved area towards the beach.

At last they saw what Strike had felt the need to see: a wide expanse of flat ocean, the colour of chalcedony, beneath a periwinkle sky. Far out at sea, spoiling the horizon, were an army of tall white wind turbines, and while Strike personally enjoyed the chill breeze coming off the wide ocean, he understood at last why Robin had brought a scarf.

Strike smoked in silence, the cool wind making no difference whatsoever to his curly hair. He was thinking about Joan. It hadn't occurred to him until this moment that her plan for her final resting place had given them a grave to visit any time they were at the British coast. Cornish-born, Cornish-bred, Joan had known that this need to reconnect with the sea lived in all of them. Now, every time they made their way to the coast they paid her tribute, along with the obeisance due to the waves.

'They were Joan's favourites, pink roses,' he said, after a while. 'What you sent, to the funeral.'

'Oh, really?' said Robin. 'I . . . well, I had a kind of picture in my head of Joan, from things you'd told me, and . . . pink roses seemed to suit her.'

'If the agency ever fails,' said Strike, as they both

turned away from the sea, 'you could come back to Skegness and set yourself up as a clairvoyant.'

'Bit niche,' said Robin, as they walked back towards the car park. 'Guessing dead people's favourite flowers.'

'No donkeys,' said Strike, glancing back over his shoulder at the beach.

'Never mind,' said Robin kindly. 'I think you'd have been a bit heavy.'

CHAPTER 66

*Speak, thou frail woman, speak with
confidence.*

Edmund Spenser
The Faerie Queene

The following evening, Strike and Robin sat down together on the same side of the partners' desk. They were alone in the office for the first time since the night Strike had given her two black eyes. The lights were on this time, there were no glasses of whisky in their hands, but each of them was very conscious of what had happened on the previous occasion, and both felt a slight self-consciousness, which manifested itself, on Strike's side, in a slightly brisker tone as they set up the computer monitor so that both could see it well, and on Robin's, in focusing herself on all the questions she wanted to ask Gloria.

At six o'clock – which was seven o'clock, Gloria's time – Strike dialled Gloria's number, and after a moment's suspense, they heard ringing, and a woman appeared onscreen, looking slightly nervous, in what looked like a book-lined study. Framed on the wall behind her was a large photograph of a family: Gloria herself, a distinguished-looking husband and three adult children, all wearing white shirts, all of them notably attractive.

Of all the people they'd met and interviewed in connection with Margot Bamborough, Gloria Conti, Robin thought, looked most like her younger self, although she hadn't made any obvious efforts to disguise the ageing process. Her hair, which was pure white, had been cut into a short and flattering bob. Although there were fine lines on her brow and around her eyes, her fair complexion seemed never to have been exposed to much sun. She was slim and high-cheekboned, so that the structure of her face was much as it had been when she was younger, and her high-necked navy shirt, small gold earrings and square-framed glasses were stylish and simple. Robin thought that Gloria looked far more like her idea of a college professor than the scion of a criminal family, but perhaps she was being influenced by the lines of books on the shelves behind her.

'Good evening,' said Gloria nervously.

'Good evening,' said Strike and Robin together.

'It's very good of you to talk to us, Mrs Jaubert,' said Strike. 'We appreciate it.'

'Oh, not at all,' she said, politely.

Robin hadn't imagined received pronunciation from Irene Hickson's descriptions of a girl from a rough background, but of course, as with Paul Satchwell, Gloria had now spent longer outside the country of her birth than in it.

'We've been hoping to talk to you for a long time,' said Robin.

'Yes, I'm very sorry about that,' said Gloria. 'My husband, Hugo, didn't tell me about any of your messages, you see. I found your last email in the trash folder, by accident. That's how I realised you were trying to contact me. Hugo – well, he thought he was doing the right thing.'

Robin was reminded of that occasion when Matthew had deleted a voicemail from Strike on Robin's phone in an attempt to stop Robin going back to work at the agency. She was surprised to see Gloria didn't seem to hold her husband's intervention against him. Perhaps Gloria could read her mind, because she said:

'Hugo assumed I wouldn't want to talk about what happened with strangers. He didn't realise that, actually, you're the only people I'd ever want to talk to, because you're trying to find out what really happened, and if you succeed, it'll be – well, it would lift a huge weight off me.'

'D'you mind if I take notes?' Strike asked her.

'No, not at all,' said Gloria politely.

As Strike clicked out the nib of his pen, Gloria reached out of shot for a large glass of red wine, took a sip, appeared to brace herself and said rather quickly,

'Please – if you don't mind – could I explain some things first? Since yesterday, I've been going over it, in my head, and I think if I tell you my story it will save you a lot of time. It's key to understanding my relationship with Margot and why I behaved . . . as I behaved.'

'That'd be very helpful,' said Strike, pen poised. 'Please, go on.'

Gloria took another sip of wine, put her glass back where they couldn't see it, drew a deep breath and said,

'Both my parents died in a house fire when I was five.'

'How awful,' said Robin, startled. The 1961 census record had shown a complete family of four. 'I'm so sorry.'

Strike gave a kind of commiserative growl.

'Thank you,' said Gloria. 'I'm only telling you that to explain – you see, I survived because my father threw me out of the window into a blanket the neighbours were holding. My mother and father didn't jump, because they were trying to reach my elder brother, who was trapped. All three of them died, so I was raised by my mother's parents. They were adorable people. They'd have sold their own souls for me, which makes everything I'm about to say even worse . . .

'I was quite a shy girl. I really envied the girls at school who had parents who were – you know

526

– *with it*. My poor granny didn't really understand the sixties and seventies,' said Gloria, with a sad smile. 'My clothes were always a bit old-fashioned. No mini-skirts or eye make-up, you know . . .

'I reacted by developing a very elaborate fantasy life. I know most teenagers are fantasists, but I was . . . extreme. Everything sort of spun out of control when I was sixteen, and I went to see the movie *The Godfather* . . .

'It's ridiculous,' said Gloria soberly, 'but it's the truth. I . . . *cleaved* to that movie. I became *obsessed* with it. I don't know how many times I saw it; at least twenty, I expect. I was an English schoolgirl from seventies Islington, but what I *really* wanted was to be Apollonia from forties Sicily, and meet a handsome American Mafioso, and *not* to be blown up by a car bomb, but go and live with Michael Corleone in New York and be beautiful and glamorous while my husband did glamorously violent, criminal things, all underpinned, you know, by a strict moral code.'

Strike and Robin both laughed, but Gloria didn't smile. On the contrary, she looked sad and ashamed.

'I somehow thought all this might be achievable,' she went on, 'because I had an Italian surname. I'd never really cared about that, before *The Godfather*. Now, out of nowhere, I asked my grandparents to take me to the Italian church on Clerkenwell Road for mass, instead of their regular

527

church – and bless them, they did it. I wish they hadn't. I wish they'd told me not to be so selfish, because their regular church gave them a lot of support and it was the centre of their social life.

'I'd always felt entirely English, which I *was* on my mum's side, but now I started trying to find out as much as I could about my dad's family. I hoped to find out I was descended from Mafiosi. Then I could get my grandparents to give me the money to go and meet them all in Sicily and maybe marry a distant cousin. But all I found out was that my Italian grandfather immigrated to London to work in a coffee shop. I already knew my dad had worked for London Transport. Everyone I found out about, no matter how far back I went, was completely respectable and law-abiding. It was a real disappointment,' said Gloria, with a sigh.

'Then one Sunday, at St Peter's, somebody pointed out a man called Niccolo Ricci, sitting at the back of the Italian church. They said he was one of the very last of the Little Italy gangsters.'

Gloria paused to take another mouthful of wine, replaced the glass out of shot again, then said,

'Anyway . . . Ricci had sons.'

Strike now set pen to paper for the first time.

'There wasn't much resemblance, really, between Luca Ricci and Al Pacino,' said Gloria drily, 'but I managed to find one. He was four years older than I was, and everyone I asked about him said

528

he was trouble, which was exactly what I wanted to hear. It started with a few smiles in passing . . .

'We went on our first date a couple of months before I was due to sit my exams. I told Granny and Gramps I was revising at a schoolfriend's house. I'd always been such a good girl; they never dreamed I could be fibbing.

'I *desperately* wanted to like Luca, because this was my way into my fantasy. He had a car, and he was definitely criminal. He didn't tell me anything about summit meetings between heads of crime families, though . . . mostly he talked about his Fiat, and drugs and beating people up.

'After a few dates, it was obvious Luca was quite keen on me, or . . . no,' said Gloria, unsmiling, 'not keen, because that implies genuine affection. He really just wanted to fix me down, to keep me his. I was so stupid and lost to my fantasy, I found that quite exciting, because it seemed – you know – the proper Mafioso attitude. But I liked Luca best when I wasn't actually with him, when I was mixing him up with Michael Corleone in my head, in my bed at night.

'I stopped studying. My fantasy life took me over completely. Gangsters' molls didn't need A-levels. Luca didn't think I needed A-levels, either. I failed all of them.

'My grandparents were really disappointed, although they were so kind about it,' said Gloria. For the first time, her voice quivered slightly. 'Then – I think it was the following week – they found out about me seeing Luca. They were desperately worried and upset, but by this time, I didn't really care. I told them I'd given up on the idea of college. I wanted to go out to work.

'I only applied for the job at the St John's practice because it was in the heart of Little Italy, even though Little Italy didn't really exist any more. Luca's father was one of the very last relics. But it was all part of my fantasy: I was a Conti, I should be there, where my forefathers had been. It made it easier to see Luca, too, because he lived there.

'I should never have got that receptionist's job. I was far too young and I had no experience. It was Margot who wanted me to have it.'

Gloria paused, and Robin was sure it was because she'd just had to say Margot's name for the first time. Drawing another deep breath, she said,

'So, there I was, on reception with Irene all day. My grandparents weren't registered at St John's, because they lived in Islington, so I got away with telling Irene a bunch of lies about my background.

'I'd created a whole persona by now. I told her the Contis were an old Sicilian family, how my grandfather and father had been part of a crime family and I don't know what else. Sometimes I used bits and pieces Luca had told me about the Riccis. Some of it was straight out of *The Godfather*. Ironically,' said Gloria, with a slight eye roll, 'the one authentically criminal thing I could have told her, I didn't. I kept my mouth shut about my boyfriend. Luca had told me never to talk about him and his family to other people, so I didn't. I took him seriously.

'I remember, a few months after I got the job, a rumour went round the local area that they'd found a body buried in concrete in one of the builder's sites up the road. I pretended I knew all about that through my underworld contacts. I told Irene I had it on good authority that the corpse had been a member of the Sabini gang. I really was a fool,' said Gloria quietly. 'A little idiot . . .

'But I always had the feeling Margot could see right through me. She told me not long after I started there that she'd "seen something" in me, at the interview. I didn't like that, I felt as though she was patronising me. She never treated me the way I wanted to be treated, as some street-smart Mafia girl with dark secrets, but always as though I was just a sweet young girl. Irene didn't like Margot, either, and we used to moan about her all the time on reception. Margot had a big thing about education and keeping your career, and we used to say what a hypocrite she was, because she'd married this rich consultant. When you're living a lie, nothing's more threatening than people who tell the truth . . .

'I'm sorry,' said Gloria, with an impatient shake of the head, 'this probably doesn't seem relevant at all, but it is, if you just bear with me . . .'

'Take your time,' said Strike.

'Well . . . the day after my eighteenth birthday, Luca and I got into a row. I can't remember what it was about, but he put his hand round my throat and pushed me up against the wall until I couldn't breathe. I was terrified.

'He let go, but there was this horrible look in his eye. He said, "You've got only yourself to blame." And he said, "You're starting to sound like that doctor."

'I'd talked to him quite a lot about Margot, you see. I'd told him she was a complete killjoy, really bossy and opinionated. I kept repeating things she'd said, to denigrate them, to tell myself there was nothing in them.

'She quoted Simone de Beauvoir once, during a staff meeting. She'd sworn when she dropped her pen, and Dr Brenner said, "People are always asking me what it's like working with a lady doctor, and if I ever meet one, I'll be able to tell them." Dorothy laughed – she hardly ever laughed – and Margot snapped right back at him – I know the quotation off by heart now, in French, too – "Man is defined as a human being and a woman as a female – whenever she behaves as a human being she is said to imitate the male."

'Irene and I talked about it afterwards. We called her a show-off for quoting some French woman, but things like that got in my head and I couldn't get them out again. I thought I wanted to be a fifties Mafia housewife, but sometimes Margot was really funny, and I watched her never backing down to Brenner, and you couldn't help admiring her for it . . .'

Gloria took yet another gulp of wine.

'Anyway, the evening Luca half-throttled me, I went home and lay awake crying half the night. The next morning, I put on a polo-neck for work to hide the bruises, and at five o'clock that afternoon, when I left work, I went straight to a call box near the surgery, rang Luca and finished with him. I told him he'd scared me and that I didn't want to see him any more.

'He took it quite quietly. I was surprised, but so relieved . . . for three or four days I thought it was all over, and I felt amazing. It was like waking up, or coming up for air after being underwater. I still wanted to be a mobster's girlfriend, but the fantasy version was fine. I'd had a little bit too much contact with reality.

'Then, at the end of our practice Christmas party, in walked Luca, with his father and one of his cousins.

'I was absolutely *terrified* to see them there. Luca said to me, "Dad just wanted to meet my girlfriend." And – I don't know why, except I was petrified of there being a scene – I just said, "Oh, OK." And I grabbed my coat and left with the three of them, before anyone could talk to them.

'They walked me to my bus stop. On the way, Nico said, "You're a nice girl. Luca was very upset by what you said to him on the phone.

He's very fond of you, you know. You don't want to make him unhappy, do you?" Then he and Luca's cousin walked away. Luca said, "You didn't mean what you said, did you?" And I . . . I was so scared. Him bringing his father and cousin along . . . I told myself I'd be able to get out of it later. Just keep him happy for now. So I said, "No, I didn't mean it. You won't do anything like that ever again, though, will you?" And he said, "Like what?" As if he'd never pressed on my windpipe till I couldn't breathe. As though I'd imagined it.

'So, we carried on seeing each other,' said Gloria. 'Luca started talking about getting married. I kept saying I felt too young. Every time I came close to ending it, he'd accuse me of cheating on him, which was the worst crime of all, and there was no way of proving I wasn't, except to keep going out with him.'

Now Gloria looked away from them, her eyes on something off screen.

'We were sleeping together by then. I didn't want to. I'm not saying he forced me – not really,' said Gloria, and Robin thought of Shifty's PA, Gemma, 'but keeping him happy was the only way to keep going. Otherwise there'd be a slap or worse. One time, he made some comment about hurting my grandmother if I didn't behave. I went crazy at him, and he laughed, and said it was an obvious joke, but he wanted to plant the idea in my mind, and he succeeded.

'And he didn't believe in contraception. We were supposed to be using the . . . you know, the rhythm method,' said Gloria, reaching again for her wine. 'But he was . . . let's say, he was careless, and I was sure he wanted me pregnant, because then he'd have me cornered, and I'd marry him. My grandparents would probably have backed him up. They were devout people.

'So, without telling Luca, I went to Margot for the pill. She said she was happy to give it to me, but she didn't know I had a boyfriend, even, I'd never said . . .

'And even though I didn't really like her,' said Gloria, 'I told her some of it. It was the only place I could drop the pretence, I suppose. I knew she couldn't tell anyone outside her consulting room. She tried to talk sense into me. Tried to show me there were ways out of the situation, apart from just giving in to Luca all the time. I thought it was all right for her, with all her money and her big safe house . . .

'But she gave me a bit of hope, I suppose. Once, after he'd hit me, and told me I'd asked for it, and told me I should be grateful I had someone offering me a way out of living at home with two old people, I said, "There are other places I could go," and I think he got worried someone had offered to help me get away. I'd stopped making fun of Margot by this time, and Luca wasn't a stupid man . . .

'That's when he wrote her threatening notes.

Anonymously, you know – but I knew it was him,' said Gloria. 'I knew his writing. Dorothy was off one day because her son was having his tonsils out, so Irene was opening the post and she unfolded one of the notes, right at the desk beside me. She was gloating about it, and I had to pretend to find it funny, but not to recognise the handwriting.

'I confronted Luca about it. He told me not to be so stupid, of course he hadn't written the notes, but I knew he had . . .

'Anyway – I think it was right after the second note – I found out what I'd been terrified about happening had happened. I was pregnant. I hadn't realised that the pill wouldn't work if you'd had a stomach upset, and I'd had a bug, a month before. I knew I was cornered, and it was too late, I'd have to marry Luca. The Riccis would want it, and my grandparents wouldn't want me to be an unwed mother.

'That's when I admitted it to myself for the first time,' said Gloria, looking directly at Strike and Robin. 'I absolutely hated Luca Ricci.'

'Gloria,' said Robin quietly, 'I'm sorry to interrupt, but could I ask you: when you were sick at Margot's barbecue—?'

'You heard about that, did you? Yes, that was when I had the tummy bug. People said one of the kids had spiked the punch, but I don't think so. Nobody else was as ill as I was.'

Out of the corner of Robin's eye, she saw Strike writing something in his notebook.

'I went back to Margot to find out for sure whether I was pregnant,' said Gloria. 'I knew I could trust her. I broke down again in her surgery, and cried my eyes out, when she confirmed it. And then . . . well, she was just lovely. She held my hand and talked to me for ages.

'I thought abortion was a sin,' said Gloria. 'That's the way I was raised. She didn't think it was a sin, not Margot. She talked to me about the life I was likely to have with Luca, if I had the baby. We discussed me keeping it, alone, but we both knew Luca wouldn't want that, that he'd be in my life for ever if I had his kid. It was hard, then, being on your own with a child. I was watching Janice the nurse doing it. Always juggling her son and the job.

'I didn't tell Luca, obviously,' said Gloria. 'I knew that if I was going to – to *do anything* – I had to do it quickly, before he noticed my body change, but most of all, before the baby could feel it or . . .'

Gloria suddenly bowed her head, and covered her face with her hands.

'I'm so sorry,' said Robin. 'It must have been awful for you . . .'

'No – well—' said Gloria, straightening up and again pushing back her white hair, her eyes wet. 'Never mind that. I'm only telling you, so you understand . . .

'Margot made the appointment for me. She gave the clinic her name and contact details and she bought us both wigs, because if she was recognised, someone might recognise me by association. And she came with me – it was a Saturday – to this place in Bride Street. I've never forgotten the name of the street, because a bride is exactly what I *didn't* want to be, and that's why I was there.

'The clinic had been using Margot's name as the referring doctor, and I think somewhere there were crossed wires, because they thought "Margot Bamborough" was the one having the procedure. Margot said, "It doesn't matter, nobody'll ever know, all these records are confidential." And she said, in a way it was convenient, if there was any follow-up needed, they could contact her and arrange it.

'She held my hand on the way in, and she was there when I woke up,' said Gloria, and now tears leaked from her dark eyes, and she brushed them quickly away. 'When I was ready to go home, she took me to the end of my grandparents' street in a taxi. She told me what to do afterwards, how to take care of myself . . .

'I wasn't like Margot,' said Gloria, her voice breaking. 'I didn't believe it was right, what I did. September the fourteenth: I don't think that date's come by once, since, that I haven't remembered, and thought about that baby.

'When I went back to work after a couple of days off, she took me into her office and asked me how I was feeling, and then she said, "Now, Gloria, you've got to be brave. If you stay with

Luca, this will happen again." She said, "We need to find you a job away from London, and make sure he doesn't know where you've gone." And she said something that's stayed with me always, "We aren't our mistakes. It's what we do *about* the mistake that shows who we are."

'But I wasn't like Margot,' said Gloria again. 'I wasn't brave, I couldn't imagine leaving my grandparents. I pretended to agree, but ten days after the abortion I was sleeping with Luca again, not because I wanted to, but because there didn't seem any other choice.

'And then,' said Gloria, 'about a month after we'd been to the clinic, it happened. Margot disappeared.'

A muffled male voice was now heard at Gloria's end of the call. She turned towards the door behind her and said,

'*Non, c'est toujours en cours!*'

Turning back to her computer she said,

'*Pardon.* I mean, sorry.'

'Mrs Jaubert – Gloria,' said Strike, 'could we please take you back through the day Margot disappeared?'

'The whole day?'

Strike nodded. Gloria took a slow inward breath, like somebody about to dive into deep water, then said,

'Well, the morning was all normal. Everyone was there except Wilma the cleaner. She didn't come in on Fridays.

'I remember two things about the morning: meeting Janice by the kettle at the back, and her going on about the sequel to *The Godfather* coming out soon, and me pretending to be excited about it, and actually feeling as though I'd run a mile rather than go and see it . . . and Irene being quite smug and pleased because Janice had just been on a date with some man she'd been trying to set Janice up with for ages.

'Irene was funny about Janice,' said Gloria. 'They were supposed to be such great friends, but she was always going on about Janice being a bit of a man-eater, which was funny if you'd known Irene. She used to say that Janice needed to learn to cut her cloth, that she was deluded, waiting for someone like James Caan to show up and sweep her off her feet, because she was a single mother and not that great a catch. Irene thought the best she could hope for was this man from Eddie's work, who sounded a bit simple. Irene was always laughing about him getting things wrong . . .

'We were quite busy, as I remember it, all three doctors coming in and out of the waiting room to call for their patients. I can't remember anything unusual about the afternoon except that Irene left early. She claimed she had toothache, but I thought it was a fib at the time. She hadn't seemed in pain to me, when she was going on about Janice's love life.

'I knew Margot was meeting her friend later in

the pub. She told me, because she had a doughnut in cling film in the fridge, and she asked me to bring it through to her, right before she saw her last patient, to keep her going. She loved sugar. She was always in the biscuit tin at five o'clock. She had one of those metabolisms, never put on weight, full of nervous energy.

'I remember the doughnut, because when I took it in to her, I said, "Why didn't you just eat those chocolates?" She had a box she'd taken out of the bin, I think it was the day before. I mean, they were still in their cellophane when she took them out of the bin, it wasn't unhygienic. Someone had sent them to her—'

'Someone?' repeated Strike.

'Well, we all thought it was that patient the police were so interested in, Steve Douthwaite,' said Gloria. 'Dorothy thought that, anyway.'

'Wasn't there a message attached?'

'There was a card saying "Thank you",' said Gloria, 'and Dorothy might've made the assumption it was Steve Douthwaite, because we all thought he was turning up a lot. I don't think the card was signed, though.'

'So Margot threw the box in the bin, and then took it out again, afterwards?'

'Yes, because I laughed at her about it,' said Gloria. 'I said, "I knew you couldn't resist," and she laughed, too. And next day, when I said, "Why don't you eat them?" she said, "I have, I've finished them."'

'But she still had the box there?'

'Yes, on the shelf with her books. I went back to the front desk. Dr Brenner's patient left, but Brenner didn't, because he was writing up the notes.'

'Could I ask you whether you knew about Dr Brenner's barbiturate addiction?' asked Strike.

'His what?' said Gloria.

'Nobody ever told you about that?'

'No,' she said, looking surprised. 'I had no idea.'

'You never heard that Janice had found an Amytal capsule in the bottom of a cup of tea?'

'No . . . oh. Is that why Margot started making her own tea? She told me Irene made it too milky.'

'Let's go back to the order in which everyone left.'

'OK, so, Dr Gupta's patient was next, and Dr Gupta left immediately afterwards. He had some family dinner he needed to attend, so off he went.

'And then, just when I was thinking we were done for the day, in walked that girl, Theo.'

'Tell us about Theo,' said Strike.

'Long black hair . . . dark-skinned. She looked Romanian or Turkish. Ornate earrings, you know: gypsy-ish. I actually thought she looked like a gypsy. I'd never seen her before, so I knew she wasn't registered with us. She looked as though she was in a lot of pain, with her stomach. She came up to the desk and asked to see a doctor

542

urgently. I asked her name, and she said Theo . . . something or other. I didn't ask her again because she was obviously suffering, so I told her to wait and went to see whether a doctor was free. Margot's door was still closed, so I asked Dr Brenner. He didn't want to see her. He was always like that, always difficult. I never liked him.

'Then Margot's door opened, and the mother and child who'd been seeing her left, and she said she'd see the girl who was waiting.'

'And Theo was definitely a girl?' asked Strike.

'Without any doubt at all,' said Gloria firmly. 'She was broad-shouldered, I noticed that when she came to the desk, but she was definitely a woman. Maybe it was the shoulders that made Dr Brenner say, afterwards, she looked like a man, but honestly . . .

'I was thinking about him last night, knowing I was going to be talking to you. Brenner was probably the biggest misogynist I ever met. He'd denigrate women for not looking feminine or talking "like a lady", but he also despised Irene, who was giggly and blonde and very feminine, you know. I suppose what he wanted was for us all to be like Dorothy, subordinate and respectful, high collars, low hemlines. Dorothy was like a really humourless nun.'

Robin thought of Betty Fuller, lying on a bed, pretending to be comatose, while Brenner poured filthy words into her ear.

'Women patients really didn't like Brenner. We

were always having them asking to switch to Margot, but we had to turn most of them down, because her list was so full. But Brenner was coming up for retirement and we were hoping we'd get someone better when he went.

'So, yes, he left, and Theo went in to see Margot. I kept checking the time, because I was supposed to be meeting Luca, and if I kept him waiting, there was always trouble. But Theo's appointment just went on and on. At a quarter past six, Theo finally came back out of the surgery and left.

'Margot came through just a couple of minutes later. She seemed absolutely exhausted. It had been a full day. She said, "I'm going to write her notes up tomorrow, I've got to go, Oonagh's waiting. Lock up with the spare key." I didn't really answer,' said Gloria, 'because I was so worried about Luca getting angry with me. So, I never said goodbye, or have a good evening, to this woman who saved my life . . .

'Because she did, you know. I never said it to her, but she did . . .'

A tear trickled down her face. Gloria paused to wipe it away, then said,

'I remember, as she put her umbrella up, she slipped. Turned over on her heel. It was raining, the pavement was wet. Then she straightened up and walked out of sight.

'I started dashing round, turning off lights, locking the records up in the filing cabinets. Then

I made sure the back door was locked, which it was – the police asked me about that. I closed and locked the front door, and ran straight up Passing Alley, which was right beside the surgery, to meet Luca in St John Street.

'And that was the last time I ever saw Margot.'

Gloria reached again for her almost empty wine glass, and drained it.

'Did you have any idea what might have happened to her?' asked Strike.

'Of course,' said Gloria quietly. 'I was terrified Luca had got someone to hurt her, or kidnap her. She'd become a bugbear to him. Every time I stood up for myself, he'd say horrible things about Margot influencing me. He was convinced she was trying to persuade me to leave him, which, of course, she was. My greatest fear was that he'd somehow find out what she'd helped me do . . . you know. In Bride Street.

'I knew he couldn't have abducted her personally, because I met him on St John Street, not five minutes after she left the surgery, and I know it can't have been his father, because his brother Marco was in hospital at the time, and the parents were with him round the clock. But Luca had friends and cousins.

'I couldn't tell the police. Luca had stopped pretending he was joking, when he threatened my grandparents. I asked him whether he was behind it, though. The anxiety was too much: I had to ask. He got really angry, called me names – dumb bitch, things like that. He said, of course he hadn't. But he'd told me stories about his father "making people disappear", so I just didn't know . . .'

'Did you ever have reason to suppose he knew . . .' Robin hesitated '. . . what happened in Bride Street?'

'I'm absolutely positive he never knew,' said Gloria. 'Margot was too good for him. The wigs and using her name and giving me a plausible story for why I couldn't have sex with him for a while . . . She's the reason I got away with it. No, I don't believe he ever knew. So, in my best moments, I thought, he didn't really have a strong enough reason—'

The door behind Gloria opened, and in walked a handsome aquiline-nosed, grey-haired man in a striped shirt and jeans, carrying a bottle of red wine. A large German Shepherd dog followed him into the room, its tail wagging.

'*Je m'excuse*,' he said, smiling at Strike and Robin onscreen. 'I am sorry for . . . *Comment dit-on "interrompre"?*' he asked his wife.

'Interrupt,' she said.

'*Oui.* I am sorry for interrupt.'

He refilled his wife's glass, handed it back to her, patted her on the shoulder, then walked out again, calling the dog.

'*Viens, Obélix.*'

When both man and dog had disappeared, Gloria said, with a little laugh,

'That was Hugo.'

'How long did you stay at the St John's practice, after Margot disappeared?' asked Strike, although he knew the answer.

'Six, seven months, I think,' said Gloria. 'Long enough to see the new policeman take over. We were all pleased, because the first – Talbot, wasn't it? – was quite strange. He bullied the life out of Wilma and Janice. I think that's what made Wilma ill, actually. She had quite enough on her plate without the police hounding her.'

'You don't think she drank, then?' asked Robin.

'Drank? That was all Dorothy's malice,' said Gloria, shaking her head. 'Dorothy was trying to pin the thefts on Wilma. Have you heard about that?'

Strike and Robin nodded.

'When she couldn't prove that Wilma was taking money out of people's bags, she put it about that she was drinking and the poor woman resigned. She was probably glad to leave, but it was still losing a salary, wasn't it?

'I wanted to leave myself,' said Gloria, 'but I was paralysed. I had this really strange feeling that, if I just stayed there, the world would right itself. Margot would come back. It was only after she disappeared that I realised . . . what she'd been to me . . .

'Anyway,' sighed Gloria, 'one night, months after she'd disappeared, Luca was *really* violent to me. I'd smiled at a man who opened a door for me as I left the pub with Luca, that's what sparked it. He beat me like he'd never beaten me before, at his place – he had this little flat.

'I remember saying "I'm sorry, I'm sorry, I shouldn't have smiled at him". And all the time I was saying it, I could see – in here—' Gloria tapped her head, 'Margot watching me, and even while I was begging Luca to stop, and agreeing I'd behaved like a little slut, and I shouldn't ever smile at strange men, I was thinking, *I'm going, Margot. I'm going where he'll never find me.*

'Because it had clicked in my head at last. She'd told me I needed to be brave. It was no good waiting for anyone else to save me. *I* had to save me.

'After he'd calmed down, he let me go home to my grandparents' house, but he wanted to see me again later. It was always like that after he'd been really violent. He wanted extra contact.

'He hadn't beaten me in the face. He never did, he never lost control like that, so I went back to my grandparents' and acted as though everything was fine. Went out to meet Luca that night, and he took me out for dinner, and that was the night he proposed, with a ring and everything.

'And I said yes,' said Gloria, with a strange smile and a shrug. 'I put that ring on, and I looked down at it, and I didn't even have to act happy, because I genuinely was. I thought *That'll buy some of my plane ticket.* Mind you, I'd never flown before in my life. The idea of it scared me. But all the time, I could see Margot in my head. *You've got to be brave, Gloria.*

'I had to tell my grandparents I was engaged. I couldn't tell them what I was really planning, because I was scared they wouldn't be able to act, or that they'd try and confront Luca or, worse, go to the police. Anyway, Luca came round to the house to meet them properly, pretending to be a nice guy, and it was awful, and I had to act as though I was thrilled about all of it.

'Every single day after that, I bought all the newspapers, and circled all of the jobs abroad that I might have a chance of getting. I had to do all of it in secret. Typed up a CV at work and got a bus to the West End to post all the applications, because I was scared someone who knew Luca would see me putting lots of envelopes in the post.

'After a few weeks, I got an interview with a French woman who was looking for an English home help, to teach her kids English. What really got me the job was being able to type. She ran her own business from home, so I could do a bit of admin for her while the kids were at nursery. The job came with room and board, and my employer would buy my plane ticket, so I didn't have to sell Luca's ring, and pretend I'd lost it . . .

'You know, the day I went into St John's and told them I was resigning, a funny thing happened. Nobody had mentioned Margot for weeks. Immediately after she disappeared, it was all any of us could talk about, but then it became taboo, somehow. We had a new locum doctor in her room. I can't remember his name. A new cleaner, too. But this day, Dorothy arrived, quite flustered, and she never showed any emotion, usually . . .

'This local . . . what's the word?' said Gloria, clicking her fingers, for the first time lost in her native language. 'We'd say *un dingue* . . . oh, you know, a crazy man, a loon . . . harmless, but strange. Big long beard, dirty, you used to see him wandering up and down Clerkenwell Road with his son. Anyway, he'd sort of accosted Dorothy in the middle of the street, and told her he killed Margot Bamborough.

'It had shaken Dorothy up, but in an odd way . . . please don't think this is awful . . . I hoped it was true. Because although I'd have given *anything* to know Margot was alive, I was sure she was dead. She wasn't the type to run away. And my worst nightmare was that Luca was responsible, because that meant it was all my fault.'

Robin shook her head, but Gloria ignored her.

'I only told my grandparents the truth the night before I was due to leave for France. I hadn't let them spend any money on the wedding that wasn't going to happen, but even so, it was a huge shock to them. I sat them down, and told them everything, except for the termination.

'Of course, they were appalled. At first, they didn't want me to leave, they wanted me to go to

550

the police. I had to explain why that was a terrible idea, tell them about the threats Luca had made, and all of that. But they were so glad I wasn't marrying him, they accepted it in the end. I told them it would all die down, and I'd be back soon . . . even though I wasn't sure that was true, or if it would be possible.

'My grandfather took me to the airport, early next day. We'd worked out a story, for when Luca came asking where I was. They were to say I'd been having doubts, because he'd been violent, and that I'd gone over to Italy to stay with some of Dad's relatives, to think things over. We even concocted a fake address to give him. I don't know whether he ever wrote to it.

'And that's everything,' said Gloria, sitting back in the desk chair. 'I stayed with my first employer for seven years, and ended up with a junior position in her firm. I didn't visit London again until I heard Luca was safely married.' She took another sip of wine from the glass her husband had refilled. 'His first wife drank herself to death at the age of thirty-nine. He used to beat her badly. I found all that out later.

'And I've never told another lie about myself,' said Gloria, raising her chin. 'Never exaggerated, never pretended, only ever told the absolute truth, except on one point. Until tonight, the only person who knew about the abortion was Hugo, but now you two know, too.

'Even if you find out Luca was behind what

happened to Margot, and I have to have that on my conscience for ever, I owe her the truth. That woman saved me, and I've never, ever forgotten her. She was one of the bravest, kindest people I've ever known.'

CHAPTER 67

There by th'vncertaine glims of starry night,
And by the twinkling of their sacred fire,
He mote perceiue a litle dawning sight . . .

Edmund Spenser
The Faerie Queene

They thanked Gloria for her time and her honesty. Having bidden her goodbye, Strike and Robin sat at the partners' desk, each of them sunk in thought, until Strike offered Robin one of the pots of dehydrated noodles he kept for snacks in the office. She declined, instead taking a bag of mixed nuts unenthusiastically out of her bag, and opening it. Once Strike had added boiling water to the plastic pot, he returned to the desk, stirring the noodles with a fork.

'It's the efficiency,' he said, sitting down again. 'That's what's bugging me. Literally no trace of her anywhere. Somebody was either extraordinarily clever, or unprecedentedly lucky. And Creed still fits that picture best, with Luca Ricci a close second.'

'Except it can't have been Luca. He's got an alibi: Gloria.'

'But as she says, he knew people who could take care of making someone disappear – because what are the odds, if Margot was abducted off the street, that this was a *truly* one-person job? Even Creed had his unwitting accomplices. The dozy landlady, giving him that safe basement, and the dry cleaner letting him have the van that day and n—'

'Don't,' said Robin sharply.

'Don't what?'

'Blame them.'

'I'm not blaming them, I'm—'

'Max and I were talking about this,' said Robin. 'About the way people – women, usually – get blamed for not knowing, or seeing – but everyone's guilty of that kind of bias. Everyone does it.'

'You think?' said Strike thickly, through his first mouthful of noodles.

'Yes,' said Robin. 'We've all got a tendency to generalise from our own past experiences. Look at Violet Cooper. She thought she knew who Creed really was, because she'd met a couple of men who behaved like him, in her theatre days.'

'Men who wouldn't let anyone in their basement flats because they were boiling down skulls?'

'You know what I mean, Strike,' said Robin,

refusing to be amused. 'Soft-spoken, apparently gentle, slightly feminine. Creed liked putting on her feather boa, and he pretended to like show tunes, so she thought he was a gay man. But if the only gay man she'd met had been Max, my flatmate . . .'

'He's gay, is he?' said Strike, whose memories of Max were indistinct.

'Yes, and he isn't remotely camp, and hates musicals. Come to that, if she'd met a couple of Matt's straight mates down the rugby club, who couldn't wait to shove oranges up their T-shirts and prance around, she might've drawn a different conclusion, mightn't she?'

'S'pose so,' said Strike, chewing noodles and considering this point. 'And in fairness, most people don't know any serial killers.'

'Exactly. So even if somebody's got some unusual habits, our direct experience tends to suggest they're just eccentric. Vi had never met a man who fetishised women's clothing or . . . sorry, I'm boring you,' Robin added, because Strike's eyes seemed to have glazed over.

'No, you aren't,' he muttered. 'You're actually making me think . . . I had an idea, you know. I thought I'd spotted some coincidences, and it got me wondering . . .'

He set down the pot of noodles, reached under the desk and pulled one of the boxes of police evidence towards him, on top of which lay the pages he'd last been re-examining. He now took these bits of paper out, spread them in front of himself again, and resumed his noodle-eating.

'Are you going to tell me about the coincidences?' said Robin with a trace of impatience.

'Hang on a minute,' said Strike, looking up at her. 'Why was Theo standing *outside* the phone box?'

'What?' said Robin, confused.

'I don't think we can doubt, now, can we, that Ruby Elliot saw Theo by that phone box near Albemarle Way? Her description and Gloria's tally exactly . . . so why was Theo standing *outside* the phone box?'

'She was waiting for the van to pick her up.'

'Right. But, not to state the bleeding obvious, the sides of the old red telephone boxes have windows. It was pissing down with rain. Theo didn't have an umbrella, and Ruby said Theo's hair was plastered down – so why didn't she shelter in the telephone box, and keep watch for her lift? Clerkenwell Road's long and straight. She'd've had a perfectly good view from that telephone box, and plenty of time to come out and show herself to the van driver. Why,' said Strike for the third time, 'was she standing *outside* the phone box?'

'Because . . . there was someone in it?'

'That would seem the obvious explanation. And that phone box at the end of Albemarle Way would give you a view of the top of St John's Lane.'

'You think someone was lying in wait for Margot? Watching out from that phone box?'

Strike hesitated.

'Do me a favour and look up Fragile X syndrome?'

'OK . . . why?' said Robin, setting down her almonds and beginning to type.

'That phone box is at the end of the Athorns' street.'

While Robin brought up the search results, Strike pulled the copy of Irene Hickson's receipt towards him. It had the time 3.10 p.m. on it. Eating noodles, Strike was still looking at the slip of paper when Robin said, reading off her screen,

'"First called Martin-Bell syndrome . . . the FMR1 gene on the X chromosome was sequenced in 1991" . . . Sorry, what exactly do you need?'

'What specific disabilities does it cause?'

'"Social anxiety",' said Robin, reading again, '"lack of eye contact . . . challenges forming relationships . . . anxiety with unfamiliar situations and people . . . poor ability to recognise faces you've seen before", but "good long-term memory, good imitation skills and good visual learning". Men are more severely affected than women . . . good sense of humour, usually . . . "can be creative, especially visually" . . .'

She looked around the computer monitor.

'Why d'you want to know all this?'

'Just thinking.'

'About Gwilherm?'

'Yeah,' said Strike. 'Well, about the whole family.'

'*He* didn't have Fragile X, though, did he?'

'No, I don't know what Gwilherm's problem was. Maybe just the Bennies.'

He didn't smile as he said the name this time.

'Cormoran, what coincidences did you notice?'

Instead of answering, Strike pulled a couple of pages of police notes towards him and read through them again. Out of force of habit, Robin reached out for Talbot's notebook, and turned to the first page. For a couple of minutes, there was silence in the office, and neither partner noticed any of the noises that were as familiar to them as their own breathing: the traffic rolling down Charing Cross Road, occasional shouts and snatches of music from Denmark Street below.

The very first page of Bill Talbot's notebook began with untidy jottings of what Robin knew to be genuine evidence and observations. It was the most coherent part of the notes but the first pentagrams appeared at the very bottom of the page, as did the first astrological observation.

(Theo? MALE?) white van speeding Aylesbury St away from Clerkenwell Green
Two women struggling by phone boxes, smaller in rainhat, taller in raincoat,
seems unsteady on feet, then VAN speeding away from Clerkenwell Green
♃ is currently retrograde in ♓ meaning planet of OBJECTIVE TRUTH
in sign of ILLUSION and FANTASY

Robin re-read this final paragraph twice, frowning slightly. Then she set aside her bag of almonds to delve in the nearest box of police evidence. It took her five minutes to find the original police record of Ruby Elliot's statement, and while she searched,

Strike remained deeply immersed in his own portion of the notes.

> I saw them beside a telephone box, two women sort of struggling together. The tall one in the raincoat was leaning on the short one, who was in a plastic rain hood. They both looked like women to me, but I didn't see their faces. It looked to me like one was trying to make the other walk quicker.

Pulse now quickened, Robin set aside this piece of paper, got back onto her knees and began to search for the record of Ruby's statement to Lawson, which took her another five minutes.

> I saw them beside the two telephone boxes in Clerkenwell Green, two women struggling with each together. The tall one in the raincoat was trying to make the little one in the rain hood walk faster.

'Cormoran,' said Robin urgently.
Strike looked up.
'The heights are round the wrong way.'
'What?'
'In Ruby's very first statement to Talbot,' Robin said, 'she said, "I saw them beside a telephone box, two women sort of struggling together. The tall one in the raincoat was leaning on the short

one, who was in a plastic rain hood. They both looked like women to me, but I didn't see their faces. It looked to me like one was trying to make the other walk quicker.'"

'Right,' said Strike, frowning slightly.

'And that's what Talbot wrote in his horoscope notes, too,' said Robin. 'But that's not how it should have been, if those two women were the Fleurys. Where's that picture?'

'Box one,' said Strike, shoving it towards Robin with his real foot.

She crouched down beneath the desk and began searching the photocopied papers until she found the sheaf of newspaper clippings Strike had shown her, months previously, in the Three Kings.

'There,' said Robin. 'Look. *There.*'

And there was the old picture, of the two women who'd come forward to say that they were Ruby's struggling women: the tall, broad, younger woman with her cheery face, and her aged mother, who was tiny and stooped.

'It's the wrong way round,' repeated Robin. 'If Fiona Fleury had leaned on her mother, she'd have flattened her . . .' Robin scanned the few lines beneath the picture. 'Cormoran, *it doesn't fit.* Fiona says *she* was wearing the rain hat, but Ruby says it was the short woman who had the rainhat on.'

'Ruby was vague,' said Strike, but Robin could see his interest sharpening as he reached out for these pieces of paper. 'She could've been confused . . .'

'Talbot never thought the Fleurys were the people Ruby saw, and this is why!' said Robin. 'The heights were reversed. It was the taller woman Ruby saw who was unsteady, not the little one . . .'

'So how come she didn't tell Lawson the Fleurys couldn't be the people she saw?'

'Same reason she never told anybody she'd seen Theo? Because she'd been flustered by Talbot trying to force her to bend her story to fit his theories? Because she lost confidence in herself, and didn't know what she'd really seen? It was raining, she was lost, she was panicked . . . by the time it got to Lawson, maybe she just wanted to agree she'd seen the Fleurys and be left alone?'

'Plausible,' admitted Strike.

'How tall was Margot?'

'Five nine,' said Strike.

'And Creed?' said Robin.

'Five seven.'

'Oh God,' said Robin quietly.

There was another minute's silence, while Strike sat lost in thought and Robin re-read the statements laid out in front of her.

'The phone boxes,' said Strike, at last. 'Those bloody phone boxes . . .'

'What about them?'

'Talbot wanted Ruby to have seen the two

struggling women beside the two boxes in Clerkenwell Green, right? So he could tie them to the van that was speeding away up Aylesbury Street, which was supposed to contain Creed.'

'Right,' said Robin.

'But after the Fleurys came forward, Talbot tried to get Ruby to agree she'd seen the two struggling women beside the first phone box, the one at the end of Albemarle Way.'

'But she wouldn't change her story,' said Robin, 'because she'd seen Theo there.'

'Precisely,' said Strike, 'but that doesn't make sense.'

'I don't—'

'She's driving round in an enormous circle in the rain, right, looking for this house she can't find, right?'

'Yes . . .'

'Well, just because Ruby saw Theo get into a van by the phone box on one of her circuits doesn't mean she can't have seen two struggling women on her second or third circuit. We know she was hazy about landmarks, unfamiliar with the area and with no sense of direction, her daughter was very clear about that. But she had this very retentive visual memory, she's somebody who notices clothes and hairstyles . . .'

Strike looked down at the desk again, and for the second time, picked up Irene Hickson's receipt and examined it. Then, so suddenly that Robin jumped, Strike let the receipt fall and stood up, both hands clasped over the back of his head.

'Shit,' he said. '*Shit! Never* trust a phone call whose provenance you haven't checked!'

'What phone call?' said Robin nervously, casting her mind back over any phone calls she'd taken over the course of the case.

'Fuck's sake,' said Strike, walking out of the room into the outer office and then back again, still clasping the back of his head, apparently needing to pace, just as Robin had needed to walk when she'd found out Strike could interview Creed. '*How did I not fucking see it?*'

'Cormoran, what—?'

'Why did Margot keep an empty chocolate box?' said Strike.

'I don't know,' said Robin, confused.

'You know what?' said Strike slowly. 'I think I do.'

CHAPTER 68

. . . an Hyena was,
That feeds on wemens flesh, as others feede
on gras.

Edmund Spenser
The Faerie Queene

The high-security mental hospital that is
Broadmoor lies slightly over an hour
outside London, in the county of Berkshire.
The word 'Broadmoor' had long since lost all
bucolic associations in the collective mind of the
British public, and Strike was no exception to this
rule. Far from connoting a wide stretch of grass-
land or heath, the name spoke to Strike only of
violence, heinous crimes and two hundred of the
most dangerous men in Britain, whom the tabloids
called monsters. Accordingly, and in spite of the
fact that Strike knew he was visiting a hospital
and not a prison, he took all the common sense
measures he'd have taken for a high-security jail:
he wore no tie, ensured that neither he or his car

was carrying anything likely to trigger a burdensome search, brought two kinds of photographic ID and a copy of his letter from the Ministry of Justice, set out early, certain, though he'd never been there before, that getting inside the facility would be time-consuming.

It was a golden September morning. Sunshine pouring down upon the road ahead from between fluffy white clouds, and as Strike drove through Berkshire in his BMW, he listened to the news on the radio, the lead item of which was that Scotland had voted, by 55 per cent to 45 per cent, to remain in the United Kingdom. He was wondering how Dave Polworth and Sam Barclay were taking the news, when his mobile rang.

'It's Brian, Brian Tucker,' said the hoarse voice. 'Not interrupting, am I? Wanna wish you good luck.'

'Thanks, Brian,' said Strike.

They'd finally met three days previously, at Strike's office. Tucker had shown Strike the old letter from Creed, described the butterfly pendant taken from the killer's basement, which he believed was his daughter's, shared his theories and trembled with emotion and nerves at the thought of Strike coming face to face with the man he believed had murdered his eldest daughter.

'I'll let you go, I won't keep you,' said Tucker. 'You'll ring me when it's over, though?'

'I will, of course,' said Strike.

It was hard to concentrate on the news now that

he'd heard Tucker's anxiety and excitement. Strike turned off the radio, and turned his thoughts instead to what lay ahead.

Gratifying though it would be to believe that he, Cormoran Strike, might trick or persuade Creed into confessing where all others had failed, Strike wasn't that egotistical. He'd interviewed plenty of suspects in his career; the skill lay in making it easier for a suspect to disclose the truth than to continue lying. Some were worn down by patient questioning, others resistant to all but intense pressure, still others yearned to unburden themselves, and the interrogator's methods had to change accordingly.

However, in talking to Creed, half of Strike's interrogatory arsenal would be out of commission. For one thing, he was there at Creed's pleasure, because the patient had had to give his consent for the interview. For another, it was hard to see how Strike could paint a frightening picture of the consequences of silence, when his interviewee was already serving life in Broadmoor. Creed's secrets were the only power he had left, and Strike was well aware that persuading him to relinquish any of them might prove a task beyond any human investigator. Standard appeals to conscience, or to the desire to figure as a better person to the self or to others, were likewise useless. As Creed's entire life demonstrated, his primary sources of enjoyment were inflicting pain and establishing dominance, and it was doubtful that anything else would persuade him into disclosures.

Strike's first glimpse of the infamous hospital was of a fortress on raised ground. It had been built by the Victorians in the middle of woodland and meadows, a red-brick edifice with a clock-tower the highest point in the compound. The surrounding walls were twenty feet high, and as Strike drove up to the front gates, he could see the heads of hundreds of Cyclopean security cameras on poles. As the gates opened, Strike experienced an explosion of adrenalin, and for a moment the ghostly black and white images of seven dead women, and the anxious face of Brian Tucker, seemed to swim before him.

He'd sent his car registration number in advance. Once through the first set of double gates he encountered an inner wire fence, as tall as the wall he'd just passed through. A white-shirted, black-trousered man of military bearing unlocked a second set of gates once the first had closed behind the BMW, and directed Strike to a parking space. Before leaving his car, and wanting to save time going through the security he was about to face, the detective put his phone, keys, belt, cigar-ettes, lighter and loose change into the glove compartment and locked it.

'Mr Strike, is it?' said the smiling, white-shirted man, whose accent was Welsh and whose profile suggested a boxer. 'Got your ID there?'

Strike showed his driver's licence, and was led

inside, where he encountered a scanner of the airport security type. Good-humoured, inevitable amusement ensued when the scanner announced shrill disapproval of Strike's metal lower leg, and his trousers had to be rolled up to prove he wasn't carrying a weapon. Having been patted down, he was free to join Dr Ranbir Bijral, who was waiting for him on the other side of the scanners, a slight, bearded psychiatrist whose open-necked yellow shirt struck a cheerful note against the dull green-grey tiled floors, the white walls and the unfresh air of all medical institutions, part disinfectant, part fried food, with a trace of incarcerated human.

'We've got twenty minutes until Dennis will be ready for you,' said Dr Bijral, leading Strike off along an eerily empty corridor, through many sets of turquoise swing doors. 'We coordinate patient movements carefully and it's always a bit of a feat moving him around. We have to make sure he never comes into contact with patients who have a particular dislike for him, you see. He's not popular. We'll wait in my office.'

Strike was familiar with hospitals, but had never been inside one with so little bustle or shuffle of patients in the corridors. The emptiness was slightly unnerving. They passed many locked doors. A short female nurse in navy scrubs marched past. She smiled at Strike, who smiled back.

'You've got women working here,' he said, slightly surprised.

'Of course,' said Dr Bijral.

Strike had somehow imagined an all-male staff, even though he knew that male prisons had female warders. Dr Bijral pushed open a door to a small office that had the air of a converted treatment room, with chipped paint on the walls and bars on the windows.

'Have a seat,' said Dr Bijral, waving his hand at the chair opposite his desk, and with slightly forced politeness, he asked, 'Did you have a good journey? Come up from London?'

'Yeah, it was a nice drive,' said Strike.

As he sat down behind the desk, Dr Bijral became business-like.

'All right, so: we're going to give you forty-five minutes with Creed.'

'Forty-five minutes,' repeated Strike.

'If Dennis wants to admit to another killing, that should be ample time,' said Dr Bijral, 'but . . . may I be honest with you, Mr Strike?'

'Of course.'

'If it had been down to Dennis's treatment team, we probably wouldn't have permitted this visit. I know the MoJ feel the Bamboroughs and the Tuckers ought to be given a last chance to ask Dennis about their relatives, but—'

Dr Bijral leaned back in his seat and sighed.

'—he's a classic sociopath, you see, a pure example of the type. He scores very highly on the dark triad: narcissism, Machiavellianism and psychopathy. Devious, sadistic, unrepentant and extremely egotistical.'

'Not a fan, then?' said Strike, and the doctor permitted himself a perfunctory smile.

'The problem, you see, is if he admitted to another murder under your questioning, you'd get the credit. And Dennis can't have that, he can't allow somebody else to come out on top. He had to give his consent to meeting you, of course, and I think he's agreed because it feeds his ego to be questioned, especially by a man who's been in the papers, and I think he'd like to manipulate you into being an advocate for him in some way. He's been lobbying to get out of Broadmoor and back into prison for a long time now.'

'I thought he was desperate to get in here?'

'He was, once,' said Bijral. 'High-profile sex offenders are usually under risk of attack in the prison system, as you probably know. You might have seen in the papers, one man nearly took his eye out with a sharpened spoon handle. Dennis wanted to come to Broadmoor when he was first convicted, but there were no grounds to admit him to hospital back then. Psychopathy isn't, in itself, treatable.'

'What changed?'

'He was exceptionally difficult to manage in the prison system. He managed to talk a young offender with Asperger's syndrome into killing himself. For that, he was put into solitary confinement. They ended up keeping him there for almost a year. By night, he took to re-enacting what had happened in the basement in Liverpool Road, screaming through the night, doing his voice and the women's. Warders couldn't stand hearing it, let alone prisoners.

'After eleven months in solitary, he became suicidal. First he went on hunger strike. Then he began trying to bite his own wrists open, and smashing his head against the wall. He was assessed, judged psychotic and transferred here.

'Once we'd had him a couple of months, he claimed he'd been faking his mental illness, which is pure Dennis. Nobody else can be cleverer than he is. But actually, his mental health was very poor when he came to us, and it took many months of medication and therapy to stop him self-harming and trying to kill himself.'

'And now he wants to leave?'

'Once he was well enough to fully appreciate the difference between jail and hospital, I think it's fair to say he was disappointed. He had more freedom in Belmarsh. He did a lot of writing and drawing before he got ill. I read the autobiography he'd been working on, when he was admitted. It was useful in assessing him. He writes very well for a man who had hardly any education, but . . .' Dr Bijral laced his fingers together, and Strike was reminded of another doctor, who'd talked of teamwork while eating fig rolls. 'You see, persuading patients to discuss their crimes is usually an important part of the therapeutic process. You're trying to find a pathway to accountability and remorse, but Dennis feels no

571

remorse. He's still aroused by the thought of what he did to those women, and he enjoys talking and writing about it. He used to draw episodes from the basement, as well; essentially producing his own hardcore pornography. So when he came here, we confiscated all writing and drawing materials.

'Dennis blames us for his deteriorating mental faculties, although in fact, for a seventy-seven-year-old man, he's remarkably sharp. Every patient is different, and we manage Dennis on a strict reward and penalty system. His chosen rewards are unusual. He enjoys chess; he taught himself in Belmarsh, so sometimes I'll give him a game. He likes crosswords and logic puzzles, too. We allow him access to those when he's behaving himself.

'But you mustn't think he's typical of our patients,' added Dr Bijral earnestly. 'The vast majority of mentally ill people pose absolutely no risk of violence, as I'm sure you know. And people do leave Broadmoor, they do get better. People's behaviour can change, if they're motivated, if they're given the right help. Our aim is always recovery. One can hate the crime, but feel compassion for the perpetrator. Many of the men in here had appallingly abusive childhoods. Dennis's childhood was pure hell – though, of course, other people have upbringings as bad and never do what Dennis did. In fact, one of our former patients—'

There was a knock on the door and a cheery blonde poked her head inside.

'That's Dennis ready in the room, Ranbir,' she said, and withdrew.

'Shall we?' said Dr Bijral, getting to his feet. 'I'll be sitting in on the interview, and so will Dennis's primary nurse.'

The woman who'd announced Dennis's arrival in the meeting room walked with Strike and the psychiatrist down another couple of corridors. Now there were doors that had to be unlocked and relocked at every passage. Through the third set of locked doors, Strike saw an obese man shuffling along in Nike tracksuit bottoms, flanked by a pair of nurses, each of whom held one of the patient's stiff arms behind his back. The patient gave Strike a glazed look as the trio passed in silence.

Finally, Strike's party reached a deserted open-plan area, with armchairs and a switched-off TV. Strike had assumed the blonde woman was Creed's nurse, but he was wrong: a burly man with tattoos down both arms, and a prominent, square jaw, was introduced as 'Marvin, Dennis's lead nurse', and the blonde woman smiled at Strike, wished him luck and walked away.

'Well, shall we?' said Dr Bijral, and Marvin opened the door onto a Spartan meeting room, with a single window and a whiteboard on the wall.

The only occupant, a small, obese, bespectacled

man, wore jeans and a black sweatshirt. He had a triple chin, and his belly kept him a foot and a half away from the white Formica-topped table at which he was sitting. Transplanted to a bus stop, Dennis Creed would have been just another old man, a little unkempt, his light grey hair in need of a trim.

(He'd pressed hot-irons to the bare breasts of secretary Jackie Aylett. He'd pulled out all of hair-dresser Susan Meyer's finger and toenails. He'd dug the eyeballs out of estate agent Noreen Sturrock's face while she was still alive and mana-cled to a radiator.)

'Dennis, this is Cormoran Strike,' said Dr Bijral, as he sat down in a chair against the wall. Marvin stood, tattooed arms folded, beside him.

'Hello, Dennis,' said Strike, sitting down oppos-ite him.

'Hello, Cormoran,' said Creed, in a flat voice which retained its working-class, East London accent.

The sunlight fell like a gleaming pane across the table between them, highlighting the smears on the lenses of Creed's wire-rimmed glasses and the dust motes in the air. Behind the dirt, Strike saw irises of such pale grey that they faded into the sclera, so that the enormous pupils seemed surrounded by whiteness. Close to, Strike could see the jagged scar which ran from temple to nose, dragging at his left lower eyelid, a relic of the attack that had almost taken half Creed's sight.

The plump, pale hands on the table were slightly shaking and the slack mouth trembled: side-effects, Strike guessed, of Creed's medication.

'Who're you working for?' Creed asked.

''Spect you'll be able to work that out, from my questions,' said Strike.

'Why not say, then?' asked Creed, and when Strike didn't answer, he said, 'Sign of narcissism, withholding information to make yourself feel powerful, you know.'

Strike smiled.

'It's not a question of trying to feel powerful. I'm simply familiar with the King's Gambit.'

Creed pushed his wire-rimmed glasses back up his nose.

'Told you I play chess, did they?'

'Yeah.'

'D'you play?'

'Badly.'

'So how does the King's Gambit apply to this situation?'

'Your opening move appears to open an easy route to your king. You're offering to jump straight into discussing the missing woman I'm investigating.'

'But you think that's a ploy?'

'Maybe.'

There was a short pause. Then Creed said,

'I'll tell you who I think sent you, then, shall I?'

'Go on.'

'Margot Bamborough's daughter,' said Dennis

Creed, watching carefully for Strike's reaction. 'The husband gave up on her long since, but her daughter'll be forty-odd now and she'll be well-heeled. Whoever hired you's got money. You won't come cheap. I've read all about you, in the paper.

'The second possibility,' said Creed, when Strike didn't respond, 'is old Brian Tucker. He pops up every few years, making a spectacle of himself. Brian's skint, though . . . or did he put out the begging bowl on the internet? Get on the computer and whine out some hard-luck story, so mugs send in cash? But I think, if he'd done that, it would've been in the papers.'

'D'you get online much?' asked Strike.

'We're not allowed, in here,' said Creed. 'Why are you wasting time? We've only got forty-five minutes. Ask a question.'

'That was a question, what I just asked you.'

'Why won't you tell me which so-called victim you're interested in?'

'"So-called" victim?'

'Arbitrary labels,' said Creed. '"Victim". "Patient". *This* one deserves pity . . . *this* one gets caged. Maybe those women I killed were the real patients, and I'm the true victim?'

'Novel point of view,' said Strike.

'Yeah, well, does people good to hear novel points of view,' said Creed, pushing his glasses up his nose again. 'Wake them up, if they're capable of it.'

'What would you say you were curing those women of?'

'The infection of life? Diagnosis: life. Terminal. "Pity not the fallen! I never knew them. I am not for them. I console not: I hate the consoled and the consoler . . ."'

(He'd slit open the corners of schoolgirl Geraldine Christie's mouth, and photographed her crying and screaming, before, as he told her parents from the dock, slitting her throat because she was making so much noise.)

'". . . I am unique and conqueror. I am not of the slaves that perish." Know who said that?'

'Aleister Crowley,' said Strike.

'Unusual reading matter,' said Creed, 'for a decorated soldier in the British army.'

'Oh, we're all satanists on the sly,' said Strike.

'You think you're joking,' said Creed, whose expression had become intense, 'but you kill and you get given a medal and called a hero. I kill and get called evil and locked up for ever. Arbitrary categories. Know what's just down the road from here?'

'Sandhurst,' said Strike.

'Sandhurst,' repeated Creed, as though Strike hadn't spoken. 'Institutions for killers, side by side, one to make them, one to break them. Explain to me why's it more moral to murder little brown children on Tony Blair's say-so, than to do what I did? I'm made the way I am. Brain scans will show you, they've studied people like me. It's how we're wired. Why's it more evil to kill because you've got to, because it's your nature, than to blow up poor brown people because we want oil? Properly looked at, I'm the innocent, but *I* get fattened up and drugged like a captive pig, and you get a state pension.'

'Interesting argument,' said Strike. 'So you had no control over what you did?'

'Control,' scoffed Creed, shaking his head. 'That shows how far removed – I can't explain it in terms someone like you would understand. "You have your way. I have my ways. As for the right way, the correct way, and the only way, it does not exist." Know who said that?'

'Sounds like Nietzsche,' said Strike.

'Nietzsche,' said Creed, talking over him. 'Obviously, yes. I read a lot in Belmarsh, back before I got stuffed full of so many drugs I couldn't concentrate from one end of the sentence to another.

'I've got diabetes now, did you know that?' Creed continued. 'Yeah. Hospital-acquired diabetes. They took a thin, fit man, and piled the weight on me, with these drugs I don't need and the pig-swill we're forced to eat. Eight hundred so-called healers leeching a living off us. They need us ill, because we're their livelihoods. Morlocks. Understand that word?'

'Fictional underbeings,' said Strike, 'in *The Time—*'

'Obviously, yes,' said Creed again, who seemed

irritated that Strike understood his references. 'H. G. Wells. Primitive beings preying on the highly evolved species, who don't realise they're being farmed to eat. Except *I* realise it, *I* know what's going on.'

'See yourself as one of the Eloi, do you?' asked Strike.

'Interesting thing about the Eloi,' said Creed, 'is their total lack of conscience. The higher race is intellectual, refined, with no so-called remorse . . . I was exploring all this in my book, the book I was writing before they took it off me. Wells's thing was only a superficial allegory, but he was groping towards a truth . . . What I was writing, part autobiography, part scientific treatise – but it was taken away from me, they've confiscated my manuscript. It could be an invaluable resource, but no, because it's mine, it's got to be destroyed. I've got an IQ of 140, but they want my brain flabby like my body.'

'You seem pretty alert to me. What drugs have they got you on?'

'I shouldn't be on any drugs at all. I should be in assertive rehab but they won't let me out of high dependency. They let the little schizophrenics loose in the workshops with knives over there, and I can't have a pencil. When I came here, I thought I'd meet intelligent people . . . any child who can memorise a seven times table could be a doctor, it's all rote learning and dogma. The patient's supposed to be a partner in this therapeutic process, and I say I'm well enough to go back to prison.'

'Certainly seem sane to me,' said Strike.

'Thank you,' said Creed, who'd become flushed. 'Thank you. *You're* an intelligent man, it appears. I thought you would be. That's why I agreed to this.'

'But you're still on medication—'

'I know all about their drugs, and they're giving me too much. I could prescribe better for myself than they know how to, here.'

'How d'you know about that stuff?' asked Strike.

'Obvious, easy,' said Creed, with a grandiose gesture. 'I used myself as a guinea pig, developed my own series of standardised tests. How well I could walk and talk on twenty milligrams, thirty milligrams . . . made notes on disorientation, drowsiness, differences in side-effects . . .'

'What kinds of drugs were these?' asked Strike.

'Amobarbital, pentobarbital, phenobarbital,' rattled off Creed: the names of barbiturates of the early seventies, mostly replaced, now, by other drugs.

'Easy to buy on the street?'

'I only bought off the street occasionally, I had other channels, that were never widely known . . .'

And Creed launched into a meandering speech that couldn't properly be called a story, because the narrative was disjointed and full of mysterious hints and oblique allusions, but the gist seemed to be that Creed had been associating with many unnamed but powerful people in the sixties and seventies, and that a steady supply of prescription drugs had been an incidental perk, either of working for gangsters, or spying on them for the authorities. He hinted at having been recruited by the security services, spoke of flights to America there was no evidence he'd ever taken, of barbiturate-addicted politicians and celebrities, and the dangerous desire of humans from all walks of life to dope themselves to cope with the cruel realities of the world, a tendency and temptation which Dennis Creed deplored and had always resisted.

Strike surmised that these fake reminiscences were designed to feed Creed's overweening craving for status. No doubt his decades in high-security prisons and mental hospitals had taught him that rape and torture were considered almost as contemptible there as they'd been on the outside. He might continue to derive sexual pleasure from reliving his crimes, but in others, they elicited only contempt. Without a fantasy career in which he was part-spy, part-gangster, the man with the 140 IQ was merely a dry-cleaning delivery man, a sexual deviant buying handfuls of downers from street dealers who'd exploited, then betrayed him.

'. . . see all that security all round me, at the trial? There were other forces at play, that's all I'll say . . .'

There'd been a solid cordon of police around Creed on his way in and out of court because the crowd had wanted to tear him apart. The details of his torture chamber had leaked: police had found the hot-irons and the pliers, the ball gags and the whips, the photographs Creed had taken of his victims, alive and dead, and the decomposing head and hands of Andrea Hooton, sitting in his bathroom sink. But the image of himself Creed now presented Strike turned murder into something incidental to a much more prestigious criminal life, a hobby that for some reason the public continued to harp on, when there was so much more to tell, and admire.

'. . . because they like salivating over dirty little things that excite them, as an outlet for their own unacceptable urges,' said Creed. 'I could've been a doctor, probably should have been, actually . . .'

(He'd poured cooking oil over dinner lady Vera Kenny's head, then set her hair on fire and photographed her while it burned, a ball gag in her mouth. He'd cut out unemployed Gail Wrightman's tongue. He'd murdered hairdresser Susan Meyer by stamping repeatedly on her head.)

'Never killed anyone by overdose, did you?' said Strike.

'It takes far more skill to disorientate them but keep them on their feet. Any fool can shove an overdose down someone's throat. The other takes knowledge and experience. That's how I know they're using too much on me in here, because I understand side-effects.'

'What were you giving the women in the basement?'

'I never drugged a woman, once I had her at home. Once she was inside, I had other ways of keeping her quiet.'

Andrea Hooton's mouth had been sewn shut by Creed while she was still alive: the traces of thread had still been present on the rotting head.

The psychiatrist glanced at his watch.

'What if a woman was already drunk?' asked Strike. 'Gail Wrightman: you picked her up in a bar, right? Wasn't there a danger of overdose, if you drugged her on top of the drink?'

'Intelligent question,' said Creed, drinking Strike in with his enormous pupils. 'I can usually tell what a woman's had to the exact unit. Gail was on her own, sulking. Some man had stood her up . . .'

Creed was giving nothing away: these weren't secrets. He'd admitted to it all already, in the dock, where he'd enjoyed relaying the facts, watching the reaction of the victims' relatives. The photographs hidden under the floorboards, of Gail and Andrea, Susan and Vera, Noreen, Jackie and Geraldine, bound, burned and stabbed, alive and maimed, their mutilated and sometimes headless corpses posed in pornographic attitudes, had damned him before he opened his mouth, but he'd insisted on a full trial, pleading guilty by reason of insanity.

'. . . in a wig, bit of lipstick . . . they think you're

harmless, odd . . . maybe queer. Talked to her for a minute or two, little dark corner. You act concerned . . .

'Bit of Nembutal in her drink . . . tiny amount, tiny,' said Creed, holding his trembling fingers millimetres apart. 'Nembutal and alcohol, potentially dangerous, if you don't know what you're doing, but I did, obviously . . .

'So I say, "Well, I got to go now, sweetheart, you be careful." "Be careful!" It always worked.' Creed affected squeaky tones to imitate Gail, '"Aw, don't go, have a drink!" "No, darling, I need my beauty sleep." That's when you prove you're not a threat. You make as if you want to leave, or actually walk away. Then, when they call you back, or run into you ten minutes later, when they're starting to feel like shit, they're relieved, because you're the nice man who's safe . . .

'It was all in my book, the different ways I got them. Instructive for women who want to keep out of trouble, you'd think, to read how a highly efficient killer works, but the authorities won't let it be published, which makes you question, are they happy for slags to be picked off on the streets? Maybe they are.

'Why're there people like me at all, Cormoran? Why's evolution let it happen? Because humans are so highly developed, we can only thin ourselves out with intraspecies predators. Pick off the weak, the morally depraved. It's a good thing that degenerate, drunk women don't breed. That's just a fact, it's a fact,' said Dennis Creed.

'I'd wind down my window. "Want a lift, love?" Swaying all over the place. Glad to see me. Got in the van, no trouble, grateful to sit down . . .

'I used to say to Gail, once I had her in the basement: "Should've gone to the bathroom instead, you dirty little bitch, shouldn't you? I bet you're the type to piss in the street. Filthy, that is, filthy" . . . Why're you so interested in drugging?'

The flow of talk had suddenly dried up. Creed's blank grey and black eyes darted left and right between each of Strike's.

'You think Dr Bamborough would be too clever to get herself drugged by the likes of me, do you?'

'Doctors can make mistakes, like anyone else,' said Strike. 'You met Noreen Sturrock on a bus, right?'

Creed considered Strike for several seconds, as though trying to work something out.

'Buses, now, is it? How often did Margot Bamborough take the bus?'

'Frequently, I'd imagine,' said Strike.

'Would she've taken a can of Coke from a stranger?'

'That's what you offered Noreen, right? And the Coke was full of phenobarbital?'

'Yeah. She was almost asleep by the time we came to my stop. I said, "You've missed yours,

darling. Come on, I'll take you to a taxi rank."
Walked her straight off the bus, arm round her.
She wasn't a big girl, Noreen. That was one of the easiest.'

'Did you adjust dosage for weight?'

There was another slight pause.

'Buses and cans of pop, and adjusting drugs for weight? . . . You know what, Cormoran? I think my second guess was right. You're here for little Louise Tucker.'

'No,' said Strike with a sigh, settling back in his chair. 'As it happens, you were spot on first time round. I was hired by Margot Bamborough's daughter.'

There was a longer silence now, and the psychiatrist again checked his watch. Strike knew that his time was nearly up, and he thought Creed knew it, too.

'I want to go back to Belmarsh, Cormoran,' said Creed, leaning in now that Strike had leaned back. 'I want to finish my book. I'm sane, you know it, too, you just said it. I'm not ill. It's costing the taxpayer five times as much to keep me in here as it would in jail. Where would the British public say I should be, eh?'

'Oh, they'd want you back in prison,' said Strike.

'Well, I agree with them,' said Creed. 'I agree.'

He looked sideways at Dr Bijral, who had the look of a man about to call a halt.

'I'm sane and if I'm treated like it, I'll act like it,' said Creed.

He leaned further forwards.

'I killed Louise Tucker,' said Creed in a soft voice, and in Strike's peripheral vision the psychiatrist and the nurse both froze, astonished. 'Picked her up off a street corner in my van, November 1972. Freezing cold that night. She wanted to go home and she had no money. I couldn't resist, Cormoran,' said Creed, those big black pupils boring into Strike's. 'Little girl in her school uniform. No man could resist. Did it on impulse . . . no planning . . . no wig, no drugged Coke, nothing . . .'

'Why wasn't there any trace of her in the basement?' said Strike.

'There was. I had her necklace. But I never had *her* in the basement, see? You want proof, I'll give you proof: she called her stepmother "Claws". Tell Tucker she told me that, all right? Yeah, we had a five-minute chat about how pissed off she was at home, before she realised we were going the wrong way. Then she starts screaming and banging on the windows.

'I turned into a dark car park,' said Creed quietly, 'put my hand over her mouth, dragged her into the back of the van, fucked her and throttled her. I'd've liked to keep her longer, but she was loud, too loud.

'Dumb thing to do, but I couldn't resist, Cormoran. No planning – school uniform! But I had work next day, I needed the van empty. I wanted to take the body back to the basement, but old Vi Cooper was wide awake when I drove back up Liverpool Road. She was looking down at me out the top window when I drove past, so I didn't stop. Told her later she'd imagined it was me. The old bitch used to sit up to see what time I came in. I usually drugged her if I was off on the prowl, but this was a spur-of-the-moment treat . . .'

'What did you do with the body?' said Strike.

'Ah,' said Creed, sitting back in his seat. The wet lips slid over each other, and the wide pupils gaped. 'I think I'm going to need a transfer back to Belmarsh before I tell anyone that. You go and tell the newspapers I've decided to confess to killing Louise, and that I'm sane, and I should be in Belmarsh, and if I'm transferred, I'll tell old Brian Tucker where I put his little girl. You go tell the authorities, that's my offer . . .

'You never know, I might even feel up to talking about Margot Bamborough when I'm out of here. Let's get these drugs out of my system, and maybe I'll remember better.'

'You're full of shit,' said Strike, getting to his feet, looking angry. 'I'm not passing this on.'

'Don't be like that, because it's not the one you came for,' said Creed, with a slow smile. 'You're coming across like a proper narcissist, Cormoran.'

'I'm ready to go,' Strike told Dr Bijral.

'Don't be like that,' said Creed. 'Oi!'

Strike turned back.

'All right . . . I'll give you a little clue about where I put Louise's body, and we'll see whether you're as clever as you think you are, all right? We'll see whether you or the police work it out first. If they find the body, they'll know I'm sane, and I'm ready to talk about Margot Bamborough, as long as I get moved where I want to go. And if nobody can figure out the clue, someone'll have to come back and talk to me, won't they? Maybe even you. We could play chess for more clues, Cormoran.'

Strike could tell that Creed was imagining weeks of front pages, as he laid a trail for investigators to follow. Psychological torture for the Tuckers, manipulation of public opinion, Strike, perhaps, at his beck and call: it was a sadist's wet dream.

'Go on then,' said Strike, looking down at him. 'What's the clue?'

'You'll find Louise Tucker's body where you find M54,' said Creed, and Strike knew Creed had thought out the clue well ahead of time, and was certain that it would have been a clue about Margot, had Strike said he'd been hired by the Tuckers. Creed needed to believe he hadn't given Strike what he really wanted. He had to come out on top.

'Right,' said Strike. He turned to Dr Bijral. 'Shall we?'

'M54, all right, Cormoran?' called Creed.

'I heard you,' said Strike.

'Sorry not to be able to help with Dr Bamborough!' called Creed, and Strike could hear his pleasure at the idea that he'd thwarted the detective.

Strike turned back one last time, and now he stopped pretending to be angry, and grinned, too.

'I was here for Louise, you silly fucker. I know you never met Margot Bamborough. She was murdered by a far more skilful killer than you ever were. And just so you know,' Strike added, as the nurse's keys jangled, and Creed's slack, fat face registered dismay, 'I think you're a fucking lunatic, and if anyone asks me, I'll say you should be in Broadmoor till you rot.'

CHAPTER 69

Beare ye the picture of that Ladies head?
Full liuely is the semblaunt, though the
substance dead.

Edmund Spenser
The Faerie Queene

After almost an hour's debrief with Dr Bijral, during which the shaken psychiatrist phoned Scotland Yard, the detective left the hospital feeling as though he'd been there twice as long as he really had. The village of Crowthorne didn't lie on Strike's route back to London, but he was hungry, he wanted to call Robin and he felt a powerful need to place himself among ordinary people going about their lives, to expel the memory of those empty, echoing corridors, the jangle of keys and the widely dilated pupils of Dennis Creed.

He parked outside a pub, lit himself the cigarette he'd been craving for the past two and a half hours, then turned his phone back on. He'd already missed two calls from Brian Tucker, but instead of phoning the old man back, he pressed Robin's number. She answered on the second ring.

'What happened?'

Strike told her. When he'd finished, there was a short silence.

'Say the clue again,' said Robin, who sounded tense.

'"You'll find her where you find M54."'

'Not *the* M54? Not the motorway?'

'He could've meant that, but he left out the definite article.'

'The M54's twenty-odd miles long.'

'I know.'

Reaction was setting in: Strike should have felt triumphant, but in fact he was tired and tense. His phone beeped at him and he glanced at the screen.

'That's Brian Tucker again, trying to ring me,' he told Robin.

'What are you going to tell him?'

'The truth,' said Strike heavily, exhaling smoke out of his open window. 'Dr Bijral's already called Scotland Yard. Trouble is, if that clue's meaningless, or unsolvable, it leaves Tucker knowing Creed killed his daughter, but never getting the body back. This could well be Creed's idea of the ultimate torture.'

'It's something to have a confession, though, isn't it?' said Robin.

'Tucker's been convinced Creed killed her for

decades. Confession without a body just keeps the wound open. Creed'll still have the last laugh, knowing where she is and not telling . . . How've you got on in the British Library?'

'Oh. Fine,' said Robin. 'I found Joanna Hammond a couple of hours ago.'

'And?' said Strike, now alert.

'She had a large mole on her face. Left cheek. You can see it in the picture of her wedding in the local paper. I'll text it to you now.'

'And the holy—?'

'It would've been on the back of her obituary. Same local paper.'

'Jesus Christ,' said Strike.

There was a longer silence. Strike's phone beeped again, and he saw that Robin had texted him a picture.

Opening it, he saw a couple on their 1969 wedding day: a blurry black and white picture of a toothy, beaming brunette bride, her hair worn in ringlets, in a high-necked lace dress, a pillbox hat on top of her veil, a large mole on her left cheekbone. The blond husband loomed over her shoulder, unsmiling. Even minutes into married life, he had the air of a man ready to wield a baseball bat.

'She wasn't Sagittarius under Schmidt,' said Robin, and Strike put the phone back up to his ear, 'she was Scorpio—'

'—which Talbot thought fitted her better, because of the mole,' said Strike, with a sigh. 'I should've gone back through all the identifications once you found out about Schmidt. We might've got here sooner.'

'What are we going to do about Douthwaite?'

'I'll ring him,' said Strike, after a moment's pause. 'Now. Then I'll call you back.'

His stomach rumbled as he called the Allardice boarding house in Skegness, and heard the familiar cross Scottish accent of Donna, Douthwaite's wife.

'Oh Christ,' she said, when Strike identified himself. 'What now?'

'Nothing to worry about,' lied Strike, who could hear a radio playing in the background. 'Just wanted to double-check a couple of points.'

'Steve!' he heard her yell, away from the receiver. 'It's *him*! . . . What d'you mean, "Who?", who d'you bloody think?'

Strike heard footsteps and then Douthwaite, who sounded half-angry, half-scared.

'What d'you want?'

'I want to tell you what I think happened during your last appointment with Margot Bamborough,' said Strike.

He spoke for two minutes, and Douthwaite didn't interrupt, though Strike knew he was still there, because of the distant sounds of the boarding house still reaching him over the line. When Strike had finished his reconstruction of Douthwaite's final consultation, there was silence but for the distant radio, which was playing 'Blame' by Calvin Harris.

So blame it on the night . . . don't blame it on me . . .

'Well?' said Strike.

He knew Douthwaite didn't want to confirm it. Douthwaite was a coward, a weak man who ran away from problems. He could have prevented further deaths had he had the courage to tell what he knew, but he'd been scared for his own skin, scared he'd be seen as complicit, stupid and shabby, in the eyes of newspaper readers. And so he'd run, but that had made things worse, and nightmarish consequences had ensued, and he'd run from those, too, barely admitting to himself what he feared, distracting himself with drink, with karaoke, with women. And now Strike was presenting him with a dreadful choice that was really no choice at all. Like Violet Cooper, Steve Douthwaite was facing a lifetime of opprobrium from the censorious public, and how much better would it have been if he'd come clean to Talbot forty years previously, when Margot Bamborough's body could have been found quickly, and a killer could have been brought to justice before others had to die.

'Am I right?' Strike said.

'Yes,' said Douthwaite, at last.

'OK, well, if you'll take my advice, you'll go straight to your wife and tell her, before the press do it. There's going to be no hiding from this one.'

'Shit,' said Douthwaite quietly.

'See you in court, then,' said Strike briskly, and he hung up, and called Robin straight back.

'He's confirmed it.'

'Cormoran,' said Robin.

'I advised him to tell Donna—'

'Cormoran,' said Robin, again.

'What?'

'I think I know what M54 is.'

'Not—'

'—the motorway? No. M54 is a globular cluster—'

'A what?'

'A spherical cluster of stars.'

'Stars?' said Strike, with a sinking sensation. 'Hang on—'

'Listen,' said Robin. 'Creed thought he was being clever, but it only takes a Google search—'

'They haven't got internet in there,' said Strike. 'He was whining about it—'

'Well, M54 is a cluster of stars in the constellation Sagittarius,' said Robin.

'Not astrology again,' said Strike, closing his eyes. 'Robin—'

'*Listen to me*. He said "You'll find her where you find M54", right?'

'Yeah—'

'The constellation Sagittarius is also known as the Archer.'

'So?'

'Brian showed us the map, Strike! Dennis Creed was a regular visitor to the Archer Hotel in Islington in the early seventies, when he was delivering their dry cleaning. There was a well on the property, in the back garden. Boarded up, and now covered over with a conservatory.'

A pair of jolly men with matching beer bellies walked into the pub across the road. Strike barely registered them. He'd even forgotten to take drags of the cigarette burning between his fingers.

'Think this through,' said Robin in his ear. 'Creed's got a body he didn't expect in the van, but he can't take it to Epping Forest, because there was still an active crime scene there. They'd just found the remains of Vera Kenny. I don't know why he didn't take the body to the basement—'

'I do,' said Strike. 'He's just told me. He drove past the house and Vi Cooper was awake and at the window.'

'OK – right – so he's got to empty the van before work. He knows his way around the Archer garden, and he knows there's a back gate. He's got tools in the back of the van, he could prise those boards up easily. Cormoran, I'm *sure* she's in the old Archer well.'

There was a brief pause, then hot ash fell into Strike's lap from his neglected cigarette.

'Bollocks—'

He flicked the end out of the window, earning himself a look of disapproval from a passing old woman pulling a tartan shopping trolley.

'All right, here's what we're going to do,' he told Robin. 'I'll phone Tucker and tell him what's just happened, including your deduction. You call

George Layborn and tell him about the well at the Archer. The quicker the police search it, the better for the Tuckers, especially if the news leaks that Creed's confessed.'

'OK, I'll get on to that right—'

'Hang on, I haven't finished,' said Strike. He'd closed his eyes now, and he was rubbing his temples as he thought through everything the agency needed to do, and quickly. 'When you've spoken to Layborn, I want you to ring Barclay and tell him he's going on a job with you, tomorrow morning. He can forget Miss Jones's boyfriend for a few hours. Or, most probably, all day, if what I think's going to happen happens.'

'What job are Barclay and I doing?' asked Robin.

'Isn't it obvious?' said Strike, opening his eyes again. 'We're up against the clock if Douthwaite talks to anyone.'

'So Barclay and I are . . .?'

'Finding Margot's body,' said Strike. 'Yes.'

There was a long silence. Strike's stomach rumbled again. Now a pair of young women entered the pub, giggling at something one had shown the other on her phone.

'You really think she's there?' said Robin, a little shaken.

'I'm sure of it,' said Strike.

'And you're—?'

'I'm going to call Brian Tucker, eat some chips, make that long-distance phone call – I think they're three hours ahead of us, so that should work fine – then drive back to the office. I'll be back late afternoon and we can talk it all over properly.'

'Right,' said Robin, 'good luck.'

She rang off. Strike hesitated for a moment before calling Brian Tucker: he'd have liked to do it with a pint in his hand, but he still needed to drive back to London, and being arrested for drink driving on the eve of catching Margot Bamborough's killer was a complication he really didn't want to risk. Instead, he lit himself a second cigarette, and prepared to tell a grieving father that after a forty-two year wait, he might soon be in a position to bury his daughter.

CHAPTER 70

. . . and lastly Death;
Death with most grim and griesly visage
seene . . .

Edmund Spenser
The Faerie Queene

The morning was so mild it might have been summer, but the leaves of the plane trees beside the telephone box at the mouth of Albemarle Way were starting to turn yellow. A patchwork blue and white sky gave and withdrew warmth as the sun slid in and out behind clouds, and Robin felt shivery in spite of the sweater she was wearing beneath her raincoat, as though a cold wind was blowing up Albemarle Way, the short side street whose tall, unbroken buildings kept it forever in shadow.

She was standing beside the telephone box where once, nearly forty years previously, the killer of Margot Bamborough had waited and watched, feeling, Robin imagined, much as she did now.

There must have been fear, and nervousness, and doubt that the plan could possibly work, and terror of the consequences of failure. But this sense of kinship didn't make Robin feel any more kindly to the killer. Looking across the road at the ancient arch of St John's Gate, she could imagine Margot Bamborough walking through it on a rainy evening forty years previously, or perhaps weaving, feeling strangely groggy and not knowing why . . . or had she realised? Possibly. Margot was a clever woman, and that was why she'd had to die . . .

Clerkenwell Road was busy with traffic and pedestrians. Robin felt entirely isolated from all of them. Nobody passing Robin could have the slightest idea of what she was about to try and do. How bizarre they'd think her morning's plans, how macabre . . . a trickle of panic ran down Robin's spine . . .

Think about something else.

There'd been a picture in the *Metro* that morning of Charlotte Ross wearing sunglasses and a long dark coat, walking along a street in Mayfair with her sister, Amelia. There had been no sign of Charlotte's husband or young twins, and the short non-story beneath the picture had told Robin nothing she wanted to know.

Charlotte Campbell was spotted enjoying a morning walk in London with her sister, Amelia Crichton, yesterday. Charlotte, who is married to Jago, heir to the Viscountcy of Croy, was recently released from hospital, following a prolonged stay in Symonds House, an addiction and mental health facility much favoured by the rich and famous.

Charlotte, who once topped *Tatler*'s list of 100 Most Beautiful Londoners, has been a favourite of the gossip columns since she first ran away from school, aged 14. Daughter of . . .

Think about something else, Robin told herself, and consciously groped around for another subject.

It was September the twentieth. A person born today would be born under the sign of Virgo. Robin wondered how long it was going to take to rid herself of the mental tic of tying dates to star signs. She thought of Matthew, who was the Virgoan she knew best. The sign was supposed to be clever, and organised, and nervous. He was certainly organised, and bright in a book-smart way . . . she remembered Oonagh Kennedy saying, 'I sometimes t'ink, the cleverer they are with books, the stupider they are with sex,' and wondered whether he was now happy about the pregnancy he'd said was accidental . . .

Think about something else.

She checked her watch. Where was Barclay? True, Robin had arrived very early, and technically Barclay wasn't late, but she didn't like standing here alone, trying to distract herself from thoughts of what they were about to do.

Theo had once stood almost exactly where Robin now was, watching the traffic roll up and down Clerkenwell Road, dark-haired Theo of the Kuchi earrings and the painful abdomen, waiting for the silver van that would take her away. Why Theo had never come forward afterwards, why she'd never felt enough gratitude to the woman who'd seen her at short notice, at least to rule herself out of suspicion and stop Talbot haring after a delusion, remained a minor mystery. But of course, that assumed that Theo felt grateful. Nobody ever really knew what happened between a doctor and patient: it was the secular equivalent of the confession box. Robin's thoughts had moved to Douthwaite when, at last, she spotted Barclay, who was approaching, carrying a holdall. When he got close enough, Robin heard the tools inside it clinking.

'Havin' a wee bit o' déjà vu, here,' he said, coming to halt beside her. 'Didn't we once go diggin' fer a body before?'

'I don't think this qualifies as digging,' said Robin.

'What's the latest?'

'He's gone out,' said Robin. 'Strike says we've got to wait until he comes back.'

'What's in there?' asked Barclay, nodding at the carrier bag in Robin's hand.

'Chocolate biscuits,' said Robin.

'Bribe?'

'Basically.'

'And has Strike—?'

'Not yet. He's in position. He wants us to . . .'

Robin waited for a group of what looked like students to walk out of earshot.

'. . . do our bit, first. Were you pleased,' Robin continued, still trying not to think about what they were about to do until it was absolutely necessary, 'about the referendum result?'

'Aye, but don't kid yerself oan,' said Barclay darkly, 'this isn't finished. That stupid fucker Cameron's playing right into the nats' hands. "English votes for English laws", the day after Scotland decides to stay? You don't fight fuckin' nationalism with more fuckin' nationalism. He wants tae get his head out of Farage's arse – is this oor wee fella now?'

Robin looked around. Silhouetted against the end of Albemarle Way was a man walking along with a strange, rolling gait, who was carrying two full carrier bags. He stopped at a door, set down his shopping, put his key in the lock, picked up his shopping bags, stepped over the threshold and vanished from sight.

'That's him,' said Robin, as her insides seemed to wobble. 'Let's go.'

They walked side by side down the street to the dark blue front door.

'He's left the key in the lock,' said Barclay, pointing.

Robin was about to the ring the bell when the door opened, and Samhain Athorn reappeared. Pale, big-eared and mousy-haired, he gaped slightly. He was wearing a Batman sweatshirt. Disconcerted to find two people on his doorstep, he blinked, then addressed Robin's left shoulder.

'I left the key.'

He reached around to pull it out of the lock. As he made to close the door, Barclay dextrously inserted a foot.

'You're Samhain, aren't you?' said Robin, smiling at him, while Samhain gaped. 'We're friends of Cormoran Strike's. You were very helpful to him, a few months ago.'

'I need to put the shopping away,' said Samhain. He tried to close the front door, but Barclay's foot was in the way.

'Could we come in?' asked Robin. 'Just for a little while? We'd like to talk to you and your mum. You were so helpful, before, telling Cormoran about your Uncle Tudor—'

'My Uncle Tudor's dead,' said Samhain.

'I know. I'm sorry.'

'He died in the hospital,' said Samhain.

'Really?' said Robin.

'My-Dad-Gwilherm died under the bridge,' said Samhain.

'That's so sad,' said Robin. 'Could we come in, please, just for a moment? Cormoran wanted me to bring you these,' she added, pulling the tin of chocolate biscuits out of her bag. 'As a thank you.'

'What's them?' asked Samhain, looking at the tin out of the corner of his eye.

'Chocolate biscuits.'

He took the tin out of her hand.

'Yeah. You can come in,' he said, and turning his back, he marched up the dark interior stairs.

With a glance at Barclay, Robin led the way inside. She heard her companion close the door behind her, and the clinking of the tools in his holdall. The staircase was steep, narrow and dark after daylight, the light bulb overhead dead. When Robin reached the landing she saw, through the open door, a white-haired woman with big ears like Samhain's, wiping the surfaces of a brown-tiled kitchen while Samhain, who had his back to her, eagerly peeled the plastic wrapper off the tin of chocolate biscuits.

Deborah turned, her neat white plait sliding over her shoulder, to fix her dark eyes on the two strangers.

'Hello, Mrs Athorn,' said Robin, coming to a halt in the hall.

'Are you from the social work department?' asked Deborah slowly. 'I phoned Clare . . .'

'We can help wi' anythin' Clare can,' said Barclay, before Robin could answer. 'What's the problem?'

'Him downstairs is a bastard,' said Samhain, who was now digging busily in the tin of chocolate biscuits, and selecting the one wrapped in gold foil. 'These are the best ones, in the shiny paper, that's how you know.'

'Is the man downstairs complaining again?' asked Robin, with a sudden upswell of excitement that bordered on panic.

'Can we have a look at whut the problem is?' asked Barclay. 'Where's he think his ceilin's crackin'?'

Deborah pointed towards the sitting room.

'I'll have a wee look,' said Barclay confidently, and he set off towards the sitting room.

'Don't eat all of them, Sammy,' said Deborah, who'd returned to the methodical wiping of the kitchen sides.

'They gave them to me, you silly woman,' said Samhain, his mouth full of chocolate.

Robin followed, fighting a sense of utter unreality. Could what Strike suspected really be true?

Two budgerigars were twittering in a cage in the corner of the small sitting room, which, like the hall, was carpeted in swirls of brown and orange. A crocheted blanket had been spread over the back of the sofa. Barclay was looking down at the almost completed jigsaw of unicorns leaping over a rainbow. Robin glanced around. The place was sparsely furnished. Apart from the sofa and the budgies' cage, there was only a small armchair, a television set on top of which stood an urn, and a small shelving unit on which sat a few old paperbacks and some cheap ornaments. Her eyes lingered on the Egyptian symbol of eternal life painted on a patch of dirty green wall.

She lies in a holy place.

'Floorboards?' she murmured to Barclay.

He shook his head, looked meaningfully down at the jigsaw of the unicorns, then pointed with his foot at the overlarge ottoman on which it lay.

'Oh God, no,' whispered Robin, before she could stop herself. 'You think?'

'Otherwise the carpet would've had tae come up,' murmured Barclay. 'Move furniture, take up floorboards . . . and would it make the ceilin' crack, down below? An' what aboot the smell?'

Samhain now came ambling into the room, eating his second foil-wrapped biscuit.

'D'you want a hot chocolate, or not?' he asked, looking at Robin's knees.

'Um . . . no, thank you,' said Robin, smiling at him.

'Does he want a hot chocolate, or not?'

'No thanks, mate,' said Barclay. 'Can we move this jigsaw? Need tae have a look beneath it.'

'Deborah don't like her jigsaw touched,' said Samhain sternly.

'We need to prove the man downstairs is lying, though,' said Robin. 'About his ceiling cracking.'

'Deborah,' called Samhain. 'They want to move your jigsaw.'

He walked out of the room with his rocking gait, and his mother took his place at the door, eyeing Robin's shoes as she said,

'You can't move my unicorns.'

'We need to have a little look underneath it,'

said Robin. 'I promise we'll take very good care of it, and not break it. We could move it . . .'

She looked around, but there was no stretch of floor big enough to accommodate it.

'In my bedroom, you can put it,' said Samhain, bobbing back into sight. 'On my bed, they can put it, Deborah.'

'Excellent idea,' said Barclay heartily, bending to pick it up.

'Close it up first,' said Robin hastily, and she folded the wings of the jigsaw mat over the puzzle, containing all the pieces.

'Good job,' said Barclay, and he carried the jigsaw mat carefully out through the sitting-room door, followed by Deborah, who looked both anxious and alarmed, and by the self-important Samhain, who seemed proud to have had his plan adopted by this new man in the flat.

For a few seconds, Robin stood alone in the sitting room, looking down at the ottoman that was far too big for this small room. It had been covered with a cloth that Robin suspected dated from the sixties, being of thin, faded purple cotton, and carrying the design of a mandala. If a tall woman curled herself up, she might fit inside that ottoman, as long as she was thin, of course.

I don't want to look, Robin thought suddenly, panic rising again. *I don't want to see . . .*

But she had to look. She had to see. That was what she was there for.

609

Barclay returned, followed by both an interested-looking Samhain and a troubled Deborah.

'That doesn't open,' said Deborah, pointing at the exposed ottoman. 'You can't open that. You leave that alone.'

'I had my toys in there,' said Samhain. 'Didn't I, Deborah? Once I did. But My-Dad-Gwilherm didn't want me to keep them there no more.'

'You can't open that,' repeated Deborah, now distressed. 'Leave it, don't touch that.'

'Deborah,' said Robin quietly, walking towards the older woman, 'we've got to find out why the ceiling downstairs is cracking. You know how the man downstairs is always complaining, and saying he'd like you and Samhain to move out?'

'I don't want to go,' said Deborah at once, and for a split-second her dark eyes almost met Robin's, before darting back to the swirly carpet. 'I don't want to move. I'm going to ring Clare.'

'No,' said Robin, moving quickly around Deborah and blocking her way back to the kitchen, with its old wall-mounted phone beside the fridge. She hoped Deborah hadn't heard her panic. 'We're here instead of Clare, you see? To help you with the man downstairs. But we think – Sam and I—'

'My-Dad-Gwilherm called me Sam,' said Samhain. 'Didn't he, Deborah?'

'That's nice,' said Robin, and she pointed at Barclay. 'This man's called Sam, too.'

'Is his name Sam, is it?' said Samhain gleefully,

and boldly he raised his eyes to Barclay's face before looking away again, grinning. 'Two Sams. Deborah! Two Sams!'

Robin addressed the perplexed Deborah, who was now shifting from foot to foot in a manner reminiscent of her son's rolling walk.

'Sam and I want to sort this out, Deborah, so you don't have any more trouble with the man downstairs.'

'Gwilherm didn't want that opened,' said Deborah, reaching nervously for the end of her white plait. 'He didn't want that opened, he wanted that kept shut.'

'Gwilherm would want you and Samhain to be allowed to stay here, though, wouldn't he?'

Deborah put the end of her plait in her mouth and sucked at it, as though it was an ice lolly. Her dark eyes wandered as though in search of help.

'I think,' said Robin gently, 'it would be good if you and Samhain wait in his bedroom while we have a look at the ottoman.'

'Knotty man,' said Samhain, and he cackled again. 'Sam! Hey – Sam! Knotty man!'

'Good one,' said Barclay, grinning.

'Come on,' said Robin, sliding an arm around Deborah. 'You wait in the bedroom with Samhain. You haven't done anything wrong, we know that. Everything's going to be fine.'

As she led Deborah slowly across the landing, she heard Samhain say cheerily,

'I'm staying here, though.'

'No, mate,' Barclay replied, as Robin and Deborah entered Samhain's tiny bedroom. Every inch of wall was covered in pictures of superheroes and gaming characters. Deborah's gigantic jigsaw took up most of the bed. The floor around the PlayStation was littered with chocolate wrappers.

'Look after yer mam and, after, I'll teach ye a magic trick,' Barclay was saying.

'My-Dad-Gwilherm could do magic!'

'Aye, I know, I heard. That make it easy fer you tae do magic, if yer dad could do it, eh?'

'We won't be long,' Robin told Samhain's frightened mother. 'Just stay in here for now, all right? Please, Deborah?'

Deborah simply blinked at her. Robin was particularly afraid of the woman trying to reach the phone on the kitchen wall, because she didn't want to have to physically restrain her. Returning to the sitting room, she found Barclay still bargaining with Samhain.

'Do it now,' Samhain was saying, grinning, looking from Barclay's hands to his chin to his ear. 'Go on, show me now.'

'Sam can only do magic after we've done our job,' said Robin. 'Samhain, will you wait in the bedroom with your mum, please?'

'Go on, mate,' said Barclay. 'Just fer a bit. Then I'll teach ye the trick.'

The smile faded off Samhain's face.

'Silly woman,' he said sulkily to Robin. 'Stupid woman.'

He walked out of the room, but instead of going into his bedroom, he made for the kitchen.

'Shit,' Robin muttered, 'don't do anything yet, Sam—'

Samhain reappeared, holding the tin of chocolate biscuits, walked into his bedroom and slammed the door behind him.

'Now,' said Robin.

'Stay by the door,' said Sam, 'keep an eye on them.'

Robin closed the sitting-room door, leaving a tiny crack through which she could spy on Samhain's bedroom, and gave Barclay the thumbs up.

He pulled the mandala covering off the ottoman, bent down, gripped the edge of the lid and heaved. The lid wouldn't budge. He put all his strength into it, but still it didn't shift. From Samhain's room came the sound of raised voices. Deborah was telling Samhain not to eat any more chocolate biscuits.

'It's like – it's locked – on the inside,' said Barclay, panting and letting go.

He unzipped his holdall and, after some rummaging, pulled out a crowbar, which he wedged the end of into the crack separating the lid from the body of the ottoman. *'Come – oan – you – fucker,'* he gasped, as the end of the crowbar lost its grip and nearly hit Barclay in the face. 'Somethin's stickin' it doon.'

Robin peeked back at Samhain's bedroom door. It remained closed. Mother and son were still

arguing about the chocolate biscuits. The budgerigars chirruped. Beyond the window, Robin
could see an aeroplane trail, a fuzzy white pipe
cleaner stretched across the sky. Everyday things
became so strange, when you were waiting for
something dreadful to happen. Her heart was
pounding fast.

'Help me,' said Barclay through gritted teeth.
He'd managed to get the end of the crowbar
deeper into the crack in the ottoman. 'It's gonnae
take two.'

After another glance at Samhain's closed door,
Robin hurried over to Barclay and gripped the
crowbar alongside him. Using all their weight and
force, both pushed the handle towards the floor.

'Jesus,' panted Robin. 'What's holding it?'

'Where's – Strike – when you need—'

There was a loud crunching, cracking noise. The
crowbar suddenly gave way as the lid of the ottoman
opened. Robin turned and saw a cloud of dust
rising into the air. Barclay pushed the lid up.

The ottoman had been filled with concrete,
which had stuck the lid down upon itself. The grey
matter was lumpy and looked as though it might
have been badly mixed. In two places, something
smooth broke through the uneven, ashen surface:
one resembling a few inches of walrus tusk, the
other, a curved surface that hinted at a dark ivory
globe. Then Robin saw, stuck to a bit of the
concrete that had adhered to the lid of the ottoman,
a few fair hairs.

They heard footsteps on the landing. Barclay slammed the lid of the ottoman down as Samhain opened the door. He was followed by Deborah.

'I'll teach you that magic trick now,' said Barclay, walking towards Samhain. 'Come in the kitchen, we'll do it there.'

The two men left. Deborah shuffled into the room, and picked up the faded purple throw that Robin had cast aside.

'Did you open it?' she mumbled, eyes on the old carpet.

'Yes,' said Robin, far more calmly than she felt. She sat down on the ottoman, even though she felt sacrilegious doing it. *I'm sorry, Margot. I'm so sorry.*

'I need to make a phone call now, Deborah. Then I think we should all have some hot chocolate.'

CHAPTER 71

Such is the face of falshood, such the sight
Of fowle Duessa, when her borrowed light
Is laid away, and counterfesaunce knowne.

Edmund Spenser
The Faerie Queene

A train came roaring and rattling along the Southeastern railway line. Strike, who was standing on the opposite side of the road, felt his mobile vibrate in his pocket and pulled it out, but for a few seconds the din was such that he couldn't immediately hear Robin.

'. . . found her.'

'Say that again?' he shouted, as the train rumbled away.

'We've – found – her. Inside the ottoman inside the sitting room. Concrete was poured in all around her, but we can see a bit of her skull and maybe a femur.'

'Shit.'

Strike had expected the presence of the body in

616

the Athorns' flat, but there was nothing routine, ever, about finding a dead human. 'Concrete?' he repeated.

'Yes. It doesn't look that well mixed. Amateurish. But it's done the job. It probably killed most of the smell.'

'Hell of a weight on a supporting beam.'

'Well, exactly. Where are you?'

'Outside, about to go in. Right: call 999, then call Layborn and tell him where I am, and why. That should speed things up.'

'OK. Good luck.'

Strike hung up. The nondescript street of terraced houses was quiet now the train had gone, birdsong replacing its thunderous clamour. Strike, who'd been waiting where he couldn't be seen, now walked up the street, passing three small houses, and at the fourth, turned left up a short garden path, then beat a tattoo on the dark red front door.

The net curtains twitched, and Janice Beattie's cross face appeared. Strike raised a hand in greeting. The curtain fell.

After a slightly longer wait than might have been expected, given the short distance from sitting room to hall, Janice opened the door. She was dressed all in black today, with sheepskin carpet slippers on her feet. Her clear china-blue eyes, rimmed in steel, looked as kind and innocent as ever. Silver-haired, apple-cheeked, she frowned up at the detective, but didn't speak.

'Can I come in?' asked Strike.

There was a long pause. The wild birds tweeted, and Strike thought fleetingly of the budgies in the Athorns' flat, where part of his mind was dwelling on the image of a skull and a femur, poking up through concrete.

'If you must,' said Janice slowly.

He followed Janice into the red sitting room, with its cheap crimson Turkish rug, its dried-flower pictures and its faded photographs. The sun was making the spun-glass Cinderella carriage and its six horses twinkle on top of the fire, which Janice had on, in spite of the mildness of the September day.

'Wanna cup of tea?' said Janice.

'That'd be great,' said Strike, fully alive to the unreality of the situation.

He listened to her sheepskin-muffled footsteps receding and the sound of the kitchen door opening. Taking out his mobile phone, he switched it to record and laid it on the arm of the chair in which he'd sat last time. He then pulled on a pair of latex gloves and followed Janice quietly out of the room, the worn carpet muffling his footsteps.

At the door, he paused, listening to the soft bubbling of boiling water against a kettle lid, and the tinkle of teaspoons, and the opening of a cupboard. With one fingertip, he pushed open the kitchen door.

Janice spun round, eyes wide. On seeing him, she grabbed one of the china mugs on the tray and raised it hurriedly to her lips, but Strike had already taken a stride towards her. Gripping the thin wrist with his latex-gloved hand, forcing the mug away from her mouth, he felt bone beneath the soft flesh and the papery skin of the elderly. With his free hand, he pulled the mug out of hers, and examined it. A good inch of viscous white liquid was swimming in the bottom of it. Still holding Janice's wrist, he looked into the teapot, which contained more of the same, then opened the cupboard over the kettle.

It was jammed with bottles of pills, weedkiller, bleach and jam jars full of what looked like home-dried plants, leaves and fungus: a poisoner's storehouse, a testimony to a lifetime's careful study of the means by which death could be delivered in the guise of healing.

'Think I'll skip tea,' said Strike. 'Let's have a chat, shall we?'

She offered no resistance as he led her by the wrist back through to the sitting room and pushed her down onto the sofa.

'A murder-suicide would be a hell of a way to go out,' said Strike, standing over her, 'but I don't much fancy being victim number . . . how many is it?'

Janice said nothing. Her round blue eyes registered only shock.

Strike looked up at the wall of old photographs. One showed a toothy, beaming brunette bride, her hair worn in ringlets, in a high-necked lace dress, a pillbox hat on top of her veil, a large mole on her left cheekbone. Just above it was a picture of a young blonde with her hair worn in a frizzy eighties perm. She was wearing a red coat. He hadn't noticed, hadn't seen, because he'd walked into the room with certain expectations, making assumptions no less sweeping than Talbot had, with his conviction that Cancerians were intuitive, gentle and perceptive. Nurses were angels, ministering to the vulnerable: he'd been as guilty of bias as Vi Cooper, seeing Janice through the prism of his grateful memories of the nurses in Selly Oak who'd helped him manage pain and depression, and of Kerenza down in Cornwall, bringing comfort and kindness every single day. And on top of it all, he'd been fooled by a veritable genius for lies and misdirection.

'I thought,' said Strike, 'I should come and tell the Athorns' social worker in person that a body's been found in their flat. You do a very good middle-class accent, Janice. I s'pose the phone Clare uses is round here somewhere?'

He looked around. Possibly she'd hidden it when she'd seen who was at the door. He suddenly spotted the hairdryer, tucked away behind the sofa, but with its lead protruding. He sidled past the coffee table, bent down and pulled it out, along with a roll of cellophane, a small phial with the label pulled off, a syringe and some chocolates.

'Leave them,' said Janice suddenly and angrily, but he laid the items on the coffee table instead.

'How ill would I have been if I'd eaten one of those dates you were doctoring when I arrived last time?' he asked. 'You use the hairdryer to fix the cellophane back round them, right?' When she didn't answer, he said, 'I haven't thanked you for those chocolates you sent Robin and me at Christmas. I had flu. Only managed to eat a couple before puking my guts up. Chucked the rest away, because they had bad associations. Lucky for me, eh?'

Strike now sat down in the armchair, beside his mobile, which was still recording.

'Did you kill *all* these people?' Strike asked, gesturing up at the wall of photographs, 'Or do some of them just have recurrent bowel problems around you? No,' he said, scrutinising the wall, 'Irene's not up there, is she?'

She blinked at him through the lenses of her round silver glasses, which were far cleaner than Dennis Creed's.

A car came trundling up the road beyond the net curtains. Janice watched it pass, and Strike thought she was half expecting to see a police car. Perhaps she wasn't going to talk at all. Sometimes, people didn't. They preferred to leave it all up to the lawyers.

'I spoke to your son on the phone last night,' said Strike.

'You never!'

The words had burst out of her, in shock.

'I did,' said Strike. 'Kevin was quite surprised

to hear you'd been visiting him in Dubai, because he hasn't seen you in nearly seven years. Why d'you pretend you're visiting him? To get a break from Irene?'

She pressed her lips together. One hand was playing with the worn wedding ring on the other.

'Kevin told me he's had barely any contact with you, since leaving home. You weren't ever close, he said. But he paid for you to fly out there seven years ago, because he thought he should give you "another chance", as he put it . . . and his young daughter managed to ingest quite a lot of bleach while you were looking after her. She survived – just – and since then, he's cut you off completely.

'We ended up talking for nearly two hours,' said Strike, watching Janice's colour fluctuate. 'It was hard for Kevin to say out loud what he's suspected all these years. Who wants to believe their own mum's been poisoning people? He preferred to think he was paranoid about all those "special drinks" you used to give him. And apparently your first husband—'

'He wasn't my 'usband,' muttered Janice. 'We were never married.'

'—left because he thought you were doing things to his meals, too. Kevin used to think his father was making it all up. But after our chat last night, I think he's seeing things very differently. He's ready to come over and testify against you.'

Janice gave a small convulsive jerk. For almost a minute there was silence.

'You're recording this,' she whispered at last, looking at the mobile lying on the arm of Strike's chair.

'I am, yeah,' said Strike.

'If you turn that off, I'll talk to you.'

'I'll still be able to testify to whatever you tell me.'

'I'm sure a lawyer would tell me not to let meself be recorded, though.'

'Yeah,' Strike acknowledged, 'you're probably right.'

He picked up the mobile, turned it to face her so she could watch, switched off the recording, then laid it down on the small coffee table beside the chocolates, the empty phial, the syringe, the cellophane and the hairdryer.

'Why d'you do it, Janice?'

She was still stroking the underside of her wedding ring.

'I don't know why,' she said. 'I just . . . like it.'

Her eyes wandered over the wall of photographs.

'I like seeing what 'appens to them, if they take poison or too many drugs. Sometimes I like 'elping 'em and 'aving them be grateful, and sometimes I like watching 'em suffer, and sometimes I like watching 'em go . . .' A prickle ran up the back of Strike's neck. 'I don't know why,' she said again. 'I sometimes fink it's because I 'ad a bang on the 'ead, when I was ten. My dad knocked me downstairs. I was out for fifteen minutes. Ever since then, I've 'ad 'eadaches . . . 'Ead trauma can do

623

fings to you, you know. So maybe it's not my fault, but . . . I dunno . . .

'Wiv me granddaughter,' said Janice, frowning slightly, 'I just wanted 'er gone, honestly . . . spoiled and whiny . . . I don't like kids,' she said, looking directly back at Strike. 'I've never liked kids. I never wanted 'em, never wanted Kev, but I fort if I 'ad it, 'is dad might marry me . . . but 'e never, 'e wouldn't . . .

'It was 'aving a baby what killed my mum,' said Janice. 'I was eight. She 'ad it at 'ome. Placenta previa, it was. Blood everywhere, me trying to 'elp, no doctor, my father drunk, screaming at everyone . . .

'I took this,' said Janice quietly, showing Strike the wedding ring on her finger, 'off Mum's dead 'and. I knew my father would sell it for drink. I took it and 'id it so 'e couldn't get it. It's all I got of 'er. I loved my mum,' said Janice Beattie, stroking the wedding ring, and Strike wondered whether it was true, whether head trauma and early abuse had made Janice what she was, and whether Janice had the capacity to love at all.

'Is that really your little sister, Clare?' Strike asked, pointing at the double frame beside Janice, where the sleepy-eyed, overweight man with smoker's teeth faced the heavy but pretty blonde.

'No,' said Janice, looking at the picture. After a short pause, she said, 'She was Larry's mistress. I killed both of 'em. I'm not sorry. They deserved it. 'E was wiv me, 'e wasn't much of a catch, but 'e was wiv me, the pair of 'em carryin' on be'ind my back. Bitch,' said Janice quietly, looking at the picture of the plump blonde.

'I assume you kept the obituaries?'

She got slowly up from the sofa, and Strike heard her knees click as she walked towards the china cabinet in the corner which housed most of her cheap spun-glass ornaments, and knelt down, again steadying herself with one hand on the mantelpiece. But now, instead of one folder, she tugged two out of the drawer in the base of the cabinet, and Strike remembered how she'd shifted things around in the drawer last time, doubtless removing those things she didn't want him to see.

'That one,' she said, showing him the fatter of the two folders, 'is all the stuff about Margot. I cut out everyfing I could find. Needed a second folder for all 'er clippings . . .'

She opened the thinner folder, which was the one Strike had seen before, and extracted an old work newsletter headed *Hickson & Co.* The blonde's colour photograph featured prominently at the top.

'Clare Martin,' said Janice. ''Eavy drinker, she was. "Accidental overdose" . . . liver failure. I knew she was taking too many paracetamol for 'er endometriosis, I watched 'er doing it. Me and Larry 'ad a bunch of people over to the 'ouse. They fort I was stupid. Eye contact between 'em all night long. Thick as mince, the pair of 'em. I was mixing drinks. Every cocktail I gave 'er was 'alf liquid paracetamol. She died eight days later . . .

'And there's Larry's,' she said indifferently, holding up a second newsletter from Hickson & Co.

'I waited six, seven monfs. That was easy. 'E was a walkin' timebomb, Larry, the doctors 'ad warned 'im, 'is 'eart was wrecked. Pseudoephedrine, that was. They never even checked 'im for drugs in 'is system. They knew what it was: smoking and eating like a pig. Nobody looked further than 'is dodgy ticker . . .'

Strike detected not the slightest sign of remorse as she shuffled the obituaries of her victims as though they were so many knitting patterns. Her fingers trembled, but Strike thought that was down to shock, not shame. Mere minutes ago she'd thought of suicide. Perhaps that cool and clever brain was working very hard beneath the apparently frank surface, and Strike suddenly reached out and removed the drugged chocolates from the table beside Janice, and put them down on the floor beside his chair. Her eyes followed them, and he was sure he'd been right to suspect she was thinking of eating them. Now he leaned forwards again and picked up the old yellow clipping he'd examined last time, showing little Johnny Marks from Bethnal Green.

'He was your first, was he?'

Janice took a deep breath and exhaled. A couple of the cuttings fluttered.

'Yeah,' she said heavily. 'Pesticide. You could get all sorts in them days, buy it over the counter. Organophosphates. I fancied 'im something rotten, Johnny Marks, but 'e made fun of me. Yeah, so they fort it was peritonitis and 'e died. It's true the doctor didn't turn up, mind. People didn't care, when it was kids from a slum . . . That was a bad death, 'e 'ad. I was allowed to go in and look at 'im, after 'e died. I give 'im a little kiss on the cheek,' said Janice. ''E couldn't stop me then, could 'e? Shouldn't of made fun of me.'

'Marks,' said Strike, examining the clipping, 'gave you the idea for Spencer, right? It was the name that first connected her with you, but I should've twigged when Clare phoned me back so promptly. Social workers never do that. Too overworked.'

'Huh,' said Janice, and she almost smiled. 'Yeah. That's where I got the name: Clare Martin and Johnny Marks.'

'You didn't keep Brenner's obituary, did you?'

'No,' said Janice.

'Because you didn't kill him?'

'No. 'E died of old age somewhere in Devon. I never even read 'is obituary, but I 'ad to come up wiv somefing, didn't I, when you asked for it? So I said Oakden took it.'

She was probably the most accomplished liar Strike had ever met. Her ability to come up with falsehoods at a moment's notice, and the way she interwove her plausible lies with truth, never attempting too much, and delivering everything with such an air of authenticity and honesty, placed her in a class apart.

'Was Brenner really addicted to barbiturates?'

'No,' said Janice.

She was shuffling the obituaries back into their folder now, and Strike spotted the clipping about holy basil, on the reverse of which was Joanna Hammond's death notice.

'No,' she repeated, as she put the obituaries back into her bottom drawer and closed it, as though it mattered any more whether she tidied these things away, as though they wouldn't soon be used in evidence against her. Knees clicking, she got slowly to her feet again, and returned to the sofa.

'I was getting Brenner to sign for drugs for me,' she said. ''E fort I was selling them on the street, dopey old sod.'

'How did you persuade him to over-order drugs? Blackmail?'

'S'pose you'd call it that, yeah,' she said. 'I found out 'e was going to see a prostitute locally. One of 'er kids told me Brenner was visiting 'er once a week. I fort, right, I'll get you, you dirty old bastard. 'E was coming up for retirement. I knew 'e didn't want to end 'is career in disgrace. I went in to see 'im one day in his consulting room and told 'im I knew. 'E nearly 'ad an 'eart attack,' said Janice, with a malicious smile. 'I told 'im I knew 'ow to keep me mouf shut, and then I asked 'im to get me some drugs. 'E signed like a lamb. I was using stuff Brenner got me for years, after.'

'The prostitute was Betty Fuller, right?

'Yeah,' said Janice. 'I fort you'd find that out.'

'Did Brenner really assault Deborah Athorn?

'No. 'E checked 'er stitches after she had Samhain, that's all.'

'Why did Clare Spencer tell me that story? Just blowing a bit more smoke around?'

Janice shrugged.

'I dunno. I fort maybe you'd fink Brenner was a sex pest and Margot found out 'e was fiddling with patients.'

'Was there ever really an Amytal capsule in Brenner's mug?'

'No,' said Janice. 'It was in Irene's mug . . . that was stupid,' she said, her pink and white brow furrowed. The wide blue eyes drifted over her wall of victims' photographs, to the window and back to Strike. 'I shouldn't of done that. Sometimes I sailed a bit close to the wind. Took silly risks. Irene was pissing me off one day on reception, flirting wiv – just flirting,' said Janice, 'so I took 'er a mug of tea wiv a couple of capsules in it. She talks till you could throttle 'er, I just wanted 'er to shut the hell up for a bit. But she let it go cold . . .

'I was sort of glad, after I'd calmed down. I got the mug and took it out the back to wash up, but Margot come creepin' up behind me in 'er flat shoes. I tried to 'ide it, but she saw.

'I fort she'd go tellin' tales, so I 'ad to get in first. I went straight to Dr Gupta and said I'd found a capsule in Dr Brenner's tea, and told 'im I fort 'e was over-ordering drugs and was addicted. What else could I do? Gupta was a nice man but he was a coward. Bit scared of Brenner. I fort 'e probably wouldn't confront 'im, and 'e didn't, but honestly, I knew even if 'e 'ad, Brenner would rather pretend to be an addict than risk me tellin' anyone about a 'is dirty little fing wiv Betty Fuller.'

'And was Margot really worried about how Dorothy Oakden's mother died?'

'No,' said Janice again. 'But I 'ad to tell you somefing, didn't I?'

'You're a genius of misdirection,' said Strike, and Janice turned slightly pink.

'I've always been clever,' she mumbled, 'but that don't 'elp a woman. It's better to be pretty. You 'ave a better life if you're good-looking. Men always went for Irene, not me. She talked shit all night long, but they liked 'er better. I wasn't bad-looking . . . I just didn't 'ave what men liked.'

'When we first met the two of you,' said Strike, ignoring this, 'I thought Irene might've wanted you interviewed together to make sure you didn't spill her secrets, but it was the other way round, wasn't it? You wanted to be there to control what *she* said.'

'Yeah, well,' said Janice, with another sigh, 'I

didn't do that well, did I? She was blabbing left, right and centre.'

'Tell me, did Charlie Ramage really see a missing woman in Leamington Spa?'

'No. I just needed to give you somefing to fink about instead of Margot prodding Kev in the tummy. Charlie Ramage told me 'e saw Mary Flanagan in a country churchyard in . . . Worcestershire somewhere, I fink it was. I knew nobody could say no diff'rent, I knew 'e was dead and I knew 'e talked such bollocks, nobody round 'im would remember one more tall story.'

'Was the mention of Leamington Spa supposed to nudge me towards Irene and Satchwell?'

'Yeah,' said Janice.

'Did you put drugs in Wilma Bayliss's Thermos? Is that why she seemed drunk to people at the surgery?'

'I did, yeah.'

'Why?'

'I already told you,' said Janice restlessly, 'I don't know why I do it, I just do . . . I wanted to see what would 'appen to 'er. I like knowing why fings are 'appening, when nobody else does . . .

''Ow did you work all this out?' she demanded. 'Talbot and Lawson never suspected.'

'Lawson might not have done,' said Strike, 'but I think Talbot did.'

''E never,' said Janice, at once. 'I 'ad 'im eating out me 'and.'

'I'm not so sure,' said Strike. 'He left a strange

631

set of notes, and all through them he kept circling back to the death of Scorpio, or Juno, which are the names he gave Joanna Hammond. Seven interviews, Janice. I think he subconsciously knew there was something off about you. He mentions poison a lot, which I think had stuck in his mind because of the way Joanna died. At one point – I was reading the notes again, last night – he copies out a long description of the tarot card the Queen of Cups. Words to the effect that she reflects the observer back at themselves. "To see the truth of her is almost impossible." And on the night they hauled him off to hospital, he hallucinated a female demon with a cup in her hand and a seven hanging round her neck. He was too ill to string his suspicions together, but his subconscious kept trying to tell him you weren't all you seemed. At one point, he wrote: "Is Cetus right?" – he called Irene Cetus – and eventually I asked myself what she could've been right about. Then I remembered that the first time we met the pair of you, she told us she thought you were "sweet on" Douthwaite.'

At the sound of Douthwaite's name, Janice winced slightly.

'Oakden said you got giggly around Douthwaite, too,' Strike continued, watching her closely. 'And Dorothy bracketed you with Irene and Gloria as some kind of scarlet woman, which implies you'd done some flirting in front of her.'

'Is that all you went on: me flirting once, and

being the Queen of Cups?' said Janice, managing to get a note of scorn into her voice, though he thought she seemed shaken.

'No,' said Strike, 'there were plenty of other things. Strange anomalies and coincidences. People kept telling me Margot didn't like "the nurse", but they got you confused with Irene a lot, so it took me a while to twig that they really did mean you.

'Then there was Fragile X. When I saw you that first time, with Irene, you claimed you'd only been to visit the Athorns once, but the second time I met you, you seemed to know a hell of a lot about them. Fragile X was called Martin-Bell syndrome back in the early seventies. If you'd only seen them that one time, it seemed odd you knew exactly what was wrong with them, and used the modern term . . .

'And then I started noticing how many people were getting stomach upsets or acting drugged. Did you put something in the punch at Margot and Roy's barbecue?'

'I did, yeah,' she said. 'Ipecac syrup, that was. I fort it would be funny if they all thought they'd got food poisoning from the barbecue, but then Carl broke the bowl, and I was glad, really . . . I just wanted to see 'em all ill, and maybe look after 'em all, and ruin 'er party, but it was stupid, wasn't it? . . . That's what I mean, I sailed close to the wind sometimes, they were doctors, what if they'd known? . . . It was only Gloria who 'ad a big glassful and was sick. Margot's 'usband didn't like that . . . ruined their smart house . . .'

And Strike saw the almost indiscriminate desire for disruption that lay behind the meek exterior.

'Gloria throwing up at the barbecue,' said Strike. 'Irene and her irritable bowel syndrome – Kevin and his constant stomach aches – Wilma swaying on her feet and vomiting while she was working at St John's – me, puking up my Christmas chocolates – and, of course, Steve Douthwaite and his vision problems, his head-aches and his churning guts . . . I'm assuming it was Douthwaite Irene was flirting with, the day you put Amytal capsules in her tea?'

Janice pressed her lips together, eyes narrowed.

'I suppose you told her he was gay to try and get her to back off?'

'She already 'ad Eddie gagging to marry 'er,' Janice burst out. 'She 'ad all these blokes down the pub flirting with 'er. If I'd told 'er 'ow much I liked Steve, she'd've taken 'im for the fun of it, that's what she was. So yeah, I told 'er 'e was queer.'

'What are you drugging her with, these days?'

'It varies,' said Janice quietly. 'Depends 'ow much she's pissing me off.'

'So tell me about Steve Douthwaite.'

Suddenly, Janice was breathing deeply. Her face was flushed again: she looked emotional.

''E was . . . such a beautiful man.'

The passionate throb in her voice took Strike

aback, almost more than the full stock of poisons she was keeping in her kitchen. He thought of the cheeky chap in his kipper tie, who'd become the puffy, bloodshot-eyed proprietor of the Allardice in Skegness, with his strands of greying hair stuck to his sweating forehead, and not for the first time, Strike had reason to reflect on the extraordinarily unpredictable nature of human love.

'I've always been one to fall 'ead over 'eels,' said Janice, and Strike thought of Johnny Marks dying in agony, and Janice kissing him farewell on his cold dead cheek. 'Oh, Steve could make you laugh. I *love* a man what can make you laugh. *Really* 'andsome. I used to walk past 'is flat ten times a day just to get an 'ello . . . we got friendly . . .

''E started dropping in, telling me all 'is problems . . . and 'e tells me 'ow 'e's mad about this married woman. Fallen for 'is mate's wife. On and on and on about 'ow 'ard 'er life is, and there's me sitting there wiv a kid on me own. What about *my* 'ard life? She 'ad an 'usband, didn't she? But no, I could tell I wasn't gonna get nowhere wiv 'im unless she was out the way, so I fort, right, well, she'll 'ave to go . . .

'She was no better lookin' than I was,' muttered Janice, pointing at the picture of Joanna Hammond on the wall. 'State of that fing on 'er face . . .

'So I looked 'er up in the phone book and I just went round 'er 'ouse when I knew 'er 'usband was at work. I used to 'ave this wig I wore to parties.

Put that on, and me uniform, and a pair of glasses I used to 'ave, but I didn't need. Rang the doorbell, told 'er I'd 'ad a tip-off about 'er domestic situation.

'People will always let a nurse in,' said Janice. 'She was desperate to talk to someone. I got 'er good and emotional, cryin' and all that. She told me about sleeping with Steve, and 'ow she fort she was in love wiv 'im . . .

'I made 'er a drink wiv latex gloves on. ''Alf of it was weedkiller. She knew, the moment she tasted it, but I grabbed 'er 'air from be'ind,' Janice mimed the motion in mid-air, 'pulled 'er 'ead back, forced it down 'er fuckin' throat. Oh yeah. Once she was on the floor, chokin', I poured some more down, neat.

''Ad to stay a while, to make sure she didn't try an' phone anyone. Once I knew she was too far gone to recover, I took off me uniform an' left.

'It takes nerve,' said Janice Beattie, her colour high and her eyes bright, 'but act normal and people don't see nothing strange . . . you just got to 'old your nerve. And maybe I wasn't showy-looking when I was young, but that 'elped. I wasn't the kind people remembered . . .

'Next day, near enough, I 'ad Steve crying 'is eyes out round my place. It was all going great,' said the woman who'd poured neat weedkiller down her rival's throat, 'I saw 'im loads after that, 'e was round my place all the time. There was somefing there between us, I could feel it.

'I never drugged 'im a lot,' said Janice, as though this was true evidence of affection. 'Only enough to stop 'im going out, make 'im feel 'e needed me. I used to look after 'im really well. Once, 'e slept on my sofa, and I wiped 'is face for 'im, while 'e was asleep,' she said, and again, Strike thought of the kiss she'd given the dead Johnny Marks.

'But sometimes,' said Janice, with bitterness, 'men fort I was the mumsy type and didn't see me as anyfing else. I could tell Steve liked me, but I fort 'e might not be seeing me the right way, you know, wiv bein' a nurse, and Kev always dragging round after me. One evening, Steve come over, and Kev was 'aving a tantrum, and Steve said, he thought 'e'd be off, let me look after Kev . . . and I could tell, I fort, you're not gonna want me wiv a kid. So I fort, Kev needs to go.'

She said it as though talking about taking out the bins.

'But you gotta be careful when it's your own kid,' said Janice. 'I needed to get an 'istory going. 'E couldn't just die, not after being perfectly 'ealthy. I started experimenting wiv stuff, I was finking, maybe a salt overdose, claim 'e did it on a dare or somefing. I started putting stuff in 'is food 'ere and there. Get 'im complaining to teachers about stomach aches an' that, and then I'd say, "Oh, I know, I think it's a bit of schoolitis" . . .'

'But then Margot examined him,' said Strike.

'But then,' repeated Janice slowly, nodding, 'that hoity-toity bitch takes 'im into 'er surgery and examines 'im. And I knew she was suspicious. She asked me after, what drinks it was I'd given 'im, because the little bastard 'ad told 'er Mummy was givin' 'im special drinks . . .

'Not a week later,' said Janice, twisting the old wedding ring on her finger, 'I realise Steve's going to see 'er about 'is 'ealf, instead of coming to see me. Next fing I know, Margot's asking me all about Joanna's death, out the back by the kettle, and Dorothy and Gloria were listening in. I said, "'Ow the 'ell should I know what 'appened?" but I was worried. I fort, what's Steve been telling 'er? 'As 'e said 'e finks there was somefing wrong wiv it? 'As someone said they saw a nurse leaving the 'ouse?

'I was getting worried. I sent 'er chocolates full of phenobarbital. Irene 'ad told me Margot 'ad 'ad freatening notes, and I'm not surprised, interfering bitch, she was . . . I fort, they'll fink it's 'ooever sent them notes, sent the chocolates . . .

'But she never ate 'em. She frew 'em in the bin in front of me, but after, I 'eard she'd taken 'em out the bin and kept 'em. And that's when I knew, I really knew. I fort, she's gonna get 'em tested . . .'

'And that's when you finally agreed to go on a date with simple old Larry,' said Strike.

''Oo says 'e was simple?' said Janice, firing up.

'Irene,' said Strike. 'You needed access to concrete, didn't you? Didn't want to be seen buying it, I'd imagine. What did you do, tell Larry to take some and not mention it to anyone?'

638

She simply looked at him out of those round blue eyes that nobody who hadn't heard this conversation could possibly mistrust.

'What gave you the idea of concrete?' Strike asked. 'That rumour of the body in the foundations?'

'Yeah,' said Janice, finally. 'It seemed like the way to stop the body smelling. I needed 'er to disappear. It was too near 'ome, what wiv 'er examining Kev, and asking me about Joanna, and keeping those chocolates. I wanted people to fink maybe the Essex Butcher got 'er, or the bloke 'oo sent the threatening notes.'

'How many times had you visited the Athorns before you killed Margot?'

'A few.'

'Because they needed a nurse? Or for some other reason?'

The longest pause yet ensued, long enough for the sun to slide out from a cloud, and the glass Cinderella coach to burn briefly like white fire, and then turn back into the tawdry gewgaw it really was.

'I sort of fort of killing them,' said Janice slowly. 'I don't know why, really. Just from the time I met 'em . . . they were odd and nobody ever went there. Those cousins of theirs visited once every ten years. I met 'em back in January, those cousins, when the flat needed cleaning out, to stop that man downstairs going to court . . . they stayed an hour and let "Clare" do all the rest . . .

'Yeah, I just fort I might kill the Athorns one day,' she said, with a shrug. 'That's why I kept visiting. I liked the idea of watching an 'ole family die togevver, and waiting to see when people realised, and then it'd be on the news, probably, and I'd know what 'appened when everyone was gossiping, local . . .

'I did a bit of experimenting on 'em. Vitamin injections, I told them it was. Special treatments. And I used to hold their noses while they were asleep. Used to pull up their eyelids and look at their eyes, while they were unconscious. Nurses don't never give anaesthetics, see, but Dr Brenner was letting me 'ave all sorts, and the Athorns just let me do stuff to 'em, even Gwilherm. 'E loved me coming over. 'E'd spend days on benzedrine and then 'e'd get sedatives off me. Proper junkie.

'I used to say to 'im, now, don't you go telling anyone what we're doing. These are expensive treatments. It's only because I like your family.

'Some days, I used to fink, I'll kill the kid and then give evidence against Gwilherm. That was one idea I 'ad. I fort, I'll get in the papers, all dressed up, give evidence against 'im, you know. My picture on the front page . . . and I fort that'd be somefing interesting to talk to Steve about, when 'e seen my picture in the paper. Men love nurses. That was the on'y fing I 'ad going for me when I was out wiv Irene, and then the bitch starts pretending she's a nurse an' all . . .

'Only fank Gawd I never did any of that, fank Gawd I saved the Athorns, because what would I 'ave done wiv Margot if I 'adn't 'ad them up the road? I'd nicked their spare key by then. They never noticed.

'I never fort it would work,' said Janice, ''cause I 'ad to frow the plan togevver in about five minutes. I knew she was onto me, when she saved the chocolates, and I was up all night, finking, worrying . . . and it was the next day, or maybe the day after, Steve went charging out of her surgery that last time. I was scared she'd warned 'im about me, because when I went round that night, 'e made some excuse not to let me in . . . I mean, 'e never went to the police, so now I know I was being paranoid, but at the time—'

'You weren't being paranoid,' said Strike. 'I spoke to him yesterday. Margot told him he ought to stop eating anything you prepared him. Just that. He understood what she was saying, though.'

Janice's face grew redder.

'That bitch,' she said venomously. 'What did she do that for? She 'ad a rich 'usband and a lover wanting her back, why's she got to take Steve off me?'

'Go on,' said Strike, 'about how you did it.'

A subtle change now came over Janice. Previously, she'd seemed diffident, matter-of-fact, or even ashamed of her own impetuousness, but now, for the first time, she seemed to enjoy what she was saying, as though she killed Margot Bamborough all over again, in the telling.

'Went out wiv Larry. Told 'im some bullshit about this poor family what needed to concrete over somefing on their roof terrace. Said they were dirt-poor. 'E was so keen to impress me, silly sod, 'e wanted to go do the building work for 'em.'

She rolled her eyes.

'I 'ad to give 'im all this crap about 'ow that would made the dad feel inadequate . . . I said just nicking a few bags of concrete mix off the building site'd be enough.

'Larry drove it to Albemarle Way for me and carried it up to their landing. I wouldn't let 'im come any further, said it would be uneffical for 'im to see patients. 'E was silly, Larry, you could tell 'im anyfing . . . But he wouldn't marry me,' said Janice suddenly. 'Why is that? Why wouldn't anyone marry me? What 'aven't I got, that ovver women 'ave?' asked the nurse who'd pulled back the eyelids from her drugged victims to stare into their unseeing eyes. 'Nobody ever wanted to marry me . . . never . . . I wanted to be in the paper in a white dress. I wanted my day in church and I never got it. Never . . .'

'You needed an alibi as well as concrete, presumably?' said Strike, ignoring her question. 'I assume you chose the demented old lady in Gopsall Street because she couldn't say one way or another whether you'd been with her when Margot disappeared?'

642

'Yeah,' said Janice, returning to her story, 'I went to see 'er late morning and I left drugs there and a note, to prove I'd been in. I knew she'd agree I was there early evening. She didn't 'ave no family, she'd agree with anyfing you said to 'er . . .

'I went from 'er place to buy a cinema ticket for the late-night show, and I called up my babysitter and told 'er I'd be later than I fort because we were getting the last viewing. I knew Irene wouldn't wanna go wiv me. She'd been makin' noises about not feelin' up to it all morning. I knew she didn't 'ave no bad toof, but I pretended to go along wiv it. Irene never wanted to go anywhere we weren't gonna meet men.'

'So, you went back to the surgery that afternoon – in through the back door, I suppose?'

'Yeah,' said Janice, her eyes slightly unfocused now. 'Nobody saw me. I knew Margot 'ad a doughnut in the fridge, because I'd been in there that morning and seen it, but there was people around all the time, so I couldn't do nuffing. I injected it wiv Nembutal sodium solution, froo the cellophane.'

'You must've been well practised by now? You knew how much to give her, so she could still walk up the road?'

'Nuffing's certain,' said the nurse. Unlike Creed, she didn't pretend omnipotence, but then, she'd also been, however reluctantly, in the business of healing as well as killing. 'I 'ad a good feeling for

643

dosages, but you can't never be an 'undred per cent sure. I'd 'eard she was going to meet some friend in a pub up the road, and she usually ate somefing before she went, but I couldn't be sure she'd eat it, or still be able to walk up the road after, or when it would really hit 'er . . .

'All the time I was doing it, getting the concrete and drugging the doughnut, I was finking, this won't work, it can't work. You're gonna go to prison, Janice . . . And you know somefing?' said the nurse, now pink cheeked and fierce, 'By then, I didn't even care. Not if she'd told Steve about me. I fort, I'll go on trial and I'll tell 'em 'ow 'e treated me like a mum and a nurse and took advantage, round my flat all hours. 'E'll 'ave to bloody notice me and 'ear me then, won't 'e? I didn't care. I just fort, I want you dead, lady. I want you dead, you wiv your 'usband and your boyfriend on the side, and my man coming to see you three times a week . . .

'Eivver she dies, I fort, and I get away wiv it, or I'll be famous, I'll be in the papers . . . and I liked the idea, then.'

She looked around her small sitting room, and Strike was certain that she wondered what her cell would be like.

'I left the surgery and went round the long way to the Athorns', but when I let myself in, Gwilherm wasn't there. I fort, OK, that's a problem. Where is 'e?

'And then Deborah and Samhain started

644

moaning. They didn't want their vitamin injections. I 'ad to get strict wiv 'em. I said to Deborah, it's these injections what's keeping you well. You don't take 'em, I'll have to ring an ambulance and get 'em to take you into 'ospital for an assessment . . . You could scare 'er into anyfing if you told 'er she'd 'ave to go outside. I give Deborah and Samhain their "vitamin injections", lying side by side in the double bedroom. Rolled 'em onto their sides. They were out for the count.

'So then I goes outside, and I waits in the phone box, pretending to be on the phone, keepin' watch.

'It didn't feel real, none of it. I didn't fink it'd work. Probably I'd go into work next day and 'ear Margot passed out in the street, and then she'd start yelling the place down saying she was drugged, and I knew she'd point the finger at me . . .

'She didn't come for ages. I fort, it's over. She's eaten the doughnut and got ill in the surgery. She's called an ambulance. She's guessed, she's got sick. There was this girl, standing in front of the phone box, and I'm trying to see round 'er, trying to see . . .

'And then I saw Margot coming up the road. I fort, well, this is it. It was raining hard. People weren't watchin'. It was all umbrellas and cars splashing. She crossed the road and I could see she was in a bad way. Wobbling all over the place. She got to my side of the road and leaned up against the wall. 'Er legs were about to go. I come out the phone box and I says, "Come on, love, you need to sit down." Kept my face down. She come wiv me, a few steps, then she realised it was me. We 'ad a bit of a struggle. I got 'er a few more feet, just inside Albemarle Way, but she was a tall girl . . . and I fort, this is where it ends . . .

'And then I seen Gwilherm coming up the other way. It was me only chance. I called 'im to 'elp me. 'E fort 'e was 'elping 'er. 'E 'elped me drag 'er up the stairs. There wasn't much fight in 'er by then. I told Gwilherm some rubbish to stop 'im phoning the ambulance. Said I could treat 'er myself . . . said 'e didn't want no police coming up, looking round the flat . . . 'E was a very paranoid man about the auforities, so that worked . . .

'I says, you go and see if Deborah and Samhain are still asleep. They've both been very worried about where you've been, and I 'ad to give 'em a little sedative.

'I suffocated 'er while 'e was out of the room. It didn't take much. 'Eld 'er nose, kept 'er mouth shut. Did to Margot what I'd been planning to do to the Athorns.

'When I knew she was dead,' said Janice, 'I left 'er sitting on the sofa and I went into the barf-room. I sat on the bog, looking at the flamingos on the wallpaper and I fort, now what? Gwilherm's here. 'E's seen 'er . . . and the on'y fing I could fink of was, let 'im fink 'e's done it. 'E's crazy enough. I fort, I'll probably 'ave to kill 'im, too, in the end, but I'll worry about that later . . .

'So I waited in the bog and let 'im go in the room and find 'er.

'I give 'im five minutes alone wiv the body, then I walk back in, talkin' to Margot, like I left 'er alive. "You feeling all right now, Margot, love?" And then I says, "What've you done, Gwilherm? What've you done?"

'And he says, "Nuffing, nuffing, I ain't done nuffing," and I'm saying, "You told me you can kill people with your powers. P'rhaps we better call the police," and 'e's begging me not to, 'e didn't mean to, it was all a mistake. So in the end I says, all right, I won't give you away. I'll make it disappear. I'll take care of it.

''E was crying like a baby and he asked me for one of my sedatives. 'E *asked* me to put 'im out, can you believe that? I give 'im some downers. Left 'im curled up asleep on Samhain's bed.

'It was really 'ard, putting her in that big box fing all on me own. I 'ad to take out all the crap they kept in there. Folded 'er up. Once I 'ad 'er in there, I checked on all the Athorns. Made sure the airways weren't obstructed. Then I ran back outside to the phone box. I says to Irene, are we still on for the cinema? And she says no, like I fort she would, fank Gawd.

'So I go back inside. I was there till midnight, near enough. I 'ad to mix the concrete bit by bit, by 'and, in a bucket. It took ages. Margot filled up most of that box fing, but it took a long time to get all the concrete round her. Then I closed the lid. It stuck to the concrete. I couldn't get it up again, so that was good.

'When they was all awake, I told Gwilherm I'd taken care of it. I said to 'im quietly, the lid on that box thing 'as jammed. Best find somewhere else to put Samhain's toys.

''E knew, obviously. I fink 'e pretended to 'imself 'e didn't, but 'e did. I was there free times a week, afterwards. I 'ad to be. Keeping 'im happy. One time I went round and 'e'd painted all those symbols on the walls, like it was some sort of pagan temple or something.

'Weeks after, monfs after, I was worried sick. I knew 'e was tellin' people 'e'd killed 'er. Luckily, everyone fort 'e was a nutcase, local. But it got bad, towards the end. 'E 'ad to go. I still can't believe I waited a year to get rid of 'im . . .'

'And around the time you killed him, you phoned Cynthia Phipps and pretended to be Margot, didn't you? To give the police another lead to hare after, and distract from Gwilherm, in case anyone had taken him seriously?'

'Yeah. That's right,' mumbled Janice, twisting the old wedding ring.

'And you kept visiting Deborah and Samhain as Clare Spencer?'

'Well, yeah,' said Janice. 'I 'ad to. They needed watching. Last fing I wanted was real social workers fiddling around in there.'

'And Deborah and Samhain never realised Clare was the same as Janice the nurse?'

'People with Fragile X don't recognise faces easy,' said Janice. 'I changed me 'air colour and used me glasses. I done a lot to keep 'em 'ealfy, you know. Vitamin D for Deborah, cause she never goes outside. She's younger'n me . . . I fort, I might well be dead before anyone finds the body. Longer it went on, less likely it was anyone would ever know I 'ad anyfing to do wiv it . . .'

'And what about Douthwaite?'

''E scarpered,' said Janice, her smile fading. 'That near enough broke my 'eart. There was me 'aving to go out on foursomes wiv Irene and Eddie, and act like I was 'appy wiv Larry, and the love of my life's disappeared. I asked ev'ryone where Steve 'ad gone, and no one knew.'

'So why's Julie Wilkes on your wall?' asked Strike.

''Oo?' said Janice, lost in her self-pitying reverie.

'The Redcoat who worked at Clacton-on-Sea,' said Strike, pointing at the young blonde with her frizzy hair, who was framed on Janice's wall.

'Oh . . . 'er,' said Janice, with a sigh. 'Yeah . . . I ran into someone 'oo knew someone 'oo'd met Steve at Butlin's, few years later . . . oh, I was excited. Gawd, I was bored wiv Larry by then. I really wanted to see Steve again. I *love* a man 'oo can make me laugh,' repeated the woman who'd planned the murder of a family, for the pleasure of watching them die. 'I *knew* there'd been somefing there between us, I *knew* we coulda bin a couple. So I booked me and Larry an 'oliday at Butlin's. Kev didn't wanna come – suited me. I got meself a perm and I went on a diet. Couldn't wait. You build things up in your mind, don't you?

'And we went to the club night and there 'e was,' said Janice quietly. 'Oh, 'e looked gorgeous. "Longfellow Serenade". All the girls went crazy for 'im when 'e finished singing. There's Larry boozing . . . After Larry went to bed in the chalet I went back out again. Couldn't find 'im.

'Took me free days to get a word wiv 'im. I said, "Steve, it's me. Janice. Your neighbour. The nurse!"'

She turned slowly redder than she'd been all interview. Her eyes watered with the intensity of her blush.

'He goes "Oh yeah. All right, Janice?" And 'e walks away. And I seen 'im,' said Janice, and her jaw quivered, 'kiss that girl, that Julie, and look back at me, like 'e wanted me to see . . .

'And I fort, *no*. After all what I've done for you, Steve? *No*.

'I did it on the last night but one of our 'oliday. Larry snoring 'is 'ead off as usual. 'E never noticed I wasn't in bed.

'They all used to go to Steve's chalet after work, I found that out, following 'em. She come out on 'er own. Pissed. Two in the morning.

'It wasn't 'ard. There wasn't anyone round. They didn't 'ave cameras around like they do nowadays.

I pushed 'er, and I jumped in after 'er, and I 'eld 'er under. It was the surprise what killed 'er. She took in a load of water on the way down. That was the only one I ever did wivvout drugs, but I was angry, see . . .

'Got out, towelled meself off. Mopped up all the footprints, but it was a warm night, you couldn't see nuffing by morning.

'Next day, I seen 'im. I says, "Terrible fing, that girl, Steve. You look awful. Wanna get a drink?"

'E went white as a sheet, but I fort, well, you used me, Steve, and then you left me high and dry, didn't you?'

A police siren sounded somewhere in the distance, and Strike, glancing at his watch, thought it was likely to be heading here, for Nightingale Grove.

'You took my sympafy and my kindness and you let me cook for you,' said Janice, still addressing an imaginary Steve Douthwaite. 'I was even ready to kill my kid for you! And then you go off messing around wiv ovver women? *No.* Actions 'ave consequences,' said Janice, her cheeks still burning. 'Men need to learn that, and take some responsibility. Women 'ave to,' she said, as the police siren grew ever louder. 'Well, I'll see 'im again in court, won't I? You know, I'm quite looking forward to it, now I'm finking about it,' said Janice. 'It's not fun, living 'ere all on me own. It'll be funny seeing Irene's face. I'll be all over the papers, won't I? And maybe some men

651

will read about why I done it, and realise they want to be careful 'oo they lead on. Useful lesson for men everywhere, if you ask me. Actions,' repeated Janice Beattie, as the police car drew to a halt outside her front door, and she squared her shoulders, ready to accept her fate, ''ave consequences.'

PART VII

Then came October full of merry glee . . .

Edmund Spenser
The Faerie Queene

CHAPTER 72

*. . . they for nought would from their worke
refraine . . .*

Edmund Spenser
The Faerie Queene

Success, as Cormoran Strike had long since
learned, is a much more complex business
than most people suppose.

It wasn't the first time that the press had turned
its sights upon the detective agency, and while
the acclaim was undoubtedly flattering and a
good advert for the business, it was, as ever,
severely prejudicial to the partners' ability to keep
working. Robin, whose home address was swiftly
discovered by the press, took refuge at the house
of Vanessa Ekwensi, and with the aid of a number
of wigs and some skilful make-up, managed to
continue to cover a certain amount of work, so
that Barclay and Hutchins didn't have to do
everything themselves. Strike, on the other hand,
was forced back into Nick and Ilsa's spare room,

where he let his beard grow, and lay low, directing the agency's subcontractors by phone. Pat Chauncey alone remained based at the office in Denmark Street, taking care of administrative matters, stolidly opening and closing up each morning and evening.

'I've got no comment. You'd all do better sodding off,' she croaked twice a day at the knot of journalists hanging around Denmark Street.

The eruption of publicity that followed the twin discoveries of a woman's body encased in concrete in a quiet flat in Clerkenwell, and a teenager's skeleton hidden beneath debris in the depths of an underground well in Islington, showed no sign of abating quickly. There were far too many exciting angles to this story: the separate excavations and positive identifications of the bones of Margot Bamborough and Louise Tucker, the comments from two bereaved families, who scarcely knew whether they felt more relief or grief, the profiles of two very different killers and, of course, the private detectives now widely acclaimed as the capital's most talented.

Gratifying though this was, Strike took no satisfaction in the way the press hounded either Gregory Talbot ('What would you say to people who say your father had blood on his hands?') or Dinesh Gupta ('Do you regret giving Janice Beattie that glowing reference, doctor?') nor in seeing the Athorns led out of their flat by genuine social workers, frightened, displaced and uncomprehending. Carl Oakden made a brief appearance in the *Daily Mail*, trying to sell himself as an expert on both Strike and Margot Bamborough, but as the article began with the words 'Convicted con man Carl Brice, son of the old practice secretary, Dorothy . . .' it was perhaps unsurprising that Oakden soon slunk back into the shadows. Strike's father, on the other hand, was happy to continue associating his name with Strike's, issuing a fulsome statement of pride in his eldest son through his publicist. Fuming quietly, Strike ignored all requests for comment.

Dennis Creed, who for so long had received top billing in any news story including him, was relegated almost to a footnote in this one. Janice Beattie had outdone him, not only in the number of her suspected victims, but in remaining undetected for decades longer. Photographs of her sitting room in Nightingale Grove were leaked to the press, who highlighted the framed pictures of the dead on the walls, the folder of obituaries kept in her china cabinet, and the syringe, the cellophane and the hairdryer that Strike had found behind the sofa. The store of drugs and poisons retrieved from her kitchen were carried out of her house by forensics experts, and the rosy-cheeked, silver-haired nurse dubbed 'the Poisoner Granny' blinked impassively at news cameras as she was led into court and remanded in custody.

Meanwhile, Strike could barely open a newspaper or switch on the TV without seeing Brian Tucker, who was giving interviews to anybody who'd speak to him. In a cracked voice he wept, exulted, praised Strike and Robin, told the world they deserved knighthoods ('Or the other thing, what is it for women?' 'Damehood,' murmured the sympathetic blonde presenter, who was holding the emotional Tucker's hand), cried as he reminisced about his daughter, described the preparations for her funeral, criticised the police and informed the world that he'd suspected all along that Louise was hidden in the well. Strike, who was happy for the old man, nevertheless wished, both for his own sake and for Tucker's, that he'd go and grieve quietly somewhere, rather than taking up space on an endless succession of daytime television sofas.

A trickle of relatives, suspicious about the way their loved ones had died under Janice's care, soon turned into a tide. Exhumation orders were made, and Irene Hickson, the contents of whose food cupboards had been removed and analysed by the police, was profiled in the *Daily Mail*, sitting in her swagged and flounced sitting room, flanked by two voluptuous daughters who closely resembled her.

'I mean, Jan was always a bit of a man-eater, but I never suspected anything like this, never. I'd've called her my best friend. I don't know how I could've been such a fool! She used to offer to go food shopping for me, before I came back from staying at my daughter's. Then I'd eat some of the stuff she'd put in the fridge, get ill, call her and ask her to come over. I suppose this is a comfier house than hers, and she liked staying here, and I sometimes gave her money, so that's why I'm not dead. I don't know whether I'll ever get over the shock, honestly. I can't sleep, I feel sick all the time, I can't stop thinking about it. I look back now, and ask myself, *how did I never see?* And if it turns out she killed Larry, poor Larry who Eddie and I introduced her to, I don't know how I'm going to live with myself, honestly, it's all just a nightmare. You don't expect this from a nurse, do you?'

And on this count, if no other, Strike was forced to agree with Irene Hickson. He asked himself why it had taken him so long to look closer at an alibi he'd known from the first was barely adequate, and why he'd taken Janice's word at face value, when he'd challenged almost everyone else's. He was forced to conclude that, like the women who'd climbed willingly into Dennis Creed's van, he'd been hoodwinked by a careful performance of femininity. Just as Creed had camouflaged himself behind an apparently fey and gentle façade, so Janice had hidden behind the persona of the nurturer, the selfless giver, the compassionate mother. Strike had preferred her apparent modesty to Irene's garrulity and her sweetness to her friend's spite, yet knew he'd have been far less ready to take those traits at face value, had he met them in a man. *Ceres is nurturing and protective. Cancer is kind, instinct is to protect.* A hefty dose of self-recrimination tempered Strike's celebrations, which puzzled Ilsa and Nick, who were inclined to gloat over the newspaper reports of their friend's latest and most celebrated detective triumph.

Meanwhile, Anna Phipps was longing to thank Strike and Robin in person, but the detective partners postponed a meeting until the first effusion of press attention died down. The hyper-cautious Strike, whose beard was now coming along nicely, finally agreed to a meeting over two weeks after Margot's body had been found. Though he and Robin had been in daily contact by phone, this would also be the first time they'd met since solving the case.

Rain pattered against the window of Nick and Ilsa's spare bedroom as Strike dressed that morning. He was pulling a sock over his false foot when his mobile beeped from the bedside table. Expecting to see a message from Robin, possibly warning him that press were on the prowl outside Anna and Kim's house, he saw, instead, Charlotte's name.

Hello Bluey. I thought Jago had thrown this phone away, but I've just found it hidden at the back of a cupboard. So, you've done another amazing thing. I've been reading all about you in the press.

I wish they had some decent pictures of you, but I suppose you're glad they don't? Congratulations, anyway. It must feel good to prove everyone who didn't believe in the agency wrong. Which includes me, I suppose. I wish I'd been more supportive, but it's too late now. I don't know whether you'll be glad to hear from me or not. Probably not. You never called the hospital, or if you did, nobody told me. Maybe you'd have been secretly glad if I'd died? A problem solved, and you like solving things . . . Don't think I'm not grateful. I suppose I am, or I will be, one day. But I know you'd have done what you did for anyone. That's your code, isn't it? And I always wanted something particular from you, something you wouldn't give anyone else. Funny, I've started to appreciate people who're decent to everyone, but it's too late for that, too, isn't it? Jago and I are separating, only he doesn't want to call it that yet, because leaving your suicidal wife isn't a good look and nobody would believe it's me leaving him. I still mean the thing I said to you at the end. I always will.

Strike sat back down on the spare bed, mobile in his hands, one sock on, one off. The rainy daylight illuminated the phone's screen, reflecting his bearded face back at him as he scowled at a text so Charlottian he could have written it himself: the apparent resignation to her fate, the attempts to provoke him into reassurance, the vulnerability wielded like a weapon. Had she really left Jago? Where were the now two-year-old twins? He thought of all the things he could have told her, which would have given her hope: that he'd wanted to call the hospital, that he'd dreamed about her since the suicide attempt, that she retained a potent hold over his imagination that he'd tried to exorcise but couldn't. He considered ignoring the message, but then, on the point of setting the mobile back down, changed his mind, and, character by careful character, typed out his brief response.

You're right, I'd have done what I did for anyone. That doesn't mean I'm not glad you're alive, because I am. But you need to stay alive for yourself and your kids now. I'm about to change my number. Look after yourself.

He re-read his words before sending. She'd doubtless experience the words as a blow, but he'd done a lot of thinking since her suicide attempt. Having always told himself that he'd never changed his number because too many contacts had it, he'd lately admitted to himself that he'd wanted to keep a channel of communication open between himself and Charlotte, because he wanted to know she couldn't forget him, any more than he could forget her. It was time to cut that last, thin thread. He pressed 'send' on the text, then finished dressing.

Having made sure that both of Nick and Ilsa's cats were shut up in the kitchen, he left the house. Another text from Charlotte arrived as he was walking up the road in the rain.

I don't think I've ever felt so envious in my life as I am of that girl Robin.

And this, Strike decided to ignore.

He'd set off for Clapham South station deliberately early, because he wanted time for a cigarette before Robin picked him up and drove them the short distance to Anna and Kim's flat. Standing beneath the overhang outside the station, he lit up, looking out over a row of bicycles at a muddy corner of Clapham Common, where ochre-leaved trees shivered in the downpour. He'd only taken a couple of drags on his cigarette when his mobile rang in his pocket. Resolving not to answer if it was Charlotte, he pulled it out and saw Polworth's name.

'All right, Chum?'

'Still got time for the little people, then, Sherlock?'

'I can spare you a minute or two,' said Strike,

watching the rain. 'Wouldn't want people to think I've lost the common touch. How's things?'

'We're coming up to London for a weekend.'

Polworth sounded about as excited as a man facing a colonoscopy.

'I thought London was the heart of all evil?'

'Not my choice. It's Roz's birthday. She wants to see the fucking *Lion King* and Trafalgar Square and shit.'

'If you're looking for somewhere to stay, I've only got one bedroom.'

'We're booked into an Airbnb. Weekend after next. Just wondered if you were up for a pint. Could bring your Robin along, so Penny's got someone to talk to. Unless, I dunno, the fucking Queen's got a job for you.'

'Well, she has, but I told her the waiting list's full. That'd be great,' said Strike. 'What else is new?'

'Nothing,' said Polworth. 'You saw the Scots bottled it?'

The old Land Rover had appeared in a line of traffic. Having no desire to get onto the subject of Celtic nationalism, Strike said,

'If "bottling"'s what you want to call it, yeah. Listen, I'm gonna have to go, mate, Robin's about to pick me up in the car. I'll ring you later.'

Chucking his cigarette end down a nearby storm drain, he was ready to climb into the Land Rover as soon as Robin pulled up.

'Morning,' she said, as Strike hoisted himself into the passenger seat. 'Am I late?'

664

'No, I was early.'

'Nice beard,' said Robin, as she pulled away from the kerb in the rain. 'You look like a guerrilla leader who's just pulled off a successful coup.'

'Feel like one,' said Strike, and in fact, right now, reunited with Robin, he felt the straightforward sense of triumph that had eluded him for days.

'Was that Pat you were just talking to?' asked Robin. 'On the phone?'

'No, Polworth. He's coming up to London weekend after next.'

'I thought he hated London?'

'He does. One of his kids wants to visit. He wants to meet you, but I wouldn't advise it.'

'Why not?' asked Robin, who was mildly flattered.

'Women don't usually like Polworth.'

'I thought he was married?'

'He is. His wife doesn't like him.'

Robin laughed.

'Why did you think Pat would be calling me?' asked Strike.

'I've just had her on the phone. Miss Jones is upset at not getting updates from you personally.'

'I'll FaceTime her later,' said Strike, as they drove across the common, windscreen wipers working. 'Hopefully the beard'll put her off.'

'Some women like them,' said Robin, and Strike couldn't help wondering whether Robin was one of them.

'Sounds like Hutchins and Barclay are closing in on Dopey's partner,' he said.

'Yes,' said Robin. 'Barclay's offering to go out to Majorca and have a look around.'

'I'll bet he is. Are you still on for interviewing the new subcontractor together, Monday?'

'Michelle? Yes, definitely,' said Robin

'Hopefully we'll be back in the office by then.'

Robin turned into Kyrle Road. There was no sign of press, so she parked outside a Victorian terraced house divided into two flats.

When Strike rang the bell labelled 'Phipps/Sullivan', they heard footsteps on stairs through the door, which opened to reveal Anna Phipps, who was wearing the same baggy blue cotton jumpsuit and white canvas shoes as the first time they'd met her, in Falmouth.

'Come in,' she said, smiling as she retreated so that they could enter a small square of space at the bottom of the staircase. The walls were painted white: a series of abstract, monochrome prints covered the walls, and the fanned window over the door cast pools of light onto the uncarpeted stairs, reminding Robin of the St Peter's nursing home, and the life-size Jesus watching over the entrance.

'I'm going to try not to cry,' said Anna quietly, as though scared of being overheard, but in spite of her resolution, her eyes were already full of tears. 'I'm sorry, but I – I'd really like to hug you,' she said, and she promptly did so, embracing first

Robin, then Strike. Stepping back, she shook her head, half-laughing, and wiped her eyes.

'I can't ever express to you how grateful . . . how grateful I am. What you've given me . . .' She made an ineffable gesture and shook her head. 'It's just so . . . so strange. I'm incredibly happy and relieved, but at the same time, I'm grieving . . . Does that make sense?'

'Totally,' said Robin. Strike grunted.

'Everyone's here,' said Anna, gesturing upstairs. 'Kim, Dad, Cyn, and Oonagh, too. I invited her down for a few days. We're planning the funeral, you see – Dad and Cyn are really leaving it up to me – anyway . . . come up, everyone wants to thank you . . .'

As they followed Anna up the steep stairs, Strike using the banister to heave himself along, he remembered the tangle of emotions that had hit him when he'd received the phone call telling him of his own mother's death. Amid the engulfing wave of grief had been a slight pinprick of relief, which had shocked and shamed him, and which had taken a long time to process. Over time, he'd come to understand that in some dark corner of his mind, he'd been dreading and half-expecting the news. The axe had fallen at last, suspense was forever over: Leda's appalling taste in men had culminated in a sordid death on a dirty mattress, and while he'd missed her ever since, he'd be a liar if he claimed to miss the toxic mixture of anxiety, guilt and dread he'd endured over her last couple of years of life.

He could only imagine the mixture of emotions currently possessing Margot's husband, or the nanny who'd taken Margot's place in the family. As he reached the upper landing, he glimpsed Roy Phipps sitting in an armchair in the sitting room. Their eyes met briefly, before Kim came out of the room, blocking Strike's view of the haematologist. The blonde psychologist was smiling broadly: she, at least, seemed to feel unalloyed pleasure.

'Well,' she said, shaking first Strike's hand, then Robin's, 'what can we say, really? Come through . . .'

Strike and Robin followed Anna and Kim into the sitting room, which was as large and airy as their Falmouth holiday home, with long gauze curtains at the windows, stripped floorboards, a large white rug and pale grey walls. The books had been arranged by colour. Everything was simple and well designed; very different from the house in which Anna had grown up, with its ugly Victorian bronzes and chintz-covered chairs. The only art on the walls was over the fireplace: a black and white photograph of sea and sky.

Rain was beating on the large bay window behind Roy, who was already on his feet. He wiped his hand nervously on his trousers before holding it out to Strike.

'How are you?' he asked jerkily.

'Very well, thanks,' said Strike.

'Miss Ellacott,' said Roy, holding out his hand to Robin in turn. 'I understand *you* actually . . .?'

The unspoken words *found her* seemed to ring around the room.

'Yes,' said Robin, and Roy nodded and pursed his lips, his large eyes leaving her to focus on one of the ragdoll cats, which had just prowled into the room, its aquamarine eyes shrewd.

'Sit down, Dad,' said Anna gently, and Roy did as he was told.

'I'll just go and see whether Oonagh's found everything; she's making tea,' said Kim cheerfully, and left.

'Please, have a seat,' said Anna to Strike and Robin, who sat down side by side on the sofa. The moment Strike was settled, the ragdoll cat leapt up lightly beside him and stepped into his lap. Robin, meanwhile, had noticed the ottoman that stood in place of a coffee table. It was upholstered in grey and white striped canvas, and far smaller than the one in the Athorns' flat, too small for a woman to curl up in, but even so, it was a piece of furniture Robin doubted she'd ever own, no matter how useful they might be. She'd never forget the dusty mass of hardened concrete, and the skull of Margot Bamborough curving up out of it.

'Where's Cyn?' Anna asked her father.

'Bathroom,' said Roy, a little hoarsely. He threw a nervous glance at the empty landing beyond the door, before addressing the detective:

'I – I have to tell you how ashamed I am that I never hired anybody myself. Believe me, the thought that we could have known all this ten, twenty years ago . . .'

'Well, that's not very good for our egos, Roy,' said Strike, stroking the purring cat. 'Implying that anyone could have done what we did.'

Roy and Anna both laughed harder than the comment deserved, but Strike understood the need for the release of jokes, after a profound shock. Mere days after he'd been airlifted out of the bloody crater where he'd lain after his leg had been blown off, fading in and out of consciousness with Gary Topley's torso beside him, he seemed to remember Richard Anstis, the other survivor, whose face had been mangled in the explosion, making a stupid joke about the savings Gary could have made on trousers, had he lived. Strike could still remember laughing at the idiotic, tasteless joke, and enjoying a few seconds' relief from shock, grief and agony.

Women's voices now came across the landing: Kim had returned with a tea tray, followed by Oonagh Kennedy, who was bearing a large chocolate cake. She was beaming from beneath her purple-streaked fringe, her amethyst cross bouncing on her chest as before, and when she'd put down the cake, she said,

'Here dey are, then, the heroes of the hour! I'm going to hug the pair of you!'

Robin stood to receive her tribute, but Strike, not wanting to disarrange the cat, received his hug awkwardly while sitting.

'And here I go again!' said Oonagh, laughing as she straightened up, and wiping her eyes. 'I swear to God, it's loike being on a rollercoaster. Up one minute, down the next—'

'I did the same, when I saw them,' said Anna, laughing at Oonagh. Roy's smile, Robin noticed, was nervous and a little fixed. What did it feel like, she wondered, to be face to face with his dead wife's best friend, after all these years? Did the physical changes in Oonagh make him wonder what Margot would have looked like, had she lived to the age of seventy? Or was he wondering anew, as he must have done over all the intervening years, whether his marriage would have survived the long stretch of icy silence that had followed her drink with Paul Satchwell, whether the strains and tensions in the relationship could have been overcome, or whether Margot would have taken Oonagh up on her offer of refuge in her flat?

They'd have divorced, Robin thought, with absolute certainty, but then she wondered whether she wasn't tangling up Margot with herself, as she'd tended to do all through the case.

'Oh, hello,' said a breathless voice, from the doorway, and everyone looked around to see Cynthia, on whose thin, sallow face was a smile that didn't quite reach her anxious, mottled eyes. She was wearing a black dress, and Robin wondered whether she'd consciously put it on to suggest mourning. 'Sorry, I was – how are you both?'

'Fine,' said Robin.

'Great,' said Strike.

Cynthia let out one of her nervous, breathless laughs, and said,

'Yes, no – so wonderful—'

Was it wonderful for Cynthia, Robin wondered, as Anna's stepmother pulled up a chair, and she declined a piece of the cake which, it transpired, Oonagh had gone out in the rain to purchase. How did it feel to have Margot Bamborough back, even in the form of a skeleton in a box? Did it hurt to see her husband so shaken and emotional, and to have to receive Oonagh, Margot's best friend, into the heart of the family, like a newly discovered aunt? Robin, who seemed to be on something of a clairvoyant streak, felt sure that if Margot had never been killed, but had simply divorced Roy, Cynthia would never have been the haematologist's choice of second wife. Margot would probably have begged the young Cynthia to accompany her into her new life, and continue looking after Anna. Would Cynthia have agreed, or would her loyalties have lain with Roy? Where would she have gone, and who would she have married, once there was no place for her at Broom House?

The second cat now entered the room, staring at the unusually large group it found inside. She picked her way past the armchairs, the ottoman and the sofa, jumped up onto the windowsill and sat with her back to them, watching the raindrops sliding down the window.

'Now, listen,' said Kim, from the upright chair she'd brought out of a corner of the room, 'we really do want to pay you for the extra month you put in. I know you said no—'

'It was our choice to keep working on the case,' said Strike. 'We're glad to have helped and we definitely don't want more money.'

He and Robin had agreed that, as the Margot Bamborough case looked likely to pay for itself three times over in terms of publicity and extra work, and as Strike felt he really should have solved it sooner, taking more cash from Anna and Kim felt unnecessarily greedy.

'Then we'd like to make a donation to charity,' said Kim. 'Is there one you'd like us to support?'

'Well,' said Strike, clearing his throat, 'if you're serious, Macmillan nurses . . .'

He saw a slight look of surprise on the family's faces.

'My aunt died this year,' he explained, 'and the Macmillan nurse gave her a lot of support.'

'Oh, I see,' said Kim, with a slight laugh, and there was a little pause, in which the spectre of Janice Beattie seemed to rise up in the middle of them, like the wisp of steam issuing from the teapot spout.

'A nurse,' said Anna quietly. 'Who'd suspect a nurse?'

'Margot,' said Roy and Oonagh together.

They caught each other's eye, and smiled: a rueful smile, doubtless surprised at finding themselves in agreement at long last, and Robin saw Cynthia look away.

'She didn't like that nurse. She told me so,' said Oonagh, 'but I got the woman confused with that blonde at the Christmas party who made a scene.'

'No, she never took to the nurse,' said Roy. 'She told me, too, when she joined the practice. I didn't take much notice . . .'

He seemed determined to be honest, now, however much it hurt.

'. . . I thought it was a case of two women being too similar: both working class, both strong characters. When I met the woman at the barbecue, I actually thought she seemed quite . . . well . . . decent. Of course, Margot never told me her suspicions . . .'

There was another silence, and everyone in the room, Strike was sure, was remembering that Roy hadn't spoken to his wife at all in those few weeks before her murder, which was precisely the time period during which Margot's suspicions of Janice must have crystallised.

'Janice Beattie's probably the best liar I've ever met,' Strike said, into the tense atmosphere, 'and a hell of an actress.'

'I've had the most extraordinary letter,' said Anna, 'from her son, Kevin. Did you know he's coming over from Dubai to testify against her?'

'We did,' said Strike, who George Layborn was

briefing regularly on the progress of the police investigation.

'He wrote that he thinks Mum examining him saved his life,' said Anna.

Robin noticed how Anna was now calling Margot 'Mum', when previously she'd only said 'my mother'.

'It's a remarkable letter,' said Kim, nodding. 'Full of apologies, as though it's somehow his fault.'

'Poor man,' said Oonagh quietly.

'He says he blames himself for not going to the police about her, but what child would believe his mother's a serial killer? I really *can't*,' said Anna again, over the purring of Cagney the cat in Strike's lap, 'explain adequately to you both what you've done for me . . . for all of us. The not knowing's been so terrible, and now I know for sure that Mum didn't leave willingly and that she went . . . well, quite peacefully . . .'

'As deaths go,' said Strike, 'it was almost painless.'

'And I know for sure she loved me,' said Anna.

'We always—' began Cynthia, but her step-daughter said quickly,

'I know you always told me she did, Cyn, but without knowing what really happened, there was always going to be a doubt, wasn't there? But when I compare my situation with Kevin Beattie's, I actually feel lucky . . . D'you know,' Anna asked Strike and Robin, 'what they found when they – you know – got Mum out of the concrete?'

'No,' said Strike.

Cynthia's thin hands were playing with her wedding ring, twisting it around her finger.

'The locket Dad gave her,' said Anna. 'It's tarnished, but when they opened it up, it had a picture of me in it, which was as good as new,' said Anna, and her eyes suddenly shone with tears again. Oonagh reached out and patted Anna on the knee. 'They say I'll be able to have it back, once they've completed all the forensics.'

'How lovely,' said Robin quietly.

'And did you hear what was in her handbag?' asked Kim.

'No,' said Strike.

'Notes from her consultation on Theo,' said Kim. 'They're completely legible – protected by the leather, you know. Her full name was Theodosia Loveridge and she was from a traveller family. Margot suspected an ectopic pregnancy and wanted to ring an ambulance, but Theo said her boyfriend would take her. Margot's notes suggest Theo was scared of her family knowing she was pregnant. They don't seem to have approved of the boyfriend.'

'So that's why she never came forward, afterwards?' said Robin.

'I suppose so,' said Kim. 'Poor girl. I hope she was OK.'

'May I ask,' said Roy, looking at Strike, 'how strong you think the case against Janice Beattie is? Because – I don't know what your police contacts

676

have told you – but the latest we've heard is that forensics haven't been able to prove Margot was drugged.'

'Not so far,' said Strike, who'd spoken to George Layborn the previous evening, 'but I've heard they're going to try some new-fangled way of getting traces of drugs and chemicals out of the concrete surrounding the body. No guarantees, but it was used successfully in a case in the States recently.'

'But if they can't prove she was drugged,' said Roy, his expression intense, 'the case against Janice is entirely circumstantial, isn't it?'

'Her lawyer's certainly trying to get her off, judging by his comments to the press,' said Kim.

'He'll have his work cut out for him,' said Strike. 'The defence has got to come up with reasons the police found a phone belonging to a non-existent social worker in her house, and why the Athorns had the number. The Athorns' cousins in Leeds can identify her as the woman who helped them muck out the flat. Gloria Conti's willing to come over to testify about the doughnut in the fridge and the vomiting attacks she and Wilma suffered, and Douthwaite's going to take the stand—'

'He is?' said Oonagh, her expression clearing. 'Oh, that's good, we've been worried about him—'

'I think he finally realises the only way out of this is going through with it,' said Strike. 'He's ready to testify that from the moment he started eating food prepared by Janice, he had symptoms of poisoning, and, most importantly, that during their last consultation, Margot advised him not to eat anything else prepared by Janice.

'Then we've got Kevin Beattie testifying that his daughter drank bleach while Janice was supposedly looking after her, and that his mother used to feed him "special drinks" that made him feel ill . . . What else?' said Strike, inviting Robin to continue, mainly so he could eat some cake.

'Well, there are all the lethal substances they've taken out of Janice's kitchen,' said Robin, 'not to mention the fact that she tried to poison Cormoran's tea when he went round there to confront her. There's also the drugged food the police have found at Irene's, and the framed photographs on her wall, including Joanna Hammond, who she claimed never to have met, and Julie Wilkes, who drowned at the Clacton-on-Sea Butlin's. And the police are confident they're going to be able to get forensic evidence out of other victims' graves, even if Margot's results are inconclusive. Janice had her ex-partner, Larry, cremated, but his lover Clare was buried and she's being exhumed.'

'Personally,' said Strike, who'd managed to eat half his slice of chocolate cake while Robin was talking, 'I think she's going to die in jail.'

'Well, that's good to hear,' said Roy, looking relieved, and Cynthia said breathlessly,

'Yes, no, definitely.'

678

The cat at the window looked around and then, slowly, turned to face the rain again, while its twin pawed idly at Strike's sweater.

'You two will come to the funeral, won't you?' asked Anna.

'We'd be honoured,' said Robin, because Strike had just taken another big mouthful of cake.

'We're, ah, leaving the arrangements up to Anna,' said Roy. 'She's taking the lead.'

'I'd like Mum to have a proper grave,' said Anna. 'Somewhere to visit, you know . . . all these years, without knowing where she is. I want her where I can find her.'

'I can understand that,' said Strike.

'You really *don't* know what you've given me,' said Anna, for the third time. She'd reached out a hand to Oonagh, but she was looking at Cynthia. 'I've got Oonagh, now, as well as Cyn, who's been the most wonderful mother . . . Mum certainly chose the right person to raise me . . .'

As Cynthia's face crumpled, Strike and Robin both looked tactfully away, Robin at the cat at the window and Strike at the seascape over the mantelpiece. The rain drummed against the window, the cat in his lap purred, and he remembered the lily urn bobbing away. With a twist in his chest, and in spite of his satisfaction at having done what he'd set out to do, he wished he could have called Joan, and told her the end of Margot Bamborough's story, and heard her say she was proud of him, one last time.

CHAPTER 73

For naturall affection soone doth cesse,
And quenched is with Cupids greater flame:
But faithfull friendship doth them both
*   suppresse,*
And them with maystring discipline doth
*   tame,*
Through thoughts aspyring to eternall fame.
For as the soule doth rule the earthly masse,
And all the seruice of the bodie frame,
So loue of soule doth loue of bodie passe,
No lesse then perfect gold surmounts the
*   meanest brasse.*

Edmund Spenser
The Faerie Queene

Robin woke a few days later to autumn sunshine streaming through the gap in her curtains. Glancing at her mobile, she saw to her amazement that it was ten in the morning, which meant she'd just enjoyed the longest sleep she'd had all year. Then she remembered why she was having a lie-in: today was the ninth of October, and it was her birthday.

Ilsa had arranged a dinner in her honour the following evening, which was a Friday. Ilsa had chosen and booked the smart restaurant, to which she and Nick, Vanessa and her fiancé Oliver, Barclay, Hutchins and their wives, Max, his new boyfriend (the lighting director on his TV show) and Strike were all invited. Robin had no plans for today, her actual birthday, which Strike had insisted she take off. She now sat up in bed, yawning, and looked at the packages lying on her chest of drawers opposite, which were all from her family. The small package from her mother had the appearance of a piece of jewellery, doubt-less in tribute to this milestone birthday. Just as she was about to get out of bed, her phone beeped and she saw a text from Strike.

I know you're supposed to be having a day off but something's come up. Please can you meet me at the Shakespeare's Head, Marlborough St, 5pm. Dress smart, might need to go on somewhere upmarket.

Robin read this twice, as though she might have missed a 'happy birthday'. Surely – *surely* – he hadn't forgotten again? Or did he think that, by planning to turn up at the dinner Ilsa had planned, he was doing all that was required, and the actual

681

day of her birth required no acknowledgement? True, she felt at a slightly loose end without work and with none of her friends available, but Strike wasn't to know that, so it was with very mixed feelings that she texted back: **OK**.

However, when she arrived upstairs in her dressing gown to fetch a cup of tea, Robin found a large box sitting on the kitchen table, with a card on top of it, her name on the envelope in Strike's unmistakeable cramped, hard-to-read writing. Max, she knew, had left the flat early to film outdoor scenes in Kent, taking Wolfgang with him, who'd sleep in the car and enjoy a lunchtime walk. As she hadn't heard the doorbell, she had to conclude that Strike had somehow transferred both box and card to Max ahead of time, to surprise her with this morning. This argued degrees of planning and effort that seemed highly uncharacteristic. Moreover, she'd never received a proper card from Strike, not even when he'd bought her the green dress after solving their first case.

The front of the birthday card was somewhat generic and featured a large glittery pink number thirty. Inside, Strike had written:

Happy birthday. This isn't your real present, you'll get that later. (Not flowers)
Love Strike x

Robin looked at this message for far longer than it warranted. Many things about it pleased her, including the kiss and the fact that he'd called himself 'Strike'. She set the card on the table and picked up the large box which, to her surprise, was so light it felt empty. Then she saw the product name on the side: Balloon in a Box.

Opening the lid, she pulled out a balloon in the shape of a donkey's head, tied by a thick ribbon to a weighted base. Grinning, she set it down on the table, made herself tea and breakfast, then texted Strike.

Thanks for the balloon donkey. Perfect timing. My old one's nearly deflated.

She received an answer sixty seconds later.

Great. I was worried it was so obvious, everybody would've got you one. See you at 5.

Light-hearted now, Robin drank tea, ate her toast and returned downstairs to open her family's presents. Everybody had bought her slightly more expensive versions of last year's gifts, except for her parents, who'd sent a beautiful pendant: a single round opal, which was her birthstone, shimmering green and blue, surrounded by tiny diamonds. The accompanying card read: 'Happy thirtieth, Robin. We love you, Mum and Dad x.'

Robin felt her luck, these days, at having two loving parents. Her work had taught her how many people weren't that fortunate, how many people had families that were broken beyond repair, how many adults walked around carrying invisible scars from their earliest childhood, their perceptions and associations forever altered by lack of love, by violence, by cruelty. So she called Linda to thank her, and ended up talking to her mother for over an hour: inconsequential chatter, most of it, but cheering, nevertheless. It was easier to ring home now that her divorce was over. Robin hadn't told her mother that Matthew and Sarah were expecting a baby: she'd let Linda find that out in her own time, and work off her initial outrage out of Robin's earshot.

Towards the end of the call, Linda, who'd disapproved of Robin's dramatic change of career ever since her first injury incurred on the job, mentioned the continuing press coverage concerning Margot Bamborough.

'You really did an incredible thing, there,' said Linda. 'You and, er . . . Cormoran.'

'Thanks, Mum,' said Robin, as surprised as she was touched.

'How's Morris?' her mother asked, in a would-be casual tone.

'Oh, we sacked him,' said Robin cheerfully, forgetting that she hadn't told her mother that, either. 'His replacement's starting next week. Woman called Michelle Greenstreet. She's great.'

After showering, Robin returned to her bedroom to blow dry her hair properly, ate lunch watching

TV, then returned downstairs to change into the figure-hugging blue dress that she'd last worn when persuading Shifty's PA to give up her secrets. She added the opal necklace, which, since she'd left her engagement ring behind when leaving Matthew, was now the most valuable piece of jewellery she owned. The beautiful stone, with its iridescent flecks, lifted the appearance of the old dress, and for once pleased with her appearance, Robin picked up the second of her handbags, which was slightly smarter than the one she usually took to the office, and went to pick up her mobile phone from her bedside table.

The drawer of the bedside table was slightly open and, looking down, Robin glimpsed the Thoth tarot pack, sitting inside. For a moment, she hesitated; then, under the smiling eyes of the balloon donkey she'd installed in the corner of her bedroom, she checked the time on her phone. It was still early to leave the house, if she wanted to meet Strike in Marlborough Street at five. Setting down her bag, she took out the tarot pack, sat down on her bed and began shuffling the cards before turning the first card over and laying it down in front of her.

Two swords intersected a blue rose against a green background. She consulted the *Book of Thoth*.

Peace . . . The Two of Swords. It represents a general shaking-up, resulting from

the conflict of Fire and Water in their
marriage . . . This comparative calm is
emphasized by the celestial attribution:
the Moon in Libra . . .

Robin now remembered that this first card
was supposed to represent 'the nature of the
problem'.

'Peace isn't a problem,' she muttered, to the
empty room. 'Peace is good.'

But of course, she hadn't actually asked the cards
a question; she'd simply wanted them to tell her
something today, on the day of her birth. She
turned over the second card, the supposed cause
of the problem.

A strange green masked female figure stood
beneath a pair of scales, holding a green sword.

Adjustment . . . This card represents the
sign of Libra . . . she represents The Woman
Satisfied. Equilibrium stands apart from
any individual prejudices . . . She is there-
fore to be understood as assessing the virtue
of every act and demanding exact and
precise satisfaction . . .

Robin raised her eyebrows and turned over the
third and last card: the solution. Here again were
the two entwined fish, which poured out water
into two golden chalices floating on a green lake:
it was the same card she'd turned over in

Leamington Spa, when she still didn't know who'd killed Margot Bamborough.

> Love . . . The card also refers to Venus in Cancer. It shows the harmony of the male and the female: interpreted in the largest sense. It is perfect and placid harmony . . .

Robin took a deep breath, then returned all the cards to their pack and the pack to her bedside drawer. As she stood and picked up her raincoat, the balloon donkey swayed slightly on its ribbon.

Robin could feel the new opal resting in the hollow of the base of her throat as she walked towards the Tube station along the road, and having slept properly for once, and having clean hair, and carrying a feeling of lightness with her that had persisted ever since she took the balloon donkey out of his box, she attracted many pairs of male eyes in the street and on the train. But Robin ignored all of them, heading up the stairs at Oxford Circus, and then proceeded down Regent Street and, finally, to the Shakespeare's Head where she saw Strike standing outside, wearing a suit.

'Happy birthday,' he said, and after a brief hesitation he bent down and kissed her on the cheek. He smelled, Robin noticed, not only of cigarettes, but of a subtle lavender aftershave, which was unusual.

'Thanks . . . aren't we going into the pub?'

'Er – no,' said Strike. 'I want to buy you some new perfume.' He pointed towards the rear entrance of Liberty, which lay a mere ten yards away. 'It's your real birthday present – unless you've already bought some?' he added. He really hoped not. He couldn't think of anything else to offer her that didn't take them back into the realm of awkwardness and possible misunderstanding.

'I . . . no,' said Robin. 'How did you know I've . . .?'

'Because I phoned Ilsa, last Christmas . . .'

As he held open the glass door for her, which led to a chocolate department now full of Hallowe'en treats, Strike explained about his failed attempt to buy Robin perfume, the previous December.

'. . . so I asked the assistant, but he kept showing me things with names like . . . I dunno . . . "Shaggable You" . . .'

The laugh Robin failed to repress was so loud that people turned to look at her. They moved past tables stacked with expensive truffles.

'. . . and I panicked,' Strike admitted, 'which is why you ended up with chocolates. Anyway,' he said, as they came to the threshold of the perfume room, with its cupola painted with moon and stars, 'you choose whatever you want and I'll pay.'

'Strike,' said Robin, 'this is . . . this is *thoughtful*.'

'Yeah, well,' said her partner, with a shrug. 'People can change. Or so a psychiatrist in

Broadmoor told me. I'm going to stand here,' he said, pointing at a corner where he hoped his bulk wouldn't impede anyone. 'Take your time.'

So Robin spent a pleasurable quarter of an hour browsing among bottles, spraying testers onto strips, enjoying a brief consultation with the helpful assistant, and finally narrowing her choice down to two perfumes. Now she hesitated, wondering whether she dare do what she wanted . . . but surely, if they were best friends, it was all right?

'OK, there are two I really like,' Robin said, reappearing at Strike's side. 'Give me your opinion. You've got to live with it, in the Land Rover.'

'If they're strong enough to cover up the smell of that car, they aren't fit for human inhalation,' he said, but nevertheless, he took the two smelling strips.

The first smelled of vanilla, which reminded him of cake, and he liked it. The second put him in mind of warm, musky skin, with a suggestion of bruised flowers.

'That one. The second one.'

'Huh. I thought you'd prefer the first.'

'Because it smells like food?'

She grinned as she sniffed the smelling strips.

'Yes . . . I think I prefer two, as well. It isn't cheap.'

'I'll cope.'

So he carried a heavy cube of white glass which

bore the unexceptional name 'Narciso' to the desk.

'Yeah, it's a gift,' Strike said when asked, and he waited patiently as the price sticker was peeled off and a ribbon and wrapping added. He couldn't personally see the point, but he felt that Robin was owed a little ceremony, and her smile as she took the bag from him told him he'd answered correctly. Now they walked together back through the store and out of the main entrance, where buckets of flowers surrounded them.

'So where—?' asked Robin.

'I'm taking you to the Ritz for champagne,' said Strike.

'Are you serious?'

'Yeah. It's why I'm wearing a suit.'

For a moment Robin simply looked at him, then she reached up and hugged him tightly. Surrounded by banked flowers, both remembered the hug they'd shared at the top of the stairs on her wedding day, but this time, Robin turned her face and kissed Strike deliberately on the cheek, lips to stubble.

'Thanks, Strike. This really means a lot.'

And that, thought her partner, as the two of them headed away towards the Ritz in the golden glow of the early evening, really was well worth sixty quid and a bit of an effort . . .

Out of his subconscious rose the names Mazankov and Krupov, and it was a second or two before he remembered where he'd heard them, why they sounded Cornish, and why he thought of them now. The corners of his mouth twitched, but as Robin didn't see him smiling, he felt no compulsion to explain.